Praise for Alyssa Day's *Bane's Choice*

"A revved-up supernatural tale that takes some impressively sharp turns."
—Kirkus Reviews

"Don't miss an Alyssa Day book! One of my favorite authors in paranormal romance."
—*NYT* bestselling author Jeaniene Frost

"Vampires, motorcycles and magic! *Bane's Choice* offers heart-pounding action and sizzling heat!"
—*NYT* bestselling author Gena Showalter"

"Smoking hot! I couldn't put it down."
—*NYT* bestselling author Yasmine Galenorn

"Gritty and sexy. A must read!"
—#1 *NYT* bestselling author Helen Hardt

"This action-packed paranormal romance is a thrill ride."
—Publishers Weekly

HUNTER'S HOPE

HUNTER'S HOPE

ALYSSA

NEW YORK TIMES BESTSELLING AUTHOR

This book is a work of fiction. Names, characters, places, and incidents are the product of the author's imagination or are used fictitiously. Any resemblance to actual events, locales, or persons, living or dead, is coincidental.

Entangled Publishing, LLC
10940 S Parker Road
Suite 327
Parker, CO 80134
Visit our website at www.entangledpublishing.com.

Amara is an imprint of Entangled Publishing, LLC.

Edited by Liz Pelletier and Lydia Sharp
Cover design by Bree Archer
Cover photography by Wander Aguiar
and passigatti/GettyImages
Interior design by Toni Kerr

Print ISBN 978-1-64937-091-4
ebook ISBN 978-1-64937-103-4

Manufactured in the United States of America

First Edition December 2021

AMARA

ALSO BY ALYSSA DAY

VAMPIRE MOTORCYCLE CLUB

Bane's Choice
Hunter's Hope

WARRIORS OF POSEIDON SERIES

Atlantis Rising
Atlantis Awakening
Atlantis Unleashed
Atlantis Unmasked
Atlantis Redeemed
Atlantis Betrayed
Vampire in Atlantis

TIGER'S EYE MYSTERIES

Dead Eye
Private Eye
Evil Eye
Eye of Danger
Eye of the Storm
A Dead End Christmas
Apple of My Eye

POSEIDON'S WARRIORS SERIES

January in Atlantis
February in Atlantis
March in Atlantis
April in Atlantis
May in Atlantis
June in Atlantis

This one is for Lydia Sharp, because wow do they deserve it! Thank you for your sharp eye and enthusiasm, even at three in the morning. You're a rock star!

CHAPTER ONE

"I bet this never happened to Dracula," muttered the man—now vampire—hanging upside down after falling off the roof of the Savannah riverfront hotel. He watched his keys and wallet fall out of his pockets and plunge to the street several stories below.

Again.

Hunter Evans was having a bad damn day.

Night.

"This vampire thing is not for weaklings," Luke told him, his voice filled with laughter. "The first thing you learn is to keep your pockets empty."

No. The first thing you learned was that the thirst was everything. All-consuming.

Fire.

They—the vampires who had Turned him—had promised that this would pass. That soon the thirst would be manageable. In time, it would be a mere background presence in his life. That he'd be able to eat normal food again. Drink a beer without gagging.

Be normal.

Almost normal.

He laughed, a sound so bitter it rasped like the screech of rusty nails being pulled from metal. Who was he kidding? He'd never be normal again.

Luke sighed. "I know, man. Believe me, though. It gets easier."

Luke Calhoun had been Turned decades ago. He'd had plenty of time to adjust. Hunter had been a vampire for all of three weeks. Nothing at all was easy or even getting easier.

Most evenings, when he woke up out of a sleep so heavy he may as well have been dead or in a coma, he was afraid he'd actually turned feral, like a lion maddened by starvation. He woke up wanting to rip and tear and rend.

To drink.

Most of all, to drink.

"Why don't you go back to the house and find a few more bags of blood? I know they keep plenty in the walk-in refrigerator in the basement," Luke said in a crooning, singsong tone that sounded like what Hunter might have used with a rabid dog.

Before, when he was the man, not the rabid dog.

"I don't want more bagged blood," he growled. "I want it fresh and hot and pumping out of the vein that I sink my teeth into. And I'm disgusted by myself for wanting it. How can I ever get used to this? How can it ever get easier?"

Luke hopped down lightly onto the balcony of a darkened room. Hopefully an unoccupied room, or some tourist was going to get the surprise of a lifetime. Then he held out his hand and a tiny flame appeared above his palm.

"It gets easier," he said again. "When I first became a vampire, this fire-starter power was so far out of my control that I nearly burned down an entire town. Nearly killed myself and my family. Ironic, a fire starter teaching a firefighter how to be a vampire, isn't it?"

"*Former* firefighter, it looks like." With some effort,

Hunter managed to right himself and climb onto the balcony. "And you said you nearly killed your family. Meara and Bane?"

Luke's laugh was as bitter as Hunter's had been. "No. Not this family. My human family."

"What happened?"

"Nothing I plan to share," Luke said flatly. "I'm tired of this. You're on your own the rest of the night. Try not to kill any innocent humans."

"What happens if I do?"

Luke hopped up onto the balcony railing and turned his head to look at Hunter. "If you do, you're a murderer. Do you want to spend the next few hundred years with that on your conscience?"

Hunter's throat tightened. "Few hundred *years*?"

But Luke just shook his head, leapt out into the dark night, and was gone.

Hunter blew out a frustrated breath and headed down to the street to find his keys and wallet. This time, though, he walked through the empty hotel room and out the door and then punched the button for the elevator. Nothing in the vampire handbook—*was* there even a vampire handbook? If not, should he write one?—mandated that he had to climb back down the outside of the building for twelve floors, although Luke or Bane would probably have something to say about it. He had been climbing around rooftops, learning the patrol routes, because part of his job now was to help his new family protect the city.

"Like Batman." His innate sense of humor kicked in then, and he grinned a little. Batman. Bats. Vampires.

Heh.

The elevator door opened just then, empty except for a man and a woman who both looked like they were about a hundred years old. Hunter nodded politely and stepped in, pressed the Lobby button, and thought about flashing his new fangs just for fun, but it would probably send them into cardiac arrest. He wasn't sure his attempt at CPR—something he'd done hundreds of times as a firefighter—would work all that well, since he still wasn't completely in control of this new vampire strength.

And there were probably cameras in the elevator, so the news would be something like:

Missing Firefighter Crushes Elderly Couple's Ribs for Fun

And wouldn't Bane have a cow about that. Vampires were a big damn secret, after all.

"Freaking elevator music," he muttered, the thirst squashing his momentary amusement.

The old man scowled at him, but, to Hunter's surprise, the old woman peeked at him from behind her husband and flashed a cheeky grin. "If I were twenty years younger—"

"You'd still be old enough to be his grandmother," the man grumbled, putting a possessive arm around his wife.

Hunter couldn't help but grin a little, even sunk in a foul mood. When they reached the lobby, he stepped back for them to exit first, and the woman winked at him. "Whoever she is, she's a lucky woman," she whispered, chuckling when her husband snorted.

Right. How *lucky* a woman would have to be to meet a man whose main desire was to drain her dry.

Maybe he would have been better off dead.

As he started to step out, an odd-looking dog raced in front of him and darted inside the elevator.

"Marigold!" a woman's voice called. "Marigold! Stop!"

Hunter looked up to see a flurry of color as a woman rushed down the hallway toward him. Or, presumably, toward the dog.

"She's inside. She's not going anywhere," he said, moving to block the entry to keep the animal in, surprised to find himself amused for the second time in ten minutes. For only the third or fourth time in the weeks since he'd died.

"She might push the button for a floor, and then where would I be? Chasing her all over the hotel all night?" The woman, a colorful whirlwind of purple silk, wild red curls, and flashing green eyes, ducked past him and bent down. "You naughty thing! Hotels are dangerous! What if somebody tried to eat you?"

"This may not be a five-star hotel, but I doubt they've resorted to eating dogs," Hunter drawled.

She lifted the animal into her arms and stood, turning to face him but still looking at the animal in her arms.

"Marigold is a raccoon, as you can see. And this is the South. They eat raccoons in the South, or haven't you read *Nathaniel Porter's Field Guide to Local Fauna*?"

"I…can't say that I have," he said slowly, because his brain cells seemed to be melting.

It *was* a raccoon.

In a hotel.

And the raccoon rescuer was the most beautiful woman he'd ever seen.

She was nearly as tall as he was, so maybe five-ten. She had cheekbones that could cut glass, and her smile, directed at the raccoon, was wide and lit up her face. Her eyes were the brilliant green of a spring apple, and her mass of red curls reached nearly to her waist. The purple dress she wore was a complicated thing made of scarves or loose flutters of fabric, and the entire picture gave him the impression of a forest nymph or fortune-teller.

"A raccoon," he finally said, simply because the situation seemed to call for him to speak, but he had no idea what the hell to say.

"Yes. As I said. If you'd move out of the way?" She finally glanced up at him. Her eyes narrowed, and her glossy red lips tightened. "Oh. I should have known it would be that kind of night."

He knew she was talking, but he couldn't quite make out the words or the meaning, because every single molecule of his body was suddenly, painfully focused on one thing and one thing only.

The pulse beating in her throat.

"What?" he finally managed.

"Are you listening?" She narrowed her eyes, but then a look of dawning comprehension spread across her face, and she sighed. "Oh. Oh, right. Well, I'm sorry, but you'll have to learn the rules. I'm only available for consults from ten until two on Wednesdays, and this is decidedly not that."

Suddenly, Hunter's confusion had nothing to do with the thirst, as the meaning of her words penetrated his dazed mind.

"What? The rules?"

"Shush, Marigold," she told the raccoon, which seemed to be trying to climb onto the woman's shoulders and into her tangle of hair. "Yes, the rules."

She glanced left and right and then leaned forward and whispered. "You see, I know what you are."

Hunter rocked back a step. She knew? But how? He hadn't flashed his fangs or done anything to expose his new nature…

"You *know*?"

She nodded, her beautiful eyes warm with something that looked a lot like compassion. "Yes, I know. I can sense when someone is…has passed on. I'm Alice Darlington. You may have heard of me."

"I don't think so," he said slowly. Alice Darlington. It wasn't a name he'd forget. And her face—damn. He was sure he wouldn't forget that face.

A flash of what looked like resignation crossed her face so quickly he wasn't sure he'd really seen it, but then she raised her chin. "Right. You just happened to show up in my elevator."

But then she took a deep breath and shook her head. "I'm sorry. That was petty, especially in light of what must have happened to you when you were alive. You can come tell me what you need, just like everyone else. Just pop by between ten and two on Wednesday, okay? The rest of my time is my own and—"

"When I was *alive*?" How did she know he'd died? And he was damn sure still alive.

He jerked his head to the right at the sound of footsteps and laughter. People coming. But he needed this conversation to continue. He put an arm around Alice Darlington and gently guided her down the hall to a windowed alcove, trying all the while to ignore the scent of her hair and the pulse in her throat. He closed his eyes and reached desperately for control when he realized he didn't want to let her go, because—somehow, some way—holding her was sending a warm sensation of peace through him.

And he hadn't known a moment of peace since he'd gotten caught in the fire that had killed him.

When he opened his eyes and slowly exhaled, she was staring up at him, her green eyes suddenly enormous in her pale face.

"How are you so solid?" Her voice was barely a whisper; she trembled in his arms. "You're manifesting this strongly, and you can't be more than six months dead… Please stop touching me. I can't help you if I'm afraid."

Hunter immediately, reluctantly, dropped his arm from her waist and took two steps back. Manifesting? What the hell?

Maybe all of this was a strange dream he was having.

A dream about *raccoons*?

Nope, didn't seem likely.

"Three weeks, not six months. How do you know about me?"

"I—It's my gift." She laughed, but it was a bitter sound. "My curse. I know you're a ghost, but I can't help you right now. Please—I have to go." With that, she edged past him and raced off down the hallway, still clutching Marigold the raccoon, leaving Hunter standing there staring after her.

A *ghost*?

She thought he was a ghost.

And she had regular consulting hours with ghosts?

Her scent still floated around him, teasing his heightened vampiric senses, and then a real smile—the kind he hadn't felt since before he'd become a vampire—spread across his face. To hell with Dracula, climbing around on buildings, and vampire lessons.

He was going to follow Alice Darlington.

His new life had just gotten a hell of a lot more interesting.

CHAPTER TWO

Alice secured Marigold in her crate in the back of the old and battered minivan, then made her way through the midnight-painted streets of her adopted hometown. Savannah was beautiful in the moonlight, taking on the magical shadows of a city that embraced its haunted past, took pride in its golden present, and looked forward to a brilliant future.

Best of all, it held no painful memories for her.

She caught a flash of deeper shadow in the darkness along the edge of the street in her peripheral vision. Something—a furtive movement?—out of the ordinary that tickled the edge of her mind. Or maybe that was only the remnant of her encounter in the hotel.

She'd never seen a ghost that *real* before.

Usually they were more…hazy. Edges not clearly defined. Sort of wavery. Shimmery.

Some of them—the ones that had been dead the longest—were almost hard to see in certain light. There was a feeling of transparent impermanence to them, as if a strong breeze would blow them to wherever they should be going.

Which, in her opinion, was never:

In her house, or

In her rescue, scaring the animals, or, really,

Anywhere she happened to be.

The ability to "see dead people," *The Sixth Sense* and

Ghost to the contrary, was highly overrated. Anyone who looked like Patrick Swayze had never once appeared to her. Nobody sang the *Ghostbusters* theme song when she arrived.

Although, admittedly, she had hummed it to herself on occasion.

This man, though, and man he was, no matter if he'd been dead three weeks, as he claimed, or a hundred years, this man had sparked electricity—or magic—in her that had crackled and sizzled across her skin. His aura had been strange. Caught somewhere on the spectrum between the colors that formed human auras—or the colors she'd learned characterized human auras; the living were not her specialty—and the darker hues that comprised a ghost's aura.

She'd caught her breath in surprise and a feeling harder to characterize than mere surprise when he'd put his arm around her, pulling her against his hard, muscular body.

His *hard, muscular* body.

His very much *not* ghostlike body.

And his eyes. They'd been so blue, and they'd shone as if lit from within, blazing as they stared down into her own.

She shrugged, trying to put it out of her mind. He'd show up for her office hours, or he wouldn't. More than likely, she'd never see him again.

She wondered at the feeling of regret that pinched her chest at the thought. She'd only spent a few minutes in his company. It didn't make sense that she'd care if she saw him again or not.

And yet...

She punched the radio on, determined to put the

encounter out of her mind, and sang along with Billie Eilish for the rest of the short drive to the small property that held both her home and her pride and joy: the Little Darlings Rescue.

No more than a ten-minute drive due west from Savannah's historic district, Little Darlings occupied a space on Kollock Street almost equidistant between two cemeteries.

Being a person who not only saw but also spoke to ghosts on a regular basis, Alice had no fear of either cemeteries or of their occupants. People were people, dead or alive, and although some of those she'd encountered had been nastier than others, she'd never met one who truly scared her.

Yet, a small voice in the back of her mind whispered.

But she dismissed that, too, since she was absolutely a person who could put unpleasantness out of her mind, after what she'd endured.

Unpleasantness, her mind jeered.

Okay, the Institute had been about more than unpleasantness.

But the word *torture*, even just whispered in her darkest memories, brought too much pain.

Someday she'd bring them down.

Someday.

But for now, she had animals to feed and care for. "Forever homes" to find for society's most helpless creatures. In a little less than a year, Little Darlings and Alice herself had earned a reputation for having a way with the most desperate cases, and the rescue facility was at its maximum capacity.

She stopped at the curb to unlock the gate to the driveway—drunken tourists had the ability to show up in the strangest places, so locked gates were common in the city—and climbed into the van, feeling the hair on the back of her neck stand up. She knew better than to ignore the feeling.

Someone or something was watching her.

"No ghosts until Wednesday at ten," she called out. "I'll see you in order of appearance then, okay? And I'll help if I can. But right now, I need to work and get some sleep."

She sighed, drove carefully into the driveway, and then jumped out and relocked the gate. If any of her neighbors were up, they'd think she was paranoid. Luckily, Savannah was *filled* with so-called "paranoid" people, and those who claimed to see ghosts, and even psychics and mediums, and charlatans and con artists. So, at best, they'd believe she had a gift. At worst, they'd think she was a con artist or in need of medical attention.

She'd dealt with far worse. In fact, she'd picked Savannah as her own forever home for exactly that reason. A city that made part of its living from ghost tours was just about the most welcoming place she could imagine.

And, even better, Savannahians loved their animals. Her rescue organization had benefitted from their love and benevolence from the first day it had opened.

She pulled up in front of her lovely home and parked in the driveway. The garage had long since donated its space to become a pet food and supply storage room, but it wasn't like the ancient minivan would be harmed by Savannah's mild weather.

The house wasn't historic—it was around fifty years old,

built on the foundation of a much older home that had been condemned and torn down—but it was lovely, and it was all hers. A modest life insurance policy she was sure her family had never known about, or they would have found a way to steal it, had paid its proceeds to her on her beloved great-aunt's passing. It hadn't been a huge amount of money, but it had been enough for a down payment, and a friendly banker with a love for animals had helped her get the loan.

Two stories of white-painted coziness with shutters that gleamed darkly now but shone bright blue in the sunshine. An interior that she was slowly but surely making her own with estate sale finds and small furnishings and decorations she built and sewed herself.

Things the Institute was good at: crafting classes and electroshock treatment.

Suddenly impatient with the uncharacteristic bitterness of her thoughts, she blew out a breath and climbed out of the van, slinging her tote bag onto her shoulder and heading for the back to retrieve Marigold, who'd chirped impatiently all the way from the hotel.

But when she rounded the back of the van, it was to discover that Marigold was no longer in her crate.

Or even in the van.

Instead, she was being held in the muscular arms of the man—ghost—from the hotel.

And the normally good-natured raccoon was hissing.

Alice froze and then forced herself forward. "What are you doing? Give her to me."

He flashed a wickedly sensual smile that caused a ripple of sensation to wash through her, carrying an unexpected heat to every nerve ending in her body. She suddenly felt too hot, too breathless, too...*alive*.

"She clearly would prefer to be held by you," he said easily. "I can't say that I blame her."

His blue eyes gleamed, glowing in the reflected brightness of the lantern lights affixed on either side of her front door. When he stepped toward her, she automatically took a step back. This man—this ghost—most definitely didn't belong in her yard, holding her raccoon. He was... too much.

Too tall, too big, too intense, too *gorgeous*.

Her breath gave a funny little hitch in her throat.

He was *beautiful*.

Maybe her age? Late twenties? Or early thirties? Tall; he was easily six feet, maybe a couple of inches more. Broad shoulders angled down to a slim waist with no softness showing anywhere. And he had amazing bone structure. She suddenly wanted to dig out the paints she'd tried out a few times when she was enjoying her new freedom and try to capture the strength in his jaw, the sharpness of his high cheekbones, and the glow in his eyes. His face held a slight beard, as though he hadn't shaved in the days before he'd died, and those long, dark lashes shaded not just his incredible eyes but the shadows beneath them. His dark hair was swept back from his forehead, as if he'd impatiently shoved it out of his way with one of the large, capable hands that currently held an armful of unhappy raccoon.

Marigold hissed again, snapping Alice out of her trance, and she edged forward, took the angry creature, and stumbled back and away from her unexpected visitor. She swallowed, hard, and tried to regain control of the situation.

The only way to deal with ghosts was to take the reins at the very beginning of each encounter. She thought she'd done this at the hotel, but she'd been caught off guard by the man's—the ghost's—*aliveness.* She'd encountered ghosts who could manipulate objects before, of course, but nothing like this.

"Listen. I—" The amusement in his gaze threw her off, and she forgot what she'd been about to say. So, she asked a basic question to give herself time to regroup. "What is your name? I can't keep thinking of you as 'that man' or 'that ghost.'"

His devilish smile flashed again. "I like that you keep thinking of me."

"That's not what I meant! I just—I actually—Oh! Good *night*!"

What was she doing? The simplest and quickest way to remove herself from the situation was to do just that. She backed away until she was on the other side of the van, and then she ran for the porch, holding a trembling Marigold tightly. When she glanced back, afraid the stranger would be right behind her, he was gone.

"Well, that's better, isn't it?" She kissed the top of Marigold's silky head as she slowed to take the steps to the porch. "I guess he can take a hint, at least."

The deep voice that answered her was husky with suppressed laughter. "Sadly, no. I'm terrible at hints. Perhaps you should be more direct."

She looked up just in time to avoid running him down, but not in time to stop herself from plowing right into him. He caught her with those strong hands on her arms and pulled her closer, Marigold between them.

Instead of struggling, though, Alice opened her senses—the ones that comprised what she thought of in her more fanciful moments as her Third Eye—completely, reaching for that icy sense of connection that always opened between her and the ghosts. If he wouldn't leave, she at least needed to get a more comprehensive understanding of what kind of ghost she was dealing with; then she could determine how to make him go away.

Her gift, once a flickering sense of the "other," and then, later, a more fully-fleshed-out recognition of the dead, now responded easily and quickly to her call. She stayed right where she was, trying to ignore the strength of his arms around her, trying not to surrender to the impulse to inhale as deeply as possible his wonderful scent of pine and soap and *man*, and closed her eyes to allow her senses to reach out for that connection to his essence—to what she thought of as the remnant of humanity that sometimes remained after a person died.

Only for her eyes to snap open again when there was no connection. No essence for her to touch, because this man, odd aura or not, was very much alive.

"You're not a ghost! You're not even dead!"

The smile still played around the edges of his sensual lips but faded from his eyes. "That's a matter of some debate, apparently."

Alice realized she still stood in the circle of his arms and shoved at his hard, muscled chest with one hand. "Get back! I have…I have pepper spray! And an attack raccoon!"

He released her and raised his hands, palms out, and

took a step back. "I'm sorry. I didn't mean to scare you."

"I don't believe you. You followed me to my home. I read books. I know that's a classic warning sign of a dangerous man. You might be a serial killer, for all I know."

Those fey eyes seemed to glow with blue flames. "**I am no danger to you. I swear it.**"

A shiver of awareness at the electrically charged sound of his voice raced down her spine. There was something almost hypnotic about him, and she found herself nodding.

Of course, he was no danger to her. He'd sworn it. In fact, he…

He…

What?

"No!" She shook her head hard, trying to dispel the compulsion she'd been falling into. "What is that? Were you trying to hypnotize me? Do you think that makes you feel like *less* of a danger? Now, I'm going to call 911, when before I would have just asked you to leave."

She lifted Marigold to one shoulder and dug inside her bag, searching for her phone.

"Damn. Well, it was worth a try," he said, raising one shoulder in a casual shrug. "I guess I'm not good enough at this vampire stuff yet. Maybe we could just talk? I find that I'd really, really like to get to know you. And my name is Hunter Evans."

"Pleased to meet you," she said automatically, before realizing what an absolutely untrue statement it was. She was *not* pleased to meet him. He'd invaded her space, tried to hypnotize her, and, and, and…*manhandled her raccoon.* She was *not*—

Wait.

"This *vampire* stuff?" She blinked, captivated by the sudden stillness with which he held himself. It was as if his body had tensed in a fierce readiness; a predator focusing his entire concentration on her. A shiver raced through her at the gleam in his eyes, and she had the overwhelming urge to run fast and far and hide away from this dangerous man.

But she was nobody's prey. Never again.

"So," she began gently, changing tactics. "Mr. Evans. You think you're a vampire. I was sure you were a ghost, but, well, that doesn't matter. The truth is you're just a man, and I was tired and confused. I'm sorry for the misunderstanding. If you'll just leave now, no harm, no foul, and—"

He leaned against one of the wooden pillars on the porch, and she could tell he was deliberately attempting to appear nonthreatening, which only made her more wary. He wore a dark, long-sleeved shirt, blue jeans, and boots, all of which should have made him seem ordinary, but instead only highlighted his dark, deadly beauty.

If fallen angels tried to look like normal humans, they would look like Hunter Evans.

"Call me Hunter, Alice. But first, tell me I can come back tomorrow, and I'll go."

She considered the request. Her instincts shouted at her to say no, but common sense said she could take precautions by tomorrow. Right now, she was vulnerable and in danger. If he'd agree to go, she was better off consenting to his request.

"Fine. You can come back tomorrow. During our normal hours of operation. Ten to six."

"Thank you, Alice." His eyes narrowed in lazy speculation. "Now invite me into your home."

"What? No! You said you'd go!" She took a step back, and then another. "Please, just go."

"**Invite me in**."

A curious warmth settled on her shoulders, relaxing them. Yes, she should invite him in; why would she refuse? He was her guest, he was…

No.

No.

"No!"

"Alice," he said, her name a sensual caress in his whiskey-rough voice. He took a step toward her, that startling blue gaze hot and fixed on her face, but then he slowly blinked and an odd expression crossed his face. "All right. I'm sorry. I didn't mean to frighten you. I'll leave."

Before she could respond, he leapt off the porch, bypassing the steps entirely, and then turned to take a long, last look at her. "But I'll be back. I can't make it during your official office hours. I'm sorry. Will tomorrow evening be acceptable?"

"I—what? Why?"

He glanced at Marigold, then flashed a totally unexpected and boyish grin. "To adopt an animal, of course. Isn't that why you're here? I bet Bram Stoker would love a raccoon to play with."

"I—what?"

"Good night, Alice Darlington. Thank you for making this the most memorable evening of my new life."

Before she could respond to that, he was gone, and she was left staring after him at nothing but shadows.

CHAPTER THREE

One of the shadows in her yard, perhaps the most insignificant of the shadows, waited until the vampire was gone and the woman had locked herself into her home. He trembled as he waited, for Minor demons were small and powerless.

This demon, who'd forgotten his nest-name, if in fact his mother had ever bestowed one before the warlocks stole him, had been in this territory for long enough to learn to fear vampires almost as much as he feared warlocks and necromancers. The vampire he'd been tasked to follow many long days before had killed the demon's master and destroyed the necromancer's warlock servants.

That vampire's woman, who'd seemed kind, at least from a distance, had turned out to be angel-kin, and those could be deadly to Minor demons.

This was a different vampire that his new master—after beating him—had ordered the Minor demon to follow. And he'd never interacted with the woman before. He would have to report it. And report *her*, the woman whose aura glowed gold and who had held a forest creature in her arms with kindness and caring.

The Minor demon cringed, his own wounds aching from the master's beating. One of his wings was bent, and he couldn't fly at all—could only hope that it would heal correctly. He could recognize kindness, even if he'd never received any.

He could recognize caring, although he had only the most distant memory of it.

If only…but no. He would not hope or even pretend to hope.

Hope was the cruelest lie of all. When one of the monsters who commanded him died, another, even more terrible, took its place.

Hope had no place in the world of a Minor demon.

A hot tear splashed onto his face, but he angrily scrubbed it away with one claw-tipped hand. He had no time for self-pity, either.

Suddenly, an amazing smell of cooking and food wafted along the breeze from the house and toward him. His stomach growled so loudly he was afraid that someone might have heard it. He was so very, very hungry. He'd had no food for days.

The master had forbidden him to eat, laughing at his hunger.

The Minor demon curled up in a ball, arms clutching his aching, empty stomach, filled with so much pain and desperation that he didn't hear the soft footsteps coming toward him until it was almost too late.

Shocked into action, he transformed into the last creature he'd seen of comparable size to himself and huddled in a ball on the ground, hoping against hope that the woman—for it was her; he could smell her delicate scent of flowers and honey now—wouldn't see him in the darkness.

But she had a light in her hand, and suddenly it was pointed directly at him.

"Oh, no," she breathed out. "Not another one. Why do people keep dumping their pets in the yard?"

The Minor demon closed his eyes and tucked his tail, which was now luxuriously furred, instead of scaled and claw-tipped, tightly around him.

"Oh, my beautiful boy, it's all right, my lovely one, let me have a look at you," she said in a lyrical voice, almost singing, a voice of bells and light and goodness, a voice designed to put any damaged and terrified creature at ease.

And he learned that even a damaged and terrified Minor demon was susceptible. He dared to open one eye.

"A beautiful golden retriever, oh, sweetheart, let me see if you're hurt, won't you?" She carefully approached, her voice calm and gentle and filled with love. "May I touch you? You'll let me help you, won't you, sweet boy?"

He knew he shouldn't.

He *knew* he *shouldn't.*

She called him a lovely boy.

He put his head in her hand.

CHAPTER FOUR

Hunter raced his Harley down the road that bordered the Wilmington River, his vampire senses wide open to the sounds and scents of a cool December night. It was maybe high forties, with a sharp breeze from the river that made it even colder. He didn't feel the cold the way he used to, though.

He didn't feel hardly anything in the same way he had before.

Before he'd died. Before he'd agreed to be Turned into a vampire.

Before his Turn had gone wrong and caused him so much pain.

These days, he didn't feel much of anything, except thirst and exhaustion and anger.

Anger at himself for agreeing to become a vampire. Maybe he should have died. Maybe it had been God's plan.

But he wasn't damned or broken or cursed. He was just a vampire. None of the worst myths seemed to be true. He'd even gone into his old neighborhood church one night, just to see if he'd burst into flames or if a lightning bolt would strike him dead.

Instead, he'd sat in the front pew, alone in the light of the candles he'd lit, feeling oddly comforted. He'd thanked God for this second life and the chance to continue to do good in the world, and then he'd gone back to the mansion and ripped into a few more bags of blood.

No irony there, right?

He slowed his bike just enough to take the turn without flipping and roared up the driveway to the mansion, still finding it hard to believe that he lived there.

In a mansion.

The house was more than a century old. It was a stately manor home that overlooked the river and was big enough for dozens of vampires to live there, although in fact only five did.

Well, five vampires, two staff members, one woolly mammoth they called a dog, and an angel.

An actual, honest-to-heaven angel. Half angel, at least. Dr. Ryan St. Cloud, the angel, had tried to explain how she'd found out she was Nephilim—half angel and half human—but his attention had wandered when he'd realized that the incredibly ambrosia-like scent he was smelling was probably her angel blood. That's when Bane, the owner of the mansion and Ryan's soon-to-be husband, had strode into the room with a glare promising Hunter's impending death.

Since Bane was the three-hundred-year old master vampire who'd Turned Hunter in the first place, it probably would have made him feel bad to kill his newest family member, so Hunter had speedily excused himself from the situation and gone to the basement freezer for more bags of blood.

Hunter scowled as he braked, sensing a theme.

Thirst? Bags of blood.

Stress? Bags of blood.

Impending death? Bags of blood.

Realizing you're seconds away from attacking a

beautiful woman, despite the fact that she's holding a raccoon in her arms? Bags of blood.

He bleakly wondered if he'd ever be able to have sex again without waking up to discover that he'd ripped his partner's throat out while climaxing. Or if he'd have to take bags of blood on all dates. Then he wondered if this was the kind of thing he felt comfortable asking Bane or Luke.

Hell, no.

"Allo! Back so soon?" Meara blinked into existence in front of him, balanced on his handlebars.

He almost crashed the bike.

"Damn it, Meara, I've asked you to quit doing that!"

She just laughed and gracefully flipped backward off the bike and onto the lawn. "Don't be so boring. I get enough 'Meara, don't do that, Meara, don't do this, Meara, don't eat the tourists' from my brother to last me another three centuries. I don't need it from you, too, little one."

She meant "little one" in terms of their relative ages. Although she looked maybe twenty-five, Bane's sister had been a vampire for three hundred years. The two of them had been Turned at the same time. Something about a wild night at an English village festival, from what he'd been able to pick up. He needed to ask for the full story sometime. Although he had no idea the etiquette involved—was it bad manners to ask another vampire how they'd been Turned?

"Fine, just stop using your invisibility powers on me like a jump scare. I'm having a hard enough time figuring this all out." He heard the snappishness in his voice and rolled his eyes at himself. "Sorry. Don't mean to sound like a whiner. It's been a difficult night. And yes, I'd have to agree with Bane that you shouldn't eat the tourists."

The thing was, he wasn't sure whether or not she'd been kidding about that. Meara Delacourt was the kind of vampire you'd expect to meet if you believed in the movie-star version of vampires. Or if vampires all looked like Norwegian supermodels.

She was tall and slender, loved to wear designer clothes and expensive jewelry that complemented her golden hair and eyes, and she had a wicked sense of humor. In other words, if she'd decided to munch on a few tourists, they'd probably consider it to be their privilege. She was so beautiful that he'd been tongue-tied and completely unable to form words the first time he'd met her, a few years back in a nightclub.

But then one night she'd been caught out by the dawn and nearly died. Purely by chance, he'd been on his way home from work and seen a woman collapse onto the road in front of his car, smoke rising from her skin, and he'd rescued her and learned about vampires all at the same time. For some reason he still didn't quite understand, neither she nor Bane had shown any inclination to either kill him or enthrall him to safeguard their secrets. Instead, they'd repaid him with their trust.

Vampires were definitely not about to come out of the coffin, so to speak, and announce their existence to the world. Protecting their secret was paramount. But Hunter had told them he would keep their confidences, and Meara and Bane had believed him.

To this day, Hunter didn't know if Bane or Meara had spied on him or followed up in any way to be sure he wasn't spilling the bloodsucking beans, but he and Bane had met for a semi-regular chess game ever since.

Now it was Hunter's secret to protect, too.

His eyes widened as the realization punched him in the gut—he'd told Alice Darlington that he was a vampire.

That was about as far from protecting a secret as you could get.

Son of a bitch.

"You look distraught, little brother. What's wrong? Perhaps you ate a few tourists yourself?" Meara's intelligent golden gaze fixed on his face. "You don't have to figure this out alone. When you and Luke tire of each other's company, come find me."

"You were unhappy that Bane Turned me," he said, not in accusation but in simple fact. Unhappy was an understatement, though. She'd been furious. He'd heard a lot of their conversation, even when he'd been trapped in unconsciousness. "The last thing I wanted to do was bother you with my problems."

She waved one hand in dismissal. "My brother takes too many chances. Turning a human to vampire is dangerous to the one doing the Turning. I don't want to lose him, just as I don't want to lose you, now that you're part of our family. But you're changing the subject. Why do you look so distressed?"

"There was this woman…" he began, reluctance fighting every word. But before he could go on, the sound of Bane's bellow roared across the yard from the back of the house.

"*Ryan!* Not again!"

Hunter threw a questioning look at Meara, who started to laugh. "Our angel is trying to learn to fly."

"What? How?"

"She keeps jumping off the roof."

A loud, high-pitched, and decidedly female shriek rang out next, and Meara raced around the house, Hunter hot on her heels. By the time they arrived, Ryan was floating in midair, halfway between the roof of the three-story manor and the grass, laughing wildly.

Bane, almost six and a half feet of deadly vampire, levitated in the air next to her and held his hands out, palms up, clearly using his powers to keep her from smashing to the ground.

And he wasn't laughing.

Not even a little.

"I fail to understand why you find your own impending death so funny," Bane said through teeth gritted so hard that his fangs might be in danger of breaking.

Ryan, still laughing, raised her own hands and flicked her fingers at Bane. Twin bolts of pure white light shot out from her hands and arrowed toward Bane, who waited until the last moment and then performed a flying somersault to avoid them. The light beams struck the topmost branches of one of the graceful old southern live oaks on the gently sloping lawn and sheared the branches clear off the tree.

Bane narrowed his eyes and moved his own fingers, and Ryan suddenly plunged toward the ground, only to catch herself with a cushion of light just before she landed, bouncing gently off it as though it were some kind of celestial trampoline.

"You are the most infuriating woman I have ever met," Bane said, floating down to the ground. "Were you planning to slice off any of *my* limbs with that light?"

Ryan ran over and threw her arms around him. "Of course not. I like your limbs just where they are. The beams would have bounced off you, just like I bounced off the light, instead of smashing into the ground. Nephilim, remember? You have to quit treating me like I'm fragile."

"You're half human," Meara drawled, stalking toward the pair. "You *are* fragile."

"Well, compared to you, an armored tank is fragile," Ryan said, still grinning. She was shorter than Meara, maybe five foot six, and curvier, too. Her long, dark hair, blue eyes, and ready smile combined to make her a lovely woman; her intelligence and warmth made her one of the kindest and most approachable people Hunter had ever met. She'd even put her own life at risk in order to help him when she'd thought Bane had abducted him from her care in the hospital for some evil purpose.

Then she'd found out about vampires and fallen in love with Bane, who, frankly, worshipped the ground she walked on—or, in this case, floated over.

Meara had confided in Hunter that the manor had been a dreary and often angry place to live before Ryan moved in. Only a few short weeks later, the entire atmosphere in the home had lightened.

"Love," Meara had said, with one of her characteristically French shrugs. "It makes so many things better."

"Hunter!" Ryan beckoned him to come closer. "How are you? I'm sorry I missed you before you went out. I had to work late at the clinic."

Ryan, a doctor with a special gift of healing, thanks to her angel father, had resigned from Savannah General to work full-time at the Delacourt Free Clinic. She was its new director and was already making improvements, according to Meara, who funded the entire endeavor.

Bane and Meara were *serious* multimillionaires, the nearest Hunter could figure, which was just another surreal thing about his new life. He'd been surviving just fine on his firefighter's salary before. Now he lived in a mansion with rich vampires and an angel.

It was like he'd died and woken up in the Twilight Zone. No wonder Alice had thought he was a ghost. The thought of her—the memory of how she'd felt in his arms—short-circuited his brain for a moment.

Alice.

He realized everybody was staring at him. Right. Ryan had asked how he was.

"I'm fine," he told Ryan. "I was out having vampire lessons with Luke."

She studied him with perceptive blue eyes. "And something else happened, too?"

"What do you mean?"

"I don't know. Something is different about you. You've been so downcast these past few days, we were worried about you." She glanced up at Bane, who'd walked up and put his arm around her waist, pulling her closer to him.

"*I* wasn't worried about you, not being a girl," Bane said drily.

Meara exploded into movement and threw a lightning-fast kick at Bane's head, stopping with perfect precision when her booted foot was an inch from her brother's face. "Yes, we *girls* are so emotional."

Bane calmly moved her foot aside with two fingers.

"Exactly. Nice form, though."

Meara laughed and lowered her leg and then put an arm around Hunter's shoulders. "Come, little brother. Tell us about your night. And the woman you mentioned."

A sharp pain in his gut reminded him of the reason he'd raced back. "Okay, sure. But I, ah—"

"Yes, of course. First, we will get you a snack. Then, we will have pie and discuss all manner of things, including why you smell like a wild animal." Meara sniffed delicately, wrinkling her perfect nose. "This is sure to be an excellent story."

He laughed. "Well, actually, there was this raccoon named Marigold..."

CHAPTER FIVE

Alice lifted the golden retriever into her arms, noting with dismay how little he weighed and how bad he smelled. He winced when her hand touched his shoulder, too, so there was probably an injury there. Thankfully she'd changed into old jeans and a sweatshirt before going back out to her van to retrieve the various bags and boxes she'd brought home with her. That's when she'd seen the poor dog shivering in the chill night air next to one of her azalea bushes.

She carried him into her home and then through the corridor to the building behind her house. The shelter was a haven of warmth and soft lighting, and soothing classical music played at a low volume night and day.

She gently lifted him into a crate in the special needs room, next to the bathing station, and laid him down on a soft blanket, murmuring to him all the time, and then closed the door and fastened it. He watched her carefully with a wary intelligence in his eyes but made no move to escape or protest, only curling up in what looked like total exhaustion.

"I'll bring you some food and water in just a moment, sweet boy," she crooned, and his ears perked up as he watched her, almost as if he understood.

Since she knew nothing at this stage about his health except there was no blood from any wounds and she'd seen no fleas, she decided to feed him before anything else. She filled a bowl with a light supper of her special homemade creation of ground turkey, rice, and vegetables, guaranteed to be easy on a dog's stomach, and put that and a bowl of fresh water in the crate with him. His eyes fixed instantly on the food, and he made a quiet moaning sound, but he made no move to lunge for the bowl. He waited politely for her to put the dishes down, pet the top of his head, and then refasten the crate before he reached out with one paw, pulled the food bowl close, and began to eat.

"Good job, sweetheart," she told him. "You eat that and keep it down, and we'll try a second helping, okay?"

Again, his ears perked up and he looked up at her. Then he bobbed his head in what she would have been prepared to swear in court was a nod before returning to his food.

"You are definitely not a stray. You've had training, for sure," she murmured. "I wonder…"

She took a deep breath and opened up to what she thought of as her second, more valuable, gift. With the same senses that allowed her to recognize and communicate with ghosts on an almost-telepathic level, she could connect with animals. Not in words, precisely, but through an emotional connection. She had never been quite sure how to label it, but the fact was that she could reassure and rehabilitate animals who had suffered trauma…even those that the rest of the world was prepared to give up on.

She knew she needed to get to work tending to everyone else—they were loudly making their demands known—but she couldn't resist trying.

Hey, sweet boy. You're going to be safe now. I don't know what happened to you, but we'll find out if you're okay at the vet and if you have a microchip, and we'll get you back home if you're just lost, okay?

When she projected the emotions associated with the word "home," the dog stopped eating, dropped into a crouch, flattened his ears against his head, and stared up at her. Sudden waves of terror lashed out from him so powerfully that they made her recoil, and he lifted his lips away from his teeth, baring unusually long canines. A low growl spilled out of his throat, but it was definitely fear, not aggression, causing it. She knew that as well as she knew her own name.

"Okay, okay. No home. We won't take you anywhere. You will stay here, and you will be safe. Do you hear me?"

The growling stopped, but he still crouched in a fight-or-flight pose, the waves of fear receding but still there.

I promise you. You will be safe. I will protect you and care for you. Do you understand?

The dog suddenly wiggled his body like he was shaking off water. Then he returned to his food as if okay now that the crisis had passed.

Alice felt a sharp stab of pure rage that anyone had treated this sweet boy so badly as to cause that kind of bone-deep fear. But then she closed her eyes, took a deep, centering breath, and returned to calm. Animals were extremely sensitive to variations in mood. If she went out to the main room in this state of agitation, she'd have a growling, hissing, snarling riot on her hands.

When she was calm again, she walked out to the large space at the heart of her shelter. "Hello, my darlings. I'm home. How is everyone tonight?"

The shelter was at capacity with twenty—now twenty-one, with the new addition—cats and dogs, four guinea pigs, two rabbits, and a ferret. And Marigold. Alice walked up and down the rows, giving a bit of attention to each, projecting waves of peace, and looking for signs of distress. Then she started in on feeding, giving them a late second dinner, carefully modulating food choices depending on their needs. Some, like Petunia the pug, were so emaciated from being loose in the wild, probably abandoned, that they had to be carefully fed with special foods and nutrients to avoid the sickness and regurgitation of refeeding syndrome.

Others, like Cleopatra the Persian cat, had specific needs that depended on the illnesses or injuries they were recovering from. Cleopatra's fur was only now beginning to grow back after the house fire she'd been caught in had burned her so badly she'd nearly died. Her family, financially devastated by the fire and their lack of insurance, had moved up north to live with a relative who was desperately allergic to cats, so they'd believed they'd had no choice but to let her go. The veterinarian who'd taken Cleo in had called Alice as soon as the situation became clear. Dr. Geary had donated her time, but Little Darlings needed to pick up the cost of the medicines and other expenses Cleo had incurred during her stay at the hospital.

Alice winced at the thought. She'd need to find a way to raise more money soon; a rescue group couldn't succeed without the help of kind and generous people who donated money, time, and supplies. Some people at the event that evening had promised donations, which would help. She did her best with what she had and didn't take any salary at all, but her roof needed repair, and food and medicines for the animals were always a priority.

The animals under her care had all been through difficult times. The rescue community knew her place as a special resource for damaged or severely injured or traumatized pets, and they sent her their most fragile. Cats, dogs, the very occasional wild animal, like Marigold—there were wildlife rescue organizations that were far more able to provide the special care that such animals needed, but those who'd been kept as pets, like Marigold, had somewhat different requirements.

Hamsters, guinea pigs. She'd even taken in her first ferret, just the day before.

All of them wanted and needed love and attention—even those who were too afraid to realize it. Even those who claimed they needed nobody. Alice didn't even try to pretend that she didn't include herself in that number. She'd been fiercely alone for so long, but what wouldn't she give for the chance at a real connection?

The answers came too quickly: her freedom. Her safety. Her life. Those were all things that she wouldn't give up for a temporary fling that would probably go bad. Except… Hunter's face popped into her mind again.

Those moments she'd been in his arms…she'd suddenly realized why people fell into bad relationships. There were times when soul-deadening loneliness smashed into intense attraction, and even she, who had to protect herself at all times, had felt the sweet, deceptive urge to succumb. To turn her face up to Hunter's and ask him to kiss her.

Or, even better, for her to kiss *him*.

She laughed at how utterly fearless she was in the safety of her own mind and opened the crate to another wounded being who liked to pretend he needed no one. Ajax the German shepherd mix. She fed him and sat cross-legged on the floor of his kennel to give him the ear scratching he loved. He pretended to be aloof, sitting regally with his head held high, facing slightly away from her, until she paused in the ear scratches. Then he glanced at her and scooted closer until he was practically in her lap. Ajax had been rescued from a dog-fight ring, and his scars proved that he'd been through some very hard times. He'd been with her for four months, and it had taken her every bit of the first three to get him to trust her. Now he was finally receptive to attention and beginning to believe he wouldn't be put back in danger at any second. His second-favorite activity of the day, close behind runs in her fenced-in yard, was listening to the schoolkid volunteers when they came to read stories to the animals.

He was still a volatile combination of wariness and a poignant need for attention, and she suddenly realized that she'd sensed the same cocktail of emotions in Hunter Evans.

"Not that I should be thinking about him. *Again.* Luckily, I'm sure I'll never see him again. Okay, sweet boy, eat your dinner."

She gave him a few final pats and then moved on to finish her rounds. She should have asked Veronica to stay later, but she'd had no idea the Small Business Association dinner would run so late. But the members had wanted to ask lots of questions after her talk, and she couldn't afford to cut any potential future sponsor or donor short. And she'd walked away with three firm commitments of support, so it had been a good night.

A *great* night.

And then…well. And then she'd encountered Hunter. Twice.

She was washing her hands when she realized she'd completed her work on autopilot, thinking of her mysterious guest all the while. Those glowing eyes—it had been almost enough to make her believe in his talk of vampires. After all, she did live in Savannah, city of a thousand ghosts.

She knew lots of people didn't believe in ghosts, either. And yet, she *knew* they existed. Who was she to say that other supernatural creatures didn't?

She laughed and hung up the towel she'd used. "Sure, and next it will be leprechauns and mermaids. I really need to get a life."

The golden retriever had cleaned his bowl but wasn't waiting for more food. He'd curled up in the back corner of the crate, wrapped the blanket around himself, and now slept the sleep of the truly exhausted. Every few seconds, he twitched or whimpered slightly, but he hadn't seemed to be injured or in pain during her brief examination. Just suffering from malnutrition, extreme fatigue, and fear.

"Sleep well, lovely boy," she murmured. "And if you don't have a name, well, we'll figure one out for you then. You look like a…Rodeo? Cranberry? No, not those. Maybe a Bob? Sam? Hmmm…"

A huge yawn escaped, cracking her jaw open, and she realized she was too tired to stand around thinking of names. Or thinking about lovely men with delusions of vampirehood, no matter how sexy they were.

She finished her nighttime routines, locking up, cleaning

up, and then double-checking crates, before heading for bed. She'd adopted out Perseus, the large tabby cat who'd most recently shared her home, so she was temporarily alone in her bedroom. Probably she'd let Ajax have the run of the house with her beginning tomorrow; he could use the socialization. But tonight, she washed up, brushed her teeth, and fell into bed, mentally beginning the many lists of all the tasks she needed to accomplish the next day. The work of running an animal rescue never ended, but the rewards were there every time she found a new family for one of her precious charges.

Even if, at times, she was so very lonely.

She'd probably never see him again, she reminded herself, not quite understanding the vague wave of sadness that trailed in the wake of that thought. She didn't need that kind of distraction in her life, anyway.

But he'd smelled *so* good…

She wrapped her comforter around herself, flashing back to the feel of Hunter's arms, and fell asleep remembering the scent of his skin.

• • •

When she woke in the middle of the night from a confusing dream of dragons and beautiful men with glowing blue eyes, the golden retriever was curled up on the foot of her bed, fast asleep.

Which was impossible.

She sat up in bed and stared at him. "How did you get out of your crate?"

The dog opened one eye and glanced up at her, his

body hunching into a ball, as if he expected a blow.

"No, no, honey. It's okay. I'm not mad at you," she soothed. "I'm just wondering how you unfastened the door to your crate and opened the two locked doors between my home and the shelter."

Impossible. Unless…unless she'd had a break-in. If somebody had picked the locks and opened the doors, it was entirely possible that the dog would have run for the only source of safety he recognized. But wouldn't he have been more excited? Barked or growled? She would have woken up at the sound. She was a light sleeper.

Instead, he'd been stealthy. She needed to get up, though, and check it out.

Or call 911?

No, she couldn't waste police time if the only real crime here was that she'd been too tired or too distracted by thoughts of her gorgeous and mysterious visitor to remember to lock the doors. The door handles had old-fashioned latches; easy enough for a clever dog to open.

That must be it.

Still. She needed to check.

She swung her legs out from under the covers and glanced ruefully down at her My Best Friend Is a Dog pajamas—not necessarily the best for scaring off burglars—and tucked her feet into her slippers. Then she stood and grabbed the softball bat she kept propped up against the side of her dresser, took a deep breath, and raised her voice.

"I'm calling the police right now, so if you're in my house, you should run away!"

The dog stretched, winced, and then climbed slowly off

the bed and followed her into the hallway. She'd have to check him thoroughly later to see what the wince was about; maybe she could do something for that shoulder until the trip to the vet.

She imagined she heard a *thud*, and her mind flipped from worrying about the dog to worrying about who was in her house.

"I called the cops! They're on the way! You should run now!"

No sound of feet running out the front door met her shout, but then again, neither did the sound of feet running toward *her*.

She edged down the hall, trying to look in all directions at once, even at the ceiling, which didn't make any damn sense, but then again, she'd been having a conversation with a man who thought he was a vampire. Stranger things had probably happened in Savannah.

Step by heart-pounding step, she cleared the upstairs, and then, after yet again talking herself out of calling the police for real, she started down the steps.

"I really mean it! Sirens, cops, jail! Ugly orange jumpsuits. I mean, who looks good in that?"

Nothing.

Feeling like she might hyperventilate any moment, she checked out the downstairs. Nobody was in the kitchen, the family room, the downstairs bathroom, or the formal dining room she'd turned into a library.

The basement.

Great. All the scariest things in horror movies happened in basements.

But, no, the door off the hallway was still locked and

bolted from her side.

"So I have a thing about creepy basements, sue me," she muttered to the dog, who was still following close behind. "Stop judging me."

When she looked down at him, he was grinning that wonderful golden-retriever smile, tongue slightly out, like he thought she was funny. Which, to a dog, she probably was. He was likely hoping she'd let him play fetch with the bat.

Finally sure her house was clear of thieves, murderers, or men who believed they were vampires, she strode over to the door that led to the covered walkway between her house and the shelter.

Closed but unlocked.

"I could have sworn I locked that door when I came in," she said, feeling her face scrunch up in confusion. She always locked doors at night.

Always.

She'd had bad dreams for years about somebody from the Institute hunting her down to carry her back to *that* hell, and she was only now finally free of the nightmares.

Please, let this not bring those back.

She stepped out into the walkway and crossed to the shelter, and, sure enough, that door was unlocked, too.

She shook her head. She must have been more exhausted than she'd realized. She started to pull the door closed, hoping not to wake any of the animals, and the office phone rang. Clearly, she hadn't turned off the ringer for the night, either.

She rushed into the office, hoping to catch the phone before her old-fashioned answering machine kicked on.

She really needed to get voicemail, but it cost money, and she'd found the old answering machine in the house when she bought it. Every penny saved was more money toward food and medicine, so…she had an answering machine.

"You've reached Little Darlings Animal Rescue. Please leave a message," her own voice sang out at her.

Beep.

"This is Meara Delacourt. I plan to donate one hundred thousand dollars to your rescue organization tomorrow, with possibly more to come after I see what you're doing. I'll be at your place at six p.m."

Click.

Alice stumbled across the room and dropped into a chair.

Meara Delacourt?

The Meara Delacourt?

Alice might be new to Savannah, but even she had heard of the famous socialite-philanthropist who funded the clinic named after her family.

But how had *Meara* heard of Alice?

The dog put his head in her lap, and she absently fondled his ears while she tried to come to grips with the idea that a famous philanthropist was giving her a small fortune, completely out of the blue.

"What a day! First I found three new sponsors, then I met a ghost who turned into a vampire, and now I'm getting a hundred grand from Meara Delacourt. Maybe I should have bought lottery tickets." She shook her head, feeling dazed, and glanced down at her newest charge. "What do you think, sweet boy? That much money covers a lot of dog food and vet bills."

The dog leaned heavily against her knees and let out a soft snore and—for just a fraction of a second—she thought she saw a puff of smoke come out of his nostrils.

"And now I'm hallucinating—"

A loud chattering noise startled her out of her daydreams of hiring another employee or maybe even expanding the shelter, and a pair of bright eyes peered down at her from the top of the office bookcase.

Ferret Bueller was out of his cage again.

Alice started laughing. *Now* life was back to normal.

CHAPTER SIX

Hunter felt his fangs drop down—a sensation that still took him by surprise. "What the hell?"

Meara shrugged. "Anger, hunger, lust. Even shock. Extreme emotion or reactions can make your body think it's under attack. You'll gain more control as you get older and more accustomed to your new life. It's a matter of time and patience."

"Yeah, yeah, great. Patience blah blah blah. But I was mostly talking about how you just called Alice out of the blue and pretended you were going to give her a hundred grand." Hunter looked around the kitchen, where they'd been chatting after he'd returned from privately ripping into a few blood bags in his room. Sadly, the pots and pans held no answers.

"I pretended nothing! You spent the past two hours—"

"Ten minutes."

"—telling me about this amazing woman you met who carries forest creatures around in hotels. She is eccentric at the very least, dangerous at the most. I must protect my new baby brother."

Hunter studied the stunning woman who looked like a supermodel and had the strength and skills of a deadly assassin and shook his head. "It's not your job to protect me, Meara. It's my job—my *literal* job as a firefighter—to protect other people."

"Like you protected me when I almost died," she said

quietly. "You should stop arguing with me. There are so many better ways to spend your time."

"Anyway," Hunter stubbornly continued. "She's probably a weirdo. Nobody that beautiful can be entirely normal."

Meara's smile held a hint of fang.

"Not talking about you. Although, you're not exactly normal either, are you? It's just that Alice thinks she talks to ghosts."

"Says the vampire," Mrs. C said, bustling into the kitchen and heading straight to the oven. "Maybe *I'm* the weirdo, since I think I talk to vampires every night."

"But—"

"Pie, dear? It's apple—your favorite."

Edge sauntered in, dressed in black jeans, black T-shirt, and black leather jacket and boots. He'd either taken the idea of vampire fashion to heart or he thought colors were beneath his notice. His glowing silver gaze snapped across the room to Meara, as always.

Hunter had spent less time with Edge than with any of the other residents of the house. The former scientist kept himself separate, somehow, even in a roomful of people. From what little Bane had told him, Edge—Dr. Sebastian Edgington, in fact, with a boatload of degrees—had been a scientist working for the government on very hush-hush classified stuff. Probably weapons, but Bane had said the details were Edge's to tell. His shoulder-length hair was prematurely white as a result of the torture a black-ops site had put him through when he hadn't complied with a particularly heinous objective. By the time he'd escaped the torture and imprisonment, he'd been near death. Bane had found him and Turned him, but Hunter didn't know any of the details of that, either.

Really, his total knowledge of Edge could be summed up as this: unbeatable computer hacker, brilliant scientist, and completely and utterly in love with Meara, although neither he nor she seemed to realize it.

Meara was very deliberately not looking at Edge, toying with the slice of pie Mrs. C had put in front of her, but the barely noticeable flush of rose along her cheekbones gave her away. Hunter wasn't exactly sure what was going on or not going on between the two of them, but the last thing he'd ever do is stick his nose into Meara's business.

People had probably died for less.

Edge smiled at Mrs. C, who gave him an enormous slice of pie, and then seated himself at the table, still watching Meara. When he finally turned that eerie silver stare to Hunter, Edge narrowed his eyes. "What's happening? Why are you annoying Meara?"

Hunter blew out a sigh. "I'm not trying to annoy anybody. I'm just explaining that I don't need her to protect me."

Edge very deliberately took a bite of pie, chewed, and swallowed before he replied. "We all protect one another. I thought you realized that. Also, Meara is an alpha female, and you are now part of her flock of ducklings. She will protect you whether you need it or not, and, believe me, you need it."

"Duckling?" Hunter laughed. "Maybe. I feel like a wobbly newborn these days, especially when it comes to this vampire stuff."

"Speaking of this *vampire stuff*, who is Alice to you?"

"How did you know about Alice? Were you eavesdropping?"

Edge raised an eyebrow and tapped his ear. "I was out in the yard."

"Oh. Right. Vampire super senses."

"Alice is the woman Hunter just met who got his blood flowing, so to speak," Meara said, with a laugh like music.

"So long as it's only *his* blood that's flowing," Edge said darkly, giving Hunter the stink eye.

"I haven't fed on any people," Hunter gritted out. "Not one. And I sure as hell wouldn't start with Alice if I were going to fall off the wagon."

"Who's Alice?" Mrs. C paused in her puttering and gave Hunter a bright-eyed glance.

"She's just this woman I met tonight at the hotel. She was chasing a raccoon, of all the ridiculous things. She runs an animal rescue, and—"

"And she fascinated our newest brother," Meara put in

Hunter pushed his plate away. "Fascinated may be too strong. I'm just interested, that's all. She was interesting. She had this way with animals, and she, well, she was just—"

"Interesting?" Edge's smile was the definition of smug.

Meara elbowed him. "Behave. Hunter is having a hard time acclimating, as we all did when we were baby vampires. We're going to help by giving him a present."

Hunter shook his head. "Baby vampire? Okay, I guess I can go along with that. But I don't need a present. You've been more than generous. The Harley—"

Edge whistled. "Sweet ride, isn't it? When you really think about the science, the physics of acceleration, gravity, and momentum—"

"Stop. Please, I beg you, stop. If I have to hear another word about physics or the stupid motorcycle, I will pin you both to the ceiling and leave you there. For *days*." Meara glared at them.

With her magical power to levitate objects, this was no small threat. It had only been a few days since she'd pinned Hunter to the wall in the upstairs hallway—for an hour—for leaving the seat up on the guest toilet.

"Not in the kitchen, please," Mrs. Cassidy said briskly. Mrs. C, all pink cheeks and white curls, served as housekeeper, cook, and surrogate mom to the vampires in the mansion, and her husband worked as handyman, chauffeur, and man-of-all-work. "And remember, Tommy and I are going to visit Molly in Paris in two weeks. You'll be on your own for Christmas. Now, I'm off to bed. Behave, you three."

Molly Cassidy, their daughter, was studying art restoration in Paris and working at a museum. They were wildly excited about this trip, so he'd picked guidebooks up for them as a thank-you gift for being so good to him.

They all chimed in with goodnights, and then Hunter turned to Meara and held up his hands in surrender. "Sorry. I'm sorry. No more Harley talk."

Edge said nothing, just aimed a sardonic glance at Meara.

"Anyway," she continued, "the gift is your friendship with Alice. Already I love her. She has the name of a storybook character. Alice Darlington. It's too perfect. And you say she is beautiful and kind, much like myself. Who could resist her?"

"*Kind?*" Edge raised an eyebrow. "Kind. Like you?"

Meara narrowed her eyes, and Edge quickly returned his attention to the pie.

"I can resist," Hunter muttered. "I'm trying very hard to resist. And you can't *give* me a friendship, Meara. When she finds out you were just kidding about that money, it will be bad."

"I *never* joke about money," she told him. "I'll have the money transferred into her account today while I sleep. Then she'll know I'm serious when I arrive at her rescue."

"When *we* arrive," Hunter said. "I'm going with you, of course."

"There's no 'of course' about it," she said, shrugging. "If you're awake, you may accompany me. If not, I'll tell you all about it when I get home."

"That's not fair," he said hotly. "I can't go until after sunset, as you keep telling me."

"For your own good, we keep telling you," she said, frowning in frustration. "We cannot bear the sun even a little bit for the first century after the Turn. Later, *much* later, if you can stop being a dunderhead for long enough to learn how to survive, you will be able to withstand brief exposure in the early morning or late afternoon. Or even a bit on the cloudiest of days, bearing in mind that the sun can break through the clouds at any time, so an afternoon excursion is not a smart move even for me, even now."

"I know. I *know*." He shoved his hair back out of his eyes. "And I have to sleep most of the daylight hours. I know. It's just so damn frustrating."

"It's better than being dead," Edge put in, staring into the distance at something only he could see.

Hunter couldn't argue with that.

Meara shrugged, clearly dismissing the subject, and moved on to another. "Why aren't you married? You're delicious. Those muscles. That face. You're an actual hero, rescuing children from burning buildings. Plus, you have that bad-boy ink. I'd think the women would be climbing all over you."

Edge narrowed his eyes and studied Hunter as if he were deciding how to dismember him. "Yes, please, tell us about how you escaped all the women climbing over you," he said, voice dry as dust.

"Yes. The climbing women," Hunter said, grimacing at both the topic and the awkwardness of the situation. "They climb over me to get to the guy standing next to me. I'm firmly in the friend zone. Just a nice guy. *Too* nice. As in, nice guys finish last." He snorted. "The last woman I was really interested in, my best friend wound up marrying."

Meara leaned forward, her lovely golden eyes glowing with enthusiasm, and put her hand on his. "Do you want me to kill them for you?"

"Sure, why not?" Hunter grinned but then realized she was dead serious.

Emphasis on *dead*.

"Damn, you gotta be careful how you joke around vampires. No, Meara, I don't want you to kill anybody for me! Or give them a hundred thousand dollars, either. I—"

Meara pushed back from the table and stood. "Do you hate kittens and puppies, then?"

"What? No, I don't—"

"Raccoons?"

"Well, I'm kind of indifferent to raccoons, but—"

"Then why are you arguing with me about giving Alice

money to care for them?"

"I'm not!" His head started to ache.

Meara crossed to the freezer and pulled out a carton of strawberry cheesecake ice cream, then took a spoon from a drawer and waved it at him. "Is this friend-zone problem why you got the ink? To get a little bad-boy cred?"

Hunter sighed and glanced down at his arms. "No. I just like the art. And the artist is a friend. He has a shop downtown."

Edge tapped his finger on the table. "Speaking of friends, we need to deal with your disappearance. So far, I've built the cover story that your burns were not as bad as originally thought. You've been in a private burn facility in Colorado, but it will be two or three months before you can believably return to Savannah. Or you can just leave the city. I can create an entirely new identity for you, but that's more involved, so I'd need a little time."

"A little time," Hunter said, feeling dazed.

"Six to eight, maybe?"

"Weeks?"

Edge rolled his eyes.

"Days?"

"Who do you think you're talking to? Six to eight *hours*."

"You can't leave town," Meara said. "You need us, at least now, while you learn how to deal with your new life. And you're part of our family now. I would be sad if you left."

Hunter swallowed a sudden lump in his throat. He had the feeling that Meara wasn't quick to consider anyone part of her family, so it meant a lot to him not only that she'd feel that way, but also that she'd admit it.

Plus, he was concerned that when Meara was sad, she went hunting for tourists to eat.

"You can always use enthrallment, judiciously," Edge pointed out. "Not too much or too often, because things get confused. But on a few select friends or colleagues, to back up your story, if you run into them."

"I can't, though. I'm no good at it. I..." He broke off, realizing that he'd been about to tell them that he'd tried to enthrall Alice.

"When did you try it?" Meara's gaze sharpened. "On this Alice? Did you drink from her?"

"No!" He pushed his chair back and started pacing restlessly around the kitchen. "No, I didn't—I wouldn't—I... Oh, *fuck*. Yeah, I sort of tried, I think. To enthrall her—not to drink from her," he hastened to clarify. "Suddenly I was trying to compel her to let me in her house, because all I could see or hear or want was the pulse in her neck."

The confession out, Hunter stood, head bowed, waiting for someone to banish him from the house and their lives forever. Or at the very least to kick his ass.

Instead, Meara laughed. "You're very precocious for being such a new baby vampire. It took me months to work up the nerve to snack on the coachman."

Edge paused, his fork midway between his slice of pie and his mouth. "What happened? Did you kill him?"

"He would have died a happy man," she purred, aiming a wicked smile at the scientist, who dropped his fork.

Hunter almost smiled at the red flush that rose on Edge's cheekbones, but he was too sunk in misery for the amusement to last long. "I'm doomed, aren't I? I'm going to hell. The first woman I've been interested in...*that* way...

for more than a year, and mostly I just wanted to get my fangs in her neck."

"What did you mean, you 'sort of tried' to enthrall her?" Edge leaned back in his chair and folded his arms over his chest. "Either you tried or you didn't. And I'm guessing it didn't work, anyway?"

"I tried," Hunter muttered. "It seemed to work for a few seconds, but then she yelled at me to get off her property or she'd call 911 on me. Some irony there, since I used to be the one who *responded* to emergency calls, not the one who caused beautiful women to make them."

"She's beautiful?" Meara's eyes glowed hot. "Even better. I cannot wait to meet your Alice."

"She's not my Alice."

"Listen, some people are just resistant to enthrallment," Edge said, shrugging. "Ryan was, too, but then of course we found out she's Nephilim."

"There can't be another Nephilim we just happen to discover right here in Savannah after not encountering one for hundreds of years," Meara scoffed, but then she bit her lip and glanced at Hunter. "This Alice doesn't glow, does she?"

"Not a bit."

"Like I said, some people, even ordinary humans, are resistant to enthrallment," Edge said. "We have to kill them."

A wave of white-hot rage seared through Hunter like a flash fire—sudden, intense, and definitely flammable—and he glared at Edge through a red haze. If looks from a vampire could kill, Edge would be a blackened smudge on the immaculately clean tile floor. "You're not killing Alice.

If you even harm a single hair on her head—"

Edge rolled his eyes. "Yeah, yeah, I get it. Doom, despair, dire threats. I've been living with Bane for years. You think *you* could scare me, human?"

"I'm not human," Hunter growled, but then he thought of what Edge had said a moment before. "But neither is Alice—at least not an 'ordinary' human. She thinks she sees ghosts."

"Yeah, I heard you say that before I walked in. But maybe she does see ghosts."

"But—"

"Bane and I can see them, too," Meara said. "One of the side benefits—curses?—of our Turn. But since she's a human, she must be a ghost whisperer."

Hunter blinked. As happened so often lately, the conversation was taking a weird turn. "Ghost whisperer?"

Edge nodded. "I've actually heard of those. A few even advertise on the dark web. 'Will find your grandmother's will' kind of thing. Might be helpful."

Meara licked her spoon, staring at Edge. "You lost your grandmother's will?"

Edge, eyes focused on her mouth, didn't seem to be able to find the words to answer.

"I think he means being a ghost whisperer. And quit playing with the poor scientist, Meara." Hunter shook his head. "Anyway, I don't think it's like that for Alice. She told me, when she thought I was a ghost—"

"When she thought *you* were a ghost?" Edge laughed. "She must not be very good at it."

But Meara nodded, a thoughtful expression on her face. "No, I can see that. The auras must be similar. What did she say?"

"She said she only took appointments between ten and two on Wednesdays," Hunter said flatly. "And she was talking about appointments with the *ghosts*, not with poor suckers willing to pay big money to talk to dear, departed Aunt Ethel or whatever."

"I've only met a couple of ghost whisperers in all these years," Meara said slowly, still eating ice cream. "They don't usually like vampires, for some reason. And we can't control ghosts. They mostly ignore us. One of the whisperers, a man, used his power over ghosts to force them to attack me. Very unpleasant."

Edge stood up so fast he knocked over his chair, his eyes silver fire. "What happened? Where do I find this man?"

Meara widened her eyes. "I killed him, of course. It was self-defense. He would have killed me if I hadn't. After he was dead, the ghosts dispersed."

"I'm *not* killing Alice," Hunter repeated, somewhat desperately, wondering how much danger he'd put her in just by having this conversation.

"Of course you're not," Meara soothed. "We'll see what we see tomorrow. If there's any killing to be done, I'll handle it."

"Let me rephrase this," Hunter growled, biting off every word. "Nobody is killing Alice. Not now, not ever. Do you understand?"

A shimmer of energy formed a large oval shape just in front of the refrigerator, and Hunter had a moment to think that the contrast of ancient vampire magic forming a portal next to a brand new, expensive Sub Zero was every bit as weird as it sounded before Bane and Ryan stepped out, holding hands and laughing.

"That's weird as hell," Edge muttered.

Hunter wondered if the scientist could read minds. "The portal and the fridge?"

"What? No, the sight of Bane laughing."

"Because love and happiness make an enormous difference in the world, and all the scientific apparatus in the world will never be able to measure that," Meara said, ice edging her words.

"What's funny?" Hunter asked the newcomers, to change the subject from the weird tension between Meara and Edge and, more important, the topic of killing Alice.

Bane aimed his glowing blue gaze at Ryan, who was still laughing. "My beloved has decided that we need to host a new form of recreation here at, as she insists on calling it, Castle Dracula."

Ryan grinned up at him. "I only say that to you, not where anybody could hear me."

"We have recreation," Edge objected. "Just a few weeks ago we killed all those necromancers and zombies."

"Plus you bought us the VR goggles," Meara added.

Ryan shook her head, groaning. "Vampires are weird. Killing zombies and necromancers is not recreation."

"It is if you do it right," Bane said, showing a hint of fang, but his eyes were laughing.

Hunter agreed with the doctor about vampires being weird but knew enough not to say it, especially now that he was one. "So, what is this new recreation?"

Ryan beamed at him. "We're going to have our first monthly supernatural volleyball tournament!"

CHAPTER SEVEN

The warlock hissed at the owl that flew toward him. The bird, possibly as wise as its species' reputation proclaimed, changed course and headed for a different tree. Not that the warlock made a habit out of perching in trees like night-flying predators, but that's what he smugly believed himself to be.

A very *deadly* nocturnal predator, as the vampire who'd visited this house was about to find out.

The Chamber had commanded the warlock to learn anything and everything about the vampires who ruled this eastern territory of the United States. Knowledge was power, and power was everything. So the warlock had given orders to the Minor demon, and the pathetic creature, probably still cringing and whining about being hungry or injured or some such nonsense, had followed the newly Turned vampire to this place and then surprisingly taken the initiative to do something without being told. This woman, whom the warlock's phone had told him was named Alice Darlington—and why was that name so familiar? had taken the ratty little demon into her house.

Of course, the creature had been disguised as a fluffy dog at the time.

Success, at any rate. So now the Minor demon had infiltrated the house and was hopefully learning the woman's secrets, which quite possibly included new information about the vampires that the warlock could take to his masters.

Perhaps even information valuable enough to give directly to Lord Alastair Neville, who ruled the Chamber and all of its members with iron-tipped claws.

But if the Minor demon failed or, worse, if the woman realized what it was and captured the useless creature, the warlock would be forced to kill them both.

He smiled, and the leaves on the branches nearest to his face withered and died from the rotting stench of his glee. He didn't even notice.

He'd be delighted to kill them both. Maybe he'd play with the woman first. All that red hair… And the shelter! An entire glorious buffet of furry sacrifices ready to serve his blood magic.

He laughed and looked around for the owl. Maybe he'd kill it now, just for a little practice.

For *fun*.

Delayed gratification was so boring.

But the bird had been wise after all, because it was gone. Probably winging its way to safer places. Oh, well. The night was young.

Before any fun could be had, however, the warlock dropped out of the tree, raced down the street, and found a dark corner of an alley to hide in so he could make a call. Failure to report in was not an option. He'd once seen what was left of a warlock who'd failed Lord Neville.

The sight still haunted his nightmares.

And the Chamber would want to know all about the very new vampire Hunter Evans and his interest in Alice Darlington.

If only he could remember why her name felt so familiar…

CHAPTER EIGHT

Alice's day felt like it would last a week. Everything was going wrong. The animals who needed pills didn't want to take them. The animals who needed to consume more calories didn't want to eat. Even Ajax avoided her in the exercise yard and stayed close to Veronica and a couple of the volunteers.

She sank down in her office seat and sighed. She needed to pay bills but wanted to hold off to see if the promised visit and donation from Meara Delacourt was really going to happen. That money would make a huge difference in what checks she wrote this month. In the meantime, she felt like she could nap for an hour or six. She hadn't gotten nearly enough rest the night before, and, even when she'd finally fallen asleep, she'd tossed and turned through disjointed dreams of sexy Hunter Evans and his glowing blue eyes.

But in some of the dreams he'd been snarling at her.

And he'd had fangs.

She shivered and tried, yet again, to put the mysterious man out of her mind. She'd never see him again, she was sure, despite what he'd said before he left.

"Because he's clearly at least mildly disturbed, and I'm definitely qualified to recognize that," she muttered. "At least *you* wanted to spend time with me, Charlie."

Her newest addition, the golden retriever who'd shown up in her yard the night before, grinned up at her, gently nudging his head into her lap for petting. Susan, Veronica's girlfriend who volunteered at the rescue every Friday morning, had given him the name.

"Oh my goodness, with that beautiful golden fur, you look like you belong on *Charlie's Angels*," she'd exclaimed in her soft Southern lilt.

And the name had stuck. He seemed to like it and had responded to it when Dr. Geary stopped by for a quick visit on her way to work. She'd pronounced Charlie to be malnourished and bruised but otherwise healthy, but Alice thought she'd seen an odd expression on the vet's face when she'd examined him, as if she'd been puzzled about something. She'd said nothing was wrong, though, and Alice was a big fan of not "borrowing trouble," as they said here in the South.

Veronica popped into the office, rolling down the sleeves of her Georgia State sweatshirt. She was a recent graduate and working hard on applications to veterinary school. She smiled at Charlie. "I'm glad our new boy is going to be okay. He really is a lovely dog. I can't believe somebody dumped him."

"Sadly, I can," Alice said, stroking Charlie's head to soothe him. His muscles had tightened while Veronica was speaking. "I used to think that only monsters would abandon a pet like this, but the real monsters would have just dumped him in the street or out in the woods. At least whoever gave him up made an attempt to be sure he'd be found and cared for by leaving him here. We never know how bad things are for people until we've—"

"Walked a mile in their sneakers. I know, I know," Veronica said, laughing. "Yes, Mom. Anyway, if you don't need anything else, I'm out. The dinner feeding is done, and I'm off to my own dinner with Susan and her clueless brother—he keeps calling me Ronnie and trying to talk football, because he thinks all lesbians should be into sports."

Alice sighed. "I'm sorry. And yes, go. Have fun. I'm good. I may have a potential sponsor stop by, but I can handle that on my own. And Henry will be here at six thirty for the night shift, so we're all good. I'll feed Charlie and put him in his crate for a while."

She wanted to tell Veronica that a raise was in her future if the new donation came through—her employee worked for far less money than she deserved, but that was the nature of nonprofit animal rescues. Working for one was more of a calling than just a job and, sadly, nobody was ever going to get rich doing it. But she'd hate to raise hopes only to have to dash them if it didn't come through.

And, it just occurred to her, that might not have been Meara Delacourt on the phone at all. Maybe it'd been a horrible practical joke or something.

"What?" Veronica studied her face. "You suddenly look like you just lost your best friend."

Alice forced a smile to her face. "No, don't be silly. I was just thinking about paying the bills, which is never fun. But this month I think we'll at least balance after the checks I got at my talk last night."

Most months, they operated firmly in the red, and her savings were running out. She really needed to work on networking and booking more speaking gigs where she could explain their mission and why help was needed.

Or maybe, just maybe, Meara Delacourt was really

going to become their golden goose.

Alice glanced down at her watch. In twenty minutes, she was about to find out.

• • •

No more than ten minutes after the sun went down, the vampire stepped out of her BMW convertible and climbed out in the Little Darlings parking area. She quite deliberately hadn't waited for Hunter to wake, because she wanted time with this woman who was *possibly* a ghost whisperer and was *definitely* someone who had captivated Meara's newest family member.

Meara was the protective type.

The old house that must be Alice's residence had charm and was surely listed on Savannah's historic register or, if not, it should be. She vaguely remembered visiting someone here in the late 1800s for…dinner? A party? No, but wait. This was lovely, but it looked like a reproduction or restoration of that old house and surely far newer.

She shrugged. So many years, so many humans. It all ran together in her mind these days. But she had no time to reminisce, because a woman who must be Alice Darlington walked out the front door of the building behind the house and hurried toward her.

Hunter hadn't exaggerated. Alice was lovely. Too thin, too pale, and somewhat haunted-looking, with those dark, almost-bruised circles beneath her eyes, but even in faded and ripped jeans and a plain white cotton long-sleeved shirt, the animal rescuer was beautiful. Her masses of red curls were tied back in a thick braid, and her brilliantly green eyes were sparkling with excitement.

Meara, who quite enjoyed beauty in both objects and people, smiled. Yes, she'd promised Hunter she wouldn't kill Alice, but she'd never said anything about not taking a little sip.

"Ms. Delacourt?" Alice's nervous smile told Meara that the woman knew exactly who she was but wasn't quite sure if the promised donation would become reality. Fair enough. The internet existed, after all. It would be impossible to completely hide one's existence these days, not that Meara really tried, what with the clinic and the other charities. And a hundred thousand dollars was a lot of money for most people to promise sight unseen.

But Meara was far from being "most people," and money only existed to give pleasure and comfort. Meara had plenty of material pleasures, so it gave her happiness—no matter how fleeting—to use her wealth to give comfort to others. Not that she'd ever admit that part out loud. She just made vague comments about tax deductions when Bane teased her.

Humans, mostly, although she'd donated to wildlife organizations in the past. She had a special fondness and even sisterly affection for tigers, who were, much like herself, both deadly and beautiful. But funding scruffy, rescued pets would be a new venture.

She wondered what Alice would say if she opened the conversation by simply suggesting they kill any human who had abandoned a pet, then sighed. Horror, shock, running, probably.

So many of Meara's best ideas resulted in horror, shock,

and running.

It was *wonderful.*

But all this ran through her mind in a matter of seconds, and then she walked forward, holding out her hands. "Let us be friends, yes? You will be Alice, and I will be Meara. Now, show me your facility, my new friend."

"I'm just delighted you're here, Ms. Dela… Meara. Please, won't you come inside? I'll introduce you to some of our residents and explain what we're trying to accomplish."

"That would be lovely," Meara said, allowing her gaze to drop to Alice's neck for only the length of a single heartbeat.

No. Mustn't. This human was Hunter's.

If Meara didn't have to kill her, of course. Then all bets were off.

She followed Alice into the building, which immediately erupted into frantic barking, meowing, hissing, and other assorted noises.

"Hush, now. I need to talk to the nice lady," Alice said, a comforting smile on her face, and—miracle of miracles—the noise subsided.

Meara narrowed her eyes. Ghost whisperer, perhaps, but a natural animal rescuer? The evidence said yes.

Alice turned to face Meara, indicating the room with one hand. "As you can see, we have large, roomy spaces for each of our rescued animals and…"

She kept talking, but Meara quit listening, because although her eyes told her a story of a spotlessly clean and well-kept facility, filled with animals that clearly liked and trusted Alice, her nose told her a different story.

Meara Delacourt's last financial statement had listed her overall wealth at a number so high that she'd had a hard time believing it. And yet, she was still the woman who'd grown up playing in her father's stables, learning from the grooms how to feed and care for her horse. Shoveling out stalls and getting so filthy that her governesses had despaired of her.

She was not, in other words, a vampire who recoiled at the smell of an animal shelter, and this one was clean and fresh, in any event.

However.

Something in this building did not smell like animal, either wild or of the domesticated variety.

Something—or someone—smelled like sulfur.

There was a demon in the house.

The door they'd just entered crashed open with far too much force, and suddenly there was another vampire in the house, too.

"Hello, little brother," Meara drawled, not the least bit repentant about leaving him behind.

"Little brother?" Alice's eyes widened as her gaze traveled back and forth between the two of them. "Hunter? You're…here? And you're Meara Delacourt's brother?"

Hunter devoured the human with his gaze, his eyes glowing a bright, hot blue, and Alice stumbled back a step.

"Your eyes! I thought that was a reflection of the lights last night, but they're actually *glowing*. What is going on?"

"I told you to wait for me," Hunter said, pointing at Meara.

She raised an eyebrow. "That was your first mistake. Nobody tells me what to do. I wanted to meet this woman you couldn't stop talking about and be sure she was not a fraud or a charlatan."

"Don't fraud and charlatan mean the same thing?" Alice blinked when they both turned to stare at her. "Well, they do. And anyway, I'm neither."

The human put her hands on her hips, gaining steam as she came to some undoubtedly incorrect conclusion. "Actually, *you're* the charlatan or fraud here, if you promised to give me a large donation over the phone but you're really here under false pretenses. Maybe you should both leave."

Meara rolled her eyes. "So dramatic. But in fact, you may have a teensy point. So, here. Please take this, and let's start over." She pulled the folded check out of the pocket of her red silk dress and held it out. Checks were so much more tangible than funds transfers.

"One hundred thousand dollars, payable to Little Darlings Rescue. I'd apologize for the slight subterfuge, but I don't feel like it. So just take the money and consider yourself lucky I don't bite you."

But the contrary human took a step back instead of forward, away from the promised check and toward the door that must lead to a corridor to her residence.

"Bite me? What is this biting nonsense?" Alice got a wild look in her eyes. "Oh, God, do you think you're a vampire, too? Are you *both* delusional? I think you may need help, Ms. Delacourt. And I'm certainly not going to take your money if you're not quite, um, of sound mind."

Meara, whose temper had been rising, suddenly tilted her head and stared at the human. "You would refuse such a large amount of money out of concern for my state of mind?"

"Of course I would! And you…you shouldn't go around offering such large sums of money. People might take advantage of you." Alice bit her lip. "And I know this sounds selfish, but it's not fair to the people you offer it to, either. People who might have been already figuring out how they'd spend it, like buying a new transport van that doesn't quit working every other day or giving raises to hardworking staff."

"People might take advantage of me," Meara murmured, suddenly *very* interested in Hunter's human. "That is unexpectedly kind of you, Alice Darlington."

"I—"

"You are coming to dinner with us, please, and I will demonstrate to you just how boringly sane and normal we are," Meara said.

"As long as she's not the dinner," Hunter said in such a quiet whisper that nobody but a vampire could have heard him.

Meara laughed. "I promise you she is not."

Then, at a volume that Alice could hear, too, she repeated her invitation. "The check is yours. I will have my lawyer discuss its validity with you, if you prefer. And, if you'll have dinner with us, out in public if you like, I will also replace that disreputable van in the driveway that you were just talking about."

Alice blinked. "Replace the van? I…I don't think…" But then she swept her gaze across the cages and kennels, taking in all the animals who sat quietly within them.

Finally, she took a deep breath and then nodded. "Yes. I accept. Which day would be good for you? I can—"

"No time like the present," Meara broke in, trying not to

grin like the proverbial Cheshire Cat had at another Alice. "Come with me."

Hunter turned pale, and his skin even took on a slightly green tinge, which was not a color Meara had known vampires could turn. "No!" he shouted, then amended, "I mean, not with you. You're a menace on the roads. She can ride with me."

Alice looked panicked. "Now? But I—"

Meara aimed a flat stare at Hunter. "You came on your bike?"

"Yes, and—"

"Did you bring even an extra helmet?"

"No, but—"

"Then she rides with me."

"*Meara!* You—"

"Fine. *Fine.*" Meara threw her hands in the air. "If I promise to obey all posted traffic laws?"

"This is not good," Alice mumbled, staring wide-eyed at the two of them as if they were actors in a particularly bad play. "If you're trying to prove you're of sound mind, this conversation is not a great start. Just saying."

Meara sighed. "And I was on my best behavior. I haven't even mentioned the demon in the house yet."

CHAPTER NINE

Alice blinked a few times to clear her vision, but everything was still dim and sort of flashy. Plus, there was loud music assaulting her eardrums; something with a hard beat screaming lyrics she couldn't quite make out.

And, oddly enough, a delicious scent of grilled meat that caused her empty stomach to growl.

She had to try three times to force the words out of her dry throat. "What…what is happening?" She licked her dry lips and tried again. "Where am I?"

A strong arm wrapped around her and pulled her close to a hard, muscular body, and she looked up to see Hunter's dizzyingly blue eyes. He raised his head and spoke to someone behind her.

"Why did she react like this? What did you *do*?"

"I'm sorry! I've never seen anyone react like this to a bit of a compulsion push."

That voice—Alice knew that voice.

"Ms. Delacourt? What? Hunter, what happened? Am I sick?"

He closed his eyes and rested the side of his face on the top of her head for a few moments, then sighed and looked at her. "No. I mean, maybe, but not really sick. It's just a reaction to the mental invasiveness of the enthrallment, the best we can tell."

"The…enthrallment?" Her mind was racing now. She felt like she'd been roofied, and that was a feeling she'd had many, many times before; whenever the Institute had decided she'd been too unmanageable, in came the orderlies with their pills and injections.

She'd tried to refuse, resist, rebel.

After a while, she'd given up, like everybody else trapped there.

"It's so loud here." She put her hands over her ears, and within seconds the pounding music was replaced with something very quiet with a lot of piano and silken, feminine singing. Alicia Keys, maybe. She breathed a sigh of relief and looked around, telling herself she'd push Hunter away as soon as she felt steadier, not admitting that she was comforted by his warm, strong presence at her side.

"Water, please?"

She heard Meara murmur something, and a minute or so later a glass of water appeared in front of her, held in Hunter's large hand. She gulped down the entire contents and held it out wordlessly for more. By the time she'd finished the second glass, somewhat more slowly, she was practically back to normal, with only the slightest headache remaining.

"Okay. Okay." She took a step or two away from Hunter and looked at the two of them, trying not to notice how ridiculously sexy Hunter was, all hard muscles and attitude in dark blue jeans and a forest-green long-sleeved shirt. "Okay," she repeated, getting her bearings. "What happened? Where are we? Just a minute ago, we were at the rescue, and you two were arguing about Ms. Delacourt's speeding problem—"

"Meara," Ms. Delacourt, wearing a red silk dress that probably cost as much as the shelter's yearly operating budget, reminded her. “Please call me Meara.”

Alice laughed a little wildly. “Sure. Why not? Meara, you and Hunter were arguing about who would drive me to dinner, and now we’re…where?” She scanned the large room and realized it was a restaurant or hotel dining room filled with elegant little tables but no other patrons. The moonlight shining through the huge floor-to-ceiling glass windows on one side of the room was the only light other than candles flickering dimly on some of the tables.

Wherever it was, it was too fancy for Alice to have ever been there before, that was for sure.

“We’re at the Savannah River Wine Bar,” Meara said. “I rented out the place for our dinner.”

“Of course you did,” Alice said mechanically, thinking crazed thoughts of rabbit holes and other alternate universes. One minute she’d been talking to a potential donor, and then the hot guy she’d met the night before—the one who *thought he was a vampire*—showed up, and then the two of them started babbling about who was a charlatan and whether Meara should drive and about buying her a new van.

Which, come to think of it, was the only reason she’d agreed to come to dinner with them in the first place. Not that she was greedy for herself, but a new vehicle with increased capacity for holding the animals she rescued, with maybe a first-aid station inside, and with an engine that worked seven days a week instead of three or four…

She shook her head, hard, to snap herself out of fantasies about rescue vans and backed another couple of steps away from them.

“Did you *drug* me?”

"No!" Meara looked offended. "Of course we didn't drug you. I just tried to *convince* you to come along with me, and my convincing skills are a little rusty."

"What does that even mean?" She glanced behind herself to be sure she had a clear path to the double doors, which were closed but hopefully not locked from the outside. "Convince me of what? How?"

She edged farther toward the door, keeping an eye on both of them at the same time.

Hunter leaned forward as if he wanted to chase after her, but he stayed where he was. "Convince you to come out to dinner, that's all. I'm sorry. I made the huge mistake of telling *some people* about you and that I'd like to get to know you, and suddenly Meara is making phone calls and personal visits and trying to compel you to come to dinner."

Meara tossed her gorgeous golden-blond hair. "I was only looking out for you, as you did for me on that day a few years ago. You're part of my family now."

"None of this makes any sense," Alice finally said, halting her escape attempt as her mind, now clear, raced to catch up. "Hunter, who is not a ghost but thinks he's a vampire, met me last night and followed me home."

"Like one of your strays," Hunter muttered, his glowing blue gaze inexplicably dropping to her throat before he wrenched it back up to her face.

She made a flicking motion with one hand, pushing the question of glowing eyes away for a moment, because it made her fear that she was the one not quite right here. "And then Meara, your family, calls to offer me a huge amount of money for the rescue—"

"Not just *offer*," Meara interjected. "I *gave* you the money."

"You gave me a check," Alice agreed. "Whether it's cashable is another matter. I've got to admit that I really have no idea what the heck is going on, and I don't like it. I have nothing that you might want—no money, no valuable possessions. Even the house, rescue, and property are almost entirely owned by the bank, not that a millionaire philanthropist needs my money. And I'm kind of doubting that I'm in the presence of the world's next pair of notorious outlaws who kidnap women just for fun."

"Notorious! I love that. I am certainly notorious." Meara's sudden smile was enormous and practically lit up the room, but Alice wasn't paying all that much attention to her smile, because Meara's eyes started glowing exactly like Hunter's did, except hers were golden to his blue.

"Oh!" Suddenly she got it and felt like a fool. "This is some kind of prank, right? You get trick contacts and play games with the gullible pet-rescue lady, right? And then..."

She trailed off as she realized that the "logical" explanation her brain had been trying to push at her made zero sense. Why would they want to play a prank on her? Why would one of the richest women in Savannah want to play this kind of weird game?

Sure, rich people could be weird, even if they called it "eccentric," but this was far over the line. So, if not that, then what?

"We're back to my original question," she said. "What the heck is going on?"

A pale, glowing form floated through the window to her right and headed straight toward her.

Great. This was *exactly* what she needed.

"Please, not now," she gritted out. "I'm a little busy here. I can help you later. Next Wednesday. Stop by the rescue."

Meara, in a move that looked like a badass stuntwoman crossed with a martial arts master, suddenly threw herself back and up into the air, turning a perfect somersault and landing in a crouch on *top* of a table. From this new perch, she stared at Alice and then delicately shuddered.

Hunter took a step toward Alice but immediately stopped moving when she held out her hand, palm facing him.

"I'll stop," he said. "But just tell me, who are you talking to?"

She glanced at him but turned her attention back to the ghost, because of course that's what—*who*—had come to join the party, and she'd had an unexpected idea.

"I spend time every week helping your kind. Helping find answers to your questions," she told the ghost, who had resolved its shape into that of a woman wearing what looked like a flapper costume from the 1920s, complete with headband and feather.

The ghost nodded, empty eyes fixed on Alice's face.

"So maybe this time you can answer a question for me." She pointed first at Hunter and then Meara. "Who are they, and what do they want with me?"

The ghost stared at Alice for a long moment. Then she threw back her head and howled. The eerie sound lasted for what seemed to be forever, and a wave of shocking cold blasted out of the howling figure and coated everything within three feet of her with frost.

Including Alice.

"That's great. I ask a simple question, and you splatter me with freezing ghost snot." Alice shook her head to dislodge the frost from her hair and shook out her hands and body to do the same with the rest of her.

"Let's break this down. First, who are they?" Again, she pointed at Hunter and Meara, who silently watched her talk to someone they almost certainly couldn't see.

The ghost floated even closer, until her glowing face was only inches from Alice, grimaced, and opened her mouth really, really wide again.

"Please, no more howling," Alice begged.

The ghost slowly closed her mouth. She leaned even closer, until Alice felt the spirit's icy breath on her face.

"*Vampiresss*," the ghost whispered. "*They are vampiresss.*"

Alice swayed as the shock of the answer reached out and punched her in the gut. Wanting to deny it but knowing it must be true.

Ghosts didn't lie. She wasn't sure why, or if it only *seemed* to be a hard-and-fast rule, but it had always been her experience. This one must really believe that Meara and Hunter really were vampires.

Which led her to the second, more immediately pertinent question. "And what do they want with me?"

"What did it say, Alice?" Hunter called out. "Please tell me what's happening, so I can explain."

She ignored him and repeated her question for the third time. "What do they want with me?"

"*They want you to die.*"

CHAPTER TEN

Hunter snapped into motion the second Alice swayed. He shot across the space between them and caught her in his arms before she could hit the floor.

She blinked up at him, her brilliant green eyes huge in her pale face, and then she smiled a little. "This is not how I imagined the evening going."

Something in Hunter's chest clenched at her courage. She'd faced down vampires and now a ghost—and probably had a demon in her house, if Meara had been right—and she still had a sense of humor. He could feel a part of his heart, the small, icy, closed-off part that had faced one too many rejections, take a small, tentative step toward warmth and hope.

He automatically stepped on the feeling. Hard.

Now was not the time.

"What happened?" he asked.

She blew out a shaky breath and pushed gently away from him to stand on her own. "Well, I guess you're telling the truth about being vampires, because the ghost just told me that you are, and ghosts never lie."

"Is that all?" Meara hopped gracefully off the table and stalked toward them. "Seemed like a longer conversation than that."

Alice shrugged, the casual motion contradicted by the wary look in her eyes. "She also told me you want me to die."

"We do *not* want you to die," Hunter said firmly. "We—"

"I know," Alice said, smoothing wisps of hair away from her face.

"You do?" He was confused. "You just said ghosts don't lie."

"Well, they don't, as far as I know. It's not like I've met all the ghosts in the world or know the secret ghost rulebook." She gave them just a hint of a smile. "But they can be wrong. How would a dead flapper from a hundred years ago know what your intent is?"

"Exactly!" He was pleased. "And—"

"And simple logic tells me that you probably didn't rent out an entire restaurant just to kill me, when you could have murdered me at the rescue and left me bleeding out on the floor. Or, I guess, not bleeding out so much as drained."

His smile faded, but he couldn't disagree with her logic.

"Look, I've never killed anybody and don't plan to start now, Alice. In fact, I've never even bitten anybody," he growled. "Maybe you could take that much on faith, while we get to know each other."

"Are we going to get to know each other?" She wrapped her arms around her waist, her body language pure self-protection combined with a touch of fear, but her eyes and raised chin signaled defiance and courage. "I'm not sure that's such a good idea, no matter how beautiful you are."

Hunter felt a slow, wicked smile spreading across his face. "Beautiful? I can work with that."

She closed her eyes and covered her face with her hands. "Argh! Clearly I spend too much time with nobody but my rescued animals for company. I didn't mean to say that out loud."

"Yes, we all agree Hunter is gorgeous," Meara said impatiently. "But why was there a demon in your rescue facility? Clearly, you're a ghost whisperer. But what else? And I warn you now, if you have anything to do with blood magic—"

Hunter stepped between them, facing Meara.

"Don't threaten her again," he said quietly, but Meara must have heard the deadly intent in his voice, because she stared at him for a long moment and then smiled.

"Fine. But if you want the lovely Alice to become part of our merry band, we need to know everything about her. Agreed?"

"Everybody has secrets, Meara."

This time, the other vampire looked away.

"I still don't understand what's going on," Alice said. "Why do you need to know all about me?"

Hunter didn't know how to say "because I plan to see you in my bed within the week" any more than he understood the fierce rush of heat that seared through him at the thought. He didn't react to women this way. He believed in long, slow courtships. Getting to know someone as a friend and then working his way up to more.

He...

Fuck.

No wonder he kept getting friend-zoned.

But he'd never had such an overpowering *want* for anyone before.

Need.

He wanted Alice. Needed her.

All of her.

He wanted to caress, comfort, consume her.

He wanted to *keep* her.

It didn't make a damn bit of sense.

Alice tilted her head, her forehead furrowing in puzzlement, and he suddenly realized he'd been silent for far too long. What had she asked?

Meara came to his rescue. "Consider it a job interview or an ordinary grant request. Have you applied for a grant before?"

"Of course. Never get them, though," Alice said, still watching them both warily.

"Yes, and they're miles long and ask for a ton of information, correct?"

Alice nodded.

"Consider this that, then. I just gave you one hundred thousand dollars of the foundation's money, and tomorrow I'll buy you a new van. Don't we deserve to know about you?"

"And we should just put aside the vampire thing?" Alice looked skeptical. "Normal grant application?"

Meara's eyes flashed. "We should just put aside the ghost-whisperer thing?"

Suddenly Alice's shoulders slumped. "Fine. Maybe we can start over?"

Hunter walked over to a table next to the window and pulled out a chair. "Why don't we start with dinner? I can smell something delicious. Alice?"

She stood there, clearly caught up in an internal debate, for a long time. Then she shrugged. "Sure. I could eat."

Hunter concentrated with every fiber of his new being on not showing the wave of fierce triumph washing through him. "Thank you."

When she walked over to the table, he waited until she turned away from him to sit down to close his eyes and inhale the fragrance of her silky hair. Flowers and sunshine. A hint of dog or cat, perhaps. And even a touch of…burned charcoal?

Sulfur?

He'd been at far too many fires to miss even a faint whiff of burning.

"Were you barbecuing?" he said.

She twisted in her seat to look up at him, and the view from above, looking down at her lovely face and neck and slight hint of cleavage made his body tighten to an uncomfortable and wildly inappropriate degree. He moved slightly to position his lower body behind her chair and out of her view before she saw and he died of embarrassment.

But damn, he was relieved. He hadn't been sure if his new vampire self was even able to have erections. All it took, apparently, was a few minutes in Alice's company to answer that question.

Halle-fucking-lujah.

Meara suddenly hit him with what he'd come to think of as vampire brain-mail.

IT WAS A DEMON. BANE AND RYAN ARE ON THEIR WAY HERE NOW WITH THE CREATURE.

The telepathic communication that all of them could send to and receive from one another had been an unwelcome surprise until Bane had explained that it wasn't mind reading and nobody was going to be able to rummage around in the deep, dark secrets he kept in his brain.

Like Hunter had told Meara, everybody had secrets. If his were uglier than most, that was his business, right? He shut dark memories away where they belonged and took a chair next to Alice, pushing it back a bit so she didn't feel crowded.

"Alice. We need to ask you a few questions now." He tried to keep his tone and expression calm and unthreatening, although he wasn't exactly sure what would seem unthreatening to a human about talking to a vampire.

She nodded, biting her lip. "Right. Like the grant. Fire away. I can give you copies of my financials, too, if you want. Profit and loss and the like. We're doing our best, but a startup nonprofit has a tough time these days, and of course there are other rescue groups already operating in Savannah, and—"

"Not about the rescue," he said gently. "About the demon. Why was there a demon in your shelter?"

Alice was a person whose every thought and emotion showed on her face, and right now her expression showed that, without a doubt, she had no idea what he was talking about.

"Okay. Look, I'm not even entirely freaked out to learn that vampires exist—if you really are one—"

He dropped his fangs and smiled.

She flinched but then lifted her chin. "Fine. You're a vampire. But I'm someone who has seen ghosts all my life, and I communicate with them, so vampire isn't that much of a stretch for me to believe. But I'm not particularly religious, so *demon* is a bit far out of my range of comfort. As in, I don't actually believe that there is such a thing."

"Wait till she meets the angel," Meara said, dropping

into a chair across from them. "I asked the staff to begin serving dinner."

"The staff? Isn't that dangerous?"

Meara laughed. "For them, maybe. No, just kidding. I've told them they will only hear us talking about perfectly dull things, like the weather."

"You hypnotized them? Like you tried to do with me?" Alice's eyes narrowed. "Are they going to get sick, too?"

"No, they're fine. I don't quite understand why you reacted so badly, either. Perhaps you have a unique type of resistance to enthrallment because of your ghost-whisperer abilities?"

Alice rolled her eyes. "Please don't call it that. It sounds silly. But maybe. I have what I think of as a Third Eye. It's what lets me understand the ghosts and what they want and even…"

Her face took on a closed expression, and she stopped talking, clasping her hands tightly in front of her on the table. Hunter reached out and put a hand on hers without even thinking about it, just wanting to protect her from whatever was frightening her.

And if it's me who is frightening her? Then what?

But he had no answer for the nasty voice in his head, so he ignored it. To his surprise, Alice didn't pull her hands away from his, but her eyes widened as she glanced up at him.

"I can also communicate with animals, in a small way. Not like Dr. Dolittle, but I can sort of feel their emotions and project mine back to them," she admitted in a small voice. "And I've never told anyone that, even in the Institute, when they tried to torture all my secrets out of me."

"Doctor who?" Meara looked confused.

During the past few weeks, Hunter had come to realize that Meara's pop-culture knowledge was spotty and based mostly around her love of laughing at shlocky horror movies and misinterpreting love stories. She and Ryan had argued for an hour about whether or not somebody called Elinor Dashwood was really planning to have an affair with Mr. Palmer after she pushed wimpy Edward out of the way.

This Edward was not the same Edward as a vampire who sparkled, they'd told him, laughing. He hadn't understood a single word of the discussion, but he'd enjoyed the banter before he'd crashed to the floor mid-sentence in a deep sleep.

Since then, he'd learned to be near or in his bed at dawn.

"Dr. Dolittle. A fictional character who can talk to animals, and they talk back to him in complete sentences," he said absently, studying Alice. "When did you first realize you could see and talk to ghosts?"

Her lips tilted up into a shadow of a smile, and she pulled her hands away from his and put them in her lap.

He was surprised at the depth of the sense of loss he felt just from losing the touch of her skin, but he forced himself not to fixate on the pulse in her throat. The urge was becoming unbearable, though. He stayed still but called out for help.

MEARA.

Meara glanced up at him and nodded.

EXCUSE YOURSELF AND HEAD PAST THE BATHROOM TO THE ALCOVE IN THE BACK. THEY HAVE BAGS OF BLOOD FOR YOU.

"I'll be right back," he told Alice. "Please excuse me and wait till I get back to tell us."

He shoved back from the table, trying not to show how desperate he was to get away from Alice and the hot, fresh blood racing through her veins. The silent waiter approaching from the other side of the table with a tray of wineglasses and a bottle was also starting to look like lunch, so Hunter got moving.

Fast.

Within two minutes, he'd ripped into the bags of blood, drained them, rinsed his mouth, and returned to the table, feeling like he could face Alice without turning into the monster she probably thought he was.

When he got back, Meara was staring wistfully at the waiter but only drinking wine, and Alice was toying with her fork.

"You were telling us when you started talking to ghosts," he prompted, seating himself again, this time just a bit closer to her.

"Was I?" She raised an eyebrow but then sighed. "Well, why not? I'm still not quite convinced you're not going to kill me for knowing your secret, so I may as well get this story off my chest. I've been wanting to tell somebody about it for a very long time."

Just then, the long, glowing oval that announced that Bane was imminently to arrive started to form near them, and Alice put her head in her hands and groaned.

"Not again. One ghost per hour is more than enough," she said from between clenched teeth.

"Oh, it's not a ghost. Just another vampire," Meara said cheerfully.

Bane stepped out of the Between with a struggling animal in his arms, Ryan just behind him. Hunter was sure the wriggling creature was a golden-furred dog, but two seconds later he was sure it was a giant lizard.

He pushed his chair back and stood, instinctively putting himself between Bane and Alice. "What the hell is that?"

"That's the demon," Meara said, also jumping up. "I *told* you!"

Alice stared at Bane, her mouth falling open, and then made a squeaky noise and shoved up out of her chair, too. "Where's the demon? Wait, the hot blond guy is the demon? Or the smiling woman? And what in the world are you doing with my dog?"

CHAPTER ELEVEN

Alice was suddenly completely fed up. Talking to ghosts always took a certain amount of mental energy, and throw on top of that learning that vampires really did exist—and meeting two of them!—being kidnapped and, if not drugged, at least hypnotized, and now add in dognapping… Well.

She was done.

"Put Charlie down," she ordered the tall surfer-looking blond guy with the serious muscles. He was almost as hot as Hunter, Meara was supermodel-gorgeous, and the new woman in the room was absolutely lovely.

Had she fallen into some weird vampire cult of extreme beauty? Were all vampires beautiful, like in the movies?

Was all of this a hallucination, and she was still under the influence of whatever drugs Meara had foisted on her?

The blond guy, who'd just walked out of a *magic mirror*, stared at her. "Who's Charlie?"

The woman who'd followed him out of the magic mirror, or portal, or whatever it was, put a hand on scary surfer guy's arm. "Bane. I think she means the Minor demon."

Hunter caught Alice by the hand when she started to rush over to the man holding Charlie. "Wait, please."

Then he turned toward the woman next to the one called Bane—*that* wasn't an ominous name, was it? "Ryan, why does the golden retriever look like a dog one moment and a giant lizard the next?"

The woman patted Charlie's head. "He's a Minor demon, Bane says. More dragon than lizard, really. I admit I don't see it, either. I healed his shoulder, though."

Alice stopped struggling and blinked at Ryan. "You healed my dog? Are you a vet?"

• • •

"You healed a demon?" Hunter asked. He couldn't quite wrap his head around that one. An angel healing a demon.

"He's not a demon!" Alice yanked her hand away from his and started toward Bane and Ryan, her face set in grim lines. "Okay, I've had enough of this. All of it. The magic movie special effects, the dramatic pronouncements, the nonsense about demons."

She stopped for a moment, dug in her pocket, and then tossed Meara's check on the floor. "No amount of money is worth this. Give me my dog. Now. Or my next step is to call the police."

One of the blank-faced waiters, still under enthrallment, of course, picked that moment to walk up to Bane and hold out a tray. "Canapé?"

Bane snarled at the waiter, flashing fangs, and Alice missed a step but then kept right on going. Damn but she was brave as hell. Hunter caught up with her just before she reached Bane, who was still holding the dog.

Lizard.

Minor demon.

Whatever.

"Wait. Alice, please. Wait. Let's at least find out—"

She shoved past him. "I will not wait. This poor traumatized animal has been through enough, and I won't let him be part of whatever bizarre charade you've got going on here. Give him to me."

Bane ignored her and looked at Hunter. "Easier to kill him, really. We can't let him hurt your human or—worse—lead whoever he's working for to her."

"She's not my human," Hunter growled, wondering why the words tasted like dust in his mouth. Did he want her to be his human?

He glanced at Alice's face, taking in the determination in her eyes and her trembling lips. She was a fighter, but this situation was too much, and now was not the time for fanciful thoughts about what he might or might not want.

"Tell me—us—about this. What is a Minor demon, and why do you think this poor dog is one?"

"Smell for yourself," Bane said. "The trace of sulfur."

Hunter sniffed, though he didn't need the confirmation. He'd smelled the sulfur before and even wondered if Alice had been barbecuing. Still, it wasn't much to go on.

"That's it?" He shook his head, still holding Alice back from getting to the dog. "Maybe he was caught in a fire. Maybe he was near a barbecue or firepit. Maybe—"

"Maybe you're all seriously disturbed individuals," Alice shouted, finally giving in to frustration. She kicked Hunter in the leg and took advantage of his surprise to twist past him and get to Bane and the dog.

She'd kicked him hard. But he'd barely felt it.

It would have hurt just a few short weeks before, when he'd still been human. Vampires were stronger, tougher.

Almost indestructible.

And here he was again, having irrelevant epiphanies about vampire life when he should be paying attention to the here and now.

Alice reached out for the dog, who whined furiously and strained to get to her. A dog didn't have much chance to get away from a three-hundred-year-old master vampire who wasn't in the mood to let him go, though.

Neither did a Minor demon, apparently.

"Bane," Ryan said, looking worried. "Are you sure about this? He looks like a dog to me, too."

Bane's entire expression lightened when he turned to Ryan. "Yes, my love. Vampire eyes can see through a Minor demon's glamour. Evidently Nephilim eyes can't, or you just haven't learned the trick yet."

Hunter put an arm around Alice's waist to pull her back. He didn't want her in contact with any demon, Minor or otherwise. That said, he didn't see it. He shook his head. "Bane, I don't see it, either. I only see a terrified golden retriever. Is it possible you're wrong on this one?"

"Look again," Bane advised.

"Really look. With your mind, not just your eyes," said Meara, who'd come up next to him and was holding a glass of wine in one hand and what looked an awful lot like a dagger in the other. "Do we need to salt the grave like we do with warlocks?"

"That's it," Alice shouted, and the dog started howling.

"I see it now," Ryan whispered. "Wow."

Hunter tried to ignore everything else and focus on the struggling creature in Bane's arms. At first, nothing changed. But then, all at once, the golden fur disappeared, and the truth was revealed. Bane was holding what looked like a tiny, perfectly formed dragon.

"It's beautiful," he said, and Alice froze at the sound of the awe in his voice.

"What? What are you saying?"

He pointed at the dragon. Demon. Whatever.

"It's *beautiful*."

The dragon's head snapped up, and it fixed its large golden eyes on Hunter's face. He blinked at the sight of the vertical pupils but then had to smile with the pure joy of seeing a creature that had stepped right out of mythology and into his new life.

"Beautiful things can be dangerous," Ryan said, her eyes sad. "Maybe—"

"Maybe what? You kill him just in case he *might* be dangerous? No," Alice said, no longer shouting, her voice as cold as the ghost ice that had spread through the room earlier. "I don't see what you see, but I can tell from Hunter's expression that there really is something. So you let me and my dog—demon—go home, and we're out of your way. No harm, no foul."

"That's not how it works, Alice," Meara said gently. "We mostly try to protect your kind. Except for the occasional obnoxious tourist, but that's more like a surcharge, really."

Hunter had the horrible urge to laugh at the idea of tourist blood as a surcharge, but he knew Alice would never forgive him and, for some more and more powerful reason, that mattered to him.

Suddenly the dragon made a pained groaning noise, and its entire body slumped in Bane's grasp. Then it shook once, twice, from head to tail and looked up at Alice.

When Alice gasped, Hunter realized the creature must have dropped its glamour, so now she saw the truth, too.

"But—but—" Alice raised a hand and then let it fall. "I don't—how is this possible?"

Meara opened her mouth, but Ryan pointed at her. "Don't say it. Nothing about Horatio."

Meara pouted. "Shakespeare hater."

Alice ignored the byplay, her gaze fixed on the dragon. "He *is* beautiful." She reached out tentatively. "Charlie?"

The dragon, in one powerful wiggling, thrusting movement, pushed his feet against Bane's chest and launched his little body at Alice, who caught him in her arms before Hunter could intervene.

"Alice!" He reached for the creature, but Alice backed away, and both of them—human and dragon—growled at him.

"He may be dangerous," Hunter said quietly, using the same persuasive tone of voice that he'd used to coax people to climb out of windows when their homes were on fire.

"He's not dangerous to me," she insisted, tightening her arms around the dragon and backing away. "And I won't let you kill him."

Before Hunter could think of anything else to say, the dragon spoke up, shocking all of them.

"I am dangerous, but never to you, Lady. Never. Please don't let them hurt me."

• • •

Alice almost dropped her dog.

Dragon.

Talking dragon.

And then the room started to spin around her.

"I think I need to sit down now," she told Hunter, realizing that, for no reason that made sense, he felt like safety. He caught her with one strong arm around her waist and helped her, still holding Charlie, to the long, low banquette seat that ran the length of the wall of windows.

She caught sight of the stunning river view through the glass but had nothing left in her to be appreciative. Scenery, no matter how gorgeous, couldn't hold a candle to an evening of vampires, ghosts, and dragons.

"Dragon," she murmured, ignoring for the moment both the vampires gathered around her with varying expressions of concern and disapproval on their faces and the waiter who offered her a glass of wine.

"On second thought," she said, gesturing to the waiter. She took the glass of wine and drained half of it in one gulp. "That's—actually, that's amazing wine."

Hunter crouched down next to her, his gaze on the dragon—still golden-retriever-sized—on her lap. "You can talk?"

The dragon's ears, which had been pinned flat against his sleek, angular head, lifted an inch or so. He was absolutely, surreally beautiful. His scales lay with geometric precision on his body, ranging from dark red to a brilliant ruby. His eyes were a deep gold, with vertical pupils, like a cat's. His tail, no longer furred but scaled, was maybe two feet long and ended in a clawed tip, probably to be used as a defensive weapon. His feet ended in talons, like an eagle's, but he seemed to be taking care not to dig them into Alice's legs.

And…he could talk.

She was holding a talking dragon in her lap in a room filled with vampires.

She started laughing, and there was a tinge of hysteria in it. The woman, Ryan, who'd arrived—

Alice refused to believe in magic portals right now. She'd already had her six impossible things, and she'd never even had breakfast. Or lunch, come to think of it.

The woman who'd arrived with Bane started toward her, but Alice shook her head. "Stay back, please, vampire. I need to think."

Ryan shook her head. "I'm not a vampire. I just want to check your pulse. You are dangerously pale and a little diaphoretic."

"Diaphoretic?" Alice blinked. "If you're not a vampire, what are you?"

Ryan smiled. "I'm a doctor. We like to use big words, like diaphoretic for sweaty, to make ourselves feel good about all those student loan bills."

Bane frowned. "I paid off those bills."

"Yes, and we're going to talk about that. Later," Ryan said firmly, which, oddly enough, made Alice relax enough to allow the doctor to come closer.

"It's just a lot," she explained, almost apologetically, holding tight to Charlie.

Ryan's quiet laughter was kind as she took Alice's wrist in her hand. "Don't I know it? I was first drunk and then having the worst hangover of my life when I found out that vampires exist. You're handling all of this much better than

I did, and I didn't even have a talking Minor demon in the mix."

"Dragon," Alice murmured, stroking the little dragon's head because he seemed to like it so much. He was making a small, contented sound that was a cross between a growl and a purr.

Ryan took a small flashlight from somewhere and shined it in Alice's eyes. "Okay. You seem basically fine, but have you had anything to eat recently?"

"I...don't think so." Alice had to think about it. "Actually, not since some appetizers at the hotel yesterday evening. No wonder I feel lightheaded."

Hunter took her hand in his when Ryan released it, and then he sat on the bench next to her, still holding her hand. Oddly enough, she didn't mind the contact; it was reassuring, even.

His fingers tightened around hers as if he were loaning her some of his strength, and then he looked around the room. "Hey, excuse me," he called out to one of the servers, who were all lined up against the wall chatting as if nothing at all out of the ordinary had been happening. "Can we get some food?"

"I hope you give them a really big tip," she murmured, feeling a wave of hysterical laughter trying to escape her lips.

"Huge," Meara said, smiling wryly. "Enormous. And I promise they'll come to no harm, nor will they remember any of this. Not you, not us, not your demon."

"Dragon," Alice countered. Then she took a moment to think while Hunter, still holding her hand, quietly conferred with the waiter about getting her some dinner.

She took a deep breath and let it out slowly. She didn't have a fancy college education, but she was smart enough to ask for expert help when she needed it. She'd asked for help from Small Business Association mentors when she'd started Little Darlings, for example, and right now she was surrounded by experts on all things supernatural.

"I'd really, really like some food. And, if it's okay, I'd like to learn more about vampires and…and demons. I can tell you about ghosts, if you like. Knowledge is power, right? Or at least it helps."

She turned to see what Hunter thought, but her tentative smile died when she caught sight through the window of the man behind him.

The man who'd somehow appeared on the previously empty terrace and headed for the French doors.

"I I—" She couldn't force the words out, so she just pointed.

"That's Edge. He's one of us," Meara said, and the man—who looked like a ghost himself, all dressed in black, with long white hair and silver eyes—shoved the door open and strode inside, holding something in one hand.

Edge's gaze immediately snapped to Meara, then to Alice. "Who is the human, and why is she holding a Minor demon?"

CHAPTER TWELVE

Edge took a menacing step toward Alice, and Hunter, who'd spent his entire life being a very nice guy, shot to his feet as a wave of fierce protectiveness swept through him.

"Back the fuck off," he growled, and suddenly he was seeing the room through a hazy wash of red. "And what the hell just happened to the lights?"

Ryan, in soothing doctor mode, made a patting movement with her hands. "Let's all just calm down, okay? Edge, please stay away from Alice. She seems to have ignited Hunter's protective instincts in a huge way. Hunter, you're seeing red because your eyes have just turned red. It will go away when you calm down."

"My eyes *what*?"

To his surprise, he felt Alice, still behind him on the bench, touch his hip. "Really? Can I see?"

He flinched. He didn't want her to see him looking like a monster out of one of the bad horror movies Meara loved to watch. He wanted to go back to the part where she thought he was beautiful and erase the past hour out of her memory entirely, but he had no idea why what Alice Darlington thought of him felt so vitally important to him.

"We're going to get some dinner, okay? That's why we came here in the first place, before Alice reacted badly to enthrallment and before the ghost showed up," Meara said, taking Hunter's arm and leading him away from the group.

When he resisted, unwilling to leave Alice alone, she

scowled at him and then turned to Edge. "Protect the human with your life, Sebastian, or I will have your head on one of these platters."

"Yes, *Sebastian,*" Hunter said, snickering.

"Shut up, Evans," Edge growled. "It's a family name. I will happily kick your ass for you, though, if you have anything else to say."

"No, you won't," Hunter heard Alice say fiercely. "You'll leave him alone or I'll…I'll set my dragon on you."

The red haze disappeared entirely from Hunter's vision, and he spun around to stare at Alice in disbelief. She was willing to protect him? Why? All he'd brought into her life was chaos and pain.

From the uncertain look on her face, she was wondering the same thing. And the dragon in her arms seemed to be trying to hide its head beneath her arm, its little body shaking. It squeaked something, but Hunter didn't quite catch it.

"What was that?"

Alice sighed. "He said that he would try, for me, but he had no chance against a vampire and would certainly die. So, great, I've had a tiny dragon for less than ten minutes and I'm already scaring the poor little guy."

She stroked the dragon's head until he stopped trembling, and then she glanced up at Hunter and offered a brave smile. "Let's have that dinner now. And an extra portion of chicken for Charlie, please."

• • •

Hunter pushed his barely touched plate away, but he kept an eye on Alice to be sure she ate enough to get her strength back up. He was almost but not quite to the point where he'd need to go back and find another one of the blood bags Meara had thoughtfully put on ice for him. Vampires still ate food, which had surprised him when he'd first discovered it, but it didn't satisfy the need to drink blood.

Miraculously, they'd all managed to carry on normal dinnertime conversation, everyone pretending to ignore the supernatural reality of the situation. Ryan was responsible for much of that. The woman absolutely refused to let any charged silences linger.

At the moment, she was telling a funny story about how the werewolves had reacted when she showed up at their clubhouse with an invitation to a volleyball tournament. From the look on his face, Bane didn't know whether to be amused or outraged.

"You went to the *wolves* without me?"

Apparently he'd decided on outraged.

"It was lunchtime! You were sleeping. Anyway, they're our allies now, and there's no reason in the world why they shouldn't be our friends," Ryan said, looking to the rest of them for support.

Meara just laughed, but Edge frowned.

"You could have been hurt or killed."

"Well, *Sebastian*," Ryan said sweetly, grinning when Edge growled. "I called first. And Carter said it would be fine. Max was looking forward to meeting me properly, after she saw me kick warlock ass."

"You call him Carter?" Bane's expression darkened. "Were you alone with him?"

Ryan rolled her eyes. "Yes, I call him Carter. That's his name. Or were you expecting that we'd Mr. Reynolds and

Dr. St. Cloud each other all afternoon?"

"You were there *all afternoon*?"

Ryan turned her exasperated gaze to Alice, who'd just finished feeding a second dinner roll to Charlie.

"Funny, but I don't remember human men being as annoyingly alpha male overprotective as this. Vampires have shockingly territorial, possessive instincts, just to warn you for future reference," Ryan told Alice, pointing her chin at Hunter.

"What? No! I just, I don't—" he started to say.

"We're not, we don't—" Alice started to say at the same time.

Then they looked at each other, and he grinned, noticing a deliciously adorable flush of pink sweep up Alice's cheeks.

"It's not just *male* vampires who have these tendencies," Meara drawled, selecting a tiny cheesecake from the tiered dish in the center of the table. She shot Edge a glance from beneath her lashes. "Perhaps something for everyone to keep in mind."

Edge's posture went from casually relaxed to rigidly upright, his gaze locked on Meara's face, but his voice remained calm. "Is that right?"

"Maybe," Bane interrupted, "we could get back to your ill-advised venture into wolf territory, my love."

Alice dropped her glass and watched as water and ice spilled across the table, making no move to retrieve it. Hunter picked it up and righted it, throwing his napkin over the water, and then he noticed the silence.

Everybody was staring at Alice, whose eyes had gone wide.

"Wait," she said, the word coming out strangled. "Wait. I admit that first I wasn't paying that much attention, and then I thought you were joking, but you weren't, were you?"

"About Ryan not going alone to the wolves? No, I certainly was not joking," Bane growled, his glowing blue eyes flashing a hot red for an instant and then fading back to blue.

"No. No! About—" Alice grabbed Hunter's arm in a fierce grip. "About... There are *werewolves.*"

He looked down at her hand, a sensation like warm honey spreading through him. She was reaching out to him.

To *him*.

For comfort.

He put his hand on top of hers, sure that she'd come to her senses and pull away, but instead she tightened her grip on him for a moment and then relaxed her hand but didn't let him go.

"Werewolves," Alice repeated.

Meara sighed and twirled her wineglass. "No offense, Ryan, but this 'oh! There are supernatural beings!' part was tedious enough when we had to go through it with you."

Ryan just shook her head at Meara and then gave Alice a sympathetic smile. "Yes, I'm sorry. They just casually drop these things into conversations. There are shifters, and I guess wolves aren't the only kind, but they're the only ones I've met."

"You met werewolves," Alice said slowly. "You spent the *afternoon* with them."

The dragon raised his head from where he'd been curled up on the chair next to Alice and hissed a little.

"Nasty creatures that like to eat Minor demons."

"We won't let anybody eat you, Charlie," Alice said firmly, but then she winced. "I'm sorry. Of course your name isn't Charlie. What should we call you?"

The little creature preened, lifting his wings and extending them in a stretch before settling back down. "Wing is better. Thank you, doctor lady. Charlie is a good name. Warlocks stole me before I had a naming."

"You're welcome," Ryan said. "I didn't realize it was a wing at the time, so I'm glad it worked."

"Those bastards have a lot to answer for," Meara said. "They stole you from your nest?"

Charlie tucked his head beneath a wing and didn't respond, which was as good as an answer, from what Hunter had learned about warlocks and necromancers in the past few weeks. They were seriously bad news, practiced blood magic, wanted to take over the world, territory by territory, and had attacked Bane's territory and tried to kill all of them. Luckily for the human population of Savannah, Bane, Ryan, Luke, Edge, the vampires in the Vampire Motorcycle Club, and the wolves had all joined up to fight back, and the good guys had won.

This time.

But the Chamber, the organization that ruled the warlocks and demanded unconditional surrender from all other supernatural beings, wasn't the type to give up, so Bane and the gang had been working out contingency plans for defensive reactions to any kind of possible attacks.

So far, Hunter's only real contribution had been putting fire-prevention and firefighting plans in place. For very smart vampires, they hadn't even thought of having fire extinguishers in the mansion. Apparently when you were centuries old and practically invulnerable, a little thing like fire didn't scare you.

"*Warlocks?* And Charlie, you really are a…a demon?" Alice closed her eyes and mumbled something that sounded a lot like "hallucinating" beneath her breath.

"Alice? Are you okay?" Hunter leaned toward her, careful not to dislodge her hand from his arm. "We can go somewhere away from all these vampires and talk, if you want."

Edge laughed. "You *are* a vampire."

Right.

Damn.

"I need to go home," Alice said, opening her eyes. "My nighttime help, Henry, is only supposed to be there for a little while longer, and I don't want to keep him out late. He's getting older."

She let go of Hunter's arm and stood, looking around the table at everyone. She swallowed audibly before she spoke. "Okay. I'm not really sure what's happening here, but let's give it a shot. Hunter met me and wanted to get to know me, which triggered Meara coming to check me out—"

"And giving you money. For the animals," Meara said pointedly, holding the abandoned check out to Alice, who bit her lip but then took it.

"Thank you. For the animals."

She put the check in the pocket of her jeans, and Hunter tried really, really hard not to stare at the sweet curve of her ass—and considered himself a big damn hero when he succeeded, since he was sitting right next to her. He hurriedly stood before he did something unforgivable like lean over and bite it.

"Never had that kind of urge when I was human," he muttered and then caught Edge giving him a wry smile before the man's silvery gaze returned to Meara.

"Then a ghost appeared and confirmed that you're vampires and told me you want to kill me—" She held up a hand at the chorus of denial.

"Like I said before, ghosts don't seem able to lie to me, but that doesn't mean they know what they're talking about all the time." She glanced down at the dragon, who appeared to be asleep. "Then I found out my newest rescue dog is really a demon who looks like a dragon, and I learned that there's a whole boatload of vampires in Savannah." She glanced at Edge.

"And now I've learned that werewolves and other shapeshifters exist. Plus warlocks. I think you'll all have to admit that the average person would be running and screaming by now, so I'm kind of proud of myself."

Meara sighed, a dreamy expression in her bright golden eyes. "I loved the running and screaming. Not so much the pitchforks and wooden stakes, but the running and screaming was so much fun."

"You're scaring Hunter's human," Bane said drily.

"Not really anybody's human," Alice said. "But I would appreciate a ride home, because I don't quite know how to take a dragon in an Uber."

Charlie raised his head and blinked his large eyes, a look of fervent devotion on his little dragon face. "Lady takes me?"

"Yes, of course. You have a home with me for as long as you want it," Alice told him firmly.

The little dragon unfolded his wings and launched himself into the air, but instead of landing in Alice's arms, as Hunter had expected, he landed on Hunter's shoulder.

"Oof. You must weigh fifty pounds."

The dragon ignored the half-hearted protest and curled his tail around Hunter's upper arm.

"Charlie and the nice vampire will protect Lady from the Chamber," the dragon said, hissing at the word "Chamber."

"The Chamber?" Bane shoved his chair back so hard it flew through the air and crashed into the wall on the opposite side of the room. "What do you know about the Chamber?"

"Master—no. Not master anymore. The bad warlock sent me to spy on the new vampire, and he led us to Lady. She found me and took me into her nest with her other foundlings. Chamber knows about her now. Must protect. Chamber is very bad."

The dragon snorted out a breath, which felt suspiciously hot against the side of Hunter's head, leading him to an uncomfortable thought. "You don't breathe flame, do you, Charlie?"

"Of course not."

Whew.

"That's a relief. The last thing we need—"

"Minor demons only breathe fire when they reach one year old."

Alice's mouth fell open, but it took her a couple of tries to get out the question that Hunter had been wondering about.

"How old are you now, Charlie?"

The little dragon preened, lifting its wings, one of which smacked Hunter in the side of the face. "Charlie is eleven months, three weeks, and six days old."

Hunter rubbed his cheek and calculated. "So tomorrow is your birthday?"

"No!"

"But—"

"Not birthed. Hatched. Tomorrow is the anniversary of my hatch day. I will try to breathe much fire then."

"Oh, goody," Alice said faintly.

"Luckily for you, Hunter is a firefighter," Ryan said cheerfully.

"Oh, goody," Alice repeated, looking dazed. But then she shook her head, as if shaking it off, and smiled at Hunter. "Okay, firefighter. Will you please escort me and my dragon home?"

"Take my car," Edge said, tossing the keys to Hunter. "It's out front."

"We should go now," Alice said. "I'm not sure I can take one more revelation tonight."

"Unfortunately, you're going to have to," Bane said. "Better yet, let's enthrall her to forget all this now."

"No," Hunter snarled, his vision going red again. "Leave her alone."

"She doesn't take enthrallment," Meara said, pouring herself more champagne. "It made her really sick when I tried. Trying harder might kill her. I think it's due to her ghost-whisperer thing."

Hunter took Alice's cold hand in his own. "I'll explain what she needs to know and call you if I need any help."

Bane hesitated but then finally nodded. "Do you swear to keep our secrets, Hunter's human?"

"My *name* is Alice Darlington." She raised her chin. "And yes, I swear to keep your secrets. Trust me, with my background, nobody would believe me if I ran naked through the streets of Savannah shouting them out, anyway."

Hunter tried, unsuccessfully, to keep from picturing her running naked, with that long, lush, red hair flying out behind her. When he felt his fangs start to descend, he snapped himself out of it.

Meara's attention fixed on his face, and she sent a message to him, mind to mind.

TAKE THE CASE OF BLOOD BAGS.

He nodded.

"I'll just be a moment. Hold Charlie," he told Alice, handing her the dragon. Then he raced down the hall to retrieve the case, pausing to drain one of the bags. When he returned, not even a minute later, Charlie was in Alice's arms, and she was moving toward the elevator.

"Thank you for dinner," she said, turning to face everyone after Hunter caught up with her. "And for the check, Meara. I promise to put it to good use, and I'll email you an accounting."

Meara waved a dismissive hand. "No need. I trust you. Anybody who would so bravely protect a Minor demon could scarcely do less for more helpless animals."

Alice just nodded and then reached out to Hunter. When he clasped his hand around hers, he stumbled, shocked by the sense of electricity in the skin-to-skin connection. But instead of letting go, he tightened his grip, feeling almost that the moment was destined.

That here was the place he was meant to be—in this place and time, with this woman.

And dragon. Demon.

He started laughing and pushed the button for the elevator.

She quirked a glance at him. "What's funny?"

"Did I mention that Edge has a Ferrari?" He shot a grin over his shoulder at Edge. "And that I've never driven a Ferrari before? I hope the dragon is potty-trained."

"Hey!" Edge started toward them just as the elevator doors opened. "Wait just a minute."

Hunter laughed all the way down to the car.

CHAPTER THIRTEEN

Lord Alastair Neville, supreme ruler of the Chamber, took a private phone call from Hanford Kurchausen in his study in London.

Dr. Kurchausen had been the director of a private institute on the east coast of the United States before it burned down, and he was also a member of the Chamber's highest echelon. The Institute had purported to be a therapeutic environment for mentally disturbed individuals.

In actuality, the place had served more as a stepping stone to hell for its unfortunate residents.

Kurchausen had gleefully manipulated—and contributed to—the patients' mental and physical agony in order to fuel ever deeper and more depraved magics.

Lord Neville quite approved.

However, there had been one particularly powerful patient who'd managed to escape. Kurchausen had demonstrated an unpleasant tendency ever since to whine about the "ghost whisperer who got away."

Now that Lord Neville had found her, quite by accident, he decided he'd prefer to capture her for his own use. The only problem was getting her out of Bane's territory. That upstart vampire had caused the Chamber quite a few problems, but he had plans for Bane and his motley group of bloodsuckers. And even more exciting plans for Bane's Nephilim mate or, at least, for Dr. Ryan St. Cloud's blood.

Lord Neville's smile, had anyone seen it, would have

terrified years off their lives.

Literally.

He pushed the button that took the call off hold.

"Hanford? Yes, Neville here. No, we still have no idea where Alice Jones might be. Such a common name, Jones. No. No idea at all."

CHAPTER FOURTEEN

Alice considered the fancy sports car in front of her and the tall, muscled man next to her. Not to mention the dragon—who now looked exactly like a golden retriever again—standing on the sidewalk next to her.

"I don't think we're all going to fit."

"We'll fit," Hunter said confidently. "Charlie can sit in this space between us."

She leaned down and peered in the window. "That's a very small space."

"He's a very small dragon. We're not talking Smaug here."

Charlie growled but said nothing, which was just as well, since an elderly couple was strolling past them just then. Alice smiled at them and exchanged hellos but waited until they were out of hearing range to respond.

"You're a *Lord of the Rings* fan?"

"Books *and* movies. Did you hear there's a TV series coming out, too?"

"Really? That's amazing! But I don't know if they can ever compete with the movies. They were wonderful." She'd watched the DVDs at least five times, loving every moment. A battered old copy of *The Hobbit* had kept her company through some of the really bad times in the Institute, but happily the story had come to be associated with escape and peace in her mind, instead of with pain and torture. She felt her smile fade, and Hunter noticed it right away.

"It's okay. We really will fit. Which was your favorite character? Let me guess: Legolas." He unlocked the car, rolling his eyes. "My sister and her friends were all gaga for that elf."

"You have a sister? I always wanted a sister! And, no, I'm an Aragorn girl all the way. But Galadriel is my number one. All that power offered to her, and she turns it down to stay true to herself. I admire that so much." She realized he was chatting about nothing to put her at ease after the evening's revelations, but she found herself perfectly content to go along with it. Her nerves needed a break.

He opened the door for her. "Galadriel is a badass. But why Aragorn?"

She grinned but felt her cheeks get hot. "All that dark, bad-boy deliciousness. How could it *not* be Aragorn?"

Hunter, all dark, bad-boy deliciousness himself, with the muscles, and with the tattoos peeking out at his wrists and at the open neck of his shirt, flashed such a wicked smile it was a wonder her clothes didn't melt off on the spot.

"It's a good thing you're a firefighter, with a smile like that," she mumbled, and he laughed.

The car was cramped, and he needed a couple of tries to figure out the gears and whatnot, but they all fit just fine. Charlie curled up on her lap and refused to move, and she stroked his ears.

She leaned back in her seat, turned her face to the window, and closed her eyes, mostly to avoid conversation. Her brain was full to bursting with new information, new people, and new problems. Since her escape from the

Institute, she'd been careful to stay away from drama and danger. Even changed her name, which had amused her at the time.

Most people trying to disguise their identity changed their name *to* Jones. She'd gone in the opposite direction.

"I know it's too much," he said, his voice gentle, but when she turned to look at him, she noticed his knuckles were white on the steering wheel. "I'm sorry. I was...I was drawn to you, and I just wanted to get to know you. I never meant for you to get caught up in my dangerous new world."

The sincerity in his voice was unmistakable, and she liked him for it.

"It's not all about you. Between the ghosts and the animals and my...past, I have enough baggage of my own."

He said nothing, but the tension in his hands eased. They rode in silence the rest of the way to her house, but it was a peaceful silence, not a tense one. When Charlie, boneless in sleep in her lap, let out a little burping snore, Hunter chuckled.

"That demon—"

"Dragon."

"That dragon is sure in love with you."

Her smile faded as she stroked Charlie's head. "It doesn't seem like he has had much love in his life. Stolen from his nest and forced to serve warlocks? That's horrible."

"If those warlocks come looking for him, they're going to be in for a big surprise," Hunter said, his face set in hard lines. "We're never letting them get him back."

She liked that he'd said "we." She'd never been part of a

"we" before…not that she really was now. She'd just met the man—vampire—and the feelings she was having for and about him made no sense.

Well, the attraction, that made sense, of course. The man was a walking fantasy. Even now, after the night's shocking revelations, she caught herself wanting to reach over and run her fingers through his silky dark hair.

But the feeling of safety—of comfort—she had no idea where that had come from. The man was a vampire, for heaven's sake, and she'd even caught him looking at her throat a few times. Planning to get her alone and drink her blood?

But if he'd planned to kill her, or even hurt her, or treat her like a snack, he'd already had plenty of chances. Instead, he'd stood between her and any sign of danger—like the casual "we could just kill you" attitude the other vampires seemed to have about humans.

She still didn't quite know what to do or even think about the check burning a hole in her pocket.

Cash it? Shred it?

Move to Montana?

So many decisions. Before she could work out her answers to any of them, Hunter was pulling into her driveway. She shifted Charlie so she could get out and unlock the gate, but Hunter narrowed his eyes at her and held his hand out for her keys. She started to protest, but he cut her off.

"We may be in danger. One of us is more vulnerable than the other. How about we focus on keeping you safe so you can care for your animals?"

She handed him the keys and nodded her thanks. He

wasn't wrong, and she wasn't going to argue about her right to be put in equal danger. Not that she knew any details, but humans undoubtedly were more fragile than vampires.

When he got back in the car, she asked him. "You said I'm more vulnerable. What superpowers do you have, being a vampire? Or invulnerabilities or whatever? Are you bulletproof?"

"Well, seeing as how I have three whole weeks of experience, I'm not sure I'm the right person to tell you all about it. I can try. Luke and the rest of them, especially Meara, have been telling me what I need to know, but it's a lot. Sometimes she forgets that she has three hundred years of experience living this life, and I'm not going to be able to pick it up in a day."

Hunter pulled the car up past where she normally parked and around to the side of the house that was hidden from the street. "If people are after us, and it's pretty clear somebody is, we don't need to make it easy for them to find us."

When they exited the car, Charlie jumped out of Alice's arms and flew up into the branches of a tree, and she wasn't quite sure what to do about it. Now that she knew he was a dragon who talked, she wasn't going to treat him the same way she did her rescue animals. He deserved to make his own choices about his life. Although, in some ways, he was very much the same as her charges. Clearly the warlock had been mistreating him. Abuse was abuse, and she'd dedicated every moment of her life since escaping the Institute to fighting against it.

"Penny for your thoughts," Hunter said.

Startled out of her reverie, Alice shook her head.

"They're not worth so much. Just dark thoughts about dark days. My childhood wasn't easy."

Understatement of the year.

Even in the dim illumination cast by the porch light, she could see Hunter's face tighten.

"Mine was great, up to the point when I almost destroyed everything."

She waited for him to explain, but he just stood silently, waiting for her to open the door to the house. Instead, she led him back to the outside door of the rescue.

"I have to check on the animals and let Henry know it's okay to go home."

Henry was a gentle man in his late seventies who had retired from a busy and successful corporate life and recently lost his wife of fifty years. There was such a wealth of sadness hidden in his reserve that she knew it had been a wonderful marriage and he still missed her very much. She occasionally caught herself wistfully imagining what it would be like to find someone with whom she could share her life and love like that. For now, she gave all of herself to the animals in her rescue. But sometimes, usually in the dark, quiet hours of the night, she was forced to admit that she wanted more.

Needed more.

Didn't all people long for a sense of connection? She'd always imagined it as a warm, quiet feeling of utter contentment when they knew someone was their person, believed in them, and had their back.

She only realized she was standing there, lost in thought, when Hunter put a hand on her arm. "Henry?" he said.

She glanced up at him and immediately wondered if he

realized how his eyes had narrowed. Did he see Henry as a possible threat?

"Yes, Henry. I absolutely adore him and don't know what I'd do without him." She put a little more enthusiasm into her voice than she was actually feeling at the moment, just to reassure Hunter that Henry was no danger. Tensions had been high all evening, and Hunter was a vampire. She didn't want Henry to become collateral damage.

Hunter scowled. "Is this Henry young and handsome and desperately in love with his boss?"

She blinked at him, caught completely off guard. That was *not* the danger she'd thought he'd be contemplating. "He's definitely handsome. But not in love with me even a little. He does have a very reciprocated lovefest going on with Cleo, though."

"Who's Cleo?"

"A very spoiled cat who thinks she's a princess. She was caught in a house fire, long story."

Hunter shook his head. "It's a sad statistic that we never keep track of, the number of pets who are hurt or killed in fires. We try to rescue them when we can, but of course the priority is always the people in the house. Not that it didn't almost kill me sometimes when I was not allowed to go back in for the family dog or cat because the entire structure was in imminent danger of coming down around our heads."

"I think everybody understands that," Alice said. "But it doesn't make it any easier. For so many of us, our pets are part of our families. Sometimes our only family."

She pulled her keys out, and, at the sound of the keys rattling, Charlie flew down out of the tree and landed next to them.

"No intruders, Lady," the little dragon said before he resumed his golden retriever glamour, and just in time, too, because before Alice could open the door, Henry did.

"Welcome back, Miss Alice. I hope you had a good time on your dinner out. It has been a very quiet evening here."

Henry was maybe five feet six inches of pure Southern gentleman. He had a thick head of white hair brushed back from the dark brown skin of his high forehead, and dark brown eyes that shone with curiosity as he looked at Hunter. He'd been with her almost the whole time she'd operated the rescue, and she'd never once shown any sign of a social life, so he was probably curious. Henry, though, was too much of a gentleman to ask questions.

"Thanks, Henry," she said. "It was definitely interesting."

He moved back to give them space to enter but then knelt down and put his hands on Charlie's head. "Oh, aren't you a fine boy? Yes, you are."

The general noise level in the shelter rocketed up to an eleven, either because Alice was back or because the animals sensed the presence of a vampire and a dragon. Who could know? Alice sighed. It was going to be an interesting couple of hours.

Charlie, though, immediately moved in closer and leaned his head on Henry's shoulder. Evidently dragons were very good judges of character.

"Henry, this is Hunter Evans, a friend of mine. He's going to volunteer here, and he'll be staying with me for a while this evening to learn something about the rescue."

Hunter played along, nodding. "Yes, I have some spare time on the evenings I'm not on call. Nice to meet you, Henry. Alice said she couldn't manage without you."

He held out his hand to Henry, who stood, and the two men shook.

"Doctor?"

"Firefighter."

Henry gave Hunter a shrewd glance, clearly sizing up the younger, taller man. Finally, he smiled and nodded as if giving his tacit approval. "Thank you for that. Firefighters are heroes, that's for sure. I'm glad to see our Alice getting more help around here. She's a dynamo, always working hard for these animals. Savannah is lucky to have her."

Alice felt her cheeks turn hot; she was still unable to take a compliment well or without looking for the hidden agenda behind it. Maybe that was something else she could work on.

She put past insecurities aside. "How is everyone tonight?"

"Things are good. Ajax had a hard time settling, and that ferret gave me a heart attack a time or two, but mostly everyone is settled. And who is this gorgeous boy?" Henry leaned down to give Charlie a good scratch behind his ears, and the dragon-turned-dog stretched his head up to be sure that Henry got all the good spots.

"Somebody dumped him in the yard. I really hate that," she said before remembering that wasn't how it had happened at all. Still. It was something that *did* happen, far too often. "Maybe we should put up a sign on the fence? Something like 'no dumping, all animals accepted' with our hours posted?"

Henry nodded. "I can pick that up tomorrow. A friend of mine has a sign shop."

The man had friends all over Savannah after living

there his whole life, so this wasn't surprising.

"Thanks, Henry. We named him Charlie—well, Susan did—and he seems to like the name. And he's doing really well. We just need to fatten him up a little bit. I've been giving him my special homemade food, and he'll be back to his fighting weight in no time."

She didn't mention the pound or three of food that the dragon had consumed at the restaurant, figuring there were some things that Henry just did not need to know. Hunter, on the other hand, had looked mildly concerned at the phrase "fighting weight," which made her remember that Charlie had told them that he planned on breathing "much fire" the next day.

She almost laughed at the direction her life had taken. Vampires and shifters and ghosts, oh my! And now dragons, too. She glanced at Charlie again, struck by a sudden thought.

Just how big did a dragon demon grow?

"Well, if everything is okay, then, I'll be heading out," Henry said. "I need to get some sleep, because I have to help a friend of mine move tomorrow. She's downsizing into assisted living, and she has sixty years of 'I can never give anything away' to sort through before her overly excitable daughter shows up next weekend and throws it all in a dumpster." Henry shook his head with a rueful smile. "I've never been able to understand this need to hoard every possession, but then again, my wife did like her collections, and I admit I'm finding it hard to part with them..."

She impulsively took his hands in hers and kissed his wrinkled cheek. "Thank you again, Henry. Yes, everything's fine, and I'll be heading to bed myself soon."

Henry's gaze shifted to Hunter for a second, and Alice wanted to die of mortification on the spot, realizing the implication he'd probably gotten. But Hunter didn't give the slightest sign he'd heard anything suggestive. He just dug his hands into his pockets and gave Henry a reassuring smile.

"Yep. I'll be on my way as soon as I learn a little bit about the rescue," Hunter said. "Nice to meet you, Henry, and I look forward to spending some time with you here."

After they'd closed and locked the door behind Henry, Alice stood frozen for a moment, not sure what to do next or even what to think. Hunter took up so much space—he was too tall, too broad, too sexy, too…too *male*. It almost made it hard for her to think.

When in doubt, though, there was always work. She had animals to take care of.

"All right. I hope you're ready to roll up your sleeves and really help me out. We've got to check on everybody, make sure that they're all settled in for the night, and—Charlie, what are you doing?"

The cacophony of vocalizations had ratcheted up a few notches, but none of the animals were focused on Alice or Hunter. They were all watching Charlie, who was in the process of unlocking Ajax's kennel door with his front talons.

The German shepherd mix scrabbled back to the farthest corner of his kennel and started to growl low and deep.

"Charlie, no! Ajax is not ready for company—"

But Charlie ignored her. Before she could get to him,

he'd walked into the kennel and closed and latched the door behind him. By the time she reached the kennel, the dragon had released his glamour, stretched and then folded his wings, and then settled down on one side of Ajax's oversize bed.

Alice tried to keep her energy calm and assertive, so as not to agitate the rest of the animals, but this was an entirely new situation for her. She'd never before had one rescue animal move in on another animal's territory. Especially not any fire-breathing dragons. She started to unlatch the door to intervene—but stopped when Ajax reacted in a way that surprised her completely.

The dog stopped growling, and his ears perked up from the flattened mode they'd gone into when he first saw Charlie opening the door. He took slow steps, bit by bit, toward the little dragon, projecting curiosity and wariness but no aggression. When he got close enough that he was in reach, he stretched his neck and started sniffing Charlie, who returned the favor. Whatever silent communication they had going on must've conveyed the reassurance that Ajax needed, because the dog shook out his fur, climbed on the bed, turned around three times, and curled up next to the dragon, closing his eyes.

Alice almost fell down.

"From the look on your face, I'm guessing that was quite unexpected," Hunter said.

Alice was still trying to understand exactly what had happened. "To be honest, I had no idea what to expect, not having had a dragon—or at least not knowing I had a dragon—in my rescue before. Ajax has been very aloof since he got here, and only in the past week or so has he allowed me to even get close to him. So for another male, even of a different species, to invade his territory—I thought it would be a full-on battle."

"There wasn't even a fight for supremacy. This is more like two friends hanging out together," Hunter said, and the wonder in his tone made her smile.

"Yes, it's always something new and different when you're working with animals. There are things you can expect, and things you would never expect in a million years. In fact— "

Hunter made a strange noise, something between a gasp and a growl, and jumped a foot in the air, cutting off whatever she'd been about to say.

He froze and aimed very wide eyes at her. "I think a *rodent* just jumped on my *head*," he said, biting off every word.

Alice took one look at him and started to laugh. "That's no rodent. That's Ferret Bueller."

CHAPTER FIFTEEN

Hunter started laughing and gently detangled the little creature's paws from his hair. "My sister, Hope, had a ferret. Such a little thing, but it was always getting into everything. I came home from school one day and found it had taken every single one of my Boy Scout derby cars and spread them out all over the floor. I swear to this day that ferret was playing with those cars up until the minute I walked in the door."

"He probably was. They're very curious. This one is an escape artist. He manages to get out of every crate I put him into." Alice held out her hands, and Hunter carefully handed over the ferret, who was chattering away cheerfully.

"Ferret Bueller, huh?"

She laughed. "Veronica suggested Ferret Wheel, but once we saw his personality, Ferret Bueller felt more appropriate."

She carried the chattering creature over to a box lined with blankets that sat on a counter.

"No crate, no lock?"

"There's no point. He'd just find a way out. He was healing from getting his leg accidentally slammed in a door, and then he hurt a different foot when he climbed a bookcase and dislodged some books that fell out, knocking him to the ground. The owner had apparently had the last straw with that, because she'd been racking up vet bills for the poor little guy every time he got in more trouble. So that's how he came to me."

Hunter nodded, but he wasn't particularly thinking about vet bills or ferrets or even dangers like the Chamber. He was only thinking of the way Alice's face glowed when she talked about her animals, and about how much he would love it if her face glowed like that when she was thinking of him.

But that wasn't how women thought of him.

Ever.

He was the nice guy. The good friend. The buddy. His next tattoo may as well read "friend zone," and that way he could just get it out of the way right up front.

He blew out a breath, suddenly disgusted with himself. With everything going on, he didn't have time for self-pity or whatever the hell this was. He needed to stay focused.

Naturally, Bane picked that moment to reach out to him telepathically.

WE HIRED CARTER REYNOLDS AND HIS SECURITY FIRM TO KEEP AN EYE ON BOTH THE MANSION AND YOUR HUMAN'S RESCUE ORGANIZATION DURING THE DAY, WHEN WE ARE NOT AS READILY ACCESSIBLE. YOU SHOULD HAVE A TEXT FROM THEM BY NOW THAT THEY ARE ON THE PREMISES. THEY WILL NOT COME INSIDE THE RESCUE UNLESS YOU NEED THEM TO. IT WOULD BE BETTER IF YOU STAY THERE FOR THE NIGHT TO BE ON THE SPOT.

For one wild moment, Hunter wondered if Bane was trying to play matchmaker, then immediately discarded the idea as one of the most ridiculous he'd ever had. Sure, being in love with Ryan had changed the master vampire, but not to the extent that he would ever concern himself in someone else's love life.

"Why are you smiling?" Alice was already working, prepping foods and medicines to be distributed as needed.

Hunter checked his phone and confirmed that the text was there. "Nothing. But you should know that Bane just reached out. The security team is here, outside patrolling, and available to us if we need them to come inside. The only thing is, the security team is made up of werewolves, and even in their human form, the animals might sense what they are and have a problem."

Alice's eyes widened, but then she shook her head. "No. No, I'm not going to freak out over a werewolf security team, after everything else thrown at me over the past couple of days. I need to get to work."

"What can I do to help?"

For the next hour or so they worked companionably and chatted, most of their conversation Alice telling him about the work and the animals. To Hunter's surprise, very few of them had any problems with him. He had figured there would be some kind of generalized freak-out when they realized a vampire was in their midst, but for most of them, he was just another pair of hands bringing the things they wanted. A couple of them even tried to make friends, like the ferret and Cleo the cat. Since he, too, had been injured in a fire—the one that had nearly killed him—he had a lot of empathy for her.

"If my life weren't so unsettled right now, I would be interested in adopting this sweet girl," he told Alice, with Cleo in his arms. "She's clearly tough and a survivor. Maybe I could take lessons from her."

Alice stilled and looked at him for a long moment before she spoke. "But don't you know that you *are* a survivor? You're incredibly tough. First off, you're a firefighter. A career that means you run into situations most people run away from. And now you're a vampire. Just your everyday life must be a test of surviving an incredibly bizarre change in circumstances. I mean, it must be weird to wake up one day and think 'Wow. I want to drink blood today.'"

Hunter flinched because he had been thinking just that.

Not the survivor bit, although he appreciated what she'd said. But about drinking blood. About how he needed to break into one of those bags from the cooler before he reached a dangerous state of hunger while in such close proximity to Alice and the sweet scent of her hair.

Her skin.

What would her blood smell like? Or *taste* like…

His own skin began to tingle, and his thoughts started to fog over, shrouded with mist. The slightest haze of red glimmered on objects in the room, warning him of exactly how strong the thirst was becoming.

"Actually," he began, but the phone started ringing.

Phones, plural. The phone in her pocket and the old landline phone sitting on a counter. Alice pulled the phone out of her pocket, glanced at the display, and shook her head, silencing the call. Then she went to the phone on the table and grabbed it.

"Little Darlings Rescue. How can we help you?"

Hunter's vision cleared, and he steadied. He was fine. He'd go grab another bag of blood after the call. He started to ask Alice who it was but then realized he could hear the other side of the conversation clearly.

Superior vampire hearing for the win.

It was about a rescue, of course. Somebody had found a cat with a litter of kittens beneath the front porch of a house that was scheduled to be demolished the following day.

"Of course I'll come out," Alice said just as Hunter had been ready to suggest that she call another rescue to deal with the situation.

"Not the best time, Alice. With people after you—"

"People have been after me for a long time," she said, surprising him. "I'm not going to change the way I live for them now any more than I did in the past."

For an instant, her beautiful face looked unbearably sad, as if all the pain in the world had settled behind her eyes. He wanted to help her—to save her—to comfort her. He wanted to be part of her world. Even a monster deserved peace, didn't he? Maybe even—although he hardly dared to think it—happiness?

The thirst rose up again and answered.

No. No, he did not.

"I'll go with you."

She was shaking her head before he finished speaking. "We're not taking a Ferrari to rescue a litter of kittens. The last thing I need is to have to pay cleaning damages to your friend."

Hunter laughed at the visual of Edge getting into his car and finding little kitten pee spots all over it, but he shook his head. "No, you're right. Let's take that old van of yours. And tomorrow we'll see about getting it fixed or replaced."

"You vampires are very high-handed, aren't you? Here's a huge check, but I'll compel you to do what I want. I'll replace your van, whether you asked for it or not." Alice's eyes narrowed, and she looked like she was ready to launch into a tirade, but then she glanced down at the phone she still held and put it in her pocket. "Okay. Okay. Let me get a few things to restock the kit, and we'll go. If you're sure you want to?"

"I wouldn't miss it for the world."

While she restocked, so did he, so to speak, moving into what was clearly the animal bathing room to drink two bags of blood. He put the empty bags back in the cooler, closed it tightly, and took a deep breath, back in control.

"Okay, Alice, let's go. I'm ready for anything now."

• • •

Thirty minutes later, when his entire body was on the ground, in the mud, and twisted up halfway beneath a ramshackle old porch while he tried to coax kittens to come toward him, he realized he'd been a little hasty.

"Maybe not ready for *anything*," he muttered, and the enraged mama cat shot out a paw, claws fully extended, and swiped his face again. "Hey! Cut that out. I'm trying to help here, you stinky fur ball."

Alice grabbed his boot. "Hunter! I'm the expert in this. I don't need you to rescue me or protect me or save me from the cat." The exasperation in her voice rang through loud and clear. "This is *my* arena, and I already told you that I have a special connection with animals. Get out of there and let me go under the porch and convey to mama cat that we're not going to hurt her or her babies."

He didn't have to think about it long. He sure as hell wasn't doing any good, and the night was getting colder and colder. Not that vampires felt the cold very much, but Alice was already shivering, even with her coat on, and the cold, damp ground couldn't be good for those newborn kittens.

He shook off the "bullheaded male stubbornness" that Alice had accused him of just a few minutes before and crawled backward out from under the porch.

"Okay, you're up. Let's see this animal magic of yours." He hadn't meant it to come out sounding like a challenge, but he could tell that Alice took it exactly like that.

She raised her chin. "I'll have them all out within five minutes. Watch me, tough guy."

With that, she dropped to the ground and started crawling under the porch. Hunter didn't even try to lie to himself and pretend that he wasn't staring at her gorgeous ass, which was doing delightful things as she wiggled her way toward the cats.

Damn, but he loved snug jeans on a woman.

"And stop staring at my butt!"

Busted.

To distract himself, he looked around. The house itself—more like a shack—was a good ten-minute drive outside the city, in a neighborhood that had fallen upon some rough times. This place was one of many that were completely deserted and abandoned and apparently destined to be demolished, probably to build apartments or a shopping strip.

He suddenly realized that he'd just taken for granted

the fact that it was abandoned, when they could have been followed by some of the warlocks or thugs from the Chamber, and swore silently at his carelessness. Then he stood utterly still for a moment and worked at sending his new vampire senses out over the area, trying to listen and focus in case he heard any animals besides the cats who might be in distress, any stealthy movement that might signal danger, or anything else that seemed out of place.

He also listened for any sounds of humans in distress.

Bane and Meara had impressed upon him that they were guardians, of a kind. Protectors of the humans in their territory against any "dark forces that soared forth on the winds of the night," as Meara had so poetically put it. Edge had laughed and said, "Yeah. Supernatural dumbasses, in other words," and Meara had levitated his dessert to her side of the table for revenge.

He grinned at the memory but kept listening and watching. He heard nothing, though. Nothing but the everyday sounds of the night—nothing that sent up a red flag warning of danger.

Then he heard Alice say, "Good girl."

Less than a minute later, she handed him the first kitten. "Put her in the warming basket, and here comes another one. Looks like we have six altogether." She handed him kittens, one after another, like a little furry assembly line. When he had all six, she started wiggling backward to come out from under the porch, and the mama cat followed her out.

The cat was far too thin, decidedly bedraggled, and looked like she had lost part of her tail at some point, but she looked at Alice with such a trusting expression that

Hunter knew they'd established a bond already.

"Surprise!" Hunter said, grinning as he caught sight of an unexpected bonus.

Alice sat up, shook dirt out of her hair, and gave him a questioning look. "What do you mean?"

He squatted down and nodded at the cat. "She brought us another one."

Sure enough, mama cat was gently holding a seventh kitten in her mouth. Astonishingly, she trotted right up to Hunter and put the kitten in his outstretched hand.

He cradled the tiny sleeping creature, overwhelmed with an emotion he couldn't quite identify. After everything she had clearly been through, this scared, almost feral cat trusted him—a monster—to take care of her baby. It didn't make sense.

None of his new life made sense.

Being a vampire, inflicting his presence upon this kind, selfless woman and dragging her into the chaos of his life. Wanting her but wanting to protect her from danger—to protect her from himself, most of all.

None of it made sense, and he was so wrong to have pulled her into his world.

Alice smiled and stood, brushing dirt off her clothes. "Well, that's surprising. I guess mama must recognize, like I do, that you will protect her and her babies." She smiled up at him with such an unwarranted look of trust that he wanted to yank her into his arms, dirt and all, and kiss the breath out of her. Hold her and kiss her until she melted into him.

Until she *kissed him back*.

Until she wanted him as much as he suddenly, searingly,

shockingly wanted her.

He did none of that. Instead, he carefully placed the final kitten in the inside pocket of his jacket, since the warming basket was filled with the six other squirming little bodies.

"We should get back. We need to get mama and the babies cleaned up, then get mama some water and food."

He nodded. That's definitely what they should do. However, his body was not agreeing with what his brain told him.

Two bags of blood hadn't been enough, he suddenly realized with a sick feeling in his gut. Not enough, and he hadn't had the sense to ask how far they were traveling or even to bring his special cooler with him. He glanced down at the hand holding the warming basket and saw the veins in his hand begin to turn black—a clear warning sign, Meara had impressed upon him, that his thirst was becoming unmanageable.

That he would need to feed. Soon. *Really* soon, in fact, if he didn't want to become a danger to the very humans they were meant to protect.

Meara joked about snacking on tourists, but she was careful to never, ever become out of control. Luke had warned him about the same thing. Even Bane had issued dire warnings about the peril of waiting too long to feed, or not taking in enough blood, as a new vampire. His brain told him he needed to get away from Alice right that minute.

Now.

Get far away, until he could take care of this problem.

His body—the thirst—told him quite a different story.

Every fiber of his being was telling him that what he really needed to do was sink his teeth into Alice's lovely neck.

He suddenly noticed that Alice's eyes had widened and she was backing slowly away from him.

"Hunter? Why are you looking at me like that?"

He carefully put the warming basket on the ground and then took a step toward her. The mama cat who had trusted him with her baby only a moment ago arched her back and hissed at him, clearly recognizing a superior predator.

He idly wondered if she now felt like prey.

If *Alice* felt like prey.

"Hunter?" Alice's voice had turned shaky and unsure. "What's happening?"

"What's happening is I'm very much afraid someone is going to die," he snarled.

Then he took a step toward her, and his fangs snapped down into place.

CHAPTER SIXTEEN

Until that moment, Alice hadn't seen death bearing down on her since she'd escaped from the Institute. Hunter's face contorted into a snarl, and his fangs—and they *were* fangs—were on full display. She stumbled back with some disjointed idea of protecting the cat, but he raced past her, so close and so fast that she actually felt a breeze from his passage. Seconds later, he had disappeared into the woods behind the shack.

She had *never* seen anyone move like that. Just for a moment, she had been afraid.

Afraid of Hunter.

It had only been a few years since she'd escaped from the Institute, and she'd made a point of reading as much as she could find about post-traumatic stress disorder. She knew she wasn't magically cured just because she'd tried so hard to move on with her life. She probably needed therapy.

Okay, she definitely needed therapy.

Frightening situations, people, and events were always going to take her right back to that room, unless she got help. That cold, white, sterile room where they'd strapped her down and stuck needles in her. Forced her to perform on demand.

Shaking, she bent to retrieve the warming basket filled with mewling kittens. The mama cat, her fur still standing on end, twined in and out between Alice's ankles, keeping close.

"He scared me, too," she murmured to the cat, not quite sure what to do next. Should she leave him? Should she be truly afraid and run?

At the very least, she needed to take care of the animals. She headed toward the van, and just before she got there, Hunter suddenly appeared next to her. She hadn't seen or heard him approach, and it scared the crap out of her.

"Don't *do* that!"

"Sorry," he muttered. "I didn't mean to scare you. Something about turning into a vampire makes a person stealthy."

She dared a glance at his face, checking for fangs. They were gone. He looked completely normal again. Or whatever passed for normal in a vampire.

"What did you do? What happened? You know, not now but before, you almost did scare me." Her laugh was a little shaky, but she felt like she needed to tell him the effect his actions had had on her, if not the reason that she'd been so afraid. She wasn't ready to share her terrible past with him or anyone else, and maybe she never would be, but she needed to tell him the truth of her feelings.

"What are you thinking about?" Hunter moved closer and picked up the mama cat, who was now perfectly content to let him do so. "Everything you think or feel shows on your face. So something extremely heavy was just going through your mind."

"I don't really want to talk about it right now." She focused on carefully moving the kittens to the crate.

He ducked his head and looked at the ground, afraid or unwilling to meet her gaze. "And who could blame you? I'm sorry. I'm sorry I scared you. It's just that I don't have much control over the hunger at this point. Meara told me it takes a while to get the hang of it, and the most important thing is to have resources available. I didn't think about that when we got the call to come out here."

She was silent until they finished stowing the cat and kittens in the secured crates in the van, considering her response. Wondering why she wasn't afraid of him now.

Was she being self-destructive? Putting herself in danger just because of the attraction she felt for him? She wasn't sure. Had no idea how to *be* sure. So instead, she turned the question around to him.

"What did you do?" She was almost afraid to ask, because part of her didn't want to know the answer. But she *needed* to know. If Hunter was feeding on people and he had gone off to find someone to drain dry, she needed to know.

Because if that were true, she couldn't and *wouldn't* have anything more to do with him.

She felt a sharp pang of sadness at the idea, which didn't make sense. She'd just met him, she barely knew him, and what she did know was strange and frightening and dangerous.

On the other hand, he'd stood between her and the other vampires' threats. He'd stood up for her. Charlie liked him, but okay, Charlie was a demon. But Henry had even liked him. And now he'd taken time out of his night to come with her and get down in the muck to help her rescue a cat and her kittens.

"I found some deer," he said, his shoulders slumping, shame in his eyes. "There were three of them—full-grown, not babies—and I only took enough from each to make them a little tired. I didn't hurt them, Alice. They're fine, and now, so am I, which means *you* are safe. And your safety is my absolute priority."

She believed him. His sincerity was apparent in every line of his body, and now he was standing there looking at her with such sad eyes, like he expected her to tell him to leave. Like it was nothing but what he deserved.

He probably didn't even remember that he had a kitten in his coat pocket.

But then his pocket started meowing, and he jumped a foot in the air.

Alice started laughing.

In spite of everything, she laughed, and Hunter's entire face lit up with what looked a lot like hope. She always tried to live her new life in hope; the feeling that she'd shared some with him warmed her past her wariness. Past her fear.

Foolish or not, she wasn't going to send him away. She'd wait and watch and be very, very careful, but she wasn't sending him away.

Not yet.

Hunter smiled at her as if he could read her decision on her face and slowly put a hand in his pocket. "Forgot this little guy."

He carefully retrieved the kitten and put it in the crate with the others, then fastened the door shut. "And now we go back to the rescue and take care of the kittens?"

She could tell that there was much more to the question than its surface meaning. Far deeper layers. He had asked if they'd go back to the rescue, but she knew that he was really asking a more poignant question.

Am I still welcome in your home after you've seen me at my worst?

She answered both questions with a single response. "Yes, Hunter. Now we go back to the rescue, and I teach you the fine art of feral-cat bathing. Nobody can say I don't know how to show a guy a good time."

Hunter's blue eyes glowed so brightly that she could almost feel the heat from his gaze on her skin. When he answered her, there was a fierce intensity in his voice. "No. No, I would never say that, beautiful Alice. Thank you."

On the drive back to her home, she had the strangest feeling that she'd agreed to far, far more than she'd intended.

• • •

By the time they got the cats cleaned up, fed, and safely ensconced in a crate with warm blankets and plenty of fresh water, it was nearly dawn, and Hunter had begun to look tired. When he fought to hide the third or fourth huge yawn in a row, she finally put down the towel she'd been using to dry the freshly cleaned counter and turned to face him, folding her arms.

"Okay, you. It's clearly past bedtime for all helpful vampires. Do you have time to get home before sunrise?"

His gorgeous blue eyes widened, the glow in them brightening, and he looked at the window, but the darkness outside was still untouched by any light.

"I… Yes. I need to sleep. Soon. But I don't have time to get back to Bane's—I guess *my* house; it's just still hard to think of a mansion as my home. Do you have anywhere here I can sleep? It just needs to have no windows."

"How exactly do you mean no windows? I mean, will a tiny glimmer of sunshine coming in beneath a door hurt you?" She clenched her hands, her entire body tensing at the idea of him coming to harm in her home.

"I won't hurt you, Alice," he said gently, and she realized he was looking at her body language and probably interpreting it as fear *of* him, not *for* him.

"I know you won't."

Her admission caused his expression to change in some undefinable way, and she suddenly desperately wished she had the ability to read a vampire's mind.

"No, a glimmer of sunshine in the room won't hurt me. In fact, only direct sunlight will kill us, from what I understand, but any sunlight can be very uncomfortable and injure me as a new vampire." A muscle in his jaw clenched, and she realized that he was embarrassed to be seen as weak.

"That's good, then. I have a storeroom off the basement that has no windows. I think they used it to keep vegetables in or something back in the day. The house is nearly two hundred years old, you know. Should we go down there now and check it out? I have a sleeping bag you can use."

She didn't tell him she'd slept in the bag in her car for a few months after escaping. After hiding in a homeless shelter at night and then working all the odd jobs she could get during the day, usually paid under the table, since she'd had no identification. When she'd finally saved up enough to buy a decrepit old car, she'd felt safe for the first time in a while.

Cars, unlike beds in a homeless shelter, could be locked.

Cars could be driven far, far away from danger.

She'd cried when that car had finally died, a year or so after she'd bought it. But then she'd found the van that she still drove. She'd never let herself be without a car again.

"Alice? We should go check it out now, before I'm completely out of options, in case it doesn't work."

She nodded, pushing old memories away, and led him through the corridor to her house. She unlocked the connecting door and went in, but then turned around when she realized he wasn't following.

"Hunter?"

He dropped his head and swore so softly she almost didn't catch it. Then he blew out a breath and looked up at her. "You have to invite me in."

"What?"

"Turns out some of the old stories are true. I'm a vampire. Part of the magic that binds us is that we can't enter a home without being invited in."

"But you walked right into the shelter!"

He shrugged. "It's a business, I guess, even though it feels like an extension of your home. Henry and other volunteers can come and go, and the adopters, too. Hey, I don't make the rules. I just have to follow them."

She hesitated, and a shadow passed behind his eyes.

"Okay, I get it. I wouldn't want to invite me in, either. I'll just go find somewhere else to sleep and be sure the wolves are watching out for you. If you—"

"Hunter."

He stilled.

"Please be welcome into my house."

His hands clenched and then relaxed at his sides, and then he offered a not-quite-convincing grin. "Thank you."

The basement was a cluttered mess. She'd kept meaning to clean it out and decide what to do with the decades worth of junk that had been stored down there that the previous owners had so *thoughtfully* left for her to deal with.

"I'm sorry. I know it's a mess, and I'm so sorry. I have a nice guest room upstairs, but unfortunately it has huge windows, and I don't have blackout curtains, and—"

"Alice." His voice was warm but firm. "It's fine. Is this the door to the storeroom?"

She had a sudden wild thought of asking him if he needed a coffin, but she luckily managed to keep the words from escaping. "Yes. This is it. There's a string to the light bulb. I'm so sorry, it's just—"

"It's fine." But as he looked around, she could see the desolation on his face. Hunter was clearly not a man who'd been accustomed to sleeping in dusty old basements. He probably had a very nice apartment in that mansion, and maybe a very nice girlfriend who lived with him…

She was shocked by the instant recoil she felt at the thought of Hunter with a nice, gorgeous, *normal* girlfriend. One who didn't talk to ghosts, commune with animals, or have PTSD over her horrible past.

"Won't your girlfriend be missing you?" She'd intended to say that in a light, casual tone, but it came out sounding sharp. Maybe even a bit angry.

He swung around and looked at her with interest. "My girlfriend?"

"I just— I meant— I'll get that sleeping bag."

Hunter shot out a hand and blocked the doorway. "Not just yet, I think. Not when you've given me a flash of hope that you might actually be willing to let me spend time with you after we resolve the issue of the Chamber."

"I…I—" She couldn't breathe. Couldn't remember how to make her lungs work. He was just so beautiful. And kind. And…

Hunter reached out and oh-so-gently touched her face. "I don't have a girlfriend. Haven't had one in a few years, to be honest."

"Oh," she said, more breathlessly than she'd have liked. "Oh, that's…that's good."

He gave her that slow, sexy smile he was so very good at and bent his head to hers. "Alice. Can I kiss you now?"

His face was so close that she felt like she might drown in his beautiful, glowing blue eyes. "I…I don't know. I've never—" She stopped speaking and wrenched her gaze from his. How could she tell this amazing man that she'd never even kissed a man? Not even a boy when she was a girl.

Never once.

"You've never?" He tilted his head to one side, watching her with complete and utter concentration.

"I've never been kissed," she said miserably.

His sharp inhalation was quiet, but she heard it and felt totally, unbelievably humiliated, tasting shame like rusty metal in the back of her throat.

But then he took her hand and put it on his face, and the sensation of his skin beneath her fingertips made her feel like champagne mixed with lightning bolts was sizzling through her body.

"So, then, you shouldn't be kissed now," he said gently.

Despair swamped through her. Why was she surprised? Nobody would ever want to kiss her. "I shouldn't?"

"No. You should be the one doing the kissing. Taking charge. Why don't you kiss me, beautiful Alice?"

Why didn't she?

Because she was afraid. What if she was no good at it? What if he hated it and never wanted to see her again? What if he was just humoring the poor, inexperienced girl?

But then the courage she'd fought so hard for soared up through her body.

What if she was a *wonderful* kisser?

He'd be *lucky* to have such a kiss.

"Yes," she told him, taking his face in her hands. "Yes."

And then she kissed him.

Tentative—so tentative at first. Her lips barely touching his.

He held perfectly still, content to let her take the lead. She tilted her head, just a little, just to find that angle…yes.

Yes.

The warmth and sensual fullness of his lips made her want to lick them. Bite them. Feelings she'd never had in her life soared through her until she was sure she must be floating. Instead of biting, though, she kissed him again. Pressed her lips to his and then dared to trace the seam of his lips with the tip of her tongue.

He made a quiet groaning sound, and she tried to step back, but his arms came up to embrace her.

"No, please don't stop," he said roughly. "You taste like honey and strawberries. Like laughter and kindness."

"That's poetic," she managed, still breathless.

"Yes. No. Whatever you want. Please, Alice. Please kiss me again."

She grabbed onto her courage with both hands—metaphorically, of course, because her actual hands were twined in his hair and she was curled into his body. "Yes. Okay. Yes."

And then she was kissing him again. This time, when she dared to touch his lips with her tongue, he opened to her, coaxing her tongue to play with his. He took control of the kiss then, tightening his arms around her until she could feel the hardness of his erection pushing against her. Rather than frightening her, though, the feeling sent a wild thrill of feminine triumph through her.

She'd done this to him.

She had.

She felt so strong. So powerful. And almost drugged with wanting.

When she finally pulled back to catch her breath, she was clinging to him, unsure whether she'd still be able to stand on her shaking legs.

"Hunter. I—"

Buzz.

The pained frustration in his expression made her laugh.

"Don't answer it," he said, his voice husky, still not letting Alice go.

"It might be about another rescue," she said with real regret, but on the other hand, maybe the phone had saved her from rushing into something she wasn't ready for. "Let me take the call. The bathroom is right there, and there's a sleeping bag in the closet inside. When I get back, we can talk—"

Hunter tilted her face up to his and kissed her again, long and deep. Then he sighed and stepped back, letting her go. "Okay. We can talk."

For some reason, she wanted to cry at the loss of his arms around her. Yes, her body was definitely rushing to a place her heart wasn't yet ready to go. She nodded and turned to flee, running from her own feelings as much as from the vampire in her basement. At the bottom of the staircase, when the phone quit buzzing, she turned to say something—she wasn't sure what—and turned, only to find that Hunter was sprawled on the floor of the storeroom on top of the sleeping bag, eyes closed, looking like he was out cold.

She slowly walked back to the storage room. "Hunter?"

Nothing.

She left the room and quietly closed the door behind herself. "Saved by the break of dawn, apparently. At least I still have a few hours to sleep before I have to open up. If we can just avoid any more crises, I'll be okay."

And she made it all the way to the shelter and had even started to lock up before someone started pounding on the door. On the plus side, she was too tired to be frightened. And Hunter had said that there was a security team on site.

On the minus side, however, when she opened the door, an enormous wolf stood on her porch, staring up at her.

Alice blinked. Scrubbed at her eyes, and then blinked again.

Nope. Not hallucinating. There was definitely a wolf on her porch.

"Welcome to Little Darlings," she told it.

And then she started to laugh.

CHAPTER SEVENTEEN

The wolf on Alice's porch shimmered with sparkling light and then transformed into a naked woman.

Because of course she did.

Alice's laughter sounded hysterical, but she couldn't quite get herself to stop. The woman grabbed a pile of clothes sitting next to her on the porch and quickly pulled them on with efficient, matter-of-fact movements. Then she held her hand out to Alice.

"Max Washington, Romulus Security. We're here keeping an eye on the place. Bane hired us."

Max looked like an athlete. Golden-brown skin, long, dark curls, and beautiful brown eyes set in a fine-boned face that looked slightly too delicate for the lean, muscular body now clad in a T-shirt, jeans, and sneakers.

Alice forced back her slightly hysterical laughter and took a breath. "I'm sorry. I'm Alice Darlington."

She shook Max's hand, but the woman raised an eyebrow, probably wondering what in the heck was wrong with her.

"I only learned that werewolves exist a few hours ago," Alice said apologetically. "Also vampires. And warlocks and demons, come to think of it."

Max nodded briskly, but her expression held sympathy. "It's a lot; I know. I was just wondering if we could talk before I go off shift. I may be acting as your personal bodyguard after this, but for now we'd appreciate it if you'd remain here today."

Alice didn't have the energy to discuss the "personal bodyguard" part, so she just nodded. "Sure. I... Do werewolves drink coffee?"

"Got whiskey?"

"Um..."

Max threw her head back and laughed. "Sorry. Just messing with the human. Yes, I drink coffee."

"Come on in," Alice said. Because why not? In for a penny, in for a pound. Or, in for a vampire, in for a werewolf, she guessed would be more applicable.

Max looked around, ignoring the barking and hissing that ramped up when she walked into the shelter. "Will you be okay alone, since your volunteer called in sick?"

"My what?"

"Are you okay? No offense, but you seem a little off," Max said, concern in her voice. Or maybe the concern wasn't for Alice but about the idea of watching the human with the fragile mind.

"Yeah. Sorry about that. Like I said, long day, long night. Lots of startling revelations, to say the least."

Not to mention the part where I just had my first-ever kiss.

With a vampire.

Who is currently asleep in my basement.

She kept that part to herself. "Come over to the office with me. I can make coffee. How do you know that my volunteer called in sick? Penny, right?"

Max stopped and growled at one of the dogs, Beauty, a hound mix, who immediately silenced her booming bark and rolled over, showing her belly.

"Good girl," Max crooned, putting a hand through the side of the kennel to pet the dog's head. Beauty wiggled all over with happiness while Alice looked on in shock.

"What just happened? That dog won't let anyone but me near her!"

"I let her know who was alpha in this situation. Wolf trumps dog, even a strong-willed one like this. What's her name?"

"She came here as an abandonment case, with no name. I call her Beauty."

Max's smile lit up her face. "It's nice that you gave her a joyful name. Dogs understand more than you think."

"Trust me, I know," Alice said, leading the way to the office and wondering if her special gift would work on Max when she was in wolf form. She almost asked but then realized she was so tired that her thoughts were rambling.

"Anyway, we know that Penny called in sick because we tapped your phone as soon as we took the assignment. By the way, she didn't sound sick as much as guilty, but I can only smell a lie in person, not over the phone."

Alice didn't even know where to start with that, so she focused on the more important issue, since she was very aware of Penny's partying/skipping-her-volunteer-shift lifestyle.

"You tapped my phone?"

"Yes. Standard procedure." Max evidently got frustrated with Alice's lack of progress on the coffee and took over, very efficiently prepping the pot.

Alice had the feeling that Max did *everything* efficiently.

"Your standard procedure equals my violation of privacy," she finally said. "I didn't ask for any of this."

Max shrugged. "I heard. I can sympathize. I never asked to be turned into a werewolf. But we have to play the hands we're dealt, even if those hands turn into furry paws, right? The Chamber is aware of you now, and they're going to be a danger until we can wipe their asses out so hard that they never come back to Savannah."

"So I need werewolf security," Alice said faintly, wondering how her life had turned into a late-night movie and deciding to worry about it later. She had work to do. "Okay. But as soon as the danger is over, the tap on my phone goes away, right?"

Max rolled her eyes. "Like we want to sit around listening to your phone calls for free?"

The werewolf downed a cup of black coffee and then rinsed the mug and left it in the sink. "Okay, before I go, do you need any help, since you're one short today?"

Alice automatically started to decline, but then thought about Max's effect on Beauty.

"Actually, yes. I could use some help. We're at capacity right now, with fifteen cats, five dogs, four guinea pigs, two rabbits, and a ferret. Oh, and Marigold."

"Marigold?"

"She's a raccoon."

Max stared at her for a moment and then flashed a huge smile that had way too many teeth in it. "If we count Marigold, the rabbits, the guinea pigs, and the ferret as breakfast, the work would go much faster. Got any mustard?"

• • •

Hunter woke up from a confused dream of chasing Alice through a maze of pirate ships and wildfires, which had come with its own musical accompaniment that sounded like pipes banging, making no sense at all, and it took him a breath to realize where he was. He'd had a strong enough feeling of displacement every time he'd woken up at Bane's for the past few weeks, but this was different. Instead of being in a bed, he was lying on top of a sleeping bag in a very dark room.

He inhaled deeply.

A sleeping bag that smelled like *her*.

Alice.

He needed to go find her.

Now.

His fangs descended, and he jumped up and shoved the door open, only to see a small cooler he hadn't seen before just outside the door. It had a note taped to the handle.

DRINK ME.

LOVE, MEARA

And he had to laugh, knowing she'd meant for him to get the *Alice in Wonderland* reference, both because of, well, Alice, and because he'd once mentioned it was his little sister's favorite book. He also felt a surge of gratitude for Meara, who was in a way his new sister, for taking care of him.

For protecting Alice from him.

He quickly drank his fill from the bags in the cooler, brushed his teeth, and took a quick shower, and then, refreshed, went to find the woman who'd haunted his dreams.

She was taking a nap, sprawled out in a deep sleep on

her bed, with a lovely old quilt like the ones his grandmother made covering her. Her wild mass of flame-red curls was loose from its braid and spread across the pillows, and he instantly got hard imagining what her hair would feel like on his skin.

On his lips.

On his cock.

He forced himself to breathe deeply, pushing calm and restraint into his senses. Wondering when and why the Turn had changed him so completely from Mr. Nice Guy, Mr. Friend Zone, to this savage beast who wanted to *claim*.

To possess.

Luke had warned him that vampires were at the mercy of strong territorial urges, but Hunter had thought he meant about *actual* territory. About places or even things.

Not about people.

But ever since he'd run into Alice and that foolish raccoon, he'd wanted to stake his claim on this woman. This beautiful, courageous, amazing woman. She'd taken him in as if he were one of her strays in need of rescue, which, in many ways, he kind of was. And she'd *kissed* him.

She'd kissed him after telling him that she'd never been kissed before.

The gift—of her trust, her kiss—humbled him.

The feel of her body against him had excited him.

Aroused him.

Right now, he had to fight every feral instinct in his new vampire body to keep from tearing off his clothes and climbing into that bed with her. Gently removing her clothes.

Maybe with his teeth.

Touching and kissing and licking every inch of her gorgeous body.

But it was too soon. It was stalker-ish, even.

It was…

It was…*exactly what he needed more than he'd ever needed anything in his life.*

As if he'd spoken his thoughts out loud, Alice opened her eyes, coming completely awake in an instant.

"Hunter?"

He nodded, almost unable to speak for fear of shouting out the words that would convey how much he wanted her. Needed her.

"I was dreaming of you," she whispered, staring up at him with those deep, drowning emerald eyes that entranced him almost as surely as if she'd been a vampire compelling him to her will.

In the fraction of a second between one heartbeat and the next, he pulled her up off the bed and into his arms, barely even noticing her state of undress before his mouth was on hers.

Taking.

Claiming.

Possessing.

She put her arms around his neck and kissed him back with fervor, laughing and pulling him even closer until, a few moments later, he felt her retreat. She looked down, not meeting his eyes, and pushed against his chest, and that's when he realized that she was only wearing her bra and underwear.

"Hunter! I'm not dressed. You… I have to—" She broke off, her cheeks flushing a hot pink. "This is too much. Too fast. Please leave so I can get dressed."

Hunter groaned but immediately released her. "I'm sorry. I didn't mean to overwhelm you. I don't know what's happening to me."

She yanked the quilt off the bed and wrapped it around her sweet, curvy body, but not before he had time to see the tiny pink bow on her bra, just between her breasts, and he knew immediately that the scrap of fabric would be starring in a few of his most erotic fantasies for the next few days.

Or weeks.

Or forever.

He turned around, forcing himself to be enough of a gentleman to comply with her wishes, but then realized he could see her clearly in the tall, oval, antique mirror in the corner of her room.

"Damn, but you're beautiful," he said roughly

She met his gaze in the mirror. "So are you. Which seems to make me behave very badly. So please go while I get dressed."

"I'm going to see you naked. Soon," he told her, the declaration shocking both of them.

She gasped. "You can't just say that to a person!"

"I'm not saying it to just any person. I'm saying it to you. You'll pick the time and the place, and I'll wait as long as it takes for you to trust me. But Alice, you have to know that I will spend every moment, from now until you agree, thinking of ways to get you into my bed."

Her mouth fell open, and she stared at him in shock. But then she did something completely unexpected.

She laughed.

"Maybe," she said, shrugging, a seductive smile tugging at her lips. "Or maybe I'll get *you* into *my* bed."

He blinked, taken completely off guard. "I—you—"

She grabbed her pillow and held it up to her face, which had turned bright pink. "Oh, wow. Oh, that is totally not me. I was trying to be a femme fatale. Did you buy it?"

She peeked at him over the top of the pillow's lace fringe, and she was so adorable and desirable and perfect that he could feel the walls around his heart shatter into tiny pieces.

But then the monster inside him roared, and his fangs descended.

"Yes," he managed, turning toward the door, forcing himself to take one step and then another away from her. "I bought it. One hundred percent."

"Are you…are you leaving? We could talk." She bit her lip, and it took every ounce of resolve he had to keep from pouncing on her.

"No, we can't talk in your bedroom, or I'll have you naked and beneath me in the next five minutes," he growled. "Alice. Please. Let me have some dignity and not attack you like the beast I am." Before she could say a single word, he ran down the stairs and out the front door, breathing in great, huge gulps of the cool night air.

That was how Meara found him a few minutes later when her limousine pulled into the yard.

She climbed out of the back seat, all long legs, grace, and flowing blue silk pants paired with a tiny gold top. "Hey, little brother. How are you? Rough day?"

He shook out his hands, only then realizing that he'd had them clenched into fists. "You might say that," he said drily. "How did you get through the locked gate?"

She rolled her eyes. "Really? Also, I have a gift for your human. An SUV. Or, technically, it's a gift from Ryan, but I drove it over here."

He glanced pointedly at the limo.

"Fine, *fine*. I told someone to drive it over here, so that counts, doesn't it?"

The SUV in question drove up through the gate just then, and he whistled. "Is that it?"

"Yes. Ryan and I thought it would be helpful for Alice to drive for her personal errands, since that piece of *merde* is falling apart and the new rescue van won't be here until the end of the week." She'd pointed at Alice's decrepit van when she said "piece of *merde*," and Hunter didn't have to speak French to get the gist.

Meanwhile, the SUV's driver tossed Meara the keys and then walked down the driveway and out the gate.

Hunter raised an eyebrow and Meara shrugged. "She probably has somebody waiting for her outside. Anyway, yes, this is Alice's new car."

"I doubt she'll accept it. She almost didn't take your money, but at least that was for the shelter. A car for her personal use? And one that's so expensive?" He shook his head. "Good luck."

The door behind him opened, and Alice, now dressed in boots, a green sweater that matched her eyes, and another pair of snug jeans that made Hunter's mouth water—*thank you, Jesus*—stepped outside.

"Good luck with what?" she said. "Oh. Hello, Meara."

Meara raised an eyebrow. "Such *enthusiasm*."

"Sorry." Alice shrugged. "It has been a long couple of

days. I only managed to get a few hours of sleep this afternoon, after convincing Max the werewolf that she couldn't eat half my rescued animals for breakfast. With mustard."

Meara started laughing. "I like that Max. She has a good sense of humor."

"Yes, but I didn't realize she was kidding at first. She found *that* hysterical. Especially after I said 'bad werewolf, no cookie.'"

Hunter tried to hold in the smile but didn't quite manage it. He could just imagine that conversation. He'd met Max a few times, too, and she was always laughing and joking, in spite of being the beta wolf—the second-in-command, just under Carter Reynolds—of the Savannah Wolf Pack.

"Did you see her in wolf form?" He hadn't yet.

"Yes, and she's beautiful, I have to admit. Chocolate brown fur with black-tipped tail and ears. She was much, much bigger than an actual wolf, though. Maybe three times the size a female red wolf would be—not that you see any red wolves in Georgia anymore. They're nearly extinct."

"I've donated money to a 'save the wolves' campaign," Meara said, sauntering over to them. "It would be a shame for such beautiful creatures to vanish."

"Speaking of beautiful creatures," Alice murmured, giving Meara a head-to-toe glance. "Are you on your way to a party?"

"No, silly girl. I've arrived to invite you to a volleyball game."

"A *what*?"

A pair of motorcycles drove through the still-open gate and up toward them. Their riders parked the bikes, nodded at Meara, Hunter, and Alice, and then walked toward the perimeter fence to talk to the two werewolves Hunter had sensed patrolling the grounds when he first walked outside.

At least vampire senses meant nobody could sneak up on him, which was all the better to protect Alice.

"More of the security team, I'm guessing," Alice said, her voice surprisingly level, considering.

"Yes. They work in shifts," he said.

"Back to Ryan's supernatural volleyball tournament," Meara said. "Tonight's the first round. She insists that you and Hunter come play and have barbecue and whatever. Vampires against the wolves, I suggested, but she plans to have us mix it up, I think."

Alice looked fascinated. "How? I mean, how are vampires and werewolves going to play volleyball? Don't you all have super strength? You'll deflate or destroy the ball every time you hit it."

"I have no idea. Ryan keeps saying she has it figured out, but I'm coming to learn that angels are overly optimistic."

Before they could ask her what she meant by that, Meara turned and strode back to the limo. "Are you coming or not?"

"I can't," Alice said. "I have nobody to watch the rescue. Henry has Saturdays off. Strangely enough, I kind of wish I could go. It sounds like fun. Bizarre, but fun."

Hunter motioned to the wolves still having a conversation by the fence, and two of them headed over while the other two went for the bikes.

"Hey, Pete."

The tall man shook his shaggy brown hair out of his face and nodded. "Evans."

"You're the night shift."

"Yep."

Pete took "strong-and-silent type" to a whole new level.

"Are you okay with checking on the animals? Taking care of anything that might arise?"

"Sure." Pete gave Alice a nod. "Ma'am. I grew up on a farm. Got a lot of experience with livestock. This can't be much different, can it?"

Bemused, Alice looked back and forth between Hunter and Pete. "No, actually, I guess not. If I could just show you a few things? I really appreciate it."

"All part of the job," Pete said, then followed her into the rescue.

"Catch!" Meara tossed Hunter the keys to the SUV and then got in the limo, which made a three-point turn and drove out of the gate, followed by the two off-shift wolves on the bikes.

Hunter just stood there, still not really believing that Alice was going to go with him, in the SUV a Nephilim had given her, to see werewolves and vampires play volleyball.

Also, his life was getting weirder and weirder by the minute.

Just then, she walked out the door of the rescue, Charlie in golden-retriever form next to her, and smiled at him. "Let's go do this!"

"Are you sure?"

Her cheeks flushed a bright pink. "Well, I figure I need to get you out of here before I jump on you, and I'm not quite ready for that, but if you leave and I stay here, I'll be lonely and miss you, so, hey."

"You are the most direct and honest person I've ever met," he told her, entranced by this facet of her personality. "Also, I loved the 'not quite ready' part of that sentence, which gives me hope for the future."

She turned an even brighter pink, but then she shrugged. "I never learned to flirt or play games, so what you see is what you get."

"I like what I see very, very much," he said quietly, and she rewarded him with a brilliant smile.

"Okay, so let's go to the volleyball game. You can drive."

"It's your car." He held out the keys, but she shook her head.

"No, it definitely is not. Now, should we stop by the store and bring something? Cake? Pie? Flowers? Beer? Do vampires even drink beer?"

"Werewolves do," the second guard said, walking up to them. "If those wimpy vampires don't want it, bring it back to us. I'm Will, by the way, Miss Darlington. My niece adopted a kitten from you a few months back. She loves that cat to pieces."

"I'm so glad to hear it." Alice beamed at him. "And please call me Alice."

"I think my new digs might need a wolfskin rug," Hunter said thoughtfully.

Will growled at him, but his eyes were sparkling with amusement. "Do your best tonight, bloodsucker, but remember that I'll be playing next week, and we'll crush you."

"There's going to be a next week?" He should have known. Ryan, being Ryan, probably had an entire year's schedule worked out. She ran the clinic with clockwork precision; why wouldn't he expect her to do the same with volleyball?

"So what the two of you are saying is that men are all the same, even if they have fangs or fur," Alice said, rolling her eyes. "Lead on to vampire-werewolf volleyball, Hunter. I have a feeling this will be worth watching."

"Don't you want to play?"

She started laughing. "Not a chance."

CHAPTER EIGHTEEN

Alice clutched the volleyball and gulped, staring down the glowing eyes of the vampires on her team and the ferocious expressions of the werewolves on the opposing team, and then she repeated her question.

"What exactly did I get myself talked into?" She glared at Hunter, who'd done the persuading.

Ryan, the only other non-wolf or vampire in the game—although she wasn't exactly human; she was a freaking half angel—grinned at her. "Get on with it, Ghost Girl. We have a game to win."

"Ha! Win, nothing. Prepare to eat that ball, Nephilim," Max called out from her side of the net.

"This has to weigh forty pounds! Are all volleyballs this heavy? I thought this was a sport for high school girls," Alice said, stalling.

"It is, but it's an Olympic sport, too. I had this ball specially made. It's Kevlar," Ryan sang out. "The better for wolves and vampires not to destroy it!"

Alice took a deep breath and heaved the ball up in the air, then hit it with all her might. It soared all of maybe six inches through the air and then started to plunge toward the ground, but suddenly a narrow beam of silvery light caught the ball and heaved it all the way over the tops of all the vampires' heads and over the net.

"Not fair using angel powers," Max shouted, jumping so high into the air that her hips were level with the top of the regulation-height volleyball net. The werewolf beta grinned at Alice and spiked the ball right at Hunter's face. He blocked it and batted it to Luke, who smashed it back over the net to the wolves.

"Anything goes," Ryan shouted back, laughing. "My angel powers versus your super wolfy muscles. Let's see who wins!"

Alice shook her hand out, wondering if she'd broken anything and seriously regretting that her ghost-whisperer powers didn't come with super strength.

"Thanks for the assist," she called out to Ryan.

"You got it, teammate!" The doctor, whom Alice still had a hard time believing was Nephilim, danced in place with excitement. "We never played volleyball like this in high school!"

They'd been picking teams when she and Hunter drove up in the ridiculously luxurious and tricked-out SUV. Charlie had immediately made friends with Bane's dog, Bram Stoker, an Irish wolfhound who towered over him and looked like he might have some buffalo DNA in his background.

Ryan had taken over then, grabbing Alice's arm and dragging her onto the volleyball court, which was a space in the mansion's back lawn delineated by a giant chalk outline. The wolves had quickly erected a net, which everyone kept assuring Alice was "regulation height," whatever that meant.

She couldn't exactly tell them that she didn't share any of their sports or cultural references, having been locked away in the Institute from the ages of twelve to twenty.

The mansion—and it was definitely a mansion; no mere

house was suitable for vampires, apparently—was enormous but graceful and beautifully designed. She didn't know anything about architecture, but she knew whoever had designed this house had been a master. She hadn't been inside yet, having gone straight from the car that Hunter kept insisting was hers now to the volleyball court. But the back lawn flowed right down to the Wilmington River, and she knew they were very close to the famous Bonaventure Cemetery.

Which meant she'd been spending a good part of the half hour since she'd arrived sneaking glances around her for the ghosts she was afraid would sense her. If they came, they'd be making demands, threatening her with impending death, or any of the other things ghosts liked to do.

She'd never yet met one who just wanted to say hey and hang out.

"Alice!"

Hunter's shout yanked her out of her thoughts just in time to see a projectile coming at her head so fast she was surprised it wasn't smoking. She didn't even try to return the ball. She just ducked.

A dark shape flew over her head, flipping upside down in midair, and hit the ball back toward the wolves. The white hair that brushed the grass just before the vampire smashed down flat on his back told her it was Edge, the one who Hunter had mentioned on the drive over was a brilliant computer hacker. Edge was helping Hunter create a slightly different identity for himself: a firefighter who'd been not quite as badly burned as everyone had thought, so his cure wouldn't be seen as miraculous. Or, worse, suspicious.

Hunter still hadn't decided whether to go back to work or not. She suspected, although he hadn't said it, that he wasn't eager to rush back into any fires after he'd nearly died in one, and she wouldn't blame him. It's not like she would ever voluntarily go back to the Institute. She'd die first.

The ball came soaring back over the net, and Meara shouted and leapt into the air, bringing her open hand down on it with such force that it exploded, blowing up into hundreds of pieces of shredded Kevlar that floated down through the air and onto everyone grouped around the net.

"I'd say that's a forfeit for your side," the alpha werewolf who'd been introduced to her as Carter Reynolds said in his deep, musical voice. He was a big man, easily six feet tall, with an unmistakable air of command. He was also as heavily muscled as Hunter, with dark brown skin and brown eyes filled with humor and intelligence. "Destroying the ball is definitely a game-ending foul."

"We have more balls," Ryan said. "I can go get one."

"Get Bane to do it," Luke, another of Hunter's vampire friends, said. "He's just slinging burgers on the grill."

"I am *not* just slinging burgers on a grill." Bane's deep voice preceded him around the side of the house. "I am a three-hundred-year-old master vampire. I do not *sling burgers*."

"Damn," Max said, laughing. "I'm only a twenty-eight-year-old beta werewolf, so I'd be glad to grill up some burgers if you don't want to get your precious vampy hands dirty."

Alice caught her breath, terrified an outright battle

would begin right in front of her on the lawn.

Bane just grinned at Max, though. “What I *do* is use my hundred-year-old certified fantastic recipe for pit barbecue on a hundred pounds of ribs, so I have enough to feed all you hungry pups when you’re done getting crushed at volleyball.”

Ryan crossed the lawn to Bane and put her arm around his waist. “Actually, Meara blew up the ball again, like she did in practice. So Carter says we forfeit, and I kinda agree with him.”

“I can’t help it if I’m so much more powerful than the wolves,” Meara said, dropping into a curtsy. The fact that she’d changed into jeans and a T-shirt didn’t make it one bit less graceful.

“If powerful means ‘I need an hour primping before I step out my front door,’ maybe,” Max said, grinning.

Then the trash talk started in earnest, and Alice was still laughing when a woman who was possibly the cook or housekeeper, or just an older vampire, called out that the food was ready.

“On our way, Mrs. Cassidy,” Ryan answered, and the group headed toward tables that were almost bowed with the weight of heavy platters and heaping bowls of food.

Hunter threaded his way through the crowd and made his way to her, slinging a casual arm around her waist. She almost flinched at the touch, another leftover from her Institute days, but shoved the instinct away and smiled up at him.

“I am terrible at volleyball,” she told him.

“But you are the most beautiful woman in the world.” He bent his head and lightly kissed her nose. “Nobody expects beautiful women to be good at volleyball. Water polo will be more your sport, I'm sure."

She laughed but then glanced at the river, which looked cold in the moonlight. "I'm definitely not trying that tonight. Maybe bowling will be my sport. Or something else you can play in a warm building. The breeze off the river is freezing my butt off."

Hunter flashed a wicked grin. "The loss of your truly fine ass would be a great sadness to the world, indeed."

She rolled her eyes. "I don't know what I'm going to do with you."

He went completely still, amusement fading, and his arm tightened around her waist. When he spoke, his voice was low and rough. "Just let me be with you. Spend time with you. That's all I ask."

Her heart skipped at least one beat—she felt it happen—and suddenly it was very hard to catch her breath. "Hunter. This doesn't make sense. How can we feel this way? We only met two nights ago."

"It doesn't make sense to me, either. But nothing about our lives makes a lot of sense, in normal terms. I'm a vampire. You can talk to ghosts and animals. There's a demon who looks like a dragon and is pretending to be a dog living in your rescue. Where's the normal in that? Maybe that's the lesson. That *normal* is for ordinary humans, and we who aren't anywhere close to normal need to find our own guidelines for living our lives."

The moment and the emotion both felt too huge, too intense. She needed to lighten the tone so she could breathe again.

So she could think.

"I agree," she said casually, pulling away from him just a bit. "New guidelines. Like dessert *before* dinner."

A flash of hurt crossed his face so fast she wasn't sure she'd actually seen it, but then he nodded and joined in, telling her without words that he'd give her space. "Riding roller coasters backward."

She reached out for his hand and twined her fingers through his, and they started walking toward the group over by the barbecue station. "Putting the syrup on the plate before the pancakes."

"Reading the ends of books first."

She gasped. "Now you go too far, my friend. We never, ever read the end first."

He tightened his hand on hers and pulled her to a stop. "Am I? Your friend?"

She stared up into his brilliantly glowing eyes. "Yes. You are absolutely my friend, and I am yours. Let's start there, okay?"

"Friends tell friends about their lives." He gently pushed a strand of hair away from her face. "Maybe someday soon you'll trust me with the story of yours."

Her stomach clenched at the thought, but the idea of having a real friend—her first that she might be able to trust enough to tell the truth—sparked something bubbly and effervescent inside her that felt almost like it might be hope.

"Yes," she promised, and it took every ounce of courage she had. "I'll tell you the whole ugly story. But if you don't want to be my friend after you know, please just tell me honestly. Don't disappear without a word."

Hunter took her face in his hands and leaned down to

press a long, gentle kiss to her lips. There was no urgency, only sweetness, but he took his time as if he were savoring the taste of her. "There is nothing you could have done or could do in the future that would make me stop being your friend."

She wanted to cry, because she knew he believed it now. But things changed, and people had told her for so long that she was the girl with the evil power and ugly soul. That nobody would ever want her.

That her own parents had thrown her away.

How could someone like her ever earn even the friendship of a man as kind as Hunter?

There were tears in her eyes when she started toward the food. "We should try the master vampire's barbecue, don't you think?"

Hunter gave her a long look that told her he wasn't fooled by her light tone, but he didn't call her on it. Which was good, because this was definitely not the place to have a deep conversation. Right at that moment, for example, two werewolves carrying icy bottles of beer were heading toward them.

"Hello, Max." Alice took the beer with a nod of thanks, although she wasn't much of a drinker. "Hopefully you brought your own mustard tonight?"

Max threw her head back and laughed, not noticing the long, speculative look Carter Reynolds, the wolf at her side, gave her. If Alice had been a betting woman, she would have put money on the idea that the alpha wanted to be more than just friends with his second. But she didn't have any real-life experience to help her judge such matters, and binge-watching HBO, the CW, and the

Hallmark Channel didn't really count.

Alice explained the mustard reference to Carter, who found it pretty funny, too, and Hunter didn't even try to hide his grin.

She narrowed her eyes and pretended to be offended. "You may all need human lessons if you think that offering to eat the animals in a rescue is in any way funny."

Max saw right through her, though. "She's kidding," she told her boss, who'd unexpectedly started to fumble for an explanation. "After she got past her shock and then her fear of offending me by explaining that her rescue animals weren't actually the buffet line, we got along just fine." She turned to Alice. "Did you get that nap?"

"I did, thanks! It helped a lot. I've been keeping vampire hours the past couple of nights, which is fine if you don't have to get up and run a business during the day."

"How is your rescue going?" Carter looked like he was really interested, not just being polite, so she told him about how Little Darlings was doing, talking probably more than she should.

Because you're such a blabbermouth, said the vicious voice in her head that she knew was an echo of Grogan, Dr. Kurchausen's chief thug who'd laughingly called himself an orderly.

Whatever she'd been saying—something about funding, maybe—trailed off as she fought to retain her composure. Hunter took her hand in his again and squeezed it lightly in support, and she squeezed back and then took a deep breath.

"Sorry. Old memories come jumping up out of the box where I locked them away and bite me sometimes," she admitted.

"We all have those memories. The trick is not to let them overpower you," Max said, her head tilted to one side, the scarlet ribbon tied around her curls catching the light. She turned to Carter. "I like this woman. She asked me all about myself. What it's like to be a werewolf. Do I like it. Would I go back to ordinary human if I could. I'm still surprised at some of the things we talked about."

Alice felt herself blush. "I'm sorry. I know I drone on too much sometimes."

"No, you do not," Hunter growled. "And you need to tell me who pounded that bullshit into your head, so I can go have a talk with them. A *serious* and painful talk."

Carter held out his bottle toward Hunter, and they clinked them together. "Amen, brother. I'd be happy to go with you and teach them a few lessons on manners and how to treat a lady."

"No!" Alice shuddered and then forced herself to smile. "No, it's— There's no need. He's long dead."

Max and Carter both tilted their heads in exactly the same way, to exactly the same degree, in an eerie parallel movement.

"No," Max said slowly. "No, he is not dead. That's the first lie I've heard you tell, Alice."

"I don't—how? How did you know?" She could tell there was no use denying it. Werewolves must be like furry lie detectors or something.

"We can smell a lie, literally," Carter said, not unkindly. "And vampires can hear your heartbeat speed up when you're not telling the truth. So there's not much use trying to lie to one of us."

Alice stared at Hunter. "You can hear my heartbeat? Know when I'm telling a lie? What else haven't you told me?"

"Speaking of things people haven't explained," Max said, pointing over Alice's shoulder to something behind her down toward the river. "Does *that* have anything to do with why Ryan keeps calling you Ghost Girl?"

Alice froze.

No, no, no, no, no. Not now, please.

She called out before she even turned around, because she could feel the icy breeze that always preceded ghostly visits. "No. Not now, please. I have visiting hours between ten and two on Wednesdays, and I'll do my best to help you then. Do you understand?"

Hunter put his arm around her and pulled her closer, and Max and Carter just stared at her wide-eyed, but she ignored all of that and pivoted so she could see what Max was still pointing at. Maybe it would be something easy. She could help one ghost with one problem and still have fun and eat barbecue, right? Maybe she—

A powerful blast of cold air smacked her in the face when she turned around, and she instinctively shut her eyes, only opening them when Hunter swore, long and creatively, beneath his breath.

It wasn't one ghost.

It wasn't *five* ghosts.

It wasn't even *ten* ghosts.

More than a dozen ghosts stood in a semicircle not ten feet away from her.

"Oh, *crap*."

CHAPTER NINETEEN

There were *fifteen* of them.

Fifteen fully manifested ghosts that looked like actual human beings. There were also maybe four or five separate glowing forms that may or may not have been remnants of ghosts. When Hunter kept swearing, Alice realized she really needed to tell him a lot more about her gift.

Later. Maybe after she figured out this new dimension of the power. Because ghosts had never before confronted her in these numbers, and right now she couldn't seem to stop trembling, shaking her head, and mumbling, "Too many. Too many, too many."

"Alice. Alice!" Hunter caught her face in his hand and forced her to look up at him. "What can I do to help?"

"They're in my *head*," she cried. "All of them. Demanding my attention, crying out for me to help them. So many voices. Too many! Too many!"

She clutched her head, flinching, and Hunter, a determined look on his face, picked her up and started to run for the mansion, only to find the way blocked by a wall of glowing spirits. She raised her head to glance over his shoulder, seeing the space behind them was empty now, and realized that these were the same ghosts, still yelling at her, but they'd somehow transported themselves to a new position in a blink. Max and Carter, meanwhile, had moved to stand back-to-back in order to face any possible danger.

Hunter noticed the wolves' stance, too. "Do you see them?"

Carter nodded, his gaze scanning the line of ghosts. "Yeah, we see them. Werewolves can see ghosts. Most natural animals do, so I guess it's a gift of our wolf side."

Max scowled. "The question is, why the hell are they here? And so many?"

Alice inhaled a long, shuddering breath and then lifted her head from Hunter's shoulder and opened her eyes. "They're here for me. Hunter, put me down. I need to deal with them, or they'll only keep coming."

"You don't have to deal with them alone," a voice called from behind her.

Ryan.

And she was walking toward Alice with Bane, Meara, Edge, and a group of other vampires and werewolves.

A fierce wave of gratitude swept through her. She wasn't alone. For the first time in her life, she didn't have to face danger alone. It was a gift worth far more than the check or car they kept trying to give her. The warmth of their support, and of Hunter's hand in hers, steadied her so she could stand on her own.

"You found me. I'm Alice," she told the spirits. "What do you want?"

Bad idea. They all started shouting their demands at the same time, and she nearly doubled over from the agony spiking through her skull.

"STOP!" she shouted at the top of her lungs, and then the strangest thing happened.

The ghosts *stopped*.

Stopped shouting at her, stopped moving, and stopped

speaking altogether.

Also, the wolves all flinched, some of them clutching their heads, and Carter Reynolds frowned and took a step toward her, growling almost inaudibly. "What did you just do to my wolves?"

Hunter immediately moved between Alice and Carter, snarling out a warning. "Stay away from her, Reynolds."

Alice put a hand on Hunter's arm and gently pulled him back to stand next to her. "It's okay, Hunter. He has a valid question. I think…" She shot a questioning glance at Max. "I think I just shoved the word 'stop' inside every one of the wolves' skulls, the way the ghosts were shouting at me in mine."

Max, still wary, nodded. "That's exactly what happened. At least to me. I heard your shout, but I heard it both with my ears and in my head. I don't know how you did it, either. Only an alpha werewolf can talk to wolves like that."

Carter, his frown lessening at Alice's obvious dismay, called out to his pack. "Everybody okay?"

All the wolves nodded except one. That guy, skinny with long hair and a scraggly beard, raised his hand. "I may need extra beer to recover!"

Several people laughed, which broke some of the tension, but Alice still needed to apologize.

"I'm so sorry," she told the alpha wolf. "I've never—well, of course I've never done that before, because I've never been around werewolves before when I was talking to ghosts. In fact, I only just learned that you guys even exist. I'm so sorry for the intrusion." She swept a glance over all the pack members. "I'm so sorry, everyone. I don't really understand how or why that happened."

"I think it's pretty clear," Bane said, one arm protectively curved around Ryan. "You somehow spoke to the wolves on the same wavelength or frequency you use to talk to the ghosts. The real question is why."

She nodded miserably, keeping one eye on the still-silent ghosts but addressing Carter. "Yes. The why. Well, this may or may not be relevant, but I, um, I can talk to animals. Is it possible that your wolf sides heard me even though you're in human form?"

From across the lawn, an unearthly howl sounded, and Charlie, still in his dog glamour, raced across the lawn toward her with Bram Stoker following, barely able to keep up despite having legs that were at least twice as long.

When Charlie reached her, he leapt up into her arms, releasing his glamour in his agitation, so every wolf and vampire there saw a perfectly formed dragon tilt his head up to hers. "Lady tells me to stop?"

That's when the crowd's mood turned dark. Evidently wolves were not fans of demons, Minor or otherwise. Reynolds growled again, deep and fierce, and Max echoed the sound. Reynolds put himself between Charlie and his beta, but Max nudged him aside so she could stand next to him.

The ghosts still hadn't moved, remaining still and silent.

Alice forced a smile to her lips. "Um, everyone? This is Charlie. He's with me."

The dragon hopped up to Hunter's shoulder and spread his wings wide before folding them and settling. Then he tilted his head in a birdlike manner. "Hello, wolves and vampires."

"Now I need another beer, too," Carter said. "It can talk?"

"Why don't you all get some food and drinks?" Ryan gestured with her hands as if herding everyone toward the tables. "Leave us to figure out the ghost issue with Alice for a minute?"

Most people, both vampires and wolves, hesitated until Bane and Carter both gave go-ahead nods, and then they moved toward the food. A slightly hysterical laugh tried to burble up in Alice's throat. That was one thing you could say for supernatural creatures. They had a seriously effective chain of command.

Hunter's face was grim, and she could feel how badly he wanted to protect her from everyone and everything. She leaned against him, taking strength from his support, and then drew in a deep breath and focused on the ghosts. "Why did you stop?"

One of them, a man dressed in clothing at least a century old, stepped forward. "You told us to stop, mistress."

Ryan gasped. "I heard that! They weren't speaking out loud before, but I heard that!"

"I heard it, too," Meara said, and the rest of the small group still standing with Alice nodded.

"We also heard the ghost speak," Carter said, his gaze still fixed on Charlie. "We'll deal with this first, but then we're going to discuss why you are harboring a Minor demon. One who was in disguise, no less."

Max was watching the little dragon with open curiosity. "He's beautiful."

Charlie preened, which almost made Alice laugh. The

myths about the vanity of dragons evidently had some basis in fact. Maybe she could introduce Charlie to Benedict Cumberbatch one day and they could compare notes.

Max touched Carter's arm. "Did you know they could talk?"

He shook his head, his face grim. "No. I didn't know they looked like dragons and could take on glamours, either. I've only ever heard tales of demons, never seen one."

"How did you know what Charlie was, then?"

"I've smelled one before," Carter answered Hunter. "Just before he burned down my house."

Max gave him a sharp look. Evidently she hadn't heard that story before.

"Not me, wolf," Charlie piped up. "No house burning. Just sneaking and spying, because the warlock ordered me to do it. But no more. I belong to Lady Alice now. She is my family."

Alice blinked. She, who had been alone since her family had abandoned her to the Institute as a child, suddenly was gaining friends and a family, however unusual they might be. But the ghosts were waiting, so now was not the time to think about it.

She took a step forward to face the spokes-ghost, shaking off Hunter's restraining hand. "Did you stop yelling at me because I asked you to stop? Out of courtesy?"

His glowing form wavered for a moment before he answered the question. "No, mistress. Because you compelled us to do so."

Oh.

Oh, *no*.

"*Magnifique*!" Meara clapped her hands. "Can you tell them to do tricks? Or patrol the grounds and watch for the Chamber?"

"I'm not going to *tell* them to do anything. They're *people*. Or, at least, they were people." Alice shook her head. "The last thing I would ever do is take away someone's free will, ghost or not. I've had that done to me, and…and I would never, ever become a monster who could do that."

Meara rolled her eyes. "Monster, shmonster. *Whatever*. At least ask this crowd of ghosts to leave so we can get back to our party."

But Alice needed to know why. Why they'd approached her in such numbers, and why they'd been so loud. What they wanted from her.

"Can you tell me why so many of you came to find me all at once? And what you want?"

The ghosts nodded in unison.

"That's not creepy at all," Hunter muttered.

"Creepy," Charlie agreed.

"Shush," she told them, then, to the ghosts, "Please? Tell me?"

The spokes-ghost bowed. "Certainly, mistress. The spirits of Savannah are restless because there are warlocks in town."

And then a shot rang out, and Max flew forward, blood spraying from a wound on her neck.

CHAPTER TWENTY

In a very expensive hotel far away from Savannah, Dr. Hanford Kurchausen woke suddenly from a disturbing nightmare of blood and fire and dragons and sat up in bed.

And then he smiled.

"I'm coming for you, Alice Jones."

CHAPTER TWENTY-ONE

Hunter dove onto Alice, taking her to the ground and covering her with his body. Reynolds threw his head back and howled—a deep, wrenching sound that should never have been able to come from a human throat. Then all the werewolves other than Reynolds and Max began to shift to wolf. The process took less time than usual, maybe a minute, so perhaps danger and rage influenced the speed of the shift.

A second later, Bane was calmly issuing mental orders to all the vampires:

GO. NOW. FIND THE SHOOTER OR SHOOTERS BUT BRING THEM BACK ALIVE. WE WILL HAVE ANSWERS.

THEY VIOLATED MY TERRITORY AND ATTACKED MY GUEST. THEIR DEATHS ARE MINE.

Luke, Edge, and Meara raced out of the yard, several of the vampires from the Vampire Motorcycle Club behind them, at such a high speed that all Hunter saw was a stream of blurring movement.

When Alice squirmed under him, he tightened his grip. "You are the most vulnerable person here. Stay down until we're sure the shooters are gone."

She quit fighting him but shoved hard. "Let me breathe, please. And I need to check on Max."

"I could use the help," Ryan said, in full doctor mode next to where Max lay on the ground, a dome of silvery light covering both of them.

Hunter didn't know if Bane or Ryan held the protective magical barrier in place, and he didn't care. He just liked the idea that Alice would be inside it, too, so he rolled off her. She immediately scrambled across the ground to help Ryan with Max.

"Tell me what to do," she said breathlessly.

Ryan ripped off her sweatshirt and wadded it up. "Hold this over the wound. We have to get pressure on it, or she'll bleed out right here on the ground."

Carter, whose face promised a very slow and painful death to whoever had shot his beta, put a hand on Ryan's shoulder. "It's okay, doc. She *won't* bleed out, actually. Wolves, remember?"

It took a moment for the words to penetrate, and then Ryan's frantic movements slowed. "It's a neck wound, though," she protested.

The alpha raised an eyebrow at her. "Kind of like the one you gave the wolf who attacked you when he was under the warlock's control?"

Hunter had heard that story. The doctor, very new to the world of supernatural creatures at the time, had defended herself with a scalpel strike to the attacker's carotid artery and been shocked when he'd healed almost instantly and come back after her.

Ryan, evidently remembering the incident, slowly sat back on her heels. "Max?"

Max opened her eyes and put a hand over Alice's where it still held the now-blood-soaked shirt to her neck, and then she tried to smile.

"You are all guts, woman," Hunter said admiringly. Shot

in the neck and already smiling. That took guts—or at least a hell of a lot of bravado.

Max grinned at him and then patted Alice's hand. "It's okay, human. I'm good."

But then she tried to sit up and flinched. When she peeled the shirt away from her neck, they could all see that the wound was still pumping out blood.

"Silver," Bane growled.

The alpha wolf snarled his agreement. "Someone is going to pay for this."

Max glanced up at Carter and winced. "Help me? I hate this part."

This part? Did people regularly shoot at the wolves? Now wasn't the time to ask, and, anyway, Hunter was sure he wasn't going to like the answer.

The big wolf dropped to his knees next to her, and she tilted her head away from him, baring her injured neck. He put his fingers, which now ended in sharp claws, to her neck and, before Ryan could protest, dug into the wound.

That's when the doctor started yelling. "What are you doing? How is that sanitary? I know you heal fast, but this is ridiculous! I—"

Carter said nothing, just showed her his bloodied fingers, which now held a bullet.

A silver bullet.

Ryan suddenly smacked herself on the forehead. "For heaven's sake—*literally*—I can do this." She leaned past Reynolds and put her hand on Max's neck, and a pure white light shone between her fingers and Max's skin.

Angel power.

Between Ryan activating her Nephilim healing gift and

Max's natural healing abilities, the wound closed up in less than a minute. Hunter blew out a sigh of relief and then looked around, suddenly aware that the ghosts were gone.

But so was Charlie.

Alice must have realized it at the same time. She stood and whirled around. "Where is he? Charlie?"

"He flew off after Max got shot," Bane told her in a voice filled with ice. "If we discover that he was part of this plot, I will kill him."

"He isn't," Alice said hotly. "He escaped those monsters. He wouldn't have anything to do with this."

Hunter said nothing but silently agreed with Bane. That gunshot could have killed Alice. If Charlie had been any part of the scheme, he was about to be a dead demon, no matter how much Hunter had begun to like the little guy.

They moved inside at Bane's insistence and convened a war council of sorts in the huge kitchen. Mrs. C bustled around, giving everyone huge plates piled high with food, which was her go-to solution for every stressful situation. In this case, it was perfect. Werewolves needed to eat a lot on normal days, since their metabolisms ran so hot and fast. When wounded, it was an important part of their healing process to consume enormous quantities of food.

Alice, dangerously pale, as if she were in shock, stared blankly into the distance, ignoring both the conversation going on around her and the untouched food in front of her. Hunter held her cold hand, but it lay limp in his, her fingers not moving.

"Alice," he murmured. "I think Ryan should have a look at you."

"Why? Why is all this happening? I don't understand

what reason this Chamber you're all so worried about would have to try to kill Max. And where is Charlie? If somebody hurts him—" She broke off and covered her face with her hand. "I promised him he'd be safe now. I *promised* him."

Bane started to speak, but Ryan nudged him, shaking her head, which Hunter appreciated. The last thing Alice needed to hear right now was another threat about the dragon and his possible involvement with a plot against the wolves.

Mr. Cassidy walked in, a shotgun cradled in his arms, his face grim, followed by Bram Stoker, who bounded over to Ryan for pets and ear scratches. "Nothing on or near the grounds. I think it's past time we invested in security cameras, though. This can't happen again."

Mrs. C rushed over and hugged her husband. "Don't you go running off like that again without telling me where you're going, you old fool. I was afraid they got you, too."

"But who?" Hunter looked at everyone around the table. "Who is it that attacked us? And why? It doesn't make sense. This volleyball game idea was spur of the moment, right? I mean, Ryan only cooked it up a few days ago. It's not like the news would have made it to Chamber HQ in England in time to set up something so dire, unless you have traitors in the wolves."

"Not a chance," Reynolds growled.

Bane shook his head before Hunter could even ask about the VMC. "I'd know."

"Then how?" Part of him found it unbelievable that he was spending a Saturday night discussing death threats by a shadowy cabal of warlocks and necromancers in England, when just a month ago his Saturday nights had usually involved darts and beer at his local bar with his friends.

Reynolds nodded. "I was wondering the same thing, to be honest. If they wanted to go after me or Max, it would have been a lot easier to find us in our daily routine and safer for them than attacking us when we were surrounded by wolves and vampires."

Max paused, her fork suspended in midair. "You think they were after you, not me?"

The alpha scowled and threw his hands in the air in frustration. "I don't have a single fucking clue. It makes sense that I've pissed more people off than you have, since I'm the one in charge. If another wolf pack is trying to move in on our territory, they'd go after me, not you."

"Not necessarily," Ryan said, drinking a cup of hot tea. "Anyone who sees the two of you together can tell that you care about Max. Hurting or killing her would harm you and perhaps make you more vulnerable."

A weighted silence descended on the group. Hunter knew that Bane had no more idea of how to respond to that than he did, and Reynolds looked like he was going to swallow his tongue. Max, who'd been caught off guard in the middle of a large mouthful of burger, choked and forced herself to swallow.

"No, that's not—" Reynolds began.

"We don't—" Max began.

"I care about every member of my pack," Reynolds finished firmly.

Ryan shrugged. "Okay. I was just suggesting another possibility."

Bane shot up out of his chair. "We're about to find out.

Edge just communicated that they've caught the warlock and his shooters and they're bringing them back here."

• • •

Alice tried to tunnel her way out of the mental fog that had wrapped around her at the sight of Max's blood spraying out of her body. She glanced down at herself and realized she had blood on her shirt. Max's blood. She'd already washed her hands—twice—but they still felt dirty. Bloody. She wanted to wash them again, but she wasn't going to turn into Lady Macbeth right there in the vampires' kitchen.

She wouldn't have even thought vampires *needed* a kitchen before she'd met Hunter and the rest of them. If she'd ever imagined that they existed, she would have thought they only drank blood and slept in coffins, but that was clearly not the case. Meara was demonstrating a fondness for pecan pie, and they'd taken her out to dinner, for Pete's sake.

She bit her lip, realizing her brain was scurrying around like a hamster on a wheel, probably to protect her from the full realization that, for whatever reason, she was in danger again. People she'd begun to consider friends were in danger.

Taking in the details of the vampires' enormous kitchen, from quartz countertops to hanging copper pots—from the fresh herbs in little pots to the huge picture window that she never would have expected—she thought it was very like a picture in an expensive magazine.

Lifestyles of the Rich and Dangerous, maybe.

"And Charlie?" she finally dared to ask. "Is he with them?"

Bane focused his gaze on something she couldn't see and then nodded. "Yes. He helped Luke and Edge find and catch the warlock."

"I *told* you he was innocent. I told you."

Hunter squeezed her hand. "I'm glad he's okay."

She noticed but didn't comment on the fact that he hadn't chimed in with his belief in Charlie's innocence. No matter. They'd all find out exactly what was going on very soon.

"Well, you're not bringing those villains into my kitchen," Mrs. Cassidy said, her cheeks flushing a hot pink. "I don't want to be offering food to someone who could hurt one of our guests." The little housekeeper put a hand on Max's shoulder. "Another piece of pie, dear? I have apple, too."

Max grinned up at her. "You are a jewel, Mrs. C, but I think four pieces is my limit, even healing from a gunshot wound. Thank you." Max looked at Ryan, then. "And thanks to you, too, angel girl."

"You would have healed on your own," Ryan said. "I'm just sorry it took me so long to remember I had access to more tools than just putting pressure on the wound. I'm still fairly new to practicing Nephilim healing in a war zone." The doctor's voice trembled on those last words, and Bane pulled her up out of her chair and into his arms.

"You were great," Max said firmly before turning to Alice. "You too, ghost girl. Thanks for stepping up."

Alice nodded, still feeling far removed from everything and everyone. "I'm just glad you're okay."

"The basement of the club," Bane said, his expression dark. "We can't let them in the house or deal with them outside, where anybody might come along."

Hunter nodded. "I'll stay here with Alice and Ryan to protect them."

Ryan started to protest, Bane immediately arguing with her.

Alice cut them both off. "I'll be going with you. I need to know why they're sending demons to my home."

"No," Hunter and Bane said at the same time.

Alice gave them a long, steady look. "You'll let me come and hear what they have to say, or you'll never see me again. I won't be locked away again, not even by someone with good intentions."

Hunter actually growled with frustration but then nodded. "Fine. But you'll do what I say, especially if it comes to any danger. Ghost whisperer or not, you're still the most fragile of us."

Alice nodded. She either would or she wouldn't when the time came; there was no point arguing about it now.

Bane started to speak, but Ryan shook her head. "I'm going."

Max started laughing when Reynolds looked at her. "Hey, I'm the one they shot. I'm damn sure going. And I'm also the beta wolf of this pack, not some helpless human. No offense, Alice."

"None taken," Alice said automatically, wondering if it were true.

No, actually. She *did* feel offended.

She leaned forward and stared down a werewolf. "But don't ever call me helpless again. I've survived more than you could possibly imagine."

Max's brown eyes flared a hot amber, and then she inclined her head toward Alice. "Noted."

As they left the house to meet Meara, Edge, Luke, several vampires, a pack of werewolves, a dragon, and the bad guys, Hunter put his arm around Alice's shoulders and leaned down to murmur in her ear. "I really, really want to hear your story. And, for the record?"

When he paused, she glanced up at him and met his fierce gaze.

"*I* never once thought you were helpless."

CHAPTER TWENTY-TWO

Hunter almost laughed at the expression on Alice's face when she saw the Vampire Motorcycle Club sign on the door of the clubhouse.

"You advertise? I thought it was a big secret." She sat back in the passenger seat of the SUV, having again refused to drive it. "I mean, the gold outline of a motorcycle on the sign out front made sense, but this?"

She was twisting her fingers together in her lap, clearly worried about Charlie but refusing to discuss it.

"That's the back door. Only a few of us use it, and Luke thought it was funny. The name of the club is public, though. Kind of Bane's jest. He says the best way to hide something is in plain sight. Would you suddenly have started believing in vampires just because you heard the name?"

She slanted him an emerald look. "I'm not sure I believe in them now, to be honest. I'm halfway sure that any minute I'm going to wake up from a long fever dream, or..."

When her voice trailed off, Hunter put the car in park and turned off the ignition. "Or?"

She said nothing, so he pushed it aside and put his hand on the door handle, almost missing her whisper.

Almost—super vampire hearing, though.

"Back in the Institute."

He climbed out of the vehicle and raced around it to open her door and pull her into a hug. "You know you can tell me anything, right?"

"Why would I? I've known you for *two days*," she said, anguish in her voice.

He closed his eyes and breathed in her scent. "But two days of this chaos is like six months in human days."

She pulled away from him, but there was a hint of a smile on her face, and he decided to take it as a win. "Later. Let's discuss this later, after we find out what these people want and why they're willing to stalk us and shoot us to get it. Also, we rescue Charlie, no matter what."

He narrowed his eyes, not sure he could agree to "no matter what," but she poked him in the chest.

"No matter what," she repeated, her eyes daring him to refuse.

"Ow. And yes, okay, no matter what."

They passed through a line of vampires and were-wolves—mostly still in wolf form—on their way into the club. With their combined forces in charge of security, nobody was getting into the club that they didn't want there.

The clubhouse itself was long and low and looked a lot like a family-style chain restaurant from the outside. On the inside, it more closely resembled an English pub—not that Hunter had ever been to one of those, but he'd seen them in movies. They weren't going inside the clubhouse part of the building, though. Bane had sent Meara, Luke, and Edge telepathic instructions to bring Charlie and the culprits here to the basement.

Again, Hunter felt that slight sense of surrealism. Suddenly he took werewolf guards and telepathic communication as a normal part of his life.

He glanced at Alice. And, possibly, a ghost-whisperer girlfriend? He shook his head, mentally smacking himself on the forehead.

Too soon for that.

When they entered the building, Hunter immediately headed for the steel door at the back end of the hall. Then he leaned forward and looked directly into the state-of-the-art retinal scanner.

"Evans, Hunter. Welcome back to Vampire Motorcycle Club headquarters," came the familiar, faintly British tones of the computerized female voice. "How are you tonight?"

The door unlocked, and Hunter walked in, turning to find that Alice hadn't moved but was staring at him with her mouth slightly open.

"You're kidding me," she said. "This is getting more and more Syfy channel every minute."

He shrugged. "You're not wrong. But when you see Edge's computers, you'll understand why."

"But they brought the attackers in here?"

"I doubt they were conscious at the time," he said flatly.

She took a shaky breath but followed him into the office, which was kept at a freezing cold temperature due to the computers he'd told her about, and he headed straight back to another steel door, this one unlocked, that led to the vault and other rooms in the basement. Her flame-red hair gleamed in the bright light, but he noticed that her fine-boned face was still extraordinarily pale. She was definitely not okay, but she hadn't uttered a single word of complaint.

She was way tougher than she looked, but he still felt an overpowering need to pick her up and spirit her away to someplace safe. He knew there was no way she'd allow that, though, so he put it out of his mind.

"What does he do with that setup?" Alice was still staring at the bank of super high-tech computers. "Run NASA?"

Hunter laughed. "He probably could. The man is a super-genius and about three different kinds of scientists all rolled up into one."

"So why is he a vampire?"

Hunter shook his head. "That's his story to tell. Or not tell, more likely. But let's head down. They're starting to question the prisoners."

She bit her lip and squared her shoulders before starting toward him, and he realized the small talk and questions had been a stalling technique. Alice pretty clearly did not want to go into the basement and face whatever awaited them but was going to force herself to do it.

And he didn't want her there, either, but he was going to stand by her side.

She'd demanded the right to confront them, and he wouldn't be the one to deny her, as much as he might want to do so. He held out a hand, instead, and held his breath until she reached out and clasped it, and they started down the stairs together.

At two flights down, they passed the weapons room. One more flight, and Hunter suddenly scented blood.

A lot of blood.

And he realized he hadn't quenched his own thirst for a while.

He glanced down at his wrists, but his veins hadn't

darkened, so he should still be fine. Someone cried out behind the door on his left, and Alice whirled around and reached for the handle.

"Not yet." He blocked her from seeing into the room when he opened the door, just in case, but the scene was still fairly benign. Bane, Ryan, Meara, Luke, Edge, Reynolds, and Max stood in a rough circle around a large open space where three men and a woman huddled.

Alice pushed past him, her focus on only one thing. "Charlie!"

The dragon, perched on a long, low table behind Meara, flew up and around the room to them, carefully avoiding getting in reach of the prisoners, one of whom stared after him with hungry eyes.

"When I get out of this, I'm going to stake your hide to a wall, you piece of demon shit," the man snarled. He wasn't tall or short, not broad or thin. He was almost entirely forgettable in every way, except for the savage rage twisting his expression.

Alice ignored him completely and gathered the dragon in her arms, holding him close. "Don't do that to me again. You scared me when you disappeared."

"Oh, *please*," the man sneered. "As if you gave a shit about a Minor demon."

Before Hunter could punch the asshole in the face, Bane flicked his fingers, and the man—warlock, actually, Hunter realized when he smelled the faint scent of rot—fell to the concrete floor, moaning.

"Keep a civil tongue in your head, you pig," Meara snarled. Her always-immaculate appearance was roughed up; her shirt was torn, and her jeans were ripped and grass-stained at the knees.

There had been a fight, then. Warlocks weren't the type to give up easily, and they had some pretty powerful magics.

"Are these the warlocks?" Alice suddenly asked, staring at the four of them. "The ones the ghosts warned us about?"

At the word "ghosts," the female prisoner raised her head and stared at Alice. "Are you her? You don't look like much. I wonder what all the fuss is about," she sneered.

"Shut up, Zela," the one Bane had shot power at hissed. "Keep your mouth shut for once in your stupid life."

Zela laughed. "Oh, I don't think so. I warned you, but you didn't listen. Now look where we are. If we survive this, I'm ratting you out to Neville at the first possible opportunity."

The man's face turned bright red, and he lunged at Zela, getting his hands around her throat for a few seconds before Max calmly walked over, picked him up by one arm, and threw him into the wall.

The wall that was nearly ten feet away.

"Damn, I don't want to make you mad at me," Hunter told Max, whistling in appreciation.

She flashed a quick grin at him but said nothing.

Reynolds crossed over to where the warlock lay in a heap, surely with at least a few broken bones, and lifted him so high into the air that his feet dangled several inches above the floor. Then he dropped him.

"Tell us. Now. Who are you, and why are you here? Why did you shoot the beta of the Savannah Wolf Pack, and how were you fool enough to think you'd survive doing it?"

The warlock just spat at him, but the other two male prisoners still in the center of the room, both human, huddled close to each other and started sniveling.

"We didn't do nothing, Mister Werewolf. We didn't shoot nobody. We were just the hired muscle. We don't even know what the plan was," one of them wailed.

The other one, who seemed to be missing a few teeth, eagerly nodded. "Yeah, what he said. We showed up just before the shooting started. All we know is we were gonna get paid five hundred bucks to help out. We didn't know, help out with *what*."

The first one wiped his nose on his sleeve. "Yeah. Yeah. And we didn't even get paid," he said indignantly.

Hunter sighed. "Right. That's certainly the important point, here."

Edge shoved his long, white hair out of his face. Hunter noticed that he was also disheveled. But of course, if Meara had been in danger, Edge would have been right there at her side. The scientist raised an eyebrow. "The big question here is do we submit this story to *Stupid Criminals in the News* or to the Darwin Awards?"

One of the thugs looked at him hopefully. "We get a reward? How much?"

"Look. These two are not the brain trust here," Hunter said, pointing out the obvious. "We should let them go."

"Yes, you totally should," said the one with the teeth. "About that reward, though?"

Bane's eyes flashed ruby red, and the men flinched away from him.

"You are lucky we're letting you live," he told them. "Don't try what's left of my patience."

They fell over themselves agreeing, and Luke walked forward and grabbed one by the arm. "I'll enthrall this memory out of their tiny brains and dump them on the side of the river somewhere."

"I'll go with you," Edge said. "Meara?"

She shook her head. "No. I'm staying here."

They all waited until Edge and Luke left with the two thugs, and then Bane grabbed a chair from the side of the room and set it down with controlled violence on the floor next to Zela.

"Sit," he commanded her. "Tell us what you know, and we'll do you the same favor."

"You shut up. He's lying," shouted the warlock.

Hunter pointed at him. "I'd suggest *you* shut up. Everyone in this room knows you're the one who shot Max. We can smell the gunpowder on you."

Alice glanced at him; he figured she was thinking that technically neither she nor Ryan could smell the gunpowder at this distance from the shooter, but it wasn't a detail the warlock needed to know.

"Shut up, yourself, Derek," Zela shouted back. "I warned you we should never have taken on a secondary mission."

"Secondary mission?" Max frowned. "Besides shooting me? And I got shot by someone named *Derek*?"

Hunter snorted.

Zela darted a quick look at Max and then rolled her eyes. "Nobody meant to shoot you, exactly. You're not important. Our job from the Chamber was to protect *her*."

Alice froze when she looked up and saw the woman pointing at her. "What? Protect me? Why? From whom?"

"Shut up," the warlock moaned, clutching his broken leg.

"The Chamber will torture you to death, you stupid bitch."

"Enough with the *bitch*, if you please," Meara snapped. Then she flicked her hands at Derek the warlock in an elegant gesture that levitated him up into the air and pinned him against the wall. "Now, *you* shut up."

He struggled and fought, trying desperately to speak, but Meara was brilliant with her vampire magics. Derek was going nowhere and saying nothing until she allowed him to do so.

Charlie, curled up in Alice's arms, peeked out. "He is the one who hurt me and made me sneak and spy on you, Lady. But I found him. I found them for the vampire friends of the Lady."

"You did good, Charlie," she said soothingly. "You're a good boy."

"All right," Bane said to Zela. "Tell us. Now. And then we'll decide if your story wins you your freedom or your death."

The woman's face turned white beneath her heavy makeup, and she pulled her jacket closer around her shivering body. "Okay. Okay. Listen, I'll tell you everything I know about the Chamber. I'm tired of that busted group of snobs, anyway. They treat women in the organization like shit, and—"

Alice suddenly thrust Charlie at Hunter and took a step toward Zela. "Do you think we give one single damn about your *employment problems*? You could have *killed* my *friend*."

Max, who'd known Alice for even less time than Hunter had, looked surprised and then pleased but again said nothing.

Zela cowered in the chair. "I'm sorry. He did it, not me. I said, do you have a death wish? Shooting somebody in the middle of a vampire party like that? But Derek had a dossier, with pictures. Said that she, the wolf, was a dangerous beast—"

Reynolds growled, and Zela backtracked, fast. "No, I know. You're not beasts. Hey, one of my best friends is a shifter. But Derek said we had to protect the property from the wolves, so he shot *her*"—she pointed at Max—"to protect *her*"—she pointed at Alice.

Several people started talking all at the same time, but Alice's clear tone cut through the chatter. "Did you say 'protect the *property*'?"

Zela nodded. "Yeah. We had double orders, I guess. The Chamber wanted Derek to capture you, and so did the other guy, and I don't know why."

"Capture Alice?" Hunter's vision started to haze red. "Capture *Alice*?"

"Yeah," Zela said, looking back and forth between all of their faces, probably seeing her lifespan dwindling to the next few minutes. "Um, they said it was too dangerous to try for the Nephilim right now, with Bane on the alert."

Bane's eyes flashed back to ruby, and, from the way everything in the room shone a brilliant scarlet, Hunter figured his eyes looked exactly the same. Then Alice made a small sound, and Hunter saw that her entire body had started shaking. He lowered Charlie to the floor and leapt across the few feet separating himself from her, then put his arms around her and pulled her close.

"Alice? Are you okay? What is it?"

"They called me *property*." Suddenly—horribly—she

started to laugh. "Property of the Institute, established 1870. We should have had T-shirts."

Now everybody was watching Alice.

"What is it, sweetheart?" Hunter touched her cheek. "Can you tell me?"

"I bet *he* can," she said, pointing at the warlock pinned to the wall. "Meara, let him talk."

Meara looked doubtful, but she flicked her fingers again, and the warlock gasped and choked out a hoarse, barking sound.

"Tell them," Alice shouted at him. "Tell them who gave you your second mission."

The warlock raked a leering glance up and down Alice's still-trembling body. "Grogan told me you were fuckable and that he was finally going to get the chance. I guess he has low standards."

"Oh, now you're going to *die.*" Hunter started toward him, fury searing through his body. His fangs snapped down into place, and he snarled out a wordless threat, but before he could reach the man, Alice screamed, and her scream was loud and long and reverberated with power.

Charlie, as if in reaction to the sound, suddenly launched himself into the air, flew over Hunter's head, and dove at the warlock, his golden eyes glowing. Hunter jumped up to try to catch the dragon but missed.

"No! Charlie, no," Alice shouted.

But it was far too late, because suddenly Hunter remembered a very important fact—Charlie had reached the anniversary of his hatch date.

So now he was "breathing much fire," as he'd told them he planned to do. So *much* fire, in fact, that Derek the warlock burst into flames.

Charlie's first attempt at breathing fire was a damn good one, by dragon standards. He was *burning a man to death.*

And Hunter, the firefighter in the room, couldn't do a damn thing about it.

Fuck that.

He raced toward the screaming man, ripping his own shirt off as he went, with some idea of using it in a "stop, drop, and roll" scenario, but damn, nobody had ever envisioned *dragon fire* when they came up with the technique, and he was just so fucking useless, and—warlock or not—the man Hunter had always been wasn't about to watch somebody burn to death.

But a shirt wasn't going to be enough.

All the anger and frustration, all the confusion and pain and helplessness of the past few weeks—of every moment since he'd first gotten trapped in that house fire and almost burned to death himself—rose up in him, and he threw back his head and *roared*.

A powerful gust of wind surrounded him and shot out toward the warlock, and then it wrapped around the man and somehow…stopped.

Stopped the fire immediately, almost as if it had suffocated it. Starved it of oxygen.

Which made no sense at all

He whirled around and stared at the vampires. "Which one of you did that?"

Meara and Bane were both shaking their heads.

"It wasn't us, my friend," Bane said gently. "I think we've discovered what your power is."

Alice, in the meantime, had started walking toward

Derek, her eyes turned to emerald ice. "Say his name."

The warlock was injured and too terrified to understand, and he just stared at her out of his reddened and shocked face.

"Say his name," she shouted. "Say it!"

But Derek just rolled over on his side and moaned.

Alice started rocking back and forth, and Hunter was very much afraid she'd gone past shock and was headed for a catatonic state. Whatever was on her mind might actually kill her if he couldn't bring her back to reality.

Back to him.

"Alice. Please, can you hear me?"

But she closed her eyes, rocking and rocking, and suddenly the room filled with white mist that was seeping through the walls. It was no ordinary mist, of course.

It was the ghosts. So many of them that they filled the room.

"We're here to help you, mistress," said the same one who'd talked to Alice at Bane's house.

Alice either didn't hear him or didn't care, because she never opened her eyes. The ghosts advanced on the injured warlock and then retreated in a tsunami of rolling fog, disappearing right through the cement walls the way they'd arrived.

And somehow, defying the laws of physics, they took the warlock with them.

The woman, Zela, fainted and fell out of the chair. Nobody rushed to catch her, but Ryan did walk over to check on her after she hit the floor.

"She's fine," Ryan said. "Didn't even hit her head."

Everybody else still in the room watched Alice like she

might be very dangerous, but nobody said anything, so Hunter, not knowing what else to do, wrapped his arms around her and held her close, hoping to share his warmth. His strength.

After a long, silent moment, she opened her eyes. "He knows where I am. He's the only person who has ever called me *property*. I'll kill him before I go back."

"You're not going anywhere you don't want to go," Hunter growled, tightening his arms around her.

"Tell us *who*," Meara demanded. "You'll kill *who*?"

"Dr. Hanford Kurchausen," Alice said. "The head of the Institute where I was imprisoned for eight years of my life."

CHAPTER TWENTY-THREE

Alice gripped the mug of coffee with both hands, looking around her at the clubhouse interior while the others poured coffee and spoke in quiet tones.

Probably about her.

The wolves had taken charge of Zela, promising to continue interrogating her until they learned everything she knew. After that, they'd call on the vampires to remove her memory of the entire encounter.

She and Ryan had made everybody promise not to kill the woman, since she'd lived up to her side of the bargain and was telling them everything she knew, thought, and speculated at a rapid pace. Seeing your colleague burning alive certainly provided incentive.

Alice pushed the memory out of her mind—it hadn't been Charlie's fault—and studied the room. It was a warm and inviting space. The long bar of polished wood was the centerpiece of the room, and tables and chairs and a few couches were scattered around in conversational groupings. There was an enormous stone fireplace and a jukebox and even a couple of pool tables. Maybe sometime Hunter could teach her to play. He'd stepped out of the room for a minute, but she could mention it to him when he got back.

Learning to play pool was something tangible she could think about—look forward to—to try to break through the terror that had swamped her since that woman had said they were meant to protect "the property."

Dr. Kurchausen had always called her that. The property. His property.

He'd done it deliberately, of course, to dehumanize her. He'd done it to all of them, the hundreds of residents—prisoners—held captive. He'd told them they were his property and existed only to serve his depraved wishes.

So, yes, she liked the idea of having something to look forward to, if she survived.

If she survived.

"I'm not going back," she announced, catching everyone's attention. "I'm telling you that right now. Kill me if you have to, but don't let him take me back there."

Edge looked up from the laptop he'd been bent over since they'd walked upstairs a half hour before, after what she'd started to think of as the Great Ghost Incursion. "That, at least, won't be a problem. There's no 'there' to go back to."

He walked over to her, carrying the computer, and put it down on the table in front of her, then turned the screen to face her. A headline screamed out at her from above a photograph of the Institute.

Hundreds Die in Fire

She clutched her stomach and bent over, gasping. *Hundreds?*

"How is this possible? I can't believe it wouldn't be a lead story on the nightly news," she whispered, still reading the article.

"It happened last year," Edge said, leaning against the table behind him. "And the reason it wasn't plastered all over the news is your boy Kurchausen."

"He's not my boy," she snapped. "He's a monster."

Hunter strode over, his own mug of coffee in hand, and sat next to her. "Well. We know about monsters here, don't we?" His face was set in grim lines, and, when she reached for his hand, he pulled away. He tried to cover the movement by reaching out to tilt the laptop screen so he could read the article, but she knew exactly what had happened.

He knew, now. Knew she was damaged goods. The pit that opened up in her stomach slammed home the truth that she shouldn't have tried to be normal. To have friends.

She shouldn't have let herself care about someone or think she was cared about in return. It hurt too much when it was taken away from her.

Charlie, curled up at her feet, whimpered in his sleep, reminding her that she wasn't the only one that the predators in the room considered to be damaged goods. She swept her gaze over all of them, the vampires and the two wolves and the Nephilim.

"It wasn't his fault. He thought he was protecting me, and he'd never breathed fire before, so he had no reason to know that he was so powerful," she said hotly, even though nobody had tried to argue with her. "You can't kill him for that."

"Kill him?" Meara snorted and poured herself another glass of something amber-colored. "We plan to give him a medal."

"Maybe the reward those thugs kept asking me about," Luke said, an incredulous look on his handsome face. Like the other vampires, Luke was ridiculously attractive. Tall and dark, with green eyes a shade lighter than hers, he seemed to perpetually find life amusing. She bet that he was never short of companionship, either. He'd even sent her a few flirtatious glances during the volleyball game, until Hunter spiked the ball "accidentally" at the back of his head.

Alice dragged her attention back to the article. She was getting squirrelly from adrenaline, shock, and lack of sleep. There wasn't much more to see, though; the piece seemed to have been toned down until it contained almost nothing in the way of facts.

She looked up at Edge. "What did you mean before?"

The vampire turned his eerie silver gaze to hers. "Been doing some digging. Kurchausen is planning to run for the U.S. Senate. Can't have a secret institute where you torture people and be a senator. Even somebody with his money couldn't hide that from the news."

Alice dismissed this. "No, you don't understand. It's not just the money. He used us—all of us whom he'd imprisoned there. He conducted horrible experiments to fuel his blood magic. And his staff—minions—perpetrated horrible abuses."

She shuddered, suddenly icy cold. This time, Hunter reached out to her, but she pretended she didn't see. Better to stand on her own than get used to looking for support that might not be there when she most needed it. She looked away from the sadness in his beautiful blue eyes, too. She had enough sadness of her own; she couldn't let him past her defenses again.

Bane, standing at the bar with an arm loosely around Ryan, looked thoughtful. "Blood magic? Although horrible, it makes sense. I've been racking my brain to try to understand how the Chamber and this doctor crossed paths over an animal rescuer."

She shrugged. "They never cared about the animal-communication side of my gift, only the ghost part. Evidently I channel a lot of supernatural energy when I talk to ghosts— "

"No kidding," Carter muttered, rubbing his head. "The inside of my skull still feels sandblasted from when you told us all to stop."

"I'm sorry. Really, I am. But, like Charlie, I had no idea I could do that, let alone so strongly."

Charlie, hearing his name, snuffled in his sleep and curled his tail around her ankles.

"Anyway, they would siphon off my energy and use it to push Kurchausen's ability to the next level. It didn't matter how much power he gained, though. It was never enough. He always wanted more and more and more. I knew that if I didn't escape, the experiments would kill me sooner or later, and the idea of being slowly tortured to death was so terrifying that I found a way to overcome my fear of the outside. I made a plan, and I escaped."

"I doubt it was anywhere close to as easy or simple as you just made it sound to escape from that nightmare," Hunter said softly. "You are a very brave woman."

Despite her resolve to keep him at arm's length, she felt a curl of warmth sweep through her at his praise. "No. It wasn't easy," she said, leaving it at that. "But now I find out that I would be dead, one way or another, if I'd stayed. I'd like to say that I can't believe he killed all those people just to further his political career, but I'd be lying."

"Well, he didn't necessarily kill them all," Edge said, taking the laptop. "The number listed as dead didn't match up with the number of residents on internal Institute documents from just before the fire."

"How did you access internal documents?"

Edge gave Alice a pitying look. "Really? Have you met me?"

"Not really—"

"Anyway, the tally was about twenty people short. Is it possible that he kept them in some other location?"

She nodded slowly. "Yes, it's possible. It's probable, actually. He used to gloat that he had two dozen of us who fueled all of his most 'productive' experiments. Then I escaped and, well, yes. It's possible."

"But I'm guessing you were one of the most powerful?" Hunter gave her a steady look. "It sounds like he may have been after you ever since you escaped."

The room started to spin around her, and Alice took a long, slow breath to try to recover her composure. "Maybe. I changed my name to Darlington—"

"From Jones?" Edge pointed to his screen. "You're listed here. Or, should I say, you were."

He typed rapidly for a few moments and then looked up. "Done. No record of any Alice having anything to do with the Institute, ever. I even removed a couple of Alices from the past fifty years, just to be safe."

She nodded. "Thank you. I don't suppose you could hide any trace of me?"

He started typing again. "Working on it. I will at least remove any trace that Alice Jones became Alice Darlington."

A hot flash of nausea struck the pit of her stomach. "There are traces there now?"

"There are always traces. It's the internet age. But I can remove them and disconnect what I can't remove, if any such thing exists." He shoved his hair back from his face and got back to work.

She almost laughed. His arrogance was probably well-deserved, but it also felt like he was showing off a little bit for Meara, who watched him when he wasn't aware of it. She glanced and caught Meara watching her, and they traded a smile, but then she looked away from the vampire. She was already too involved with these people. If she needed to run, which she almost certainly would need to do, she didn't want any ties holding her back.

Holding her down.

She deliberately did not look at Hunter or admit, even to herself, that it might be far too late when it came to him.

She leaned down to wake Charlie up with a hand on his back and then stood. "I have to go home. I need to check on my animals."

"Pete is there," Hunter began, but she cut him off.

"No. They're not Pete's responsibility, just like I'm not yours. Please take me home. Now."

Hunter scooped the sleepy dragon up into his arms. "Okay. I'll take you back now. But I'm staying there with you until this is resolved, if that's okay with you."

"What if it's not?"

He clenched his jaw. "Then I'll stay outside and protect you from there until I have to take refuge from the sun. But you won't be alone or unprotected during either the nights or days. You're in danger because of me—"

"That at least we know now isn't true," she said. "It's pretty clear that the Chamber's interest in me stemmed from Dr. Kurchausen."

"Keep Lady safe," Charlie squeaked, opening one eye.

"Yes, Charlie," Hunter said. "We will keep Alice safe."

She sighed and capitulated. She couldn't fight both of them. "Yes, of course you can stay with me until I figure out what to do next. That basement isn't very comfortable for you, though."

Meara put down her drink and pulled out her phone. "I can fix that."

When Alice started toward the door, Max, who'd been fairly quiet, suddenly stepped in front of her.

"You're not alone. You called me your friend, and I want you to know that you're mine, too. You're not alone," Max repeated, "and whatever reckless idea you're hatching, forget it. We'll protect you."

Alice wanted to cry, but she forced back the tears and smiled, just a little. "Or I'll protect you."

Max shocked Alice by throwing her arms around her in a fierce hug. "You're not alone," she whispered, and Alice closed her eyes, letting herself sink into the offered comfort and strength, just for a moment.

When she pulled back, she pointed a finger at the werewolf. "You're not alone, either. Try not to get shot anymore."

Max's laughter followed her all the way out of the clubhouse.

CHAPTER TWENTY-FOUR

Hunter tried about a thousand times to think of exactly the right thing to say as he drove them through the night toward Alice's home.

Tried and failed.

She just sat silently, staring out the window into the darkness.

Charlie was curled up in the backseat, sound asleep. Apparently, terror, danger, and breathing fire wore a dragon out. Hunter idly wondered if the fact that he hadn't quite killed the warlock was something that a Minor demon would be proud of—or regret.

"What does that mean, anyway?"

Alice sighed but slowly turned her head to look at him. "What?"

"If Charlie is a Minor demon, what does a Major demon look like? A giant dragon? A scary monster, like the demons we've seen in movies and stuff?"

She said nothing.

"I mean, there must be a reason they're called Minor, right? I just wonder what it is. Meara will probably know." He realized he was babbling, but he couldn't seem to stop.

Alice still said nothing.

When they pulled up to the gate, the werewolf security team opened it, and Hunter drove in, then stopped and rolled down the window.

"Hey," a bald, muscular werewolf said. "I'm Ian. Things

have been completely quiet here."

"Hunter. Did your alpha fill you in?"

Ian nodded. "We're on the alert for this doctor and any of his thugs, in addition to the Chamber. That white-haired hacker vampire sent photos of Kurchausen and all his known associates to our phones."

Alice finally stirred. She leaned over the console. "Hello, Ian. I'm Alice," she said, her voice polite but frighteningly empty. "Thank you for this. I hope you won't have to be here long."

"Doesn't matter how long. We're going to get these bastards who dared to shoot our Max," Ian said, a hot orange glow flaring in his eyes. "We'll keep you safe, too, ma'am."

She thanked him, but her voice held only desolation. Hunter drove on and pulled around the side of the building, then put the car in park.

"We *will* protect you," he told her.

She didn't even look at him, and he cast about furiously for something to say—something to do—that could pull her out of the terror or depression or fatalism that was slowly but surely carrying her deeper and deeper inside herself.

Further and further away from him.

"Alice? What do you want?"

She clutched her hands together in her lap so tightly that her knuckles turned white, and then she looked up at him, her green eyes huge in her too-pale face.

"I want to have sex with you."

• • •

Even an hour later, when they were finishing up the chores for the shelter, Alice still refused to discuss her declaration that had damn near knocked him off his feet. He was trying to be patient and let her speak up at her own pace, because…well, because everything.

She was an innocent, and he was a vampire.

She was everything good and pure and kind, and he was a monster.

She was unbelievably stressed and probably terrified, and he was damn sure not going to take advantage of that. He'd had to rush straight to the basement and retrieve a few bags of blood just to deal with the effect of her statement—he didn't want to think of what the actual act of making love to Alice would cause.

He could *hurt* her.

No. He'd die before he'd hurt her. Probably best to stay far, far away, once he knew she was safe.

He watched her move along the aisle of kennels, graceful and so beautiful. He was damn sure not going to take advantage of her, no matter how much he wanted her.

Charlie, who'd hopped into the rescue and made straight for Ajax's kennel, was now asleep curled up next to the German shepherd. They'd checked on, fed, and settled everyone else, even Ferret Bueller, who'd spent a good ten minutes using Hunter as a climbing gym and grooming his head.

Hunter's phone buzzed in his pocket, and he put down his cleaning rag and answered it.

"It's Edge," he told Alice. "Edge, I'm putting you on speaker. What's up?"

Edge's jubilant voice came through loud and clear. "Who's brilliant?"

"Albert Einstein," Hunter said promptly.

"Yeah, but he's dead. Who's— "

"Just tell us, please," Alice said, her voice strained. "I'll be glad to feed your ego afterward."

There was a silence, and then Edge laughed. "Okay. Sorry. I get carried away with my research sometimes. So, good news. You don't have to worry about Kurchausen, at least for a little more than a week. I have confirmation that he's at a high-level, *mandatory*, meeting in England at the Chamber HQ until a week from Monday."

Alice collapsed back against the counter behind her, catching herself with her hands before Hunter could grab her. "Are you sure?" she asked. "Really sure?"

"Absolutely. More good news? We found the house the warlock was using, and his laptop was in it—plus, one of the wolves found his phone where he'd thrown it into the woods when he saw us coming. According to his texts and emails, and confirmed by Zela, they were the only two the Chamber sent to Savannah this time."

"This time," Alice echoed, biting her lip. "Is this an ongoing battle?"

"Unfortunately, yes. We're going to have to find a way to end this. It may mean going to England."

Hunter shrugged, then realized Edge couldn't see it. "It is what it is. I'd go to England or France or the freaking North Pole if it would end the threat of the Chamber once and for all."

Alice reached out and put her hand on Hunter's arm, touching him for the first time since they'd returned to the shelter. "Does this mean we're safe? We're not under attack?"

"That's what it means. At least for now," Edge said. "We're keeping Reynolds's security company under contract, here and at your place, until we catch Kurchausen. But yes, it looks like we have a good week of freedom from these bastards."

"Thank you," Alice said, her voice steady in spite of how her body was shaking like a leaf. "Thank you so much."

"You got it, ghost girl. Remember, you're not alone anymore," he said gruffly, and then he ended the call.

Hunter stared at his phone in shock. "Evidently you're not just a ghost whisperer; you're a vampire whisperer. I've never heard Edge be so nice to anybody before."

Alice pushed past him, raced down the corridor between the shelter and her house, unlocked the door, and ran up the stairs. He followed her at a more sedate pace, locking doors as he went, and then climbed the stairs, following the heart-rending sound of her hiccupping sobs.

"Alice?" He pushed open her slightly ajar door and walked in to find her curled up on her bed.

"I'm sorry," she gasped, her voice muffled by the pillow she was clutching. "I was being so strong, but it's like the sudden relief from fear has hit me harder than the fear itself."

"Sometimes that's exactly how it happens." He thought back to a few of the more difficult fires he and his crew had fought. "The adrenaline can hold you up until the crisis passes, and when it drains out of you afterward, there's nothing left but exhaustion and nausea."

She sat up, her hair a mussed red cloud of curls around her face, her eyes sparkling with tears. "I need to blow my nose. Do you want to have sex now?"

He clamped his lips together against the laughter trying to escape, leaned over, and snagged a tissue box from her bedside table. She took one and loudly blew her nose, took another and wiped her eyes, and then jumped up to discard the tissues. When she caught sight of herself in the mirror, she gasped.

"No wonder you don't want to have sex. I look scary!"

He couldn't fight it anymore. He dropped his head into his hands and started to laugh. "Oh, Alice. Sweetheart. I don't think I have ever wanted *anything* more than I want to make love to you. But this has been a hell of a long night, and emotions are high. Why don't we just—"

"Watch TV?"

"Sure. Why not?" He took her hand and gently pulled her down to sit in his lap, and then he kissed her reddened nose. "Any ideas on what to watch?"

"*Buffy the Vampire Slayer*?"

• • •

They were halfway through the first episode, in which Buffy and her mother moved to a town with the improbable name of Sunnydale, when they heard a vehicle drive up outside.

Alice, snuggled up close to Hunter's deliciously warm and muscular body, groaned at the thought of stirring. Especially now, when it was almost dawn and he'd need to sleep soon.

"What is it?"

Hunter's phone rang again. He held it up before

answering, and she saw Meara's name.

"Hey, Meara. What's up?"

"You, apparently. It's very close to dawn, little brother."

"I know," Hunter said, pulling Alice closer to him. "I'm off to my fancy basement accommodations any minute now."

"Not so fast," Meara said. "The van that just arrived? I sent a few things over with a friend of mine. Alice, please let her in and then just get out of the way and allow her to do her thing."

"How did you know I was here?" Alice said.

"I could hear you breathing. Hunter, didn't you tell her about superior vampire senses yet?"

"We've been a little busy," Hunter said drily.

Alice smiled at him and then looked at the phone. "Who is your friend, what is she bringing, and why should I get out of her way?"

"Because she has a few comfort items for Hunter, since he'll be staying with you for a while. I assume you heard the good news about your evil doctor, but I'm guessing Hunter wants to stay with you for now, just in case."

"Definitely," he said, his cheerful expression intensifying into blazing heat as he looked into Alice's eyes. "So, so much."

He leaned toward her, and she met him halfway. Just as their lips met, the doorbell rang and Meara loudly cleared her throat.

"*Au revoir*, my darlings. I'll see you tonight."

"Tonight?"

"Girls' night in. Movie night, I think Ryan said. Later." And with that, Meara clicked off, just before the doorbell rang again and someone pounded on the door.

"I'm *coming*," Alice shouted, frustrated for so many, many reasons. She started to stand, but Hunter caught her wrist and pulled her back to him. When she overbalanced and landed in his lap, he caught her, laughing, and then he captured her mouth with his own again, as he had done several times while they watched television.

But this kiss was different. Deeper.

Somehow...*more.*

She stopped trying to analyze it and kissed him back, running her fingers through his silky dark hair. She kissed him with longing and wanting and need.

She kissed him with hope—the tiniest kernel of hope that she'd been right to consider Savannah her new home.

She kissed him, and it was a revelation of heat and passion and a blazing hot *need* that she'd never experienced before in her life.

When she finally stopped, only so she could breathe, she leaned her forehead against his.

"I didn't know," she said wonderingly. "I never dreamed it could be this way. Kissing. Touching. It's magical."

He kissed her again, fast and hard. "It's definitely magical with you," he groaned. "So magical I just want to get you naked."

She bounced up off his lap and grabbed the hem of her sweater, ready to rip it off over her head. "Yes! Let's do that right now!"

BOOM BOOM BOOM.

Hunter blew out a breath, looking as horribly frustrated as she felt. "I guess we'd better get that. If it's a friend of Meara's, she'll stand there all day."

"Fine," she growled. Then she stomped across her small sitting room and flung the front door open. "*What?*"

The neatly dressed older woman standing on her porch didn't turn a hair at Alice's rudeness. She held out her hand. "I'm here to set up the basement for a Mr. Evans, dear. I'm Janice Street, Street Designs. Meara sent me."

Alice shook her hand, stunned, and then Janice turned and loudly whistled, which must have been the signal, because two large men hopped out of the van and started carrying furniture and rugs into the house.

"Which way to the basement, dear?"

Alice silently pointed to the door.

"Thanks. Now don't worry about a thing; we'll be out of your hair in no time."

Alice turned back to Hunter in a panic when Janice Street walked off. "Meara hired an *interior designer* for my *basement*?"

Hunter shrugged. "Hey, the closest I've ever come to an interior designer was when somebody turned on HGTV at the station. Maybe she'll know what that knocking sound in the walls is, though." He started to follow Janice and her crew down the stairs.

Alice just stood there, fairly certain that her life had spiraled completely out of her control.

"*What* knocking sound in my walls?"

CHAPTER TWENTY-FIVE

Hunter woke up Sunday evening to warmth, complete darkness, and the scent of flowers tickling his nose. It only took a second for him to remember why: he was in the new bed Meara had sent over, protected from the sun by the blackout curtains the frighteningly efficient designer and her staff had hung.

He wasn't sure about the faint aroma of flowers until he rolled over and his face pressed into a mass of silken hair. He froze, inhaling the lush, rich scent for a long moment, and then dared to reach out a hand to touch what felt like the lovely—but clothed—curve of a woman's hip.

Alice's hip.

Alice's *scent.*

Alice's silky curls on his pillow.

His body hardened so fast that he was almost afraid his cock would split his pants wide open. Alice was in bed with him.

Sleeping.

In his *bed.*

With *him.*

Predatory instincts he hadn't known he possessed roared to life inside him, turning him feral.

Savage.

He wanted to take her mouth and kiss her awake. He wanted to take her body and show her what lovemaking was. He wanted to plunge his fangs…

No.

He wanted to take *everything.* To *possess* everything.

All of her. Just not her blood. Never her blood.

He wanted… He needed…

When he realized he could now see the outline of her sleeping form lit up by a dim red light, he threw himself back and away from her, leaping out of the bed. His eyes—they must have turned red like Bane's did when he was outraged. Like Meara's did when she hadn't fed in far too long.

He was looking at Alice through the scarlet glow of his own eyes…like she was prey. He stumbled away from her, having to force his feet to respond to his brain. Every inch of his new body wanted to jump on her and take and take and take. Her mouth, her body, her blood.

Especially her blood.

But the last remnant of his true self—Hunter Evans, firefighter and perennial nice guy—that part of him was shouting at him from deep inside his mind. Shouting *no* and *stop* and *get out.*

Except…those were such unimportant words, really.

Hunter took a step toward the bed.

What did it matter, just a little blood? She liked him, maybe even could come to love him. She wouldn't begrudge him such a little thing.

The scent of her skin began to drown out the scent of wildflowers from her hair, and her heartbeat was the only sound in his ears. In the room.

In the whole world.

Just a tiny bit. He would only take a sip. Just to try it. Just to understand why he craved her blood so badly—why he craved it hot and fresh and pumping, sweet and rich, into his mouth.

He took another step toward Alice. Toward what he wanted. What he needed.

What was *necessary.*

"Hunter?" The bedclothes rustled, and then he heard a *click* and the new bedside lamp lit up, bathing the room in what was probably a golden glow.

To him, though, it was still red. Just a red that shone more brightly.

"Oh. Okay. It's after sundown." Alice stretched, and Hunter avidly watched the graceful lines of her body. Listened to the slow, steady beat of her heart.

She tilted her head. "Hunter? Are you okay?"

He took a dragging step toward her. "Alice, I need you. You'll let me taste you, won't you?"

A sharp inhalation of breath was her only response for several long seconds, and then she patted the bed next to her. "I'm not exactly sure what that means, but I like holding you. I love kissing you. Maybe we could try for more?"

Her innocence acted like a splash of ice water on the savage need pounding through Hunter's body. He flew backward—literally *flew* across the entire length of the basement—to get away from her, his bare feet landing on the edge of the rug the designer had rolled out when turning the dark basement into a fully furnished bedroom suite. Hunter's feet were on a warm rug instead of cold concrete, and he realized that he was standing in the dark just beyond the edge of the lamp's glow, hiding his red eyes and undoubtedly monstrous face from her, while wearing nothing at all.

After she'd left him to sleep that morning, he'd pulled off his clothes as he usually did, pulled the new and extremely comfortable comforter over himself, and let himself sink into the deep sleep of daylight.

"Hunter?"

"I need to feed, Alice," he said roughly, ashamed. "I don't trust myself around you until I do. All I can hear is your heartbeat, and I'm afraid I would hurt you—or worse—if I don't feed quickly."

"Of course," she said, but he didn't hear the disgust that he'd expected in her voice. Instead, he heard warmth and compassion, neither of which he deserved.

She walked toward the far side of the room and indicated a large cabinet. "Meara sent over a small refrigerator, completely stocked, as part of the shipment. I didn't notice it until you were already asleep. The designer plugged it in over here, tucked inside this cabinet."

He started toward her again, drawn to her against his will. The sound of her heartbeat acted like a magnet pointing him toward true north. He knew her blood would taste more wonderful than the most expensive wine. It would taste like ambrosia.

Like life itself.

His gaze fixed on the pulse in her throat, and his fangs snapped down into place. "Alice," he pleaded, while he still could. "You must get away from me. Run. *Now*."

Instead of running, though, she opened the refrigerator door, retrieved a bag, and held it out to him. And, miraculously, even in the dim light he could see very clearly that her expression held only kindness. Not fear or hatred or revulsion.

A powerful thought arrowed into his soul. Maybe—just maybe—he was the only one in the room who believed he was a monster.

"I'll leave you to it," she said tactfully, but before she walked away, she leaned toward him, possibly to kiss him, and he was the one who was afraid. Afraid of what he might do to her. Certain that his life would be over if he harmed her in any way.

He flinched away from her, snatched the bag of blood, and leapt across the room to the side opposite the staircase to leave her an open field of retreat.

"I'm sorry. I am so sorry, Alice," he growled, running out of both patience and control. "But you should leave. *Now*. I don't know what I might do, and I'm fighting my new instincts with everything I've got right now to keep from pinning you to the bed and sinking my teeth into you."

Sinking his cock into her, too, but she was far too innocent to hear that. And he wasn't such a monster—not yet, at least—that he'd say it.

She held her ground for a moment and looked into his eyes. "Hunter, I'll leave because you asked me to go. I'll be in the shelter checking on the animals. But please remember this: I trust you. I know you would never hurt me. I think…I think you need to trust yourself as much as I trust you."

With that, she ran lightly across the room and up the stairs. He stood frozen, a feeling of warmth and possibly even happiness rising inside him, but he didn't trust the feeling. He *couldn't* trust the feeling.

Because he also still had the competing urge to chase

after her and bring her down like prey.

He ripped open the bag and drained it, then did the same with three more. By the time he finished the fourth, he was again completely in control of himself.

Then he forced himself to reach out to Bane on the telepathic communication pathway.

HOW LONG WILL IT TAKE BEFORE I CAN TRUST MYSELF WITH HER?

It took what felt like forever—but was probably only a few minutes—for Bane to respond.

I CAN'T ANSWER THAT. IT'S DIFFERENT FOR EVERYONE. BUT, I THINK, A LOT SHORTER FOR YOU THAN FOR MANY. BEFORE THE TURN, YOU WERE A MAN OF SUCH INTEGRITY, AND BECOMING A VAMPIRE DOESN'T CHANGE WHO YOU ARE. IT ONLY INTENSIFIES CERTAIN FEELINGS.

YOU SHOULD TRUST YOURSELF. YOU WON'T HURT HER UNLESS YOU TURN FERAL. BUT YOU SHOULD ALSO BE CAREFUL TO AVOID SITUATIONS WHERE YOU'RE TEMPTED. IF YOU FAILED, IF YOU DID HURT OR EVEN KILL HER, YOU WOULD NEVER BE ABLE TO LIVE WITH YOURSELF.

The master vampire's echo of Hunter's own thoughts was eerie, and Hunter knew Bane wasn't wrong. He would never forgive himself if he hurt Alice. In fact, he wouldn't be around to worry about forgiveness, because if there ever came a time that he harmed Alice—or any innocent—that would be the day he walked into the noon sun.

Coming to that realization went a long way toward

helping him regain his equanimity. He pulled his clothes on and headed for the small bathroom, where he found his toiletries kit—thank you, Meara—and brushed his teeth, then took a quick shower. By the time he was done, he felt almost human again, as the expression went.

He stared at himself in the fogged-up mirror, wondering if that's where the expression had originated—from a monster trying to be a person.

When he shook his head at his fanciful thoughts and walked out of the bathroom, Alice was waiting for him.

He blew out a breath and studied her face, searching for a hint of what she was thinking. Maybe she'd come to her senses and was about to order him out of her house. Were the vampire myths true? If she revoked her invitation, would he somehow be magically shoved out of her house like being shot out of a cannon? He realized there was an awful lot he had yet to learn about his new existence.

She looked a little nervous, but she was smiling, so maybe she wasn't planning to kick him out. On the other hand, he'd never been very good at reading the thoughts and feelings of other people, especially women. He was good at being a buddy; good at being a shoulder to lean on. Not so good at understanding the emotions. He'd worked so hard all his life at being a good guy and maintaining an even keel. The shell he was only now realizing he'd built around himself had kept him from being hurt but had also kept anybody from getting close enough to really care about him.

Was it possible that he'd figured all this out far too late to have a chance with Alice?

Also, when had his life turned into a Hallmark movie?

His mom and Hope would never believe this. Not that he'd ever tell them about it—at least not about the vampire part.

He realized he'd been silent for way too long and tried to make a joke. "I think this situation just turned awkward."

She ignored that and said nothing, biting her lip. Finally, when he was about to start singing sea shanties or telling knock-knock jokes or doing some other completely ridiculous thing to break the tension, she cleared her throat.

"I made it all the way to the hallway before I decided that I wasn't running away anymore. Not from you. Not this time." Alice stared at him, her lips trembling, her eyes huge. "I feel this enormous relief, after Edge's call. Like I have a respite from fear and danger, and enough time to decide what I want to do next, how I do it, and who I do it with."

When he managed to force words out of his throat, they sounded low and gravelly even to his own ears. "And have you? Decided what to do? Who to do it with?"

Please, let her say she wants it to be with me.

She stood there looking at him for a moment that lasted an hour or a day or a lifetime, and then she stepped toward him. That single step was all it took to unleash the control he was keeping on his emotions. He met her in the middle of the room and swung her up into his arms.

"Please tell me it's me, Alice. *Please*."

She put her arms around his neck and kissed him. "Of course it's you. It feels like it was always you. I want to—we can, I mean, Henry is here—well. Please, will you be with me? Now?"

He wanted complete clarity, so he asked, "Be with you?"

"Make love to me. With me." She blushed. "Like you said, we've really been on a dozen dates, in vampire years, so it's not too soon. I mean, the shows on the CW say that—"

He hugged her so tightly that she gasped.

"Hunter! I have to be able to breathe in order to do this properly, right? I mean, you do want to, don't you? Be with me?"

He bent his head toward hers and smiled. "Oh, sweetheart. You have no idea."

• • •

Alice had been so very afraid that he would turn her down. That he'd decide she had too much baggage, or that her past was on the verge of destroying her future and he didn't want to be any part of it.

Or, even, that the idea of being with a virgin was too much. Too ridiculous. Too stressful. Because she thought all those things about herself. She'd been kept isolated in the Institute, used for her power. But even in the six years since she'd escaped, she'd never dared to enter into any relationship. Never dared to get close. Not even to make real friends, although Veronica had been making some inroads there. It was almost impossible to keep a wonderful person like Veronica at arm's length.

But then Hunter had exploded into her life. With his impossible claims, outrageous sexiness, wonderful sense of humor, and strong protective instincts.

Not to mention his *kisses*.

The kisses were so far beyond anything that she could have ever imagined that she was almost afraid her head might explode if they really did make love.

Hunter started to laugh. "Okay. I can tell you're overthinking this. Are you making a mental plan? Lists?"

She blushed. He'd teased her gently about all the lists she had posted everywhere in the shelter, but it was the only way she could be sure to get things done.

"I'm not exactly sure what I would put on this list," she confessed. "Kisses? Hugs leading to naked hugs? Questions about safety and condoms and other responsible things?"

She paused, sure her face was now flaming bright red to match her hair.

Hunter put his hands on the sides of her face, gently tilted her head up, and then angled his wonderful mouth over hers in a long, deep kiss. When she could finally breathe again, she was not only smiling but a little bit weak at the knees.

"I love your list," he said, punctuating his words with kisses. Nibbling at her neck, gently biting her ear, and doing other things that were stealing her breath.

"At least most of your list. We don't need condoms, because vampires can't catch or transmit human illnesses. But I'll wear one if it will make you feel safe. I'll drive out to the store right now and be back in ten minutes." He took her mouth again and kissed her until someone started making tiny moaning noises.

She was pretty sure it was her.

"In fact, the way I'm feeling, I could *run* to the store and be back in ten minutes. Wait here."

She grabbed his arm when he turned toward the stairs. "No. I believe you. Just like I hope you believe me that I'm safe, since I've never done this before."

He closed his eyes for a moment, and when he opened them again, they glowed so hotly she wondered that they didn't start a fire. Or maybe they did. She was definitely burning with impatience to get back to the kissing part.

And on to the naked part.

The idea of touching all that hard, masculine muscle naked was doing funny things to her, from her nipples to her core. She still couldn't seem to catch her breath, either.

She tried to pull his head down to hers, but he resisted, his expression turning serious.

"There's something else, Alice. I will never be able to father a child." Sadness dimmed the glow in his eyes. "I didn't know that when I agreed to be Turned. On the other hand, if Bane hadn't Turned me, I'd be dead. Couldn't have been a dad like that, either."

A powerful wave of sympathy made her eyes start to burn, and she had to blink tears away so he didn't see them and think she pitied him. But she needed to tell him her truth, too.

"Not that we're having *this* conversation right now, because it's way too soon, or maybe it's a conversation we'll never need to have. But just in case it makes you feel better, I can tell you that I never, ever want to have a child—at least not a child who is mine genetically. I don't know if this ability to talk to ghosts and animals is hereditary, but I do know that I had a great-grandmother who died in an insane asylum. Possibly she had the same *gift* as I do, but nobody knew how to deal with it back then." She tried to smile. "Not that anybody knows how to deal with it very well now, either."

He twined a long strand of her hair around his fingers but never stopped looking into her eyes. "So you don't want to have children in case you might pass this along to them?" His voice held so much compassion and understanding that the tears she'd suppressed before came rushing back.

"Exactly. Please, though, can we quit talking about sad things now? And maybe go back to the kissing?"

He shouted out a laugh, picked her up, and tossed her on the bed. Then he pounced, landing partly on top of her and partly next to her. She'd been afraid, in the past, that if she ever got into a situation like this she would be too nervous or embarrassed or afraid to enjoy it.

She was absolutely thrilled to find that none of that was true. Her emotions started at delight and ended at joy. With an added bonus of sheer, primal, mind-blowing desire. She wrapped her arms around his neck and pulled him toward her. "Kiss me *now*."

And so he did. He kissed her as if kissing her was the only thing he ever wanted to do. As if she were the center of his world. His home.

His heart.

And she kissed him back in exactly the same way. She had next to no experience with kissing, but she was sure she had more than enough enthusiasm to make up for it. She explored him with her lips and her hands, tentative touches on safe places of his body—his powerful arms, his muscular chest. His shoulders, neck, and face.

And he returned the favor, teaching her so much. She learned which touches made her heart race and which ones made her skin tingle with electricity.

She learned that touching Hunter in certain ways made his breath catch in his throat; other touches made him groan. She learned so many things, just from the feel of lips to lips, skin to skin. From her fingers in his hair, from his mouth at her neck.

It was only after he'd moved down her body, now kissing her collarbone, that she realized she hadn't been even the slightest bit afraid when he'd kissed her neck that his fangs would've descended or that he'd bite into her skin.

She *did* trust him—even more than she'd said—and she realized the depth of that trust with a sense of wonder. She'd only just met him; in actual hours, days, and minutes, that was the truth. But they'd packed what felt like a lifetime's worth of experiences into a few short days, and she believed that she *knew* him—his heart, his character, even his soul—more profoundly than she'd ever known anyone before in her life.

Not that there had been any *men* in her life—not like this. She suddenly realized that he certainly had women in his past to whom she could be compared, and her newborn self-confidence took a hit. She withdrew a little and ducked her head.

Hunter raised his head from where he'd been pressing kisses along the neckline of her shirt. "I felt that. I felt you pull away from me," he said, concern clear in his voice. "Did I hurt you? Scare you? Am I moving too fast for you?" He sat up. "I'm so sorry. I'm a fool. Of course this is too much for your first time being intimate with someone. Why don't we—"

She stopped him with a finger on his lips. "No. Please don't think that. It's just that…this is silly."

"Tell me," he coaxed, taking her hands in his.

"It's just… I realized that I must compare really badly to all the women you've been with in the past."

She didn't know what she'd expected as a response to that statement, but it sure as heck wasn't that he'd start laughing and pull her back into his arms.

"Oh, sweetheart. First, there haven't been all that many women. I will explain to you in painful detail someday about just how often I've been relegated firmly to the friend zone with the women I meet. Second, it wouldn't matter if there had been a hundred women. Or a thousand women. I can tell you with complete honesty that I have never once in my lifetime felt the way I feel when I'm kissing you."

She started to ask him if he was feeding her a line, because she knew about feeding lines. She'd seen it on TV. But then she looked into his eyes, and the raw sincerity she saw there stole both her words and her breath.

He really meant it.

He really, *truly* meant it, and she felt her heart leap in her chest.

"I don't—this is going to sound ridiculous, but I suddenly feel like I'm in the middle of a love song. Not only that, but I understand the lyrics for the very first time in my life." A wave of heat rose in her face when she realized she'd just mentioned *love*, but an expression of sheer joy combined with smug male triumph flashed across his face, and, instead, she had to laugh.

"You make me feel like a hero," he told her, his voice serious. "Even though it sounds ridiculous to say, it's true. So now we've both admitted gooey, emotional things to each other."

He laughed and rolled over on the bed, still holding her, so she ended up lying on top of his long, lean, muscular body, and she had the sudden urge to rub all over him like a cat.

Before she could embarrass herself by doing it, though, he stroked her hair. "Now, you just have to promise that you'll never tell Bane or the other guys."

She kissed his nose and smiled at him. "You know, I wouldn't worry about it. From the way Bane acts with Ryan, I'm pretty sure he's said a few of these emotional, gooey things himself."

"You're right. What was I thinking?" He laughed. "So, never tell Meara."

Looking down at him and feeling his hard body stretched out beneath hers, Alice felt a sizzle of heat sweep through her and lost all desire to banter.

"Hunter. I think it might be time for us to take off some of these clothes."

CHAPTER TWENTY-SIX

Hunter had never heard more beautiful words in his life.

But there was no way in hell that Alice's first time was going to be in a basement, no matter how well it happened to be furnished.

He lifted her in his arms and leapt up and out of the bed, then ran up both flights of stairs to her bedroom, where he carefully laid her down on the bed and then opened the big picture window to let the night breeze into the room.

When he turned, she sat up in bed and sent him a questioning glance.

"You should always see the stars when we make love, beautiful Alice."

She grinned. "That's very poetic, but it's also a little cold. Also, won't the wolves patrolling the grounds, ah, hear us?"

"Oh, right. The wolves. Honestly, just the idea of making love to you has pushed everything else out of my brain," he admitted, delighted when she blushed.

He was delighted with *everything* about her, his practical darling, with her lists and common sense and hard-won independence.

His practical *Darlington*.

He laughed. "I just made a pun in my brain."

She rolled her eyes, still smiling at him. "Please, keep it in there. And close the window! Leave the curtains open, though. I do want to see the stars."

But then she bit her lip, suddenly looking shy, and he

was definitely not having that. He closed the window, pushed the curtains open even farther, and then headed toward the bed, pulling his shirt off as he went. When he heard her gasp, he might have even flexed, just the tiniest bit, because why not? All those years of working out had to be good for something besides fighting fires.

"You're beautiful," she said, awe in her voice, and he felt like a king.

• • •

Alice stared at Hunter, her heart pounding in her chest, beating a rhythmic accompaniment to the fantasy she was living, breathing, and feeling. The world fell away; her past and her present. Even worries about the future all floated away like feathers on a cool Savannah breeze. She was left vulnerable.

Fragile.

Bare to his gaze even though she was still fully clothed—her emotions and thoughts stripped of the protective shell she normally hid behind.

He *was* beautiful. Tanned and muscular, and a swirling design tattooed on his skin provided a mysterious hint of danger to the man who claimed to be only a "nice guy," only a man relegated to the friend zone. Just watching him move had changed the simple act of breathing from an automatic function to a conscious decision, and she forced herself to fill lungs that suddenly seemed tighter than they'd ever been before.

He sat on the edge of the bed but didn't reach for her.

Instead, he simply studied her face for a long time. Finally, just when she was going to either hurl herself into his arms or lock herself in her bathroom, he touched her cheek.

"You know I'm a firefighter, right?"

She nodded, confused at the subject change.

"Do you know what a flash point is?"

"I—no. Not really."

"In layman's terms, a flash point is the lowest temperature at which a substance will ignite." He moved his hand from her face and touched a strand of her hair, running his fingers down the length. "In life, a flash point is the critical point when something—or someone—causes an extraordinary or very significant action."

She said nothing, just tilted her head and waited.

"You were my flash point, Alice. When I ran into you in that elevator, your hair like living flame, you changed my life. Everything since I met you has been a reaction to your effect on me. You've ignited me. You found a monster and made him believe he can be a man."

She put her hand on his chest, just over his heart, and felt the strong, steady beat. "You've been my flash point, as well. Since I met you, I've dared to dream of a different life. A fuller life. One in which I don't live just for the animals, or in fear of my past and future, but in the present. Daring to take risks and dance into the unknown. Daring to ask you to be with me."

The smile that spread across his face warmed her heart as much as his touch, now gently caressing her wrist, warmed her body.

"Then let me love you, Alice Darlington," he murmured. "Let's dance into the unknown together."

She started to unbutton her shirt, but he stopped her with a touch.

"Not yet; just be with me for a while." He stroked her hair, her face, and her shoulders, running his hands down her arms to her wrists and capturing her hands in his. He leaned toward her, their bodies still apart—not touching—separated by a distance so small she knew she could breach it whenever she was ready.

And he kissed her. Soft, gentle kisses; barely there brushes of his lips on hers. On the corners of her mouth. On her cheeks and forehead and then back down to her mouth. His kisses were oh-so-gentle.

Until suddenly they weren't.

Now he kissed her with heat and urgency, with power and passion. He took her mouth as if he couldn't *not* kiss her, as if everything in him had risen up to meet her desire and stoke it higher and higher.

And she kissed him back with exactly the same passion.

She was desperate for more; more and more of his touch, his taste, his hardness against her softness. She made a sound—a moan or plea, she wasn't sure what—and he soothed her with gentle murmurs, coaxing her to lie back and let him love her.

When he finally began to unbutton her top, he paused and looked into her eyes. "Are you sure, Alice? This is a huge step, and I don't want you to take it with me until you're absolutely sure."

"I'm sure! I'm *so* sure. Please don't stop," she gasped, and his lips quirked as if he were fighting back laughter.

She fumbled to help him with the buttons, her fingers shaking, but stopped him before he got to the last one.

"Hunter, there's something I have to tell you."

He stopped immediately, his beautiful eyes asking a question without words.

She drew in an unsteady breath. "It's just, I've waited all my life for this. You'd better make it good."

His smile lit up the room. "Alice, you are absolutely wonderful. You know that, right?"

"I guess we're about to find out."

"I don't have a single doubt in the world." He'd managed the last button and drew the sides of her shirt away, exposing the pink lace of her bra. "Alice, you're *beautiful*."

Her heartbeat sped up, and she wanted to urge him to hurry up, or to slow down, or to do *something. Anything.*

The look of absorption on his face calmed her, a honey-warm feeling of feminine satisfaction sweeping through her at the realization that he found her beautiful.

Desirable.

He stroked her breast just above the top of the lace and then kissed her there. When he unfastened the front clasp and gently pushed the sides of her bra away so she was bared to his gaze, she thought her body would either melt or float completely off the bed.

And then he caressed her nipple with the tip of his finger, and electricity shot through her body, arching her back and stealing her breath.

"Oh! Oh, is it supposed to feel like that?"

"Better," he murmured.

"I'm not sure that's possible," she said honestly, and he bent down and took the tip of her breast in his mouth.

"Oh! I was—oh! Wrong. So wrong," she managed, clutching his head as he licked first one and then the other of her nipples, holding her breasts, stroking them, massaging them.

"Very wrong," he agreed, running his hands down her sides, down her hips, and to her legs. "Should I show you how wrong? Do you still want this? Want me?"

She clasped her hands around his back, holding him to her, not giving him the slightest chance to escape. "You just try and get away, and you'll be very sorry."

He smiled. "I'm not going anywhere, sweetheart. Wild horses couldn't drag me away."

Somehow, their clothes disappeared. Somehow, her body was tucked into the curve of his as he lay beside her.

Somehow, she was touching him, smoothing his hot, velvety skin beneath her fingertips.

"I thought your skin would be colder," she murmured.

"It probably is when you're not touching me." His hand was on her belly, stroking and caressing, and then his lips were on hers again, dark, drowning kisses that stoked the fire racing over her nerve endings to a feverish height. She couldn't get comfortable—couldn't stop straining to move closer and closer to him, to his touch, to...*something*.

His fingers moved lower, caressing her exactly at the center of where she needed him, and she jumped, arching toward him.

"More," she demanded, but he kissed her again so she couldn't talk, couldn't beg, could only feel. Feel his fingers slide through the slick wetness between her legs.

Feel him touch her in that special place connected to every single nerve ending in her body, concentrating her entire world on the feel of his fingers on her body. Her mind spun around and around, her thoughts a glittering kaleidoscope of shattered impressions.

He applied pressure in exactly the right way to make her lose her senses, and she gasped.

"Hunter!"

"Yes, love?"

"Did you know that all female mammals have a clitoris?"

He paused in what he was doing, and she wanted to bang her head on the wall.

"I'm sorry. I sometimes spout random animal facts when I'm overwhelmed," she said miserably, all but shaking with need. "Please don't stop."

He bent down and kissed her again, long and deep, and then moved his head and licked one of her nipples into his mouth, sucking gently while still stroking her clitoris, and she cried out, the sensation too much—too much.

When he raised his head to look at her, his eyes were sparkling with amusement and something more primal. "Did *you* know that Dalmatians get along very well with horses, and that's why they were trained to run in front of the first fire engines? They cleared the path and helped guide the firefighters to the fires."

She started to answer him, but then one of his fingers slid inside her body, just a little, just enough to make her moan.

"I don't—we—what was the question?"

His clever fingers stroked up and down through her heat, sliding through her body's wetness and rubbing slickly against her clitoris, up and down and around and around until her entire being was concentrated on that single point of contact.

And then he kissed her again, and the universe shattered.

CHAPTER TWENTY-SEVEN

Hunter had never been so hard in his life—not even as a randy teenager. Every muscle in his body was tense, and his cock was a steel bar in his pants, but every ounce of frustration was worth it to see and feel Alice come apart in his arms.

She was so beautifully responsive, not shy or awkward or hesitant. She'd even threatened him if he tried to get away. And now she was warm and wet and very relaxed, her eyes half closed, and his immediate plan was to take her up and over the edge again.

And again and again and again, as many times and for as long as she would let him. He never wanted to leave her side or her bed, and he didn't have the slightest idea how he'd come to need her so very much in such a short time.

He didn't care, either. Logic had no place here. Only touch and desire; only emotion and sensation.

She blinked, her lovely green eyes filled with wonder. "Is it always like that? How do people ever leave their beds?"

He laughed, again—he'd never laughed so much in bed. Life and love with her would be filled with joy.

Love?

Love?

Could it be possible that love had waited to find him until he'd died and come back transformed into a being he didn't always recognize? Could she love him as he was now?

"It's definitely not always like that. But for us? It's going to get even better."

A beautiful, sated smile spread across her delicate face. "You're the expert."

She reached for him and pulled him close, and he groaned when her hip bumped his erection.

"I'm sorry! Did I hurt you?" She tried to scoot away from him, but he only tightened his arms around her.

"No, sweetheart, it's fine. My body is just *very* excited about getting to know yours."

She hesitantly reached down and touched the tip of his cock, and he was so hard he was afraid he might go off in her hand like a teenager in the back of a car.

She was just so damn perfect. Her skin was that beautiful pale ivory that only redheads ever had, and her clouds of curls felt like silk on his skin. The way she'd flushed a delicate rose pink from her chest up through her neck and face when she came had made him want to throw her over his shoulder and carry her off to a castle, where he could treat her like the princess she so clearly was.

How did a woman who'd been through so much find the way to live with such joy? With so much kindness and compassion that even demons fell in love with her?

What chance did he have of resisting?

And why would he want to?

"I need you," he blurted out.

"Yes," she said, her body quivering—with excitement, he hoped.

"I need you, Alice. Will you let me love you again? Take me into your body?"

Her emerald eyes darkened, and he could smell her

arousal. Hear her heartbeat speed up.

"*Yes*. Yes, Hunter, yes and yes and yes. Please."

He pulled her to him and took her mouth, nibbling at her lips, letting his tongue play with hers until she got used to the sensation and then changing the tone of the kiss. Claiming her, his head angled to allow him to go deep, past her defenses. Into her heart, maybe.

Into her memories, certainly. He wanted to be sure she never forgot him; he knew he'd never forget her, even if she left him tomorrow and he lived for centuries.

Denial seared through him at the thought, and he leaned back so he could look into her eyes. "Don't leave me, Alice. No matter what happens with the Chamber, with the evil of your past—talk to me about it. Let me try to find a way that we can battle through it together."

She kissed him, her hands moving down his sides, touching his abdomen, and brushing against his erection again.

"I promise," she told him, finally, when she stopped kissing him. "But we have a bigger problem. So to speak."

"We do?"

She glanced down at his cock, and her cheeks flamed a hot pink. "There is no way that you are going to fit inside me."

Hunter threw back his head and laughed, then hugged her. "You are amazingly good for my ego, sweetheart."

She looked dubious. "It's not about ego. It's about basic physics. Or some kind of science. You're—" She waved her hand at him. "And I'm—" She gestured at her slender hips, or maybe at the red curls between her legs. He wasn't quite sure, but he wasn't going to interrupt her by asking, because he was far too entertained.

When it seemed clear she was done trying to explain the problem, he smiled at her. "We will fit very well. I promise you."

"But—"

"You know how wet you were when I was touching you?"

She blushed again but nodded.

"Let's try to do that again, but even more."

"Even more? But how can we do even more?"

By this point, he was actually shaking from wanting her so much, so he didn't try to explain. He just moved down her body, stroked her gently, and then parted her curls.

"I'm going to taste you now," he murmured, watching her face carefully for any sign of distress or that he was going too far. But she only looked fascinated—and wildly excited—so he bent his head and put his tongue on her.

Her body bucked beneath him, an involuntary reaction, and he wrapped his hands around her thighs and held her in place while he licked into her and around her clit and then, finally, when she was shaking and crying out "more, more, more," he fastened his lips around her and sucked hard.

Right where she needed him, he knew, because in seconds she was screaming his name, her hands gripping his head, her sweet honey in his mouth.

When the tremors racking her body calmed down, he moved to lie next to her again. "Alice, please let me inside you now."

She was still gasping for breath, but she opened her eyes and nodded. "Yes. Yes. I don't know how we'll fit, but yes."

He slid a finger through her wetness and showed it to her. "This is what your body was made to do. It will probably hurt a little, this first time, but I promise to do everything I can to make it better."

She winced at the word "hurt" but nodded. "I know. I trust you."

She touched his face and smiled up at him with such unreserved trust that he was almost afraid to continue. He knew the first time was painful for women, but he'd never been with a virgin, so he wasn't exactly sure how bad it would be. It wasn't the kind of thing he and his buddies had ever discussed. He could only go slowly and carefully and try his best not to hurt her too much.

His body screamed at him to *hurry up*, but his mind and heart were shouting at him to *go slow*, and he was suddenly unbelievably grateful that he'd consumed so many bags of blood, because combining this much physical need with the thirst would have been a very bad thing.

When he positioned his body between her legs, her muscles tensed for a moment, but then she closed her eyes and exhaled deeply, relaxing. He kissed her—long, slow kisses—and then he finally entered her, slowly and carefully. When he felt resistance, he paused.

"Sweetheart, this is when it's going to hurt. Are you sure you—"

"Let's get past it, then." She dug her heels into the bed and pushed herself up, driving his cock home, and he groaned, fighting his urge to thrust into her hard and fast.

"Oh," she said faintly. "That...pinched."

In a move more heroic than any he'd performed in years of firefighting, he clenched his eyes shut and froze.

"Do you want me to stop?"

"Are you kidding? Now that we got the tough part over, keep going!"

His eyes snapped open, and he studied her face. "Are you sure?"

"Yes!" She wrapped her legs around him, taking him even deeper, and he finally believed that there'd be no turning back.

He took her mouth, and then, when she clutched his shoulders, he took her body in a hard, driving rhythm, thrusting deep. Claiming her.

She shifted around a bit, finding the best angle, and then she slammed her head back into the pillow, an expression of startled desire on her face.

"Oh, Hunter! That— It doesn't hurt anymore. It feels… It feels—" She cried out. "Again? How is this happening to me again?"

Her cries and moans spurred him on, and her fingers digging into his shoulders pushed him that last little bit over the edge. He hung on to enough control to be sure he wasn't hurting her, but when he saw the waves of her orgasm crash over her, he drove his body into hers as deep as he could and let the explosion take him.

He'd never come so hard, and he wondered briefly if it was because of Alice or because he was a vampire—or both—and then he stopped thinking of anything at all, because his brain was melting out of his ears and he collapsed, panting, on the bed next to Alice.

When he could manage to speak again, he turned to look at her. "Are you okay?"

She laughed and raised her hand and then let it fall

back down on the bed. "I am so far beyond okay. If okay is a drop of rain, I'm an entire hurricane past okay."

"Good." Contentment washed through him, pulling him back toward sleep, but this time the sleep of satisfaction.

"Hunter?"

"Hmm?"

"You were right. We *did* fit."

"Always," he told her, and then he curved his body around hers, unwilling to stop touching her even in his sleep, and they both drifted off into a nap. He dreamed of sunshine and Dalmatians and Alice, always Alice, and he didn't wake up until maybe a half hour later, when his ass started buzzing.

CHAPTER TWENTY-EIGHT

Alice eventually became aware that a phone was buzzing. Somewhere. Not that she particularly cared. She might not ever care about answering phones again. It might be a rescue, though, so she forced herself to turn over even though her body was so saturated with pleasure she was finding it very hard to move. She blindly reached out, fumbling around her bedside table for the phone, and managed to knock the lamp onto the floor. Luckily, it landed on the rug, so nothing shattered. She was horrified to hear herself giggle—she hadn't done that since she was maybe five years old.

"What's happening?" Hunter sounded as dazed as she was, which utterly delighted her.

"I think it's the phone."

"Whose phone?"

"I don't know. Hey, maybe it's yours. In that case, I don't need to answer." She dropped her head back on the pillow and threw her arm over her eyes, content to drift back into sleep.

Hunter wrapped one muscular arm around her and pulled her close, and her feeling of blissful contentment grew even more wonderful.

"Was it okay?" Suddenly, she felt a little shy. "I mean, I haven't done it before so I'm probably not that good at it, but I'm sure I'll get better with practice."

He responded with a lazy grin. "If you get any better, I

might not survive. I think my brain may have exploded this time."

Alice giggled again and realized her phone or his phone or whoever's phone it was had stopped buzzing. She put her hand on the side of his face and stroked his cheek, marveling at the realization that she had both the ability and the right to do so. He *wanted* her to touch him. He wanted to touch her.

This was a truly miraculous state of affairs.

Then she had an even better thought. "Can we do it again?"

Hunter groaned and tightened his arms around her. "We can definitely do it again and again and again and again and again, but you're going to have to give me a moment or two to recover first. I'm sure I'll be up to the job soon."

She knew he was amused, but she wasn't quite sure why. No matter, though. She just loved that she could make him smile. She loved that she'd brought humor and light to his life, especially after everything he'd been through since almost dying in that fire. She loved his courage and his heart.

In fact, she was starting to believe that she might be falling in love with him. Falling so hard, so fast into love with a man who was nothing at all like what she'd ever imagined on those rare occasions when she had dreamed of meeting someone to share her life with—it was scary.

But, somehow, her heart was beginning to be convinced that he was everything that she'd never known she needed.

The phone started buzzing again, and this time she didn't have to worry about whose phone it was, because a few seconds later a second phone started buzzing.

Hunter's gaze sharpened, and he sat up. "It must be important if they're calling both of us."

He rolled over and grabbed his phone, which had been under the comforter for some reason, and then took hers off the bedside table and handed it to her. Their gazes met with a shared reluctance to open the door to anything that might ruin their time together, but he sighed and answered his.

"Bane? You're calling me on a *phone*?"

It took a moment for Alice to understand the question, but then she remembered that Hunter had mentioned the mental pathway vampires could use to speak to one another when they'd been chatting in the rescue.

"Little Darlings. Alice Darlington speaking," she answered her phone.

"Hey, Alice. It's Ryan. I'm calling you about coming over for movie night tonight."

She glanced up at Hunter, who was making a strange face.

"Seriously," he said into his phone. "You called me about *movie* night? Isn't that a little outside the guy code?"

Alice laughed but then returned her attention to her own call. "I don't know, Ryan, there's a lot to do here—"

"Oh, is that Hunter I hear? Great! Bring him, too. We'll see you in an hour."

Before Alice could even think of an answer, Ryan hung up.

"No, I don't care what kind of popcorn we have. And now I know you're just screwing with me." Hunter flinched at whatever Bane said in response to that, and then he ended the call.

"Let me guess," he said drily. "We're going to movie night."

She sighed. "It looks like it. But that's okay. It will give me a chance to return that ridiculous SUV to Ryan and explain why I can't keep it."

He dropped his phone on the rug and then snatched her phone out of her hand and tossed it onto her dresser. Then he started toward her with a very sexy, very determined look on his face. "What was it you were saying earlier? About 'can we do this again?'"

She struck her sultriest pose and then ruined it by giggling yet again. "But we have to go to movie night. Can we do this in only an hour?"

He threw back his head and laughed. "You know, you have no idea how good you are for my ego. And yes, we can do it in only an hour. Or at least I'll give it my very best try."

She sighed and pretended to look resigned. "Oh, well then. If you insist."

"No, that's okay. If you've changed your mind…"

This time, *she* was the one who pounced on *him*.

• • •

Hunter backed the car around and waited for Alice to come out of the shelter. He couldn't stop smiling and had even caught himself humming. He felt amazing. Like a million bucks. And it wasn't even about the sex—well, it wasn't *only* about the sex—it was about Alice.

About how she made him feel. About the missing piece of a life that he hadn't even realized was so empty before—before he'd almost died.

Before he became a vampire.

For years now, he hadn't even realized how alone he'd been. He'd always enjoyed his work, but a life lived with work at the center of it was hollow. He had good friends, too; it was true. But it had been a long time since he'd been in a close relationship, and he'd never been close enough to any woman to feel the things he felt for Alice after only such a short time.

It didn't make sense, and he didn't care. Maybe being a vampire had intensified his feelings, or maybe the answer was simply Alice. Her strength and her beauty. Her kindness and her compassion. Her trust and belief in him, and also her willingness to trust anyone, ever, given what she'd been through.

She was incredibly brave and fiercely independent, and he felt honored that she'd allowed him into her life. Not just allowed but welcomed him into her life and her home and her bed. He stared out the windshield at nothing in particular and caught himself humming again, and he was still smiling like a damn fool when she came out of the shelter, spoke to Ian for a moment, and then dashed over to the car and climbed in.

"Charlie says he wants to stay and hang out with Ajax. He's also making friends with Ferret Bueller, strangely enough." She looked thoughtful and a bit concerned. "I hope my understanding of what he means by 'make friends' is the same as his understanding. I'd hate to come back and find out that what he really wanted was a crispy ferret snack."

"Charlie *told* you he wants to stay? Henry didn't hear him, did he?"

Alice had told him that Henry volunteered every Sunday afternoon so she could have some time to herself, which—although she hadn't said it—was why she'd had time to come and curl up next to Hunter for a nap. He made a mental note to buy Henry a bottle of scotch.

Or a house.

She laughed. "No, Charlie is careful about that. But Pete did hear, which is okay, because he knows all about Charlie. All the wolves do, he said. He told me he'll keep a special eye on our little dragon, although he used the other D word."

Hunter leaned over and kissed her. He couldn't help himself. She was so damn beautiful, and, with her face glowing like that, she looked like a goddess. He hoped that he'd been a big part of causing the joy on her face.

No, he didn't hope. He *knew* he had. Whatever insecurities he hadn't realized he'd been carrying around, after all those times of being told he was only a buddy or too nice to take seriously—those insecurities had disappeared, or at least packed their bags and prepared to move out. He grinned. Evidently happiness was contagious.

Then he tried to focus on what she'd been talking about. Oh, right. "Yeah, Pete seems like a good guy."

Alice fastened her seat belt, nodding. "I like him a lot. He's a quiet person, never says much. But he's very calm and gentle with the animals, and they respond to that very well. He said that after this issue with the Chamber and the Institute is resolved, he'd like to be added to my volunteer roster. I think he has his eye on Cleo, too, which surprised me. I don't know why. I guess I wouldn't have thought a cat would like a werewolf. But she loves him, and he's very good with her."

"Who knew?" He put the car in drive and headed for the gate. "Cats and werewolves. Speaking of surprises, I also can't believe we let ourselves be dragged into movie night when we could've stayed home in bed and played indoor games."

He snuck a glance at her and saw that she was blushing again, which made him smile. "You can't keep blushing after I've seen and touched and tasted every part of your body, sweetheart."

Her face turned even pinker, but then she raised her chin and put on a fake posh voice. "Yes. I'm definitely a wanton, jaded woman now. With all my experience and everything, you know. I might teach classes."

Then she spoiled the effect with that charming giggle he'd heard from her for the first time only a little over an hour before.

"Well, if you do teach classes, please sign me up as your one and only student," he said lightly, forcing away the uncomfortable feeling in his gut at the idea of her with anyone else but him. He might be a vampire, but he wasn't a Neanderthal.

"It's a deal."

On the drive to the mansion, they chatted, getting to know each other even more. What kinds of foods they liked, their favorite restaurants—Alice hadn't been to very many, because she put all of her money back into the rescue. What he liked about his job and whether he thought he might go back to it now that everything had changed.

"Well, they'd certainly be happy to have someone who wanted to work the night shift all the time," he said ruefully. "I just don't know how long I could hide being a vampire from everyone."

When she didn't answer, he glanced over and saw the surprise on her face.

"What is it?"

"It's just— I mean, what are you talking about, how long you could hide it? Won't everyone realize there's something different right away when they see your eyes glowing?"

"Right. I forgot you can see that. Before I met you, I thought only vampires, werewolves, and angel kin could see the glowing eyes. Normal humans can't."

Alice shook her head. "This conversation is so bizarre. You know, sometimes I'm just fine, and then other times I feel just how much my life has turned upside down when I catch myself in the middle of surreal conversations like this about which kind of supernatural creature can tell that a vampire's eyes glow."

He laughed, steered the SUV expertly around a tourist trolley bus, and continued toward Bane and Meara's house. "I know exactly what you mean. I've known about vampires for a while, of course, because I happened to rescue Meara from being caught out after dawn once, a few years back. For whatever reason, they didn't try to wipe my memory. In fact, Bane and I started up a monthly chess game. But since it happened to me—since I became a vampire myself—everything is so much more immediate, if that makes sense."

He suddenly wondered why he hadn't realized how lonely he'd been for so long, to the point where his closest friendship had been with a vampire he only saw once a month for a chess game. Funny how being with Alice—feeling such almost-overwhelming happiness—had allowed him to see the sadness that had been hiding beneath the surface of his life even before he'd been Turned.

She put a hand on his arm; for comfort or in solidarity, he didn't know, but he didn't care which it was. He was just happy that she was touching him.

"Yes. It makes perfect sense," she said in her gorgeous, husky voice. "I've been able to see ghosts and talk to them and communicate with animals since I was about eight years old. But it's only since I met you last week and learned about this whole other supernatural community that I feel like the world really is entirely different from the way ninety-eight percent of the people on the planet imagine it to be."

"Maybe not ninety-eight percent. I keep meeting more and more people who know. For example, I didn't even know ghosts were real," he told her. "I just thought all those reports of weird noises and houses were all about old wood shifting or plumbing problems."

She looked at him in disbelief. "I can't imagine what that's like, not to believe in ghosts. I've had to live with them as part of my life for so many years."

He braked for a student driver and tapped the steering wheel with his fingers. "This is a strange segue, but I actually was going to talk to you about your plumbing. I kept hearing knocking noises in the basement pipes all day."

Alice groaned. "That's not great. Fixing the plumbing is definitely not in my budget. Although, I guess with the check that Meara gave me, I might be okay. I'm using all of her money for the rescue, of course," she hastened to add. "But since I won't have to pour all of my own money back in, at least for a little while, I might be able to afford a plumber."

"You don't even take a salary, do you?"

She snorted. "Like there's money for that. I'm lucky to be able to pay Veronica, and I have to give her far less than she's worth. But maybe…maybe things are looking up."

He wrapped his hand around hers, brought it to his lips, and kissed her fingers. "Things are definitely looking up for me. And hold off on that plumber. I'm actually pretty handy, and I'd be glad to take a look and see what we're dealing with. If it's too complicated, we'll call in the professionals. But if it's something simple, I'll be able to handle it myself."

"I can't ask you to do that," she said, sounding shocked.

"You *didn't* ask me to do it. I volunteered. That's what friends do, you know."

"No, I didn't actually know. I haven't really ever had any friends," she said in a voice filled with so much sadness that his heart ached. "But I'm trying to change that. Is that what we are, Hunter? Friends?"

He gave her a very direct look before quickly turning his gaze back to the road, because, while he was sure *he* could survive a car accident, he sure as hell didn't want to involve her in one. "I hope we're far more than friends."

Her smile lit up the world—at least his world—and he held her hand all the rest of the way to the mansion.

• • •

Wow.

Nobody could say that Alice's life hadn't changed completely. Here it was Sunday night, and she was arriving at a vampire mansion for movie night. With her…boyfriend?

No, too soon.

With the man who had only a short while before so deliciously relieved her of her virginity. She smiled a secret smile and unbuckled her seat belt, and then he was already around to her side of the car, opening the door.

True, she was a little sore in places where she'd never been sore before, but every time she'd shifted in her seat on the drive over, she'd started smiling all over again.

She'd caught Hunter humming a couple of times, too, so she hoped very much that he shared her happiness, because making love with him had been absolutely wonderful. She still couldn't believe that she'd had not one, not two, but *three* orgasms during her very first time.

That she had was all about him. The care he'd taken with her; his patience. His absolute focus on her pleasure. She felt so lucky to have had the experience with Hunter, when she thought of how badly her first time could have gone.

She'd been imprisoned and isolated for much of her life, it was true, but since she'd escaped, she'd read books. She'd watched movies. She knew very well, even if she didn't have friends to talk about such things with, that first times rarely went well and almost *never* went brilliantly, like hers had.

"I was part of it, too," she said out loud, a feeling of epiphany washing over her. Sometimes she needed to remind herself that she was a valuable person in charge of her own life and future. She'd spent far too long being told that everything she did was wrong and that she had no worth to anyone except for how they could use her powers.

Hunter, walking beside her from the car to the house, slanted a puzzled look at her. "You were part of what, too?"

"I was part of making those orgasms happen," she said, just as Ryan opened the door.

Hunter made a muffled sound that she *knew* must be laughter, and she could feel her face flame so hot that she knew it must be turning a hideous beet-red color, based on prior experience.

She considered her options and then laughed, shrugging. "So, angels don't have any way to make somebody disappear from sheer embarrassment, do they? Because I could *really* use that right now."

Ryan grinned at them and then put her hands over her ears. "I'm sorry, did you say something to me? I have a very rare medical condition that has rendered me completely unable to hear anyone or anything for the past five minutes. I'm sure it will clear up soon, if you want to hang around for movie night. But now? Nothing."

Impulsively, Alice hugged the smiling doctor. "It's no wonder everyone loves you."

Ryan hugged her back, giving Hunter a sly glance. "If only I *had* been able to hear anything, I might've said apparently everybody loves you, too, Alice. But since I have this temporary hearing loss, I'm just going to say welcome back to our home. I'm so glad you came. You can team up with me against Meara. She has terrible taste in movies, and she misunderstands the ones she does like. When we first met, she had the nerve to tell me she liked *Pride and Prejudice* mostly because of the way Elizabeth only fell in love with Mr. Darcy after she saw how big his house was."

Alice looked at her with interest. "Who's Mr. Darcy? Is he one of the werewolves?"

CHAPTER TWENTY-NINE

After Hunter kissed her cheek and excused himself to go to his room and change clothes, Alice stared—gawked, really—at everything in sight. She'd only seen the kitchen before, which was amazing, but just a kitchen. The impact of the whole house…wow. It really was a freaking mansion.

From what little she could remember of her life before the Institute, her family had been very poor. They'd lived in a trailer, but not one of the nice ones with little flower gardens and fresh coats of paint, like their neighbors. Looking back on it with an adult eye, which she tried never to do, she'd long since realized that her parents must've had a drug problem and probably had been criminals, maybe to support the habit. There had often been sketchy people over to visit, and somtimes her mama had ordered her to her room to play the "hide in your closet" game.

That was before she'd started talking to ghosts, of course. Then there had been the eight years in the Institute, in a room like a cell, with white walls and steel bars.

Now, she'd found her beautiful house, and she loved it, but this—this was a mansion. And the only thing even remotely like it that she'd ever been inside was the Telfair Academy building downtown, which had originally been a family home.

When they entered the house, the first thing she saw was a gorgeous, wide staircase that led to what Ryan told her was the ballroom.

The *ballroom*.

Because of course vampires had a ballroom.

For tonight, though, they'd transformed it into a movie room. The huge screen seemed out of place in a building filled with so much beautiful old polished wood paneling and floors, marble tables, and crystal lamps and vases. There were even those old-fashioned wall lights with hand-blown glass.

"I know. It's a lot," Ryan said quietly. "I spent most of my time wandering around lusting over furniture when I first met Bane."

Alice appreciated the attempt to make her feel less like a country bumpkin come to the big city, but she had to laugh. "You forget—I've met Bane. I doubt it was the *furniture* you were so interested in."

Bane, tall, blond, and sexy in a terrifying "don't make me kill you" kind of way, was almost as gorgeous as Hunter—not that she'd ever tell either of them that.

Before Ryan could answer, Meara stalked into the ballroom, holding a DVD case in each hand.

"So, this is called the *Blade* trilogy," she said, not bothering with *hello*. Maybe greeting people wasn't a vampire thing. "From what I can tell, it's about a vampire who hates vampires and tries to kill them. Which is a clear and classic case of self-loathing. So, is this a three-movie set about his search for a good psychiatrist? Because that would bore the crap out of me."

Ryan started laughing. "Not exactly. It's actually about—"

"*This* series, on the other hand, is about a billionaire who throws his money away by cloning or somehow creating dinosaurs, especially the ultimate-predator types, and then stuffs humans on an island with them for the dinosaurs to snack on. I don't really understand why this would be sufficient plot for more than one movie. Are humans so stupid that you keep volunteering to be the snacks?" Meara aimed an accusing stare at Alice, as if she wanted her to defend the entire action-movie genre or humanity in general.

"Well, I—"

Edge walked into the room, carrying two enormous bowls of popcorn. "Hello, Alice. Where's Hunter?"

So much for her theory of vampire greetings or the lack thereof.

"I'm here," Hunter said, walking into the room and heading straight toward her. "Meara and popular culture are kind of hit-or-miss."

"As I said," Ryan crowed.

"I guess I'm with Meara," Alice told them cheerfully. "We weren't allowed TV or movies in the Institute, in case it interfered with our 'treatment.' So I actually have no idea what either of those series of movies is about. We could watch Harley Quinn in *Birds of Prey*. I just discovered it. It's this great movie about a woman who wears amazing clothes and likes hyenas but hates clowns." She looked around the room, though, because that had puzzled her. "Doesn't everybody hate clowns?"

For some reason, Edge carefully put the popcorn bowls down on a table, smacked himself in the forehead, really hard, and strode out of the room, muttering something under his breath.

Hunter looked like he was trying really hard not to

laugh, but at least he stayed in the room. She wondered what she'd gotten wrong this time, even though it couldn't be about the clowns.

She shivered. *Nobody* liked clowns.

Anyway, before she could ask Hunter what she'd said that was so funny, Bane flew into the room.

Literally *flew* into the room—the second-story room—through an open window.

She whirled around and stared at Hunter. "Vampires can fly? You can *fly*, and you didn't tell me? I might not ever forgive you for this."

He looked sheepish and mumbled something beneath his breath.

"I don't think she caught that, little brother," Meara said, grinning at him.

Hunter sighed. "Fine. Maybe I can fly, or maybe I can't. So far, I've only been able to levitate up off the floor a few feet. And since I'm not reckless, like angel girl over there, I'm not going to jump off the roof to find out."

There was a lot there to unpack, so Alice focused on the important part. "You can *levitate*?"

Meara rolled her eyes. "Of course he can fly. He's just been too busy wandering around being all emotional over turning into a vampire to focus on it. I think he only needs the proper incentive to discover his abilities." With that, she gestured with one hand toward Alice, who immediately started floating up through the air until the top of her head touched the ceiling.

The ceiling that was maybe twenty feet above the floor.

"Put her down, Meara," Hunter growled. "You'll frighten her."

Everybody looked up at Alice, who grinned and gave them two thumbs-up. "This. Is. *Awesome!*"

Meara looked at Alice and back at Hunter, then strolled out of the room. "I'm going to go get more snacks," she said. "If you want her down, get her yourself, Hunter."

"If you want me, come and claim me," Alice said, giggling, knowing that Hunter would get the *Lord of the Rings* reference.

He smiled at her but then looked at Bane, who raised an eyebrow, saying nothing. Ryan grabbed a handful of popcorn and shoved it in her mouth, probably to keep from offering suggestions or advice.

"Fine." Hunter closed his eyes for a moment, his face fixed in an expression of fierce concentration. Then he opened his eyes, looked up at Alice, and leapt into the air.

Whatever he'd done before, this was far more than merely levitating. He shot all the way up to the ceiling and hovered there, holding his hands out to Alice.

"I guess you *can* fly."

"Apparently I can," he said drily. "On the other hand, I don't know if there's much I wouldn't try to do for you."

His confession winged its way across the space between them and straight into her heart.

There wasn't much he wouldn't do for her.

She realized she felt exactly the same way about him, but now was not the time to tell him, because she had a feeling she might cry when she did. Instead, she took his hands.

"Okay, then let's jump out the window!"

Beneath them, Ryan started laughing, and Bane groaned. "Not another one."

• • •

Hunter sat on the floor, leaning back against Alice's knees, content to let the conversation wash over him. They'd started and stopped the movie—the original *Ghostbusters*, in honor of Alice, who had never seen the entire thing—three or four times now in order to debate whatever ridiculous thing came up.

This time, it was about the physics of the Stay-Puft Marshmallow Man.

Edge, the scientist, was firmly on the side of: It was physiologically impossible for such a creature to exist. Something about height-to-weight ratio or mass-to-marshmallow ratio or something. Hunter had tuned out after the first five minutes, especially when Alice started stroking his head.

Meara, naturally, was on the opposite side of any argument that involved Edge.

Alice had admitted she had never eaten a marshmallow, so now she and Ryan had decided to head down to the kitchen and see if they had the supplies to make s'mores. Alice leaned over and kissed the top of Hunter's head, and he didn't think she even realized what she'd done, but everybody else in the room certainly did.

They all stared at him exactly the way he'd look at somebody he caught punching a kitten.

He had the feeling that he was in for a long conversation of the ass-kicking kind, at least with Bane.

"Are you coming?" Alice hopped up and followed Ryan to the doorway.

"Actually," Bane said when Hunter stood up. "We need to talk to Hunter for a minute about some business matters."

"Sure." Alice smiled and blew Hunter a kiss, then ran lightly down the stairs after Ryan.

"What did you do?" Bane's frown was forbidding, but Hunter was made of sterner stuff than to fall apart because a master vampire frowned at him. Especially when he kept kicking the master vampire in question's ass in chess on a regular basis.

"That's none of your business," Hunter told him. "And, before you ask, Meara, it's none of your business, either. But I love you for whatever you were about to say."

She walked over and hugged him and then kissed him on the cheek. "You're both adults. Since you don't want to hear it, I won't tell you to be careful with her. I won't even say that her life hasn't prepared her for a lot of the things in our world."

"Nice of you not to say it," he drawled. "On the other hand, her life prepared her for more than I've ever had to handle. So maybe it would be good if people started to realize just how incredibly strong she is."

"Well said," Meara said admiringly.

Bane made a dismissive gesture. "Fine. Enough of that. We need to talk about your accounts."

"What accounts?" He looked at them, puzzled. "Oh. Should I be paying rent, since I'm living here now? Sure. Just tell me how much. I'll give you money for the time I've already been here, too. I think I need to move back into my apartment, though—"

Meara started laughing, cutting him off.

Bane didn't laugh—he looked insulted. "Of course you don't have to pay rent. As a new member of our family, we have opened new accounts for you. Online banking, since you now can't go into a bank during the day."

Hunter still didn't understand what they were getting at. "Well, I appreciate that, I guess, but I already have online accounts. Everybody has online accounts now. Nobody goes into the bank anymore. And my paychecks are direct deposit."

Meara patted his arm. "You're not getting this. Let me be direct. We opened an account for you and put in an initial deposit of five million dollars. Edge will give you the access codes." She turned to Bane. "Now can we get back to the movie?"

Hunter, meanwhile, felt like they'd teamed up and punched him in the throat. "Wait! Wait just a minute. What are you talking about? I don't need any accounts. I sure as hell am not going to take five million dollars from you."

"Oh. Is that not enough?" Meara tapped one slender finger against her lips. "I can transfer more—up to ten—but since today is Sunday it will have to wait till tomorrow."

"No! You're not understanding me. *No* millions of dollars! I won't take any money at all from you. I can carry my own weight."

Meara glared at him and poked him in the chest. "You saved my life. Putting aside any false humility, my life is worth far more than a few million dollars. We created this new existence for you when we Turned you. Do you really think we will let you suffer for it?"

Hunter felt like he was flailing and didn't understand why, because he was clearly in the right in this conversation.

"There's a big difference between suffering and five million dollars. I won't take it. Use it for your clinic or for one of your charities. Which I am *not*. A charity, that is." He felt himself getting angry and tried to tamp it down.

Five million dollars. What the *hell*?

He knew Meara cared about him, but she didn't necessarily have a contemporary understanding of things. In fact, she was standing there with silvery tears glistening in her lashes. "You're throwing this back in my face? Fine. You've hurt my feelings. I'm leaving. When I get my feelings hurt, I have to go eat a tourist." She turned on her heel and started to stalk from the room.

"No!" He ran after her. "Meara, I'm so sorry. I didn't mean to hurt your feelings. But I can't take money from you."

Meara slanted a sideways glance at him and started laughing. "I'm just kidding. I'm not going to go eat any tourists. There are never many around on Sunday evenings, anyway."

Ryan and Alice, who were walking up the stairs with a platter of s'mores, stared at the pair of them. Alice's eyes were wide, and her mouth was hanging open just a tiny bit.

He understood the reaction. He felt the exact same way.

Ryan just gave him a rueful grin and shook her head. "Welcome to my world. I went from struggling to pay my student loans and the tiny car payment on my Prius to this." She waved her left hand in the air, and Hunter noticed the enormous diamond ring that he could've sworn she hadn't been wearing the day before.

"It's easier to just let them do it sometimes. You have to pick your battles," she said as she passed him.

Alice mouthed the words *what the heck* at him as she followed Ryan into the ballroom.

Bane took the s'mores platter from Ryan and put it down on a table, and then he pulled her close. "Speaking of your Prius—as I've told you several times, it's not safe. I've acquired a more appropriate car for you. It's brand-new, so it has a warranty, and it's much safer."

Ryan smiled up at Bane so sweetly that Hunter, who was far more familiar with independent human women then Bane was, winced and took a step back.

Better to be out of the splatter zone.

"Just what kind of car would you consider to be safe enough for me, my love? A Humvee? A tank? A bullet-proof presidential limo?"

Bane looked thoughtful. "I can buy one of those?"

Hunter shrugged. "I can look into it, but I doubt—"

Ryan actually growled at them, which was kind of funny, sort of like a mouse growling at a pair of lions, except for the fact that he and Bane both took careful steps back.

"No, we cannot buy a *presidential limo*. And I'm keeping my Prius. I bought it myself, and it has a lot of good years still in it."

"Don't argue with me," Bane said in exactly the kind of tone that meant he might be sleeping on the couch that night. "I bought you a BMW SUV. It's a far better car."

"I wouldn't dream of arguing with you about it," Ryan said, her voice dripping with sincerity.

Hunter winced. "Oh, boy."

Bane, wisely, looked suspicious. "Then where is it?"

"Where is what, darling?"

"The SUV, Ryan," Bane said through gritted teeth.

"Where is the SUV?"

Ryan smiled, triumphant. "I gave it to Alice."

Alice, who had been following the conversation with her head turning back and forth like she was a spectator at a tennis match, dropped the s'more she'd been about to bite into. Hunter reached out, caught it before it fell, and popped it in his mouth.

"Oh, no," Alice said. "Don't get me involved in this. I've already told you and anyone else who would listen that I can't accept that car."

Ryan patted Alice's arm and then handed Hunter a napkin. "Of course you can accept it. You need a safe car. What if you're out buying groceries or something and there's an injured animal lying in the middle of the road? Are you going to try to transport it in that crappy old van you have? Where's your sense of responsibility to the animals?"

"But I—"

"She won't have that crappy van for long," Meara called out, returning. "The new transport vehicle should arrive by Friday."

"Good," Hunter said with considerable satisfaction. He hated the idea of Alice driving somewhere in an unsafe vehicle during the day, when he couldn't protect her. He sat down on the couch and pulled her down onto his lap, arms wrapped around her waist. Her cheeks turned pink, but she didn't jump away from him, which he counted as a win.

Still, though, she kept trying to protest. "No, you don't understand—"

Bane threw his hands in the air. "Fine. Alice needs a safe car. She keeps the BMW, of course. But what happened to the Volvo I bought you last week?"

Ryan kissed his cheek. "I gave it to my friend Annie."

Bane just stared at her, speechless.

"You gave it to me, right?" Ryan said sweetly.

"Yes, but I— "

Ryan turned to Edge, who'd just come back in the room. "And it's titled in my name, right? Or at least until you arranged the title transfers of the Volvo to Annie and the SUV to Alice, right?"

Edge nodded, a resigned look on his face.

"There you go. Listen, she's my best friend, and she needs a safe car. Hers is about to fall apart."

"How did you explain a present like that?" Meara asked with interest.

Ryan waved her diamond ring around again. "Easiest thing in the world. I'm marrying a rich guy who's very generous."

"Well, *that's* certainly true," Alice mumbled, looking shell-shocked.

Hunter narrowed his eyes. "I'm very generous. And *way* better looking than Bane."

"Everybody's very generous," Alice said, giving him an exasperated look. "But I can't take a personal car from you, Ryan. It's too much. It's just…too much. Don't you see? And Meara, the van—it's a lot, too. Are you sure? I mean, the rescue really needs one, but I don't want to feel like I'm taking and taking from new friends."

Meara scowled and started pacing around the room, and Hunter was pretty damn sure she was swearing, quite inventively, in French. He didn't remember a lot from his high school language class, but…

He whistled and gave Meara an admiring glance. "The

rescue van is the unnatu

Really? Harsh, my friend.

but that's harsh."

Alice scooted over so she w

not on his lap, but she didn't pu

with it. She glanced up at him.

goose."

He rested his head back on th

laughing. "Of course you did."

CHAPTER THIRTY

"Okay. Enough already about the cars," Ryan said firmly. "The rescue gets the van, Alice gets the SUV, Annie gets the Volvo, and I keep my Prius. Any arguments? No? Good." She grabbed the remote and clicked the movie back on, as if saying the discussion was over.

When she put the remote down on the table, though, Bane gestured with his index finger, and the movie paused as the remote rose up off the table and floated through the air toward him. Hunter snatched it out of the air as it went by and started the movie.

Bane gave him a look. "I can just as easily levitate the screen all the way out the window."

Hunter put the movie back on pause. He liked that screen.

Alice looked like she didn't know whether to start laughing or stand up and run out of the house.

"It's like this a lot around here," Hunter confided.

"No wonder you like sleeping in my basement."

Everybody except Ryan turned to look at Alice.

Meara tapped her ears. "Remember that whispering is not really effective in a room full of vampires. Werewolves are the same way, just for future reference."

"How about that volleyball game," Alice said brightly. "That was so much fun. We should do that again."

Hunter looked at her in disbelief. "I thought you hated volleyball."

"Work with me," she hissed.

Ryan happily went along. "It was great, but I need to get a sturdier ball. I thought the Kevlar was a great idea, but apparently it's not tough enough."

Bane gave Ryan a look that said he knew perfectly well what she was doing but was going to let her get away with it, at least for now. Then everyone started debating the merits of different kinds of vampire-proof volleyballs. A few minutes later, Mrs. Cassidy bustled up the stairs, her husband right behind her, and they brought trays of freshly baked cookies with them.

The housekeeper walked right over to Alice and offered them to her first. "That was so scary, what happened with the ghosts, dear. I hope you're okay."

"Thank you. I've been dealing with ghosts for a very long time, so it doesn't bother me as much anymore, but that was definitely out of the ordinary."

Mrs. C laughed. "I never had the choice *not* to believe in ghosts, since I grew up in a house of vampires, but I've never interacted with any."

Alice gave her a puzzled glance. "Really? So you don't talk to the ghost who lives here?"

• • •

When everyone stopped talking and stared at Alice, she knew she'd blown it again. She was always careful never to speak of the supernatural with ordinary people, but she had thought that she was free to talk about such things here, with these people.

"I'm so sorry, Mrs. Cassidy. I hope I didn't frighten you. It's just that seeing ghosts is so much a part of my normal everyday existence that sometimes I don't remember that's not true of everybody."

The older woman, who had gone pale, rallied and gave her a smile.

"That's fine, dear. But there aren't really ghosts in this house, are there?" She looked around the room, but all the vampires shook their heads.

"I've never seen any," Meara said. "Are you sure, Alice?"

"It's not just some weird electrical resonance or something?" Edge put in.

Alice started to get defensive, but then she realized that they were asking because they truly wanted to know, not because they were mocking her abilities. "Yes, I'm sure. Believe me, this has been my life for twenty years. I know a ghost when I see one. In fact, she looks a lot like you, Mrs. Cassidy."

The housekeeper dropped her tray, but Hunter reached out with lightning-quick reflexes and caught it before it hit the ground. He didn't even lose any of the cookies. He carefully set it down on the table and took Mrs. Cassidy's arm, then led her to one of the chairs.

"I'm so silly," she said. "I can't believe I reacted like that. It's just that my mother—well, she's been gone for almost ten years, but people always said I was the spitting image of her." A tear rolled down her plump cheek. "It's my mother, still here as a ghost. It must be. That means she didn't go to heaven. She didn't pass on. What could be wrong?"

Alice felt terrible to have caused the woman such

obvious pain and agitation, and she hurried to correct the misimpression. "No, it's not like that. Some ghosts, yes, they're stuck here on this plane for some reason. But others—the majority of the ones who are actually roaming around—they're not really ghosts as much as they are a sort of residual echo of energy that the person left behind. Often in their homes, where they felt the most loved and at peace." She gestured to where the ghost who was almost certainly Mrs. Cassidy's mother stood with a feather duster by a maple desk. "I wish you could see her. The energy is really just an echo of the lovely woman she was in life."

Tommy spoke up for the first time since the conversation started. "You can tell that? You can tell what kind of person she is?"

Alice shrugged but then nodded. "Yes. Kind of. It's like the auras that humans have, or so I've heard. I can't see the auras of living people. You can tell when a person is basically peaceful, just like you can tell when someone is angry or violent."

Mrs. Cassidy looked all around the room as if trying to see what Alice saw, but of course she saw nothing.

Alice pointed to the desk. "She's been standing there cleaning that desk with a feather duster ever since I first got here tonight, but I caught sight of her in the kitchen yesterday. If I hadn't realized how much she looks like you, I would've thought she had been a maid in this house in the past, perhaps."

"She did love that little desk," Mrs. Cassidy said fondly. "It was actually her desk, where she would write out her lists for the week. She told me it would be mine when she was gone and to take special care of it, and I always have."

Almost before Mrs. Cassidy finished speaking, the echo of her mother looked up and caught Alice's gaze with hers. This had never happened before with a ghost who was such a faint echo, but when it had happened with stronger manifestations, it was because the person had a message for someone still living.

Alice mentally weighed the pros and cons of trying to communicate with this particular ghost, who clearly had something to say. She didn't want to upset the housekeeper any further, but on the other hand, maybe there was something important for her to know.

Hunter, as if realizing she needed support, tightened his arm around her. "Are you okay?"

It was almost funny how much that meant to her, because no one had ever thought to ask her that. They all only wanted to know about the ghosts. What the ghosts looked like, what the ghosts wanted.

Nobody ever asked what the ghost whisperer wanted.

She smiled a little when she realized she was using the label that Meara had given her. But then she turned toward Mrs. Cassidy. "Actually, and I hope this won't upset you, but your mother has just communicated with me that she has something to say. Would it be okay with you if I try to listen?"

"If I couldn't tell when a human was lying," Bane said slowly, "I might be tempted to think you were a scam artist."

Alice didn't know if the words were a warning or a threat, but she didn't care. They were in her arena now, and she was powerful here. Hunter, however, she had to restrain from jumping up and doing who knows what to his friend, the master vampire.

Mrs. Cassidy held tightly to her husband's hand and then nodded with a great deal of dignity. "Yes, child. If you can hear whatever it is my sweet mother—or her echo—wants to say, please do."

Alice nodded and closed her eyes to center herself. Then she took a deep breath and walked over to where the ghost still dusted the desk. Hunter kept her hand in his, and she held on tight.

The ghost, still maintaining eye contact with Alice, smiled at her, and the smile was identical to Mrs. Cassidy's, banishing any hint of doubt that might've remained in Alice's mind.

"Spirit. Speak to me, and you will be heard." Simple words, but she'd found through trial and error that simple was the most effective with ghosts, especially ones that were so faintly manifested.

The ghost communicated her message, then floated across the room and touched her daughter on the cheek. After that, she floated toward a growing circle of light that had appeared against the far wall.

Alice watched, in awe as always, as the familiar scene played out. The ghost or, in this case, the echo of a woman's personality slowly passed from this realm to the next. When the glowing gateway closed, Alice exhaled slowly and then turned back to face the group.

"It was very simple, really—"

Mrs. Cassidy interrupted her, holding one hand to her face. "Did she just touch me on the cheek? I could have sworn I felt it."

Alice nodded. "Yes, she did, on her way to the Golden

doorway. The echo of your mother has passed on now, I think to merge with the rest of her being, but I'm no metaphysical expert. I think most people who claim to be are really just the scam artists Bane is worried about."

Edge, looking as fascinated as everyone else in the room, in spite of his scientific leanings, leaned forward. "Well? Did she tell you anything?"

Alice nodded and gestured toward the desk. "She said to tell you that you are her sweet girl, and she is so proud of you," she told Mrs. C. "And she also said to tell you that she hid her pearls in a velvet box in her later years, when she was getting forgetful. Then she forgot to tell you where they were. Evidently there is a secret drawer in this desk that you access from the right lower panel."

Mrs. Cassidy gasped and then burst into tears. Ryan rushed to hug her and hand her a box of tissues, and they all waited for her to calm down. When she finally did, wiping her eyes, she smiled at Alice.

"Well, that certainly answers the question of whether or not you're telling the truth, young lady. When I was a little girl, I used to play on the floor next to her desk when she was working. She would keep a box of crayons in the drawer for me and said it was our secret. I always felt so special."

Her husband helped her to her feet, and they walked over to the desk. She bent down and pressed on a spot exactly where the ghost had indicated, and a tiny drawer popped open. She put in her hand, then pulled out a velvet box, and, of course, when she opened it, a beautiful triple-strand pearl necklace was inside.

Everyone burst into spontaneous applause, much of it

directed at Alice, who simply smiled and nodded, trying not to let them see the sadness on her face. When they all gathered around Mrs. Cassidy to see the drawer and admire the pearls, Hunter followed Alice back to the couch, where she curled up in a corner.

He leaned close and spoke to her in a very quiet voice. "Are you really okay?"

She sighed. "I'm fine. It drains a little of my energy to communicate with them, but not a lot in this case. It's not that, so much. It's what Mrs. Cassidy said."

He tilted his head, clearly trying to understand. "But she said you were clearly telling the truth."

"Yes." She sighed and blinked back the tears. "But, you see, I already knew that."

She could see from the look in his eyes that he understood immediately, and for once in her life, after using her gift, she didn't feel so alone.

CHAPTER THIRTY-ONE

Hunter wrapped his arms around Alice and pulled her so close she was practically sitting in his lap again, and he managed to persuade her to watch the movie with him just like that. As the minutes passed, he felt her relaxing, until she was finally laughing and throwing popcorn at the screen with Meara and Ryan. Just after the demon Zuul showed up—and, damn, but Sigourney Weaver was hot in this movie—Bane took a phone call.

Hunter leaned over to whisper in Alice's ear. "Now I know why I like this movie so much. She has the same wild curly hair as you."

A burbling laugh escaped before Alice clamped her hand over her mouth. When everyone stopped looking at them, she turned to whisper back to him. "Now I know why you want me. I'm fulfilling your twisted Ripley fixation. I watched *all* the *Alien* movies."

He pretended to think about it, and she elbowed him.

Just then, Bane's terse communication came through on the telepathic channel:

WE HAVE CONTACT. SOME OF THE CLUB MEMBERS FOUND ANOTHER PLACE. THIS ONE HAS CHAMBER MEMBERS HIDING OUT. A LITTLE HOLE-IN-THE-WALL APARTMENT BUILDING. I'M HEADING OUT THERE NOW TO INTERROGATE THE TWO WARLOCKS OUR PEOPLE FOUND INSIDE.

Edge's voice sounded inside Hunter's skull next:

PLEASE TELL ME IT'S NOT THE SAME TWO WE LET GO.

Bane again:

NO. THOSE ARE PROBABLY HALFWAY TO MIAMI BY NOW. THESE WE'VE NEVER SEEN BEFORE. LET'S GET READY TO RIDE.

Meara spoke up from where she sprawled in a comfortable chair. "I'm staying here."

When Ryan and Alice looked confused, Meara shot a narrow-eyed glance at Bane and then spoke to the two women. "What Bane and Hunter haven't told you yet is that they found more Chamber thugs and are off to question them."

Bane glared at his sister. "You didn't give me a chance. I was planning to tell Ryan."

Ryan gave her new fiancé a long, steady look. "Of course you were. Because you weren't trying to protect me in spite of myself, were you? We're never going to have a repeat episode of the locking-me-in-your-room trick, either, are we?"

Bane hesitated, but from the look on his face Hunter could tell that he would absolutely love to protect Ryan from all dangers, in spite of herself or otherwise. In fact, Hunter felt the same way about Alice.

It shouldn't have surprised him that Alice herself was as practical as ever.

"Go," she told him. "I don't have any superpowers and can't jump out of even a first-floor window, so I wouldn't be any good in the situation. I'm sure someone here can give me a ride home."

Meara started to say something, but Hunter pointed at her. "Not you. I'd like for Alice to have a chance of surviving the drive."

"Party pooper."

Downstairs, the doorbell rang, and Ryan jumped up. "Tommy and Mary Jo were getting ready to go to bed, so I'll run down to answer that."

"No, you won't, or at least not alone," Bane said. He caught her around the waist, lifted her into the air, and flew down the stairs.

"That is so cool," Alice said, nudging Hunter, who just shook his head and moved into the hall so he could see who was coming to visit. With all the activity in town and no security camera yet, he wasn't happy about any of them answering the door. He wasn't entirely sure what kind of backup he could be to a master vampire and an angel, but he knew that no matter what happened, nobody was getting through him to Alice.

When they opened the door, Hunter was surprised to recognize the deep, rumbling voice.

Edge walked over to stand next to him. "Did you know that Bane invited the alpha wolf to the party?"

Hunter shook his head. "No. But if I'm not mistaken, the beta wolf has come as well."

Alice spoke from behind him. "I'll be happy to see Max. She's lucky that she can heal so quickly from such a dangerous injury."

When he turned and saw the expression on her face, Hunter instantly wanted to murder whoever had harmed her in the past. But he didn't say that. Instead, he answered the question she'd meant to ask, not the one hidden behind the surface of her words.

"Vampires have pretty wild healing properties as well. It's the main reason I survived being burned nearly to death. The Turn healed me."

Alice reached up and touched his face. "Be careful. Do you hear me? I don't want to lose you after I just found you."

He found himself humbled by her openness and sincerity. He owed it to her to give her back the same. "I don't want to lose you, either. I'll be back. No worries on that score. And I won't be gone long, either."

"Well, if that's the case, we're going to have a double feature," Ryan said, linking her arm through Alice's and heading back toward the movie screen, where Meara was now declaring that the Ghostbusters should have fed the mayor to the ghosts.

She wasn't wrong.

Hunter caught up to Alice, swung her around, and pressed a hard, fast kiss to her mouth. "To remember me," he said.

Alice touched her fingers to her lips, smiling. "What was your name again?"

He laughed, dropped a kiss on the top of her head, and followed Edge down the stairs toward Carter Reynolds and Max, who were talking to Bane and Ryan.

"I've asked Max to stay and watch over the women," Reynolds said.

Hunter looked at Max to see how *she* felt about that, but before she could indicate her feelings one way or the other, Ryan smiled that special smile of hers—the one that seemed to be full of teeth. The smile she used with what he thought of as her "Death by Angel" voice, the one that had so much sweetness piled on it she could probably kill the listener with sugar poisoning.

"To watch over *the women*?"

Reynolds backtracked immediately, mumbling something, but Hunter could see he was out of his depth. An alpha wolf *told* the people beneath him—and *everyone* in the pack was beneath him—what to do, when to do it, and even how to do it. It had probably never occurred to him that human women and angel kin would not react the same way.

"Um—"

"I'm perfectly capable of watching over myself, and Meara is, too. If there's anybody who needs watching, we can handle it," Ryan said, her eyes narrowing.

Bane said nothing, letting the werewolf dig himself out of the hole he'd put himself in.

Max, though, reluctantly weighed in. "With all due respect, alpha, I deserve to come with you. I'm the one who got shot yesterday, after all."

"That was about some petty side mission the warlock had taken on. Not about the Chamber. Tonight is about the Chamber, and I want you to stay here and"—he glanced at Ryan—"um—"

Ryan raised an eyebrow.

"Assist the women while they look after themselves," Reynolds finished triumphantly.

Pathetic.

"Fine," Max said, not even attempting to hide her fury. "I'll stay here and watch rom-coms with the little ladies."

"We're actually watching *Ghostbusters*. Alice keeps telling us what the movie is getting wrong," Ryan confided.

At that, Max looked a fraction less disgruntled but certainly not completely satisfied. Luckily for Hunter, the werewolf hierarchy was none of his business.

"Let's go get them." Bane's gaze snapped to him. "Hunter, are you sure you want to be involved in this? We know who you are, and it's someone who *saves* lives, not someone who threatens them. If you want to bow out of this particular job, no one will hold that against you."

Hunter stood his ground. "Not a chance. When they came after Alice, they came after me."

"So soon?" It was Edge's turn to look disgusted. "You just met her! Is every man in this house turning into a lovesick fool?"

"Watch it, Edgington," Bane snapped, but then he gave the scientist a considering look and started to laugh. "From the way you've been acting around my sister, I have a feeling you're going to be singing a different tune very soon."

Edge opened his mouth and then clamped it shut, a dizzying mix of emotions crossing his face.

Max, now reluctantly following Ryan up the stairs, snorted.

"I thought we were coming over to meet with the head of the Vampire Motorcycle Club," she said. "Apparently we've ended up at a taping of *The Real Housewives of Savannah* instead."

Hunter started laughing.

She had a point.

With that, he, Bane, Edge, and Reynolds headed out the door to the Harleys. They all knew a good exit line when they heard one.

• • •

When Ryan walked back into the movie room, or ballroom, or whatever else they'd decided to call a room the size of a basketball court, Alice was surprised to see Max stomping into the room behind her. The werewolf beta seemed to be in perfect health, and she looked badass in her jeans, boots, and leather jacket with a red shirt beneath. You would for sure never have guessed that she'd been shot in the neck so short a time before. Her face, though, was set in angry lines.

"Hey, Max. How are you doing tonight?"

Max glanced up and nodded at Meara before returning Alice's hello.

"I'm perfectly fine, except for the fact that my overprotective alpha keeps trying to keep me away from situations where I should absolutely be involved."

Meara faked a giant yawn. "Surely not," she said mockingly. "A man who thinks he knows better than the women around him, no matter that they're ten times smarter than him and probably more deadly? Say it isn't *so*."

Max laughed, in spite of herself, perhaps, but then she growled with frustration. Or maybe she just growled. Alice still didn't know that much about werewolves.

"Popcorn?" Ryan handed Max the bowl and then got her a beer.

Max thanked her but looked at the beer without much enthusiasm. "I don't mean to be a diva or anything, but do you have anything stronger than this? Not really in a beer mood."

Meara jumped up out of her chair. "Let's make lemon

drop martinis."

"What's that?" Alice was always keen to try new experiences, but a martini sounded a little bit old-fashioned and overly sophisticated for her.

"It's delicious. It's kind of like a vodka martini—"

"But with lemon juice and triple sec or Cointreau," Ryan said. "They're really delicious, but you have to be careful. When something tastes like a punchier version of lemonade, and it's a hot night in Savannah... Well. Let's just say that mistakes can be made." She grinned but refused to say any more about it, even when Meara pressed her.

"That sounds like so much fun. Going out at night with your girlfriends. I've never done that," Alice said wistfully.

All three of them looked at her as if she were an alien, and she started to shrink back into herself, but then she remembered that the new, stronger Alice didn't do that anymore. "Hey, it's not like I've had much opportunity. But I'm willing to try it now. Should we go out somewhere?"

Meara, busily mixing a pitcher of drinks over at an antique bar cart, shook her head.

"Normally I'm the first to suggest a night out on the town. Love to meet tourists and all that. But right now, with all the different forces in play, I think it's better that we keep Alice and Ryan home tonight, don't you, Max?"

"Hey, what do you mean 'and Ryan'? Angel powers here, remember?"

Meara prowled across the room in her ridiculously graceful panther-meets-supermodel manner and handed Alice a martini glass, its rim dipped in sugar.

Alice took a cautious sip and then, delighted, a huge gulp. "It's delicious! I think I'm going to need lots of these."

Ryan patted the air as if to say slow down. "Hold on there, wild child. Have you had much vodka in the past?"

Alice shook her head, happily taking another drink of the delicious cocktail. "No. This is my first time. But now I know I love martinis!"

"Oh, boy." Max accepted a cocktail from Meara and nodded her thanks while still looking at Alice. "You might want to slow down a little. One of my worst hangovers in college had to do with vodka, a football game, and a boy named Bubba, of all ridiculous things."

Ryan's laughter rang through the room. "Oh no. That's impossible. I had a disastrous date with a boy named Bubba, too. It can't possibly be the same Bubba?"

Max slanted a glance at her over the rim of her glass. "Did your Bubba go to Ohio State and play football for the Buckeyes?"

"Definitely not."

Meara returned to the couch, carrying her own glass, and raised it in a toast. "To all the Bubbas in the world. May they find love with women whom they could never possibly deserve."

Alice drained her glass and then giggled when a tiny burp escaped. "But what about those poor women? Then they'll be stuck with husbands named Bubba and a bunch of little Bubbas."

She cracked herself up. And then she decided to pour herself another drink, determined to ignore all advice about moderation. It really hadn't been a moderation kind of week.

"Alice," Ryan said in a friendly tone.

"I know, doc. I *know*. But I really don't want to hear it—

not tonight. It's been a hell of a week, and it sounds like next week isn't going to be any better in terms of bad guys chasing me and shooting my new friends." She raised her glass in Max's direction. "So if I want to have a few lemon drops tonight, when I'm not even driving, I think that's okay."

"Speaking of driving—"

"No! Don't start with this SUV thing again. You people can't just go around giving everybody luxury cars."

Max raised her hand. "You can give me a car, Ryan. My piece-of-shit pickup truck is about to die any minute. I don't make a lot of money as a full-time werewolf and part-time librarian."

Ryan shrugged. "Sure. Any day now, Bane is going to give in to his worst impulses and buy me something new. That one's all yours."

Max punched the air. "Woot! And people said you angels were all bad news."

Alice giggled and finished her second cocktail while still standing right there by the cart and poured herself another. Then she turned to Max in delight. "You're a librarian? I love librarians! I'm not sure I would've survived, either in the Institute or in the years afterward, without libraries. No matter how bad things got, I could always escape into a book. I love the ones with castles and princesses, but I'm also a huge fan of a good, scary thriller."

Meara smiled at her. "I'm not surprised you like books about princesses. With that hair and those eyes, you certainly look like one."

Alice burbled out a laugh. "I don't think you have room to talk about looking like a princess, Miss Supermodel. Just being in the same room with you is enough to give a normal woman an inferiority complex."

"Speak for yourself, ghost girl," Max said. "I am inferior to no one, and you're not exactly normal. None of us are."

Ryan jumped up and opened a large cabinet. The shelves inside held what looked like hundreds of DVDs. "Okay. What movie should we watch? Since we're drinking lemon drops, should we watch *Sex and the City*?"

Meara's smile faded, and she aimed a very direct look at Max. "I think, before we watch another movie, we should discuss the current situation with the Chamber. Max, you seem like the sensible one in the wolf pack."

Max started to protest, but Meara waved that away. "I know, I know. Loyalty to the alpha and all that. But let's be real here. You must realize as much as I do that continuing to go after these minions is doing us no good. The Chamber keeps sending more. We need to take the battle to them. I'm planning to go to England, track Lord Neville down, and rip his evil, blood-magic-practicing heart out."

"Are you inviting me along?" Max narrowed her eyes in thought. "It might be difficult to arrange time off work from both of my jobs, but I think it's doable."

"Do you *need* an invitation?" Meara raised an eyebrow. "To me, you don't seem like the type of woman who would."

Alice, whose grasp of the situation seemed to be getting hazy—but that might have just been the lemon drops—raised her hand. "I want to go to London. I want to meet Sherlock Holmes."

Ryan and Alice traded a glance, and Alice realized they might think she was simple. Or at least naive. "Yes, I *realize* that Sherlock Holmes is a fictional character. Remember what I just said about books? What I'd like to do is go to the Sherlock Holmes Museum. And maybe I can talk to some English ghosts and find out the scoop on this Lord Neville for you."

Ryan, still sorting through movies, grabbed one and held it up with a triumphant look on her face. "Well then, the movie choice is obvious."

Alice looked woefully at her empty glass and then up at Ryan. "It is?"

"*An American Werewolf in London*."

"Winner!"

They spent the next hour or so making fun of the movie and mixing more and more pitchers of cocktails. Alice had finally slowed down after she didn't know how many drinks, but she was still ensconced in a warm haze of sparkling fog and bubbly joy.

That afternoon, she'd made love for the first time ever, and now she was having a movie night with three women who might very well become close friends. Even though people were still trying to kill her, she might actually be having the best time of her life.

Max threw popcorn at the screen and laughed. "Believe me, that is not how being a werewolf works."

"That's what I thought about *Ghostbusters*," Alice said. "Ridiculous!"

"They should have asked you to be a consultant," Ryan said, and all four of them thought that was pretty funny and laughed for a long time. Or maybe that was about the lemon drops, too.

"Vodka might be the devil," Alice said or tried to say. It took a couple of tries to pronounce *vodka*. She blinked.

"Russian words are hard."

"Shush. We're going to wake up Mary Jo and Tommy, and then I'll get another lecture on behaving like a lady, not drinking too much, or that old favorite: Don't snack on the tourists." Meara tossed her hair back out of her face and sighed. "Honestly, it's more than I can bear. I am more than two hundred years older than she is. As it is, we're going to have to vacuum up all this popcorn or get Bram Stoker to eat it, or we'll be in big trouble." She paused the movie and tossed the remote down on the table, then looked at Max. "Okay. On to the important things. Which of the wolves are the most fuckable?"

Alice snorted lemon drop out her nose and then fell over on the couch, laughing hysterically. "I can't believe you just said that!"

"I can't believe you said it, either, but for a different reason," Max said. "You've been around most of us, what with the battle with the necromancer and now the volleyball game. We totally won that, by the way. But I think it's pretty obvious who the hottest wolf in the pack is. Other than me, of course."

Ryan and Meara looked at each other and then at Max.

"Obvious to you," Ryan said, grinning. "Don't think we haven't all noticed the way Carter looks at you. He's got that hot alpha thing going on. Yummy!"

"Yeah. *No*. You think the oh-so-proper alpha would dare to cross the line and get involved with his beta?" Max rolled her eyes. "Absolutely not. And don't think I haven't tried, either, because I certainly have given it my best shot. And my best shot is pretty damn phenomenal. But nothing doing."

Alice sat there listening to every word, her eyes wide with surprise. She'd never thought that real people might talk like this. She knew they did on TV shows, but that was made up. She'd never had actual girlfriends that she could sit around and have girl talk with.

She could feel her face heat up so much that it must be bright red, but she was fascinated.

"Clearly you're not trying hard enough," Meara told Max. "Because that man looks at you like he wants to lick you like an ice cream cone."

"Meara!" Alice said in shocked delight.

"Hey, if you can't talk about men with your girlfriends, who can you talk about them with? Annie and I dissected the relative merits of every straight man who's ever worked at the hospital while we were there. And even some of the patients—not that we would've made a move on patients. It's just what you do." Ryan shrugged. "It's like checking out all the desserts even though you know you're only going to have one."

"Or none," Max said, slumped in a chair. "Yeah, no desserts for me. I can't make a move on any of the wolves who are lower than me in the hierarchy, for pretty much the same reason Carter won't get involved with me. And I haven't met any human guys who interest me enough to take a chance that they might learn our secrets."

"Same here, except worse," Meara said glumly. "Imagine the same problems you have with hiding your true self, then multiply it by never being able to go on a date in the daylight. There sure as hell are not a lot of male vampires around I'd even be interested in. That's why I asked about fuckable werewolves."

All three of them looked at Meara when she said the thing about not being interested in male vampires. Even Alice, who'd only just met them all, knew better than *that*.

But only Max was brave enough to speak out. "Yeah, that's a big lie. The sexual tension between you and that deliciously hot, young, white-haired vampire is enough to set the house on fire. Why don't you tap that?"

"There will definitely be no tapping with Sebastian Edgington," Meara said firmly. "His heart is probably made of chemicals and nanobots."

"You know about nanobots, but you don't know what *Jurassic Park* is?" Ryan shook her head. "Meara, you are a woman of untold depths."

"Yeah. Like I was saying, I'd like to find someone to breach my depths," Meara said primly. "So to speak."

Then she fell off the chair and lay there on the floor laughing helplessly. "This vodka is strong enough to affect vampires. Did I mention that?"

"I might be floating," Alice said, staring dreamily at the ceiling. "Can ghost whisperers levitate? Maybe I should try jumping off the roof."

"No!" all three of them shouted.

Alice just laughed. "I was kidding about the roof. I think. And I think you should give Edgingburg Sebastianana a chance," Alice told Meara, stumbling just a teeny bit over the name. "He might surprise you."

"You're cut off, little one," Meara said. "Also, this isn't exactly your area of expertise, is it? Most of the time, you act like an innocent little virgin."

Alice looked up at her, surprised. "Well, of course I do. Until earlier today, I was."

CHAPTER THIRTY-TWO

Hunter, Bane, Edge, and Reynolds drove their Harleys through the streets of Savannah at speeds that would've killed a human. Their vampire reflexes allowed them to take turns ridiculously fast, avoid obstacles, and leave any potential pursuers in the dust. Flying might have been faster, but humans had the unfortunate tendency to look up sometimes, and it might be hard to explain a squad of flying vampires. Not to mention that werewolves needed to stay on the ground.

When they arrived at the run-down apartment building just outside of town, Hunter started to get a very bad feeling about the place even before he stepped off his bike. "Something's wrong."

Bane nodded. "The place reeks of death and blood magic. We are too late."

The members of the VMC and the Savannah Wolf Pack who'd cornered the two warlocks had reported that they were safely in custody, but there was an unfortunate truth that Hunter was learning about warlocks. There was no such thing as safety when you were dealing with them. Reportedly, they could even work their foul form of magic while semi-conscious. The trick, Bane had told him, was to never, ever let your guard down.

The scent of blood and death emanating from the apartment on the ground floor with the door swinging open told them that they were definitely too late—and somebody had almost certainly let their guard down.

"Where's Luke?" Hunter had half expected the other vampire to show up at some point during the evening or even to meet them here, but there was no sign of him.

"He's dealing with a problem of his own," Bane said. "A personal issue. Someone from his past has unexpectedly shown up and is trying to cause problems for him, which would cause problems for the rest of us."

"Oh, good. More problems," Hunter said, rolling his eyes. "And just when I was becoming so accustomed to happy days and smooth sailing. Anyway, tell him to let me know if he needs anything."

Bane nodded but said nothing else, and they walked over to the apartment, having avoided it for as long as they could.

Edge and Reynolds, who'd had to veer off the road to avoid a bus full of drunken tourists, roared up into the parking lot and jumped off their bikes, both of them flinching at the smell of rot.

Inside the apartment, the scene was an ugly one, and one that Hunter had seen far too many times before. Supernatural beings weren't the only ones killing each other, after all. But there was something different about this. Far different from the usual gang shooting or murder over money, sex, or drugs that firefighters saw almost as often as police did.

This room stank of rot and foulness—the hallmarks of blood magic and its practitioners.

"You don't see a lot of decapitations in Savannah," Hunter said mildly, hoping he wasn't going to vomit from seeing a head on the kitchen table in the trashed apartment.

Even before it had become the scene of two murders, the apartment hadn't been a homey kind of place to live. The only furniture was the scarred table, now carrying the head, and a couple of lawn chairs. A spill of small plastic bags with some kind of white powder contents lay on the floor on a corner of the nasty, stained carpet.

"This is standard operating procedure, unfortunately," Reynolds said. "When supernatural predators come to town, they often zero in on local drug dealers and kill them, steal their cash and guns, and even take over shit heaps like this so they can use it as a place to hole up while they're in town."

Hunter nodded. "Make sense. Even if the warlocks weren't successful at taking over the place, it's not like crystal meth dealers were going to be reporting them to the cops."

"These weren't drug dealers, though," Bane snarled. "These are two of our own. Where are the other two?"

Edge checked out the rest of the apartment, careful to avoid stepping in blood or any other kind of evidence. Not that Hunter thought this crime scene would ever see the light of day. Edge glanced through a couple of open doors, presumably to the bedroom and the bathroom, then turned and shook his head. "Nobody here. My guess is wherever our other guys are, they're either dead or wishing they were."

Reynolds's head snapped up, and he lifted his nose, scenting the air, and then ran out of the apartment. When they followed him, he was already headed toward the bikes.

"I smell them. Or, at least, I've caught the scent of that nasty blood magic. It would be too big of a coincidence for there to be other practitioners in this neighborhood tonight. Let's go get him. Them."

"What direction?"

"That's the bad news," Carter said, looking grim. "They're headed toward Congress Street."

"She lied to us! Zela lied to us," Hunter said.

Edge gave him a sardonic look. "Shocking, I know. Warlocks have *never* lied to anybody before."

"She was a warlock, too? But—"

"They come in all genders," Bane said, swinging a leg over his bike. "I think she was still an apprentice but smart enough to lie. Do your people still have her, Carter?"

"We have her," Carter said grimly. "Or at least we did have her. Now I'm wondering if this was a concerted effort and these two met up with her. If so, this is an even bigger problem than we thought." He pulled his phone out and made a call but shook his head.

They didn't waste any more time talking but headed toward Congress Street. Luckily, on a Sunday night, the bars and clubs weren't as packed as they would've been the night before. But there were still far too many people in the streets and clubs, partying, drinking, and generally making fools of themselves.

The perfect prey for warlocks who might be on the hunt for human sacrifices, in other words. If all three of them were together, their triumvirate would be far more powerful than just two of them would be. And if they'd been injured in the battle that had gone down in the apartment, they'd be desperate for a new source of power.

Hunter might not be back to work as a firefighter right now, but the last thing he wanted to see was any of the people in his town getting hurt or possibly killed by these bastards.

Reynolds gestured, pointing to their left, and the four of them made the tight turn to head down the alley he'd indicated. The werewolf was off his bike almost before it was fully parked, running toward the back entrance of Club Red.

"Of course it would be Club Red," Hunter groaned. "We were constantly having to cite this place for being over capacity. If the warlocks want to cause the biggest possible disaster, this would be a good place to do it, even on a Sunday."

"Except that's not it," Bane said, pointing at the roof. "They're not inside the club; they're on top of it. That can't be good."

"Whatever they're planning to do, we're ending it. Now." With that, Edge launched himself into the air, Bane right behind him, heading toward the three—and it *was* three—warlocks on the roof of the club. The alpha werewolf wasn't far behind, leaping up to dig his fingers into handholds and pulling himself rapidly up the side of the building. The instant he reached the top, he started to shift into his wolf form.

"Time to fish or cut bait," Hunter muttered, and then he concentrated with every fiber of his being and leapt into the air—this time, he didn't fall back down to the ground. This time, he didn't land on his head.

This time, he flew.

Right into a fiery projectile.

"Because that's fair," he shouted, shaking off the burn on his side and heading straight for the warlock who'd thrown it at full speed.

That's when he discovered that a vampire's full speed in flight was pretty fucking fast. Just in time, too, because Bane and Edge were fighting the other male warlock and Zela. The firebolt-tossing warlock was trying to kill Carter, who was already down on his side, blood pouring out of his chest, and Hunter didn't know how bad something had to be before a werewolf lost the ability to heal.

He tackled the warlock before he could throw any more fireballs, flew off the roof with him, and twisted in midair so it was the warlock, not Hunter, who hit the pavement headfirst. His head bounced once, and then he didn't move again.

From the look of him, he was never going to move again.

Hunter had just killed a man.

He stood there staring at the dead warlock, heaving in breath after breath, and only realized the fighting on the rooftop had ended when Bane flew down with Carter Reynolds, still in wolf form, in his grasp. He put the alpha wolf gently on the ground; Edge tossed Zela's body off the roof, and Bane used his magic to cushion the body's fall. Edge jumped lightly down, an unconscious third warlock over his shoulder.

"I say we kill this one, too," Edge growled. "Although, I admit I didn't mean to kill the woman. I was hoping she'd talk again even though we know she's a liar. But she was about to skewer me in the heart with a nasty little stiletto knife she pulled out of a pocket. You never expect warlocks to use anything but magic, and that's how they get you."

"That's why I let that one live," Bane said, nodding to the man, still breathing, that Edge dumped none too gently on the ground. "We should ask him if there are any other Chamber servants or hired help in town."

"He'll only lie," Edge said.

"Not if I compel him," Bane said, fangs snapping down.

Both of them—all three of them, because Reynolds was coming back to consciousness—suddenly looked at Hunter, as if they'd only noticed his silence right at that moment.

"Hunter? Are you all right?" Bane glanced down at the dead warlock next to Hunter's feet.

"I'm a murderer now," he said dully. "I killed this man."

"Warlock," Edge corrected him.

"Does it matter?"

"It matters to Carter. You saved his life," Bane said.

The warlock that Edge had dropped on the ground started to stir, and then he jumped up into a crouch, staring wildly around himself.

"We should take this party out of here, before some human shows up and sees too much," Edge said.

"What does this one know?" Hunter pointed to the only warlock left alive. "Or should I just kill him, too? Now that I've done it once, it probably gets easier."

He heard the monotone his voice had dropped into—shock setting in. He'd seen a lot of people in shock after fires; he'd just never expected to be one of them.

"Not yet," Bane said, and the warlock recaptured his arrogance when he heard.

"You! You're the vampire hanging around Alice Jones." The captured warlock sneered at Hunter—pretty unwise, considering what had happened to his friends. "You won't be able to save her. The Chamber is after her, and that creep who ran the Institute is after her, too. One of us is going to get to her. You can be sure of that."

Alice's name broke through Hunter's fog. "I will kill you before I let you touch a single hair on her head," Hunter snarled, his fangs descending and snapping into place.

The man's nasty chuckle grated on Hunter's nerves. "You can't kill me. It would start a bigger war with the Chamber than you've already got. Do you know who my uncle is? When we get our hands on your little ghost whisperer, I'll be sure I have some private time with her first before we use her up, if you know what I mean."

The world exploded into fiery red flames, and every shred of Hunter's sanity vanished, annihilated. He became a creature of death and devastation; no longer a man, no longer a firefighter.

He was a *monster*—and he was happy to be one. If he was a killer now, he was going to be the best killer those bastards in the Chamber had ever met.

Hunter hurled himself at the warlock, who tried to duck, but Hunter grabbed his arm with a hand that suddenly ended in razor-sharp claws.

"Wait, Hunter," Edge shouted, trying to hold him back. "We need to find out everything he knows. You can't kill him. Not yet."

Hunter suddenly laughed, and the sound was long and loud and far too savage. He acknowledged at a primal level that his laughter meant death was coming—death was *here*, *now*—and they didn't even realize it. The warlock in his grip began to struggle in earnest, though, possibly recognizing what he was about to face, trying to raise his magic to fight back.

Hunter roared, and the fire-muffling wind he'd conjured before raced to his bidding. The warlock's magic snuffed out, suffocated beneath rage-conjured power. The world was ruby red, splashed scarlet with Hunter's fury—fury that they would *dare* to threaten Alice.

His Alice.

Not now. Not ever.

"Then I won't kill him. Not yet. But he can answer questions without this arm," Hunter snarled. And then, before anyone could move to stop him, he ripped the warlock's arm off at the shoulder.

Blood sprayed everywhere, and people were shouting at him, but he couldn't see. Couldn't hear. Could only focus on drinking in the hot, rich, magic-laden blood. More and more, rich and dark and sulfurous blood, sizzling from his mouth straight to his nerve endings, making Hunter so powerful that nobody would ever threaten Alice again.

He threw back his head and shouted, reveling in the blood.

In the *power*.

And the last thing he knew was the blow that hit him in the back of the head before everything went dark.

CHAPTER THIRTY-THREE

Hunter clawed his way back to consciousness, pain like molten lava searing through his body. He wrenched away from the hands trying to restrain him and leapt up into the air, landing six feet back from where he'd been.

"What the fuck just happened to me?" He looked down at himself and shuddered. He was covered in blood, a nightmare come to life. The monster he'd been afraid he'd become was now a reality. "What did you do? No—what did *I* do?"

He could hear the anguish in his own voice and saw it reflected back at him on Bane's expression. Next to Bane, Carter Reynolds still lay on the ground, but now he was in human form with what looked like multiple stab wounds and burn marks rapidly healing. The wolf was injured badly, but he was clearly healing from it. So why were the three of them all looking at him like someone had died?

Edge spoke up first. "He doesn't remember. He was blood drunk, and his short-term memory might be affected."

"Blood drunk? What does that mean?" Hunter stared at them and then back at himself. At his blood-drenched clothes. "What are you talking about?"

Bane and Edge glanced at each other and then moved aside. Behind them on the ground lay what was left of the three warlocks. Zela was simply dead with no visible signs of why. The man next to her clearly had a broken neck, from the way his head was twisted at an angle. The other one…the other one looked like he'd been attacked by a beast. A beast made of claws and teeth; a beast bent on death and destruction.

A beast of no mercy.

And…he was missing an arm.

Hunter started to ask another question, but he wasn't sure what, and then he realized his fangs were still descended. The blood—the blood that was all over his clothes and hands—he realized he could taste it.

In his mouth.

He was the beast.

He bent over and retched, vomiting up blood and bile and anguish. When he finally finished, he stood and wiped his mouth with the back of his sleeve, wanting to scream and roar and curse the world. But none of that would help, so he stood there, waiting for the judgment he knew was coming. Maybe he'd be lucky.

Maybe Bane and Edge would kill him quickly.

"It's not your fault," Bane said. "It's *not* your fault. It's mine. I should've known better than to bring a newly Turned vampire on a mission like this."

Edge nodded, but his eyes were wary. "The things I did when I was newly Turned—and I had far less reason than you did. He threatened Alice. We all heard him. If you hadn't killed him, I was going to."

Reynolds, his wounds now entirely closed, nodded and slowly stood, naked and scarred. "You saved my life. If he'd killed me, the Chamber would've had a good chance to take over the pack in the confusion and chaos that follows the unexpected death of an alpha. Who knows how many of my wolves would've died? Thank you for that." He headed over to his bike to get dressed.

Hunter laughed, but the sound was filled with bitterness and despair. They were trying to make him feel better about being a monster. About having murdered a man—*two* men—no matter that they were warlocks. Hunter had always believed in justice and fairness, and he'd murdered these men who'd had no trial, no chance of a defense.

Who'd died a painful, gory death.

A *loud*, painful, gory death. "How is it that nobody heard all this noise?" He looked around, but they were completely alone in the back parking lot of the bar.

"I went inside and did a mass enthrallment. Everybody in the bar thinks Adele is going to show up any minute to play and sing for them. Nobody is moving from their spot. Trust me."

Hunter rubbed the back of his head and winced.

"Yeah, sorry about that," Edge said, not sounding sorry at all. "I had to knock you out after you drank about a quart of warlock blood."

"I drank warlock blood?" Hunter felt like throwing up again, but there was nothing else in his stomach. Instead, he could feel the horrible power of the blood's magic racing through his system.

He deserved to *die.* And he could never, *ever* go near Alice again.

"I can tell what you're thinking, and it's self-indulgent," Bane said. "Self-defense and defense of others have always been justifiable reasons for killing someone who needs it. The first warlock almost succeeded in killing Carter, and he would've killed you next. This one bragged to us that he was the one who did the decapitating in that apartment. I would have killed him after we tried to question him. I don't feel an ounce of regret about it, and neither should you. We are the guardians of our people and of all the residents of Savannah."

"I don't know if this will matter or even if it should matter," Edge said. "But our people, the ones that these two killed, left behind families. Our people didn't deserve to die, but these two did. And we don't have time for you to sit around feeling sorry for yourself. We have to go search the city for any more of them."

With that, Edge stalked over to his bike, fired it up, and took off.

Hunter just stood there, unable to think or speak or move. He'd killed someone, but that wasn't the worst of it, was it?

He'd killed. Twice. And drank warlock blood.

"I'm sorry I didn't get to you in time to stop you from drinking that blood," Bane said. "And you drank so much—it would have been too much even of ordinary human blood, so you were blood drunk and getting worse. Blood drunkenness can send a vampire into a berserker mode or else just act as simple intoxication, depending on your emotional state when it occurs. For you, then—you were going even beyond berserker. The threat to Alice sent you over the edge of reason."

Hunter tried to take that in, forcing an unnaturally calm expression to his face. "But he is—he *was*—a warlock. Is there any… What will happen to me?"

"We're not entirely sure," Bane admitted. "Basically, we always try to avoid it. Their magical ability is inherent to some degree and not all dependent on their blood sacrifices. So you may have taken in some of that magic with the blood. Do you feel sick or wrong?"

"Or like decapitating anyone for your own nefarious purposes?" Carter said this lightly, walking back toward them, but Hunter didn't miss the wary expression in the alpha werewolf's eyes.

"I don't know what I feel, except sick. And like I need to vomit again and again and again." He gritted his teeth but forced the questions out. "Is this it? Am I ruined? Am I destined to be evil now—the monster that I've been afraid of turning into?"

Bane's eyes turned icy. "The fact that you think that, and that you have continued to think that since the Turn, tells me that you believe we, your friends—your new family—are monsters. How have you been able to be friends with monsters?"

"That's not what I meant," Hunter began.

But it was too late. Bane turned on his heel and left. Carter gave Hunter a look of disgust, but, unexpectedly, there was also compassion. "New wolves go through this a lot. The best advice I can give you is that you're going to have to decide once and for all if you want this new existence. Because if you believe that being a vampire makes you inherently evil, well, that's no way to live. And Alice deserves better."

Alice.

Alice.

Forgetting his anguish, the fact that he was covered in blood, and even the motorcycle he'd ridden over on, Hunter launched himself into the air, focused on only one thing: reaching Alice before any of the factions after her could find her.

• • •

Alice stood by the window, lifting her face to the cool night air, letting the conversation behind her wash over her without paying particular attention to it.

She liked the women and felt like they might become true, close friends. But their shock over her revelation about losing her virginity had made her feel isolated again. The only person who hadn't ever made her feel like she wasn't normal was Hunter, and she missed him suddenly so much that it was like a pain in her chest.

One thing was certain, though. She was never drinking vodka again.

The lemon drops had tasted so good, and she'd been so happy chasing the bubbly, exhilarated feeling they'd filled her with that she'd drunk far too many of them. Ryan, bless her heart, had kept urging her to slow down. Alice guessed that since Ryan was a doctor, she couldn't help herself. And she'd undoubtedly been right. Alice shuddered to think of the hangover she was going to have in the morning. Right now, she was in the process of drinking the two large bottles of water that Ryan had recommended to help with the dehydration, which apparently caused much of the headache part of hangovers.

It must be wonderful to be a doctor and understand so much about how bodies and health worked. Sometimes Alice felt so inferior. She had no college degree; she didn't even have a high school diploma. They hadn't seen a reason for her to study or learn anything in the Institute, because *property* didn't need to have any knowledge.

Property only needed to do its job.

She leaned her flushed forehead against the window, annoyed with herself but also realizing she might be learning about another side effect of drinking too much alcohol. Self-pity.

After all, once she'd escaped, she'd made it part of her master plan to learn everything that she could. When she'd been able to settle in one place for a while, she'd studied and gotten her GED. And books—there were always books. Even when she was living in the shelter, she'd gone to the library almost every day. To learn and learn and learn.

But as much as all that learning had been wonderful and had opened up the world to the mind of a woman who'd spent her life trapped in a single room, it hadn't stopped her from feeling a twinge of regret when she saw people her age wearing sweatshirts emblazoned with the names of their colleges. Maybe, someday, she would take some college classes. Maybe even get a degree. If she drummed up enough support for the rescue, she'd be able to hire another employee and have some time to herself to attend class. Time to study.

She was still young, and she didn't believe that college was only for kids fresh out of high school. She intended to look upon learning as a lifelong experience, not something you did once and then stopped. If she had to wait until she was ten or twenty or even thirty years older to go to college, well, so be it. She'd still be that much older, degree or not, so she might as well get that degree. Or even *two* degrees.

"Dr. Darlington" had a nice ring to it.

She started laughing, realizing that her thoughts were spinning off in ridiculous directions. Also, she really liked the new last name she'd taken for herself, but, given her gift of communicating with animals and the similarity of Darlington to Dolittle, maybe not.

Meara surprised her by walking over to stand next to her at the window. "I'm sorry if we teased you too much, little one. We like you, and we're just worried about you. Your innocence, your relationship with Hunter—everything is so new, and now you have to deal with bad guys after you from every direction. It's a great deal to land on your shoulders all at once."

Alice smiled, trying to reconcile this compassion and empathy with Meara's usual conversations about eating tourists. "You're a lovely person, aren't you? You try to hide it under a very tough exterior, and I'm not talking about your glamour-girl persona. I'm talking about how aloof you keep yourself. But your heart is just enormous. You've even found room in it to take in an awkward stray like me."

Meara's expression was the most vulnerable Alice had ever seen on her face. She started to speak and then stopped and simply studied Alice for a long minute.

Finally, just when Alice was starting to believe she'd shocked Meara speechless, the vampire spoke up. "You see, this is what surprises and delights me about you. In so many ways, you are so naive of the ways of the world. So unsophisticated. But you have such a directness and honesty about you, perhaps because you never learned all the little polite lies and fictions of society. However it happened, why you are the way you are, it doesn't matter." Meara shrugged. "What matters is that you are a beautiful soul, and I promise that I will do my best to protect you. Please believe, although you may have been friendless in the past, that this is no longer the case. I would be your friend—if you'll have me—and it's not an offer I make lightly."

Alice could feel the tears burning at the back of her eyes. "I would love that. Thank you."

Meara smiled at her but then noticed Max was heading toward them, and her expression changed in a heartbeat from vulnerability to mocking amusement. "Fine, already. You don't have to get all mushy about it," she told Alice, who felt totally bewildered until she realized that Meara was only putting on a show, this time for the werewolf.

So she just smiled and nodded. "That's me. Totally mushy."

Max arrived and gave them a sharp look but evidently didn't see anything out of the ordinary—whatever "ordinary" even meant on a movie night hosting a vampire, werewolf, angel, and ghost whisperer.

"I see the party's over here at the window." The werewolf had downed several lemon drops herself. "Ryan went downstairs to find the phone number to order pizza. I figured if we're going to hang out for another movie, we're going to need more snacks."

"I don't think I can stay and watch another," Alice said, shaking her head to clear the tipsiness. "I need to get home and check on the animals. I'm also worried about Charlie.

He's done almost nothing but sleep since he breathed fire. I don't know if he's in some kind of denial because he hurt that warlock, or if this is a natural reaction to breathing fire for the first time, or ever, maybe? You don't happen to have a starter manual, like *Facts for Living with a Minor Demon*, do you?"

"I actually do have something like that," Meara said, surprising her. "I keep in touch with an order of monks who are scholars and historians of supernatural beings. We were talking about demons—Minor and otherwise—just last month. I'll ask them to email me everything they have, so we can learn more about Charlie."

"You were talking to monks?" Alice blinked, trying to imagine that.

"Monks who have email?" Max laughed. "You never fail to surprise me, vampire."

"You're pretty surprising yourself, werewolf," Meara said. "Speaking of which, I think I should call my team over sometime this week, and we can give the two of you a fashion makeover. Right now, you're both naturally hot. But a little time with my glam squad, and you'd both be simply stunning."

"Great. A vampire makeover." Max looked like she'd swallowed something sour, which made Alice laugh.

"I don't know about Max, but I would love it. Does your team have somebody who cuts hair, maybe? I haven't had my hair cut in a couple of years, and the ends are getting frizzy. Plus, it would be awfully nice to have some kind of shape to this mass of curls. Or maybe I should call it a *mess* of curls." But then she remembered Hunter stroking her hair when they'd made love, and she smiled a private smile.

"My glam squad has a hairdresser, makeup specialist, and a clothing stylist. Plus, I have accounts with all the best boutiques in town. Or we could fly to New York if you want. Actually, we should probably do that anyway."

Alice's head started spinning again, but this time she didn't think it was from the lemon drops. "Wow. That would be great. I mean, here in Savannah. I'm not ready to leave the rescue and go to New York, but—"

Suddenly, Max growled—a truly frightening sound—and yanked Alice away from the window.

"What is it?" Meara's amused expression turned savage. "If those *cochons* from the Chamber dare come here, they will be very sorry."

Alice, knowing that she was the weak link in this trio of vampire, werewolf, and ghost whisperer, backed away from the window and then ran to intercept Ryan, who had just entered the room.

"I think somebody's outside," Alice told Ryan.

"Not just outside but almost here," Max said. "I can smell them, and they smell like blood. Lots of it. Whoever or whatever it is, they're coming at us through the air."

Meara made a sweeping expression with one hand, and a beautiful sword that had been on the wall display across the room flew toward her. She caught it, twirled her wrist one time, the blade flashing, and then stood in a ready position.

On the other side of the window, Max had partially shifted her fingers into claws. "No time for the entire shift to wolf. They—"

A blast of wind shoved both women away from the window, and then Hunter, blood-drenched and with glowing ruby eyes, hurtled into the room and landed six feet or so away from Alice.

His gaze snapped to hers, and he started toward her, a predator intent on his prey. "*Mine.*"

Meara leapt across the room to intercept him, landing between Alice and Hunter.

"You're not yourself, little brother," she said lightly. "Why don't you get cleaned up? And then Alice will be very glad to see you."

Hunter swept out an arm as if to shove Meara out of the way, but she gracefully somersaulted backward through the air and landed a foot or two beyond his reach.

"Alice. I need you. Come with me now," Hunter demanded, and the anguish on his face laid to rest any doubt she might've had about his appearance.

This was *Hunter*. He wouldn't harm her.

He held out his hand, and she stepped forward and took it.

"Alice, no," Ryan cried out.

Meara held up her sword, as if to block Hunter from taking Alice, and Max raced over to stand with her.

"I know what you're thinking, but you're wrong," Hunter snarled at them. "I would never hurt her. She's in danger, and she's *mine*. I must keep her safe."

"It's okay, Meara," Alice said. "I want to go with him."

Hunter tightened his grip on her hand. "Yes. Now."

Ryan, who must be one of the bravest people Alice had ever seen, took a step toward them and put her hand on Hunter's blood-soaked sleeve.

"We want to protect her, too. Why don't you get cleaned up, and we'll all protect her together? You *know* me,

Hunter. You know I would never do anything to hurt you or Alice."

For a moment, Alice thought Ryan's calm, reasonable tone had gotten through to him. But then he bared his fangs. "You don't understand. *None* of you understand. Alice, will you go with me?"

She looked into his eyes and still saw *him*, even through the brilliant scarlet color. "Yes. Always."

Before Meara, Ryan, or Max could move, Hunter wrapped Alice in his arms and shot through the air, out the window, and up into the night sky.

CHAPTER THIRTY-FOUR

By the time Alice caught her breath, they were soaring through the night air above Savannah, but she wasn't afraid.

She was *exhilarated*.

The cold air; the lights of the city behind them; the crisp, clean scent of the night sky. No wonder humans had tried to fly since the dawn of time. She would give a lot to be able to do this herself. Too bad ghost whisperers had more mundane gifts.

This was freaking *amazing*.

But she was also worried about Hunter, and he hadn't said a word to her since he'd taken her out of the mansion so dramatically. "What happened? Are you injured? Whose blood is this?"

His arms tightened around her, but he didn't respond. His eyes were still glowing a hot ruby red, and part of her knew that she should be afraid—should be terrified—but she wasn't. This was *Hunter*, and she knew somehow deep in her soul that he would never hurt her. She was, again, more afraid *for* him than of him.

"Are we going home? I need to check on the animals. We can get you cleaned up, and you can explain what happened. Let me make sure that you're okay."

He still didn't answer, only made a growling noise deep in his throat. She subsided, deciding to hold off on any more questions for the moment. The last thing she needed was for him to lose focus or drop her, especially over the river.

Away from the river, please.

She'd never learned how to swim. If she survived this, lessons were definitely going on a list.

Then, as if he'd heard her thoughts, he switched directions and swooped down toward the water, and she finally had the sense to become a little bit afraid.

"What's happening? Hunter, answer me! You're scaring me now. *I don't know how to swim!*"

He sped up, and she started shouting his name. "Hunter! *Hunter!*"

Her shouts must've finally gotten through to him, because he looked down at her as if he'd only just realized that he held her in his arms.

"Boat," he growled, and that was all, but she followed his gaze and realized he was headed for what looked like a yacht docked on the Savannah River.

Hunter had clearly managed flying and was succeeding brilliantly at it, but landing was another matter. He hit the deck of the boat too hard, stumbled a few steps, and then crashed into the railing, but even through all that he was careful to turn in such a way that his body took the brunt of the hit, and she was safe, cushioned in his arms.

Three men and a woman, all dressed alike in white shirts and khaki pants, came running toward them, all shocked and calling out excited questions. The glow in Hunter's eyes increased in intensity as he stared at each of them in turn, and the effect was eerie, like a red spotlight sweeping across their faces.

"*You will go to your beds now. You will go to bed and*

sleep, because you know all is well and secure. You will not wake up until morning. Go now," Hunter commanded, issuing the string of orders in a reverberating voice that, oddly enough, also made her feel like she should go lie down and go to sleep, even though none of it had been directed at her. She started to walk away from him, but he grabbed her arm and pulled her back toward him.

"Not you, sweetheart," he said roughly. "I would never compel you. Not you. Never you."

She stared up at him as all four staff members turned and walked calmly and silently toward the cabin.

"What did you do to them? Are they going to be okay? Hunter, you have to tell me what happened to you. You're scaring me."

"I never want to scare you."

"Too late. But I'm afraid *for* you, not of you. You look like someone tried to murder you." She took a good look at the blood on his hands, face, and clothes, and she stumbled. So much blood. Too much blood.

The memories…so much blood…

She shook her head to clear it. "Hunter? You need to tell me what happened right now, or I'm leaving."

He was on her so fast that she hadn't even seen him move, backing her into the railing, one hand on either side of her body.

Trapping her.

"You can never leave me," he snarled. "I need you."

He wasn't rational, Alice finally realized. Not even a little. There would be no reasoning with him, so she tried coaxing. "I won't leave you. I'm not going anywhere. Please, though, let's get you cleaned up. I'll go with you. I need to see your skin and make sure you don't have injuries."

His laugh was dark and wild. "I'm not the one who's injured. I'm not the one who got killed, either. I'm the killer." His eyes flared with scarlet heat, and he dug his fingers into her arms. "How safe do you feel with me now?"

• • •

"Hunter. *Hunter!*"

The anguish in Alice's voice finally got through to him—past his rage, past his self-loathing, and even past his terror for her. He tried to remember what she'd been saying to him, but all he remembered was the fear that had been in her eyes.

Something about cleaning up, maybe.

"Yes. Yes, I should shower." Suddenly, nothing in the world was as important as getting out of his ruined clothes. Scrubbing the blood off his skin. Brushing his teeth, though all the mouthwash in the world might not be enough to banish the taste. It was very likely that all of his nightmares for the rest of his life would circle around the taste of warlock blood in his mouth.

He threw himself at the railing and retched again, dry heaving, miserably aware of Alice at his side. What was he doing? He shouldn't be around Alice when he was like this. What must she think of him?

If this were a fairytale, she was Beauty and he was the beast. But not a sanitized beast like the ones who sang and danced in movies meant to entertain kids. No, he was the beast from ancient nightmares. From the terrifying tales people had told around campfires for thousands of years.

And now that he'd consumed warlock blood, how would that affect him? What would he become now? He'd just enthralled four humans with barely a thought, when he'd been unable to do it at all before. He'd flown through the sky at tremendous speed—carrying Alice. What else would he—could he—do?

Alice put her arm around his waist, in spite of the blood and the dirt. "I don't know whose boat this is, and at this point I don't care. All I want to know is if you think there's a shower in it somewhere."

The determined look on her face startled a shadow of a laugh out of him, even though just moments before he'd thought he'd never laugh again. "It actually belongs to the governor. He likes to invite firefighters and police officers who are getting medals or commendations for a day on the boat. Makes him feel important, I guess. But for some reason I remembered the fact that he's in Washington when I saw it sitting here at the dock. And yes, it has a shower. It has a couple of very fancy bathrooms, I remember, because he showed it all off to us when I was here."

It had only been six months or so since he'd gotten that commendation. Six months—only half a year—and look how his life had changed. The same yacht where he'd received a commendation for bravery was now the place where he stood, covered in the blood of a warlock, trying not to frighten the woman that he was pretty damn sure he was in love with.

That realization—that he *loved* her—made the decision for him.

"This way," he told her. He started toward the cabin and was overwhelmed with gratitude when he felt Alice slip her hand in his.

"I'm going with you," she said. "Maybe I can be useful to hand you a towel or find you clean clothes. I don't know. But I'm not leaving you alone again tonight. Who knows what might happen to you without me around to protect you?"

She tried to smile but wasn't very successful at it. The fact that she'd tried, though—it pierced his heart. The courage of this woman drove him to his knees.

And he understood in that moment that he could never deserve her.

• • •

She wanted to cry, watching him scrub and scrub and scrub. The last of the blood had swirled down the drain more than five minutes before, but still he was pouring soap in his hands and scrubbing his face, his arms, and every part of himself as if he could never get clean again.

She'd found him a new toothbrush in a drawer, torn the plastic wrap off, and handed it to him with a tube of toothpaste. He'd brushed his teeth right there in the shower for a very, very long time, which, more than anything else, terrified her.

It was pretty clear that someone had died, and a cold certainty was crystallizing inside her that *Hunter* had caused the death. Had maybe—probably—even drunk blood from the victim.

She stood leaning against the sink, feeling her mind ice over while she ran ever-more outlandish and hideous possibilities through her mind. She watched him through the frosted glass, catching glimpses of his incredible body. It shocked her that the sight of him aroused her so powerfully, in spite of the situation—even though he might be a killer. But it had only been a little while, after all, since his body had been wrapped around her.

Driving inside her.

Bringing her to unbelievable heights of amazing pleasure and ecstasy.

More than that, though, he'd made her feel wanted. *Desired.*

Even…loved? She knew, deep in her heart, that she was already in love with him. She couldn't and *wouldn't* leave him alone with whatever he was battling now.

When she saw him pour yet more shampoo into his cupped hand, after he'd already washed his hair multiple times, she decided that enough was enough. She took a deep breath for courage and then stripped off her shirt and jeans, leaving on her bra and panties, and walked into the shower with him.

The hand holding the shampoo bottle had fallen to his side, and Hunter was leaning against the tile wall, his eyes closed, anguish on every line of his face.

"You need to tell me what happened," she said, and his eyes snapped open.

"I'm a murderer again, Alice. I killed a man. *Two* men."

She tried to hide her shock but was probably unsuccessful. It was impossible to hide a pounding heart from a vampire. "You said you were a murderer 'again.' When were you a murderer before?"

He looked at her through eyes that still glowed red—that were dead, stripped of all emotion.

"When I was sixteen, I almost killed my sister."

CHAPTER THIRTY-FIVE

After Hunter's revelation, everything Alice had planned to say floated out of her mind. She was still trying to come up with a response, or a question, or *anything*, when he turned off the water and reached out for one of the clean towels she'd put on the bathroom counter for him and handed it to her, then took another for himself.

"I can't put those clothes back on," he said, looking lost. "I don't know what to do."

"That's okay. I do." She quickly dried off, dressed, and then went looking for something for him to wear. The crewmen she'd seen hadn't been as tall as Hunter, so she bypassed their rooms and found the master suite.

"Fancy," she murmured, looking around in disgust. The amount of dog food she could buy for the cost of just the furnishings in this room... She put it out of her mind. She had things to do.

She pulled the closet door open and found things that looked like they might fit Hunter. They'd be a little big, because apparently the governor was a portly guy, but that was fine. They'd be good enough to wear to get to her house. She suddenly felt the most inappropriate giggle burbling up inside her. Were they going to have to fly? They didn't have a car here. Although she guessed if Hunter could suddenly compel people to do things like he had with the crew, he could manage to compel someone to loan them a car.

It struck her that she was thinking, bizarrely enough, in completely supernatural terms. A week ago, her solution would have been much simpler: just call an Uber. She almost couldn't believe how the world had changed. Her world, at least.

She put it all aside and hurried back to the bathroom with the clean clothes.

Hunter dressed in the jeans and sweatshirt with no complaint and not even any comment, which worried her. He picked up his own socks and his boots, which were only slightly spattered, and then followed her to the deck.

"I really should clean that bathroom," she said, suddenly worried that one of the crewmembers might get in trouble for the mess. It definitely was not their fault that a vampire who needed a shower had dropped by.

"You really should not. You should come sit with me and drink champagne." He grabbed a champagne bottle out of the bucket filled with melting ice that was sitting on a table with what was apparently the remains of the crew's dinner. "Why not celebrate? All the warlocks are dead."

She had never seen a person who looked less like he wanted to celebrate than Hunter did right at that moment. And the flat, dead sound of his voice frightened her. She had to find a way to reach him soon, or she was very much afraid that she'd never be able to reach him again.

"I guess the crew members celebrate when the governor's not here," she said, looking around. "I need to ask you, though, about what you did to them. Compelling them all to obey you like that. Is that normal? That's not something you would ever try to do to me, is it?"

"No, never," he said, his voice filled with self-loathing. "I've tried compulsion before, and it hadn't worked for me yet. Luke told me it takes a while to grow into my powers. But then again, nobody knew the effect that drinking a warlock's blood might have on a vampire."

He popped the top of the champagne and took a long drink straight from the bottle, then held it out to her.

She shook her head, grimacing. "No, thanks. I may never drink again. Meara made lemon drop martinis, and I had way too many of them. Let's just leave it at that."

"Well, apparently I got drunk, too," he said bitterly, sinking down in a deck chair. "Want to hear an ugly story?"

She didn't, but she knew she must, so she nodded and sat next to him, taking his hand.

He told her everything—at least, everything he remembered—about what had happened since he'd left her earlier that evening. He didn't try to pretty it up or spare himself in the telling, but she wondered how he could possibly believe he was the bad guy in the story.

After he told her about coming to the mansion with some idea of protecting her, she held up a hand for him to stop.

"So, let me see if I understand this. The warlocks were the ones sent to capture me?"

"Yes." He took another long drink.

"And they killed two of your vampires and two wolves?"

"Yes, as far as we know. But—"

"And then," she said, speaking over him. "Then they tried to kill the alpha wolf and almost succeeded?"

"Yes, but—"

"After *that*, one of them tried to kill you, and the other

one threatened me with, at a bare minimum, sexual assault. Do I have that right?"

"Well—"

"*Do I have that right?*"

"But—"

"No. No buts. I don't want to hear it. It sounds like you did exactly what you needed to do and you saved Carter's life. It was self-defense and defense of others and protecting me all rolled up in one. Not to mention justice for all the others they've killed."

He laughed, and the sound was harsh in the quiet. "Yeah, but none of that explains the part where I drank his blood. Drank so much I got blood drunk."

She winced. "Okay, I'll give you that it's a little extreme. On the other hand, he threatened me. If it had been me, and he threatened you, I would have done *everything* in my power to end him."

She squeezed his hand to make sure he was paying attention and tried for a slightly lighter tone. "Anyway, the one guy was throwing blood-magic fireballs at you. This was not some ordinary bar fight where the worst that happens is that somebody throws a barstool through a window."

A hint of a smile crossed his face—the first sign he'd shown that maybe, just maybe, he was going to be okay. But then his amusement faded, and he shook his head. "I don't know what to think. I don't know who I am. All my life, I've tried to be the nice guy, ever since what happened to Hope. And now, suddenly, I'm not just a bad guy but a murderer. A double murderer. What will I do with that? How do I live with it?"

Alice saw a folded blanket on one of the benches that lined the sides of the boat, and she grabbed it and wrapped it around herself because she was getting cold out on the deck. Hunter took her hand and pulled her toward a hammock that was set up at the front of the boat and pulled her down into it with him. He said nothing, just wrapped his strong arms around her and held tight, his breathing eventually slowing as he relaxed.

"I don't deserve to hold you like this," he murmured, but thankfully he made no move to push her away.

She thought it might be time to make her own confession. "I had to hurt someone in order to escape the Institute. I'm pretty sure…I'm pretty sure I killed him." She didn't look at him, because she didn't want to see his expression turn to condemnation. She had never confessed this before, and the sick feeling of guilt tried to rise up in her throat again, but she forced it back the way she'd been forcing it back for years.

"He was one of the worst of them. The orderlies. He was always hitting people. Never me, because there were strict orders about not hurting me, but everybody else he could get away with hurting, he did. That night I escaped, I'd thought I had everything planned out perfectly. But he stayed late that night or changed his shifts or something. Anyway, he was in my way when I was heading through that last hallway on my way to the fire escape. I tried to be so quiet, but he heard me and caught me, and I don't know what he would've done. I just knew I couldn't survive any longer in that place. I screamed, and then I just snapped. I don't even know how—I think I kneed him in the crotch—but I got him down on the floor somehow."

She took a deep, shaky breath, remembering. Back in that hallway once again.

"And once he was down there, I grabbed his head and smashed it against the floor. At least once. Maybe twice or more. I don't know, and I can't exactly remember. I just know I was in the grip of some kind of mania—terror combined with red-hot rage—and one minute I was smashing his head on the floor, and the next minute I was running out the door. I turned to look back—I never should have, but I did—and he was lying on the floor with blood seeping out of his head onto the cold white tiles of the floor. I still see that image in my nightmares sometimes."

She finally dared to look up at him and almost didn't believe she was truly seeing such compassion on his face. And the terrifying red color was gone; his eyes had returned to their normal, beautiful, glowing ocean blue again. Maybe he had empathy for her because of what he'd just been through. Or maybe whatever damage or magic the warlock blood had wreaked on him was going away. Either way, she was so glad to see his eyes back to normal she almost cried. Instead, she hid her face against his chest.

"I'm not sorry," she told his shirt, hoping that he could hear her. Superior vampire hearing, hopefully. "That's the point of me telling you this. I guess, if asked, I would have said that only a horrible person would smash someone else's head against the tile floor until he almost certainly died. But the truth is that I'm *not* a horrible person. I was someone driven to an extreme measure, just as it sounds like you were."

He put a hand on the side of her face and coaxed her to

look up at him. "Alice. Of course you're not a horrible person. You had no choice."

She shook her head. "No. You were protecting Carter. And me. I was only protecting myself."

"But—"

"If you're a monster, then so am I."

He said nothing, but the jaw he'd been clenching so tightly relaxed somewhat, and his eyes lost some of the bleak hardness they'd carried since he'd flown into that window to get her.

She wanted to pound the point in harder, because Veronica had told her that men's skulls could be hard as rocks, but she thought perhaps it would be better to let it go.

For now.

So she lay there in silence, content just to be next to him, wrapped in a blanket, with the cool night air washing over them but still warm.

"You mentioned your sister," she said after a long while. "Tell me about her."

He tightened his arms around her and kissed the top of her head. "Her name is Hope, and she's wonderful. It was the worst thing that ever happened to me, but I realized when I grew up—especially working as a firefighter—just how much worse it could have been. And of course tonight..." He took a deep breath and blew it out slowly. "First I have to tell you that I was kind of an asshole when I was a teenager."

She laughed and reached up and touched his cheek. "I can't believe that. You're so nice."

He groaned and made a face. "Please, for the love of

God, never call me nice again. Every time a woman tells me how nice I am, I find out she's engaged to one of my friends the very next month."

"You *are* nice. Not to mention, I like your friends—at least the ones that I've met—perfectly well. But can you actually imagine me with any of them?" She started laughing but stopped when she realized his eyes were starting to shade toward red again.

She poked him in the chest, hoping that talking and calm and even a hint of playfulness would pull him away from the edge of despair. "Don't be ridiculous. You know I want nothing to do with any of your friends. You're stuck with me. Now tell me about Hope and how awful you were as a kid."

He shifted position, pulling her more fully on top of him. She couldn't *not* kiss him, then, so she did. Again and again. Long, delicious kisses, and their bodies fit together so well...she sighed with pleasure.

But there were things that needed to be spoken tonight; demons exorcised—with no offense to Charlie. "Tell me."

"Okay, but it's not a great story. I actually was fine as a kid. We had a good life. It was just me and my sister, our mom and dad. We did the typical American-family thing. Summer vacations to the beach, Sunday dinners were mandatory, that sort of thing."

She sighed wistfully. "It sounds like a movie or a scene from a book. You're very lucky, you know."

"I know. And I'm sorry. I wasn't trying to—"

"It's not your fault my childhood was what it was. But, please, I'll stop interrupting. Just tell me more."

"Well, my little sister, Hope. She was adorable when she

was little. She followed me around like I was her hero. Big brother and all that. And it was fine—great, even—until I got to high school and turned into a jackass."

She found it hard to imagine. "Really?"

"Really."

"Why did you turn into a jackass?"

"Because I was arrogant and proud. I'd almost reached my full height, and I was filling out with muscle, since I worked on a landscaping crew in the summers, and suddenly girls noticed me. And I started doing really well in sports. The last thing I wanted was a little sister following me around everywhere."

She was starting to understand, and her heart ached for the man who'd forced himself to live with the guilt of whatever tragedy he clearly still blamed himself for.

"One night, just after she turned thirteen, Hope decided that, since she was a teenager now, she could go to parties with me. But I was way too proud of my badass self to show up to a party with my baby sister, so I told her she couldn't come."

"But she came to the party anyway?"

"She tried," he said grimly. "But she never got there. She got a ride from a friend of mine—someone I *thought* was a friend—who was already drinking before heading to the party. He stopped by the house to see if I wanted a ride, and there was my cute little sister, all dolled up, looking older than thirteen and ready to go to the party. So he decided to invite her along. God knows what would've happened if he'd shown up at the party with her. I probably would've beaten the shit out of him, which still would have been a better outcome. But that's moot anyway, because they never got to the party. They were in an accident a mile away from my house. He drove the damn car right off the road and hit a tree. And he came out of it with nothing but scratches, while my sister ended up in the ICU."

Hunter's face was filled with so much pain that she wished she had a vampire's gift to be able to compel someone to forget a memory.

"I'm so sorry. If it's too painful to talk about, then don't. The last thing I want to do is bring up bad memories on a night that has already been so difficult."

He shook his head. "It's okay. I've never talked about this since that night. Instead, it's been festering inside me all these years. Maybe the magic in the warlock blood I drank stirred up every terrible memory I have. Anyway, it actually feels okay to tell *you* this story. Maybe once it's out in the open, I can finally get past it. Hope forgave me years ago, of course. Even before she was out of the ICU. That's just the kind of person she is."

"She sounds wonderful. I'm so glad she's okay. But what exactly happened? How bad was it?"

"Bad. Hope could have died," he said flatly. "And it would've been my fault."

"That's not true," she protested. "Your friend who was driving drunk—it's his fault. I also can't believe that the way you were raised, in such a good family, your sister didn't know better than to get in a car with someone who'd been drinking. Even at such a young age."

"She was too excited to go to the party. I doubt she even realized he'd been drinking. Anyway, I'm not putting the blame for what I did on a thirteen-year-old girl."

"No, of course not. Neither was I. I'm just saying that a lot of factors went into the circumstances that led up to the accident. You can't—"

"I love you for wanting to protect me from my own memories. From the pride and arrogance that nearly got my sister killed. But it's over, and she survived. She was in the hospital for almost a week, but she was so strong and healthy and had such a fierce will to live. They were worried about the swelling in her brain, and I'm pretty sure she even went into a coma for a few hours, but then she woke up and started asking about spaghetti and meatballs."

He laughed. "That girl could always eat. Spaghetti and meatballs was her favorite dinner. When she woke up and asked my mom for meatballs, Mom burst into tears, and we all sat around laughing and crying until the nurses came running into the room and kicked us out so they could do tests. I think when Mom started laughing, that's when I knew it was going to be okay."

"And after that? Did you take her to parties with you?"

"Absolutely not. I *stopped* going to any parties instead. Even if I hadn't been grounded for a month, I was punishing myself. I had nearly gotten my sister killed, and I damn sure wasn't going to have any fun, because I didn't deserve it."

She squirmed around until she was sitting up in the hammock. "*Aha!* Now I understand. It's a pattern with you. Everything that goes wrong in life is automatically your fault. Your sister wanted to go to a party, and your friend was a drunken fool, so that was your fault. A warlock killed club members—your people—and almost killed Carter

Reynolds, then was trying to kill you, too, before you killed him first in self-defense. Another warlock helped kill people and threatened to capture and assault and probably kill me, too, so you protected me. Yes, in a horribly violent way, but you're too new at being a vampire to have been able to control that. Even Bane said so. But, to you, that's your fault, too. Do you see the problem here?"

He pulled her back down into his arms, frowning. "Don't use logic on me, woman."

She started laughing. "How about I use my feminine wiles on you instead?"

Then she bent down and kissed him for a long, long time. When she raised her head a while later, gasping for air and shaking from head to toe from pure, delicious arousal, she was very pleased to see the dazed look on his face.

"Alice?"

"Yes?"

"What *are* feminine wiles?"

"I have no idea," she admitted. "Maybe we could figure it out together?"

He groaned when she lightly bit his earlobe.

"Alice. I don't deserve—"

"Nobody could possibly deserve me," she interrupted, twining a hand in his hair. "I'm just that wonderful."

"You really, really are," he said fervently, turning his head so her lips could more easily reach his neck. "Please, do that again."

"Like this?" She nibbled her way down from his neck to his shoulder and then tried something he'd done to her that had driven her wild—she bit down on the curve, just *there*, and his body jerked beneath her.

"Yes," he groaned. "Exactly like that."

She kissed him, then, kissed him like she would never stop kissing him, and when she finally raised her head, panting, he caught her face in his hands.

"Alice. Oh, Alice. I wanted to be so much more for you—a man, not a monster."

"You're not a monster," she said simply. "You're *mine*."

CHAPTER THIRTY-SIX

When she said "you're mine," Hunter's defenses shattered. How could she want him, after he'd confessed to murder? How could she try to defend him—defend *him*—after what he'd done?

And, maybe worse, how could he be starting to believe that she had a point? That what he'd done had been justice, not murder?

That he was now the guardian Bane had called him, not a monster at all?

"Mine," Alice said again, interrupting the stream of consciousness speeding through his mind.

"Alice," he said fiercely, making up his mind, for better or worse. "I need to kiss you, now. I need to be inside you, *now*. More than I have never needed anything in my life. Please—I know you must be sore, after—"

She put a finger on his lips. "Yes. *Yes*. I need you inside me. I need to feel you, to know that you're part of me. That you're safe."

She tightened her arms around him, and he knew—in some part of himself deeper than thought, deeper than reason—he knew that if he took her here and now, claimed her body right here in the crisp, clean, night air, beneath the stars, that he would never, ever be able to let her go.

She needed to know. He needed to tell her and let her make the choice. Be the hero he'd once thought he was and let her go if she changed her mind.

And then he'd walk into the sunlight, and the agony of life without her—the fear that he was becoming a monster—all of it would be gone, forever.

"Alice," he began, searching for words. "You need to know. If you give yourself to me now, you're mine. And I'm yours. Forever. I can't—I can't be casual with you."

Her beautiful green eyes got wider and wider as he spoke, and he tried to explain. "I can't— I don't know how to be this person. This vampire. But since I met you, no matter that it has been such a short period of time, I've known peace again. Laughter—real laughter."

"Hunter, I—"

He cut her off, desperate to explain, to get it right so she would stay. So she would choose him. Choose a future with him. Choose a *love* with him.

"I know it doesn't make sense, Alice, but you're *it* for me. My flash point."

"Hunter—"

He kissed her, long and deep, to postpone the denial he knew must be coming. The polite words of refusal.

The words that would end him.

She gently pushed his chest until he slowly, reluctantly released her. But before she could speak, he offered her his shattered heart.

"Alice. I love you. I'm *in love* with you. Please, please give me a chance, although I don't deserve it. I know I can never deserve it, but I swear I'll spend a lifetime trying. If only you—"

She made a frustrated sound and kissed him hard, stopping his words, and then, before he could think of what else to try or how else to plead with her, she gave him a brilliant and tender smile.

"Hunter. I love you, too."

She loved him? His dazed mind tried to comprehend it. How could she love him? She was all goodness and light, and he was...he was...

He was *thirsty.*

And her pulse beat in her neck, so very, very close to his fangs.

• • •

Alice suddenly realized that Hunter had gone very, very still.

"So thirsty," he muttered. "So thirsty."

And then he licked her neck.

No.

No, damn it, she was *not* going to lose him, not when she'd finally found him. Not to the warlocks, not to his own self-loathing, and she sure as hell was not going to lose him to the thirst.

She grabbed his face and forced it up until he met her gaze. "You listen to me, Hunter Evans. You just told me you love me, and I told you I love you, too. So you know what we're going to do right now?"

"What?" His eyes started to clear, and she breathed a prayer of thanks.

"You're going to make love to me, and it's going to be *much* better than draining my blood, and"—she took a deep breath and then said it—"if you still need to drink, I'm going to offer you some of mine. Just enough—not all of it, do you understand? We're going to have a wonderful life with our friends and Charlie and the animals, and lots and lots of sex, and the last thing you want to do is kill me, right? Because I'm a ghost whisperer, and…and I'll come back and haunt your ass!"

She gave him a triumphant smile, and, wonder of wonders, the red haze in his eyes disappeared completely, and he pulled her closer and hugged the breath out of her.

"I could never love anyone like I love you," he told her. "And I'm damned sure not going to drink your blood. If I'm desperate, I'll go find one of those crew guys and take a little, but not you. Never you."

"You love me? Really?" She suddenly felt shy, now that the crisis had, if not passed, at least abated.

He laughed and kissed her and then stared intently at her, his hands sliding up under her shirt to her breasts, which he firmly grasped. "Sweetheart, I love you so much I'm going to fuck you—so hard and so well. And then I'm going to keep on fucking you until you promise that you'll never, ever leave me."

She gasped, both at his provocative language and at the feel of his fingers, now pinching her nipples, and then she moaned, beginning to tremble with heat and desire and dark, delicious, liquid need. "Well, then," she said breathlessly. "I think we should get on with that."

He shouted out a sound of such triumph that she was worried he'd wake the crew, or the people on shore, or the freaking Coast Guard, and then he got to work removing their clothes, touching and tasting every inch of her skin as he bared it, and she forgot to worry about anything at all.

She wanted to kiss him everywhere; wanted her hands

all over him; kept making incoherent sounds of need and saying things like "more" and "mine" and "now."

And "Hunter." Always, always *Hunter.*

"Don't tell me to slow down," he rasped, his lips at her breast and his fingers on her, inside her, stroking through her slick heat. "So hot and wet for me, Alice. Only for me. Always for me. Let me inside you. Please. *Now.*"

"Yes— Now! Please, I need you," she gasped, and he grasped her thighs in his big hands and spread them, positioned himself between them, and drove into her, slowly, carefully invading her body, so hard and big—surely bigger than even before, so much of him, *so much*, and she cried out when he reached between their bodies and pressed his finger against her right where she needed him, right where…right where…oh, he was *so deep* inside her, so deep, and she couldn't…she couldn't…

"Hunter!" she screamed, and he moved back, pulling out of her, and she wanted to cry. "No, don't stop! Don't stop!"

"Never," he growled, and then he thrust back inside, deep and hard, and then she was bucking against him and he was moving, thrusting, long, slow strokes and then short, fast strokes, pounding into her, his big body shaking with the same desire that had captured her in the middle of a hurricane, a tsunami of need and pleasure.

He groaned again, burying his face in her neck, and she realized from the rigidity of his muscles that he was trying to hold on to his self-control.

"To hell with that," she said fiercely, and she tried something new, tried tightening her interior muscles around him, and he growled and started moving faster and harder and deeper, not *fucking* her but loving her, loving her, and he took her up and over the edge into a shattering release.

She cried out, holding on with every part of herself, holding on to this man she knew she was deeply, beautifully, impossibly in love with. "Hunter," she said brokenly, almost sobbing from the beauty of the feeling. "Hunter."

"Yes, my love," he said, and then he came, too, so hard and so intense, shaking in her arms.

They lay there, locked around each other, floating on waves of pure sensation, for a very long time, but then Alice saw the first hint of dawn far out in the east, and she forced herself to rouse.

"Hunter." He didn't move, and she tried shaking him. "Hunter!"

He made a contented humming sound. "Kiss me again, Alice. Love me."

"Hunter. Honey. We have to get moving. Dawn isn't very far away."

He sat up fast, suddenly wide awake. "Alice?"

"Yes, it's almost dawn."

His smile was as big as the universe. "Not that! You called me honey."

Laughing, they threw on their clothes, and he flew them home, holding her in his arms, both of them smiling every moment of the way. When they made it to her house, they raced to the basement and barely made it before the sun rose fully.

"I love you," he said. "Did you know—"

And then he fell down, sound asleep, missing the bed by at least a foot. Luckily for him, he didn't hit his head. Luckily for her, she was strong enough to lift him onto the bed, although he was so big she was almost tempted to just leave him there on the floor.

Unfortunately, though, she was going to have to wait all day Monday to find out what he'd been about to ask her.

"I love you," she whispered.

And then the basement door slammed open and Charlie, squeaking with excitement, flew down to her and almost set the bed on fire.

CHAPTER THIRTY-SEVEN

When Hunter woke up Monday evening, he was alone in the room, except for the pirate standing at the end of the bed. Given the week he'd just lived through, this did not surprise him all that much. The slight smell of burned fabric, however, did.

"You must be looking for Alice."

"The beautiful woman who talks to ghosts? Yes. But you can see me, so I guess you'll do."

"Lucky me," Hunter drawled.

The ghost—because of course he was a ghost—was dressed like a gentleman who'd lived a couple hundred years before. He wore a shirt that was surprisingly un-puffy, a vest, a coat, and breeches tucked into what must have been fairly expensive leather boots. He also had that fabric thing tied around his neck. A cravat? And, of course, a magnificent hat with a giant plume tucked into the band on one side.

Plus the sword hanging from his belt. Hunter wondered if ghost swords could actually cut people and then realized that his life had turned into a late-night movie.

Or a circus.

Finally, when the pirate showed no signs of leaving, Hunter sighed and put his hands behind his head, studying the man. "Snazzy dresser."

The pirate narrowed his eyes, as if he suspected Hunter of mocking him.

"What is this snazzy?"

"Fancy, sharp, good. Pick one."

"Ah, so it is a compliment."

"Sure. Why not? Now maybe you can get the hell out and come back on Wednesday. Alice takes appointments with, ah, people such as yourself on that day."

Naturally, that's when he heard the door that opened to the corridor between the buildings slam, and Alice ran down the basement steps, followed by Charlie, who was wearing his dog form.

"Hunter! You're awake! You'll never guess what happened. I—"

Damn, but she was beautiful. She was wearing jeans and a Little Darlings Rescue polo shirt, her hair coming out of the braid she tried taming it with for work, and her cheeks were glowing with excitement.

Charlie ran up and leapt on the bed, landing squarely on Hunter's stomach.

"Ow!"

Alice had slowed down to a walk, staring at the pirate. "Hello," she finally said. "Why are you in my house?"

The ghost removed his hat and swept a deep bow. "Captain Armand Merveuille, at your service, mademoiselle."

She sighed. "Hello, Captain. But it's not exactly at my service, is it?"

"I beg your pardon?"

"You should," Hunter muttered, finally giving up on privacy. He threw back the covers and yanked on the jeans that were on the floor next to the bed, then pulled a sweatshirt over his head, feeling just a bit smug at the way Alice stared at him like he was a box of chocolates she wanted to devour. Which led to a graphic visual of Alice licking chocolate off his cock, and he suddenly wanted to know how to banish the damn ghost.

Immediately.

Memories of the night before swirled through him. She loved him.

She *loved* him.

But Alice turned to look at the ghost, who was staring at Charlie.

"There is something wrong with your dog," the captain said. "He is not right."

"He is none of your business," Alice said firmly. "What do you want?"

"I want you to help me retrieve my treasure. You can have a ten percent finder's fee for your trouble."

• • •

Alice was having a hard time concentrating, in spite of the mention of treasure. Hunter was just so incredibly hot, and she was so incredibly frustrated, because she'd been hoping to catch him before he got out of bed so she could jump in there with his warm, cuddly, naked body.

Now he was not only not in bed, but they were not cuddling, and nobody was naked.

This was an extremely frustrating state of affairs.

"One moment, please," she told the pirate.

"I've been trying to get your attention for weeks," he said, looking extremely offended. "I've been knocking and knocking on your pipes."

Hunter gave him a hard look. "*You're* the knocking in the pipes?"

"Of course. Who else?"

"Oh, I don't know," Hunter said sarcastically. "We thought it might be an actual, you know, plumbing problem."

The pirate waved his hand in a flamboyant gesture. "No, your pipes are fine. I've been in and out of the walls for months, so I would know."

Alice's mouth fell open. "Why have you been in and out of my walls for months?"

Captain Merveuille shrugged. "I've been trying to get your attention so you can help me retrieve my treasure. But it hasn't worked until now. I was unable to fully manifest before tonight. I'm not completely sure why."

"Okay. I still don't really get it, but please hold on a moment." She turned to Hunter. "Pete and Ian's replacements are here for the night shift, but I'm supposed to tell you they took a break to go to dinner because everybody is safe now!"

Hunter studied her. "I doubt that," he finally said slowly. "The Chamber, from what I know about it, isn't going to give up so easily. And this doctor who's after you—"

"That's just it! Edge called and said Neville and Dr. Kurchausen were battling it out in England; the scoop is that Neville either killed or imprisoned Kurchausen, and both of them are in a *lot* of hot water right now."

"They're warlocks, Alice. Hot water isn't a big problem. They'd just use it to fill a cauldron or something. The last thing we need to do is let our guard down now."

"Warlocks?" the pirate said, narrowing his ghostly eyes.

"Where are the warlocks?"

Hunter's gaze snapped to the pirate. "In fact, isn't it quite the coincidence that we get this so-called news just when the pirate here shows up to distract us? How do we banish a ghost, Alice?"

She blew out a frustrated breath. "No. *Listen*. Edge started a viral campaign that he copied to all law enforcement agencies pretty much everywhere in the *world*, naming names of everyone in the top levels of the Chamber and giving a ton of evidence about the fact that they're running a human-trafficking ring."

Hunter looked interested. "They are?"

Alice shrugged. "Yes. Edge just didn't bother to add in the part that the human trafficking had to do with the supernatural."

"Probably wise," the pirate said.

Alice turned to him and frowned. "I said, one moment please."

Then she walked over to Hunter, threw her arms around his neck, and gave him a huge hug. "Do you know what this means? They're going to be *far* too busy to worry about me, so I have time to figure out my next move. If we're lucky, Neville and Dr. Kurchausen and anybody else who might've been after me—or after Ryan—will get locked away for so long they'll forget our names."

The pirate clapped his hands with all appearance of sincerity. "Congratulations, Mademoiselle Alice. This good news means that you have time to help me retrieve my treasure, yes?"

Hunter bared his teeth at the pirate, but he didn't let his fangs descend, so it wasn't nearly as threatening as it might've been. "Alice," he said, his beautiful face serious. "No. I'm sorry, and I know Edge is a brilliant computer genius, but Neville has more money than God, so I bet he has his own computer genius. Hell, he probably has an entire squadron of them, and they're all spending their lives making the 'truth' online look exactly like whatever the Chamber wants it to look like. And if Kurchausen is really as high up in the hierarchy as we believe, then he's going to be just as bad. This is not the time to relax our guard. Trust me."

The pirate took a step toward them. "If you have gold, you can hire your own genius, no?"

"Maybe," she said, thinking. Hunter had a very good point. Only her desperate need to be free and safe could have made her jump on such flimsy evidence, anyway. At the first sign of danger, in the past, she'd vanished. But she'd made Savannah a home, and she wanted to stay.

So she was ignoring all the danger signs that should be shouting at her to run, run, run. Or, at least, to be very, very careful if she stayed.

But maybe the ghost was right. Part of a treasure would certainly help. Hiring security, for one thing. Getting video cameras installed on the grounds, for another.

"Maybe we should help him," she said slowly. "It would be very cool to find treasure, not to mention the things we could do with it. For safety. For the rescue. For our future."

"Yes," the pirate agreed, his face brightening. "All of those things."

"I can think of a lot more fun things to do this evening than muck about looking for some old treasure," Hunter said, smiling down at her, which made her think of naked cuddling again.

"Perhaps," the pirate said. "But none of that will get you a fortune in gold and jewels."

Hunter's eyes narrowed. "How big a fortune are we talking?"

"Why would you trust us, though? We could have you lead us to the treasure and then steal it," Alice pointed out.

The pirate looked offended. "Don't you think I studied you before I came to you with this proposition? I've seen nothing but honesty from you in the time you have lived here."

"You've been *spying* on me? You—you—*pervert*!"

The pirate drew himself up to his full height of maybe five feet, five inches. "Certainly not. I am a gentleman."

"A gentleman *pirate*."

"A *privateer*. And one who does not spy on ladies."

"Oh, what the heck. Why not?" Hunter grinned at her. "Maybe if we get some gold out of this, we won't have to worry about the vampires trying to give me their five million dollars."

"Or give me new cars and vans," Alice said, beginning to see the upside.

The pirate looked back and forth between them, eyes wide. "Why would you refuse—no. Never mind. I don't want to know. Just tell me now. Will you help me or not?"

"Okay," Hunter said. "We'll help you for half the treasure and a promise that you'll leave forever after we find it."

"Absolutely not," the captain roared. "Ten percent. And of course I'll leave. Do you think I *like* being bound to this plane of existence?"

"Who knows?" Hunter shrugged. "Pirate."

"Privateer," the ghost said through gritted teeth.

"Fifty percent."

"Fifteen."

"One third each," Alice said. "A third for you, a third for me, and a third for Hunter."

Merveuille's mouth fell open. "That's even worse! Clearly you do not understand how to bargain, woman."

Alice narrowed her eyes. "Clearly *you* do not understand how to bargain *with* a woman. Because now I want seventy percent, split between me and Hunter, and you can have the other thirty."

The ghost threw his hands in the air and stalked back and forth, muttering to himself in French. Finally, he turned and gave them a blinding smile and an elegant bow. "Dearest lady. I was hasty and rude and offer my sincerest apologies. I would be willing to accept the initial offer of fifty percent for me and fifty percent to be split between the two of you."

Hunter gave him a skeptical look. "See, the thing I'm wondering is, how can you spend money anyway?"

The pirate nodded as if he'd expected this question. "It is of course not for me. One of my descendants, a great-great-however-many-greats grandchild, has opened a restaurant in Savannah. He's a good boy, and his wife is delightful, but the restaurant is struggling, as many do when they start."

Alice abruptly sat down on the bed, wondering what had happened to her life that she was being lectured about the economics of the current restaurant industry by a pirate who'd been dead a couple hundred years. "So you want your share to go to them?"

"Exactly! Their restaurant is named *La Tour*, which is a dreadful name. The Tower—what does that mean? It's not even located in a tower. You could, perhaps, ask them to rename the restaurant after me. The Marvelous Merveuille, for example, has a nice ring to it."

Your name *means* marvelous," Hunter said, laughing. "You want these people to rename their restaurant the marvelous marvelous? And that's better than the tower?"

"I don't plan to ask you how you spend your share," the ghost said haughtily.

"Oh, what the hell." Hunter grabbed Alice's hands and pulled her up off the bed. "Let's go find some treasure and make a couple of restaurant owners very happy."

Charlie, who had been silent and remained in dog form through all of this, looked up at them. "Charlie comes too, Lady?"

That's when the ghost drew his sword.

CHAPTER THIRTY-EIGHT

Dr. Hanford Kurchausen scanned emails on his phone as the car sped through the night but realized he wasn't seeing any of it. He was too close to his goal to think about anything else but Alice.

Alice Jones, the bitch who'd escaped him just when he was about to conduct the ultimate ritual.

She'd been his property and would be again, and *this* time she wouldn't get away.

He'd paid a small fortune to buy his freedom from Neville's cage, and the flunky he'd bribed had finally managed it just hours before police of all kinds, British and international, had landed on the Chamber headquarters' doorstep.

Clearly the dark powers of fate wanted him to succeed.

The irony—that he'd escaped a cage only to travel across an ocean to put another human being in one—had never once crossed his mind.

Grogan, who was completely loyal, if somewhat one-dimensional, glanced at him from his place in the driver's seat. "Do you have everything you need for the ritual? I'm assuming you want to do it in the city tonight?"

"Yes. I'm not waiting one more second. Once I drain Alice of her power, I'll reach heights of magic no warlock has achieved in a thousand years."

"And what about the girl? Will she survive it?"

Hanford smiled as they passed a sign welcoming them to Savannah. "Not a chance."

CHAPTER THIRTY-NINE

Hunter stared down at the sketchy-looking wooden ladder in the dark hole in the ground. "You've lived here for how long and you didn't realize you had a trapdoor in the basement?"

Alice shrugged. "Like I told you before, I've avoided the basement. It was dirty and full of clutter, and there were weird noises." She glared at the pirate. "Of course, now we know why there were weird noises."

Hunter turned to the ghost. "And you're sure about this?"

"I've been haunting the same spot for two hundred years. What do you think?"

"Okay. What do we have to lose?"

Alice groaned. "Haven't you ever seen a horror movie? You never, ever ask that question just before you go into the dark hole in the ground."

The pirate drew his sword and bowed to Alice. "You will have me to protect you, fair lady." With that, he gracefully dropped through the trapdoor to the ground below, not bothering with the ladder, although why the hell Hunter thought a ghost would need a ladder, he didn't know.

"You're not afraid of dark, closed spaces, are you?"

Alice shook her head. "No. I'm more afraid of brightly lit closed spaces. Charlie? Do you want to go with us, or do you want to stay here?"

It was a fair question, after the ghost had tried to

eviscerate the little guy with his phantom sword. Apparently, pirates were not fans of talking dogs. Charlie had been scared, so he'd transformed into his dragon shape, and then all hell had broken loose. Only Alice screaming that the pirate had better stay away from her dragon or he was never going to see his gold had calmed things down.

Now they were getting ready to climb down into a dark hole in the ground. This evening was getting better and better. And he was worried that Edge's overly inflated view of his own skills was going to make everybody relax their guard at the worst possible time.

He sighed and climbed down the ladder, then waited at the bottom to help Alice. When she was partway down, he plucked her off the ladder into his arms and kissed her, then kissed her again. "Well, there's one advantage to this adventure. You in my arms again."

She put her arms around his neck and kissed him back. "*Definitely* an advantage."

"Really? Now? *Here?*" The pirate tapped his ghostly foot with impatience, and Hunter wanted to punch him in the head. Wasn't really sure what punching a ghost in the head would do, except make Hunter feel better, but still. The urge was there.

They turned on the flashlights they'd brought and started down the tunnel—because of course it was a tunnel—after the pirate. The place smelled like mold, damp, and rat shit, and was absolutely *not* where Hunter wanted to be spending his evening.

"Where does this end?" he said.

"It ends with us having my gold, of course."

"I wasn't speaking metaphorically," Hunter gritted out.

"I was asking where the *tunnel* ends."

"Oh! It ends at a crypt."

Alice stopped walking so abruptly that Hunter ran into her.

"We're going to a crypt?"

The pirate nodded.

"We're going to a crypt, through a tunnel, at night."

"Yes, as I said."

Alice clenched her jaw so tightly Hunter was afraid her teeth might shatter.

"If we're going to a crypt," she said, "and you know which one it is, why didn't we just walk through the cemetery and get to it that way?"

"Because then everyone would see what we were doing and try to steal the gold, of course," the ghost said, speaking with exaggerated patience.

Alice clenched her hands into fists. "I'm going to punch you in the head. I swear, before this is over, I'm going to punch you in the head."

The ghost pretended not to hear her, but Hunter grinned. "I was just thinking that same thing. Clearly, we were made for each other."

They walked for what felt like half a mile but was probably considerably less—walking through the pitch black with only flashlights made it seem farther than it was—and encountered a lot of cobwebs, broken pieces of wood, and several rats. Hunter was not a particular fan of rats, plus he had to stop Alice from trying to rescue them.

"They're rats, Alice. They like it down here. It's like rat Disneyland."

"Isn't Disneyland rat Disneyland?"

"No, it's mouse Disneyland."

The pirate made an impatient growling sound. "This is one of the stupidest conversations I've ever heard, and I've been around for two hundred years."

Alice pointed a finger at the ghost. "No smack talk out of you, mister. We're doing you a favor here."

The pirate rolled his ghostly eyes. "Yes. A favor that will make you rich. Perhaps we can move along?"

Hunter was a fan of that. But he also liked the idea of giving up on the whole idea and going back to the house, because kissing Alice and getting her naked suddenly seemed infinitely more interesting than walking through this underground tunnel, treasure or not.

"Who dug the tunnel?" Alice asked.

The pirate shrugged. "I don't know. It was used for smuggling."

"Bane might know. He used to be a smuggler," Hunter told Alice.

Merveuille stopped and shouted, "Look! There's the door." He pointed at another rickety-looking ladder.

Hunter aimed his flashlight at the top of the ladder, and, sure enough, there was another trapdoor.

"I'll go first this time," Hunter said. "Unless you want to do the honors?"

The pirate sneered at him. "As you know, I cannot open physical doors." With that, he floated up to the top of the ladder and through the trapdoor.

The closed trapdoor.

Hunter had to work a little harder.

"What the hell is on top of this trapdoor? A freaking marble sarcophagus?" He really had to strain to get the door open, and that was with vampire strength. But, finally, he heard something screech across the floor above him, and the trapdoor flew open.

"Finally!" The pirate stuck his head in the opening and looked down at them. "What took you so long?"

Hunter and Alice looked at each other. "I really am going to punch him in the head," Hunter told her.

"I'm not sure it would work, him being a ghost and all. But we could just leave him here and let him suffer."

The ghost caught on and offered his abject apologies, so they climbed the ladder and entered the dark crypt.

"Would you call this a crypt or a mausoleum?" Alice looked around. "I'm not really sure. Maybe we should look it up—"

"Not now," the ghost shouted. "We're finally here!" He pointed at a marble bench on one side of the crypt. "That's it!"

Hunter looked at the bench and then back at the pirate. "Your treasure is a marble bench? We went through all this for a *marble bench*?"

The ghost was hopping back and forth with impatience now, the feather in his hat quivering. Hunter was kind of enjoying winding him up, but he noticed that Alice was biting her lip, so he let it go. "Okay, okay. Is there any special way to open this, or do I just rip the lid off or, I guess in this case, rip the seat off?"

"You're smarter than you look," the pirate said.

Hunter bared his teeth.

The pirate's tone was suddenly contrite. "Sorry. If you pull the bench away from the wall, there's a door in the back."

Alice shone her flashlight along the bench, then walked to the wall and tried to look at the back of it. "And how did nobody ever find this all this time?"

"You tell me," said the ghost. "You lived right next door to the cemetery for more than a year, and it never occurred to you to come over and search all the crypts for benches that might secretly contain treasure, right?"

Alice looked thoughtful, but then she nodded. "Okay, I'll give you that. I guess you're smarter than you look, too."

Hunter walked over to the bench and shoved it away from the wall. It weighed a damn ton. Sure enough, though, there was a door in the back. Hunter looked at the ghost—after all, it *was* his treasure—and the ghost nodded, apparently speechless with excitement.

So Hunter wrenched the door off and then stood back when a gleaming pile of gold and jewels came pouring out onto the concrete floor.

Alice gasped. "Oh my God. It's an actual pirate's treasure. Oh wow oh wow oh wow."

"I know. I have to admit, though, I didn't really believe him," Hunter said.

Charlie, who'd been following along quite timidly, suddenly got very excited. His golden eyes gleamed with avarice, and he stretched his wings to their full wingspan.

"Hunter? Do you think all the stories about dragons and their hordes are true?" Alice asked nervously, moving to block Charlie's path to the treasure.

"He's a demon," the ghost pointed out.

"He's also a dragon," Alice said.

Hunter looked from the little dragon to the gold and back again. "I guess we're about to find out."

"Keep that beast away from my treasure!" Merveuille put his hand on the hilt of his sword, but Alice glared at him, and he backed down. And then a squeaking noise sounded from the open trapdoor.

Alice whirled around. "Oh, no."

"What is it?"

"It's Ferret Bueller. He must have unlocked the door from the rescue to my house again and followed us over here."

The ferret jumped on the dragon's back and started petting Charlie's ear. For a minute, Hunter was afraid the little guy was going to become crispy fried ferret, but then he noticed that the dragon enjoyed the attention.

"You are very odd people," the pirate said.

"Maybe you should be nice to the people who found your treasure for you," Hunter drawled.

"You didn't *find* it, exactly." The pirate saw the look on Hunter's face and changed his tune. "I must thank you with all my heart for revealing my treasure at last. Now we need to take it all back to your house and divide it up. I will be in charge of that."

"Wait just a minute," Hunter said, but Alice put a hand on his arm.

"No, I think he's right. It was his treasure, so he knows what is more valuable and what is less. And he's a gentleman and won't try to cheat us."

The ghost might've been planning to cheat them right up until that moment, because an expression of pride mixed with dismay was written all over his face. "No, of course I will not cheat," he mumbled.

"Let's go get a rolling cart or something to carry this out

of here," Alice suggested, picking up a gold coin. "Wow, I'm looking at it and can still hardly believe it. No matter what, we should get a historian to look at it, too."

"No!" the pirate shouted.

"You'd be famous," she said.

"Really?"

Hunter rolled his eyes. Even ghosts wanted their fifteen minutes of fame. "Okay. Let's go get that cart and do this. I need to reach out to Bane and find out what's going on."

"But we can't just leave it," the ghost protested. "What if someone steals it, now that it's out of the bench?"

"Captain. It's been safe for two hundred years. I think it will be safe for another twenty minutes. And by the way, whose crypt is this?"

The pirate looked at her in surprise. "Mine, of course."

Alice sighed. "Of course it is. And that's not creepy at all."

Just then, the ferret jumped off Charlie's back, grabbed something in each tiny paw, and raced back to the trapdoor and then fled down the ladder. Charlie started toward the treasure again, but Alice stopped him.

"Charlie, I promise we will give you some treasure. You can guard my share for me until we figure out what to do with it, okay? But for right now, let's go back and get a cart or bags or something."

"I will stay and watch over the treasure," Captain Merveuille said.

"Probably want some time alone with your fond thoughts about all that raiding and pillaging, huh?" Hunter picked up an emerald necklace that had fallen out of the bench and lay askew on top of some gold coins. "You know,

I'd be happy to take just this one piece for my share." He turned to Alice and held it against the creamy skin of her neck. "It's the exact shade of your eyes."

She smiled at him, and for a moment he forgot where they were. What they were doing.

Maybe even his name.

"You have the most beautiful smile in the world," he murmured, touching her cheek. He looked back at the pirate. "You okay if I take this?"

For once, the pirate was gallant. "As you say, it will be beautiful with the lady's eyes. Please take it as my gift."

"Thank you both," Alice said, still smiling. "But I'd look pretty silly cleaning out kennels wearing an emerald necklace. How about we go get that cart and come back and load up the captain's treasure? And then we need to call two restaurant owners who are going to be very surprised."

With one last, longing glance at the treasure, Charlie turned back toward the trapdoor, and everyone but the ghost trooped back through the tunnel to the house. Hunter boosted Alice up, letting her go first, and he heard a little squeaking sound when she climbed out.

Hunter laughed. "Did you step on Ferret Bueller?"

When he climbed out of the trapdoor and turned around, two men were pointing guns at him, and one of them had his hand wrapped around Alice's throat.

CHAPTER FORTY

Alice knew something was wrong the moment she climbed up the ladder. It was almost as if the air itself felt electrically charged; as if some malignant evil had moved into her home and spread its scrabbling fingers into her scalp.

And her basement smelled like rot.

She tried to call out but only made it as far as a squeaking noise before she saw them.

Saw *him*.

The face of a thousand nightmares—of a hundred panic attacks.

Dr. Kurchausen was in her house.

He held a finger to his lips, shaking his head in a slow, exaggerated movement. Grogan, Kurchausen's creature, stood on the other side of the storeroom at an angle, pointing a gun at her head. He motioned toward the doctor with the barrel of the gun, telling her without words to move, but even if she'd wanted to comply, she couldn't do it.

She couldn't move. Couldn't speak.

Couldn't breathe.

She heard Hunter ask if she'd stepped on the ferret, and she yanked herself out of her frozen state to try to scream—to warn him—to close the trapdoor and keep him safe. But Kurchausen's lips were moving, and he made a gesture with one hand, and then she levitated off the floor and flew across the room to him, dropping gracelessly when she reached him. He caught her before she could fall—by grabbing her neck.

And then he dug his fingers into her throat.

"You thought you could escape me? You are *nothing*. You are my *property*," he hissed, his eyes truly wild. This close to him, the hideous smell of rot was so overpowering her eyes watered.

That's when Hunter climbed through the trapdoor and took in the scene in an instant.

"Let her go," he roared, his muscles bunching as he prepared to leap to her rescue, but before he could take a single step, Kurchausen swung the pistol up and dug the barrel into Alice's ear so hard it made her cry out.

"No," she told Hunter. "Charlie!"

He immediately understood and kicked the trapdoor shut with one foot. Alice hoped Charlie wasn't too afraid, but Kurchausen would probably know him for a Minor demon, if he really was at the top levels of the Chamber.

She couldn't take the chance that Charlie would be captured and enslaved or killed.

"Hunter. Run," she begged him, knowing he could move fast enough to get help.

Fast enough to survive.

She would gladly get shot or even face a future in captivity—the future she'd been so terrified of that she'd been willing to die to escape—if only Hunter could be safe.

"I'm not going anywhere," he said, his eyes darkening to a deep, fiery scarlet. "Not without you. Kurchausen, if you don't let her go, you're going to be very sorry for a very short while."

The doctor sneered at him. "A very short while?"

"Yes. Because after that, you're going to be dead."

Kurchausen looked at Grogan. "Shoot him."

"Stop!" Alice screamed, but it was too late. Grogan shot Hunter in the chest, knocking him back against the wall, and she started to cry, sure he was dead.

But then he pulled himself up to stand, leaning on the wall.

"What are you waiting for? Finish him," Kurchausen shouted at Grogan.

"No! Wait!"

The doctor raised an eyebrow at Alice's plea and motioned to Grogan to hold off. "If I wait—if I let your precious vampire live—what will you give me for his life?"

"Alice, no," Hunter groaned, clutching his chest. "No! I've called Bane. The troops are on the way. Don't do this."

Kurchausen nodded. "Then we'd better hurry. Grogan, kill the vampire and set him on fire. In fact, burn down this entire establishment—the house, the rescue, everything."

"No," she screamed. "No, stop! Doctor, please. Don't hurt him. If you promise me you won't hurt him, I'll go with you."

"You're going with me anyway," he said dismissively and started dragging her off. "Shoot him, Grogan."

She wildly cast about for what she had worth bartering for Hunter's life, and then, remembering, dug in her pocket for the gold coin she'd picked up. "Wait! I have pirate gold. Treasure! You can have all of it!"

He let go of her neck and slapped her face hard. "Right. And next you'll offer me the Brooklyn Bridge. Shut up, you stupid bitch. You're coming with me right now and— "

"Stop!" She felt the blood run down her chin from her split lip, just like she'd felt it so many times before. It had always been one of the doctor's favorite ways to discipline his *property.* But she ignored it and played her last card, tears streaming down her face. "Let him live, and I'll do whatever you want. *Voluntarily*. I'll even try to *help* you with your rituals instead of fight you."

Kurchausen froze, narrowing his beady eyes at her. In his bland gray suit, with his bland gray hair, he could have looked like any middle-aged businessman if it weren't for the madness in his black, black eyes.

Or the overpowering scent of rot from the blood magic he practiced.

"*Anything* I want? And you'll help?"

Hunter roared out his denial, but he was trapped by Grogan's gun pointed at him and by Kurchausen's gun pointed at her. His beautiful face was twisted with anguish and pain, and his skin seemed to be turning paler right in front of her eyes as the blood drained out of him.

"No! Alice, *no*!"

But it was too late, because Kurchausen nodded. "Yes. What do I care about one vampire's life? He can live, if I have your word."

She started to answer, but he twisted the pistol barrel in her ear, hurting her enough to make her cry out. He'd always loved it when he could make her cry—when he could make her scream in pain.

"Not your promise. Why would I trust you? No, you will swear an oath on your power that you will obey me and even take the initiative to help me. My magic will bind you to the oath."

She shuddered, because she knew she would be truly trapped with him for the rest of her life if she swore a blood oath, but one glance at Hunter firmed her resolve.

"Yes," she whispered, but then she took a deep, shaky breath and tried again. "Yes. I so swear it, on my power."

He muttered some words in a language she didn't know, and an excruciating pain like the searing burn of a brand flamed across the palm of her hand. She cried out again, and when she looked down, a blackened symbol that looked like writhing snakes was imprinted on her skin.

"There's no going back now," the doctor said, a death's head smile spreading across his face. "That binding is unbreakable until the death of the one who cast it. Even after you die, you will have to obey me."

Alice's soul cried out in denial, but she'd had no choice. She'd had to do anything she could to save Hunter. She loved him.

She hung her head, miserable, waiting for the doctor's first command.

She didn't have to wait long.

He handed her the gun and laughed, a horrible, high, evil laugh, while all but dancing with glee. "Shoot the vampire."

CHAPTER FORTY-ONE

Hunter felt his life draining away, ounce by ounce, for almost a minute, but then his vampire recuperative powers began to kick in. He was very careful not to let them see, though, and forced himself to play almost-dead while he figured out a way to save Alice from that bastard.

He'd screamed down the mental communication path that they needed help, and he knew Bane, Edge, and Meara were on the way, but even flying, they would never make it on time. It was up to him. He *would* figure out a way to save her, and Kurchausen and his thug would die.

But then the son of a bitch bound her with an oath and told her to shoot him.

"No!" she screamed, dropping the gun, but he could see the horrible strain in her face when her free will smashed against the rock wall of the binding oath.

And free will died.

She moved, jerky like a marionette on a string, bending down at an impossible angle to retrieve the gun, fighting herself, fighting the oath, and fighting the doctor's power over her.

The sight of her fighting the oath, to the point where he heard her wrist bone actually snap, was so compelling that even Grogan glanced at her, taking his eyes off Hunter for only a second or two.

But Hunter was a vampire. He'd been Turned by the most powerful master vampire on the east coast of the U.S., and he'd drunk his fill of warlock blood only the night before.

A second or two was all he needed.

He knocked Grogan down and then launched himself at Kurchausen, exploding through the air like a rocket and slamming into the monster, smashing him *through* the wall and into the next room.

And then Hunter ripped the bastard's throat out with his bare hands.

The gunshots sounded, two in rapid succession, seconds after he threw Kurchausen's body aside.

When he raced back into the storeroom, Grogan was already dead. Alice's eyes were wide and shocked, and she held the gun in her hand again.

And blood poured from the gunshot wound in her stomach.

CHAPTER FORTY-TWO

Hunter roared out his denial and rushed to catch Alice before she hit the floor. He leapt into the air and flew up the stairs with her, then lay her down on the couch in her parlor, putting pressure on the horrible, gaping wound, and screamed at Bane.

HE SHOT HER, HE SHOT HER, HE SHOT HER! SHE'S DYING. WHAT DO I DO? THERE'S NO TIME FOR AN AMBULANCE. SHE'S DYING IN FRONT OF ME!

Bane's voice came back instantly.

WE'RE STILL FIVE MINUTES AWAY FROM YOU. YOU ONLY HAVE ONE CHOICE, IF YOU'RE SURE SHE'S DYING. IF SHE AGREES.

Hunter suddenly knew exactly what that one choice was. Hadn't he been in the exact same place only a month before?

Alice suddenly opened her eyes and squeezed his hand. "Are you safe? Did I save you?"

"Yes," he told her, his beautiful Alice. His love. He kissed her forehead, not even realizing he was crying until he saw a teardrop land on her cheek.

"I love you, Hunter," she whispered, all color fading from her face. "You're not a monster. You never were. Please find someone to love and live your life with. Please be happy. I don't think I could stand it if you aren't happy."

"I love you, too. More than I ever believed I could love

anyone," he told her, his heart shattering in his chest.

Her eyes fluttered shut, and fear sliced into him. "Alice! Alice, listen to me."

She opened her eyes again, the beautiful green already going dim, and he knew he was out of time.

"Alice, there's a way we can be together. You could be like me. Like Meara and Bane. Would you be willing to be Turned? I know it's frightening, but—"

She murmured something so faintly that he never would have heard it without vampire hearing, but he still couldn't believe it.

"What?"

She said it again. "Will you marry me?"

Joy swept through him, sweeping the fear out before it. "Yes, my love. Yes, of course I'll marry you."

Her eyes started to close again. "Then yes, please, with all my heart, I agree to become a vampire. But Hunter?"

"Yes?"

"I think it's too late," she whispered.

And then her heart stopped beating.

Hunter tightened his grip on her hand and plunged his fangs into her throat.

CHAPTER FORTY-THREE

For three days, Hunter Evans, previously a highly decorated firefighter and currently a vampire, sat by Alice's side as she slept.

Meara kept him company most of the time, but Bane, Edge, Luke, and the Cassidys all also stopped by to bring him food or blood or just sit with him. Even the wolf alpha and beta, Carter and Max, stopped by once, stuck their heads in and saw Alice's still form, and offered their best wishes.

Bane told him that this was normal. That his, Hunter's, Turn had been the one that was out of the ordinary, with the way he'd kept waking up out of the coma. That this was how it was *supposed* to go.

For three days, Hunter ignored all of them and waited and watched, holding Alice's hand.

For three days, Charlie waited with him, curled up on the end of the bed in the mansion's safe room, his tail wrapped protectively around Alice's ankles.

Apparently, although he had no memory of it, he'd told them about Charlie being trapped in the tunnel. He'd even told them about the pirate, when they'd finally reached the house and found him draping the emerald necklace over Alice's icy throat.

She'd died, technically, just before he'd begun the process of the Turn. The blood exchanges.

He'd heard them, when they thought he was asleep,

discussing the odds of whether she would wake up at all or, if she did, whether she would be whole. Or sane.

Or still herself.

He was almost afraid to hope. If she died, he would gladly walk into the noon sun.

For three days, he waited.

On the third day, just after dusk, she opened her brilliantly green eyes and smiled at him, and the sun began to shine again in his world.

For the first time in three days, he could draw in a full breath. For the first time in three days, he didn't curse his heart for beating without her.

She smiled at him, and his soul shattered into tiny, crystalline shards of joy and hope and love. And then he started shaking, and he couldn't seem to stop.

She tried to speak but only made a croaking sort of sound.

He scrubbed at his face, pushing the tears away, and then took her hand, trying to pull himself together. "Alice? Can you hear me? Are you okay?"

She stretched, rolling her neck, and then glanced down as if surprised that her legs didn't move, smiling when she saw Charlie asleep at her feet.

But she still didn't say anything, and Hunter's heart began to plummet. "Alice! Please, sweetheart. Please talk to me."

She glanced up at him and licked her dry lips. "Hunter?" Her voice was a rusty croak, and it was the most beautiful sound he'd ever heard.

"Yes, love? What is it? Anything you need, I'll find a way. Just tell me."

She squeezed his hand. "Can we have spaghetti and meatballs?"

When everyone raced up to find out what was going on after Hunter shouted out his joy, they found the two of them together, laughing and crying, and the little dragon hopping around the room, dancing with happiness.

"She's going to be okay," Hunter told them, stroking Alice's beautiful red curls and holding a glass of water for her to sip. "She's going to be just fine."

"Of course she is," Meara said, her golden eyes suspiciously wet. "She's a badass. And I'm planning the wedding."

Alice blinked. "Wedding? Who's getting married?"

Hunter kissed her cheek, holding her and never wanting to let her go. "We are. Don't you remember? You proposed."

"I what?"

"Oh, no. You can't back out on me," Meara said. "I've already begun wedding plans. You're stuck with him now."

Alice smiled, her entire heart shining in her eyes for everyone to see. "Then I must be the luckiest woman in the world."

Hunter kissed her again, only letting her go when he heard a chittering sound at his feet.

"You have another visitor, by the way. He wouldn't stay at the rescue without you, so Meara brought him over here until you recovered."

Before Alice could ask, Ferret Bueller hopped up into her lap, chattering excitedly, clutching something in his tiny paws. Alice reached out a finger and stroked his head, and he closed his eyes and leaned his head into her palm.

Her *unmarked* palm. The doctor's binding had died with him, as he'd unwittingly told them it would.

"What's that you've got there?" Alice coaxed the little creature to drop his treasure into her hand and then gasped.

It was an enormous diamond-and-emerald ring.

"Oh! The treasure! Poor Captain Marvelous. What happened?"

Edge snorted. "Poor Captain Marvelous nothing. By the time we calculated the current value of the treasure, taking into account market fluctuations, the price of gold, the—"

Meara poked him in the chest. "Get on with it!"

"Yes, well. The treasure is worth around twenty million dollars. His half, which he wants to go to his heirs, is, of course, ten million. We're working out the details now."

Alice's eyes widened. "We have ten million dollars? Ten *million* dollars? The rescue—it's going to be amazing!"

"The wedding is going to be amazing," Meara said dreamily.

Ryan came over and hugged Alice, her eyes tearing up, but then she shook a finger at her. "No ugly bridesmaids' dresses, okay?"

Meara snorted. "What do you think you're talking about, ugly bridesmaids' dresses? It's going to be a double wedding. You and Bane and Alice and Hunter!"

Ryan made a squeaking sound that sounded exactly like Ferret Bueller, but Bane's expression, looking at Ryan, was pure satisfaction.

Hunter gazed down at Alice and knew *exactly* how Bane felt.

Meara caught Hunter's attention and nodded discreetly

to the ice chest in the corner of the room and then herded everyone out, even Charlie and the little ferret. Alice was going to need to feed very soon, and Hunter would have to introduce her to the things he'd been learning about his—their—new existence.

But for now…

"I know you don't remember, and you were dying, and it all happened too fast," he began.

"Hunter—"

"No. I need to tell you this before life and the rest of the world push their way back into this moment. Alice, I love you. I love you with everything I am and everything I will ever be. I love your kindness and your courage. I love your beauty, inside and out. I love everything about you and want nothing more than for you to share my life forever."

He kissed her hands, one after the other, and got down on one knee, holding out the ring that Ferret Bueller had so helpfully stolen from his jacket pocket. "Will you marry me?"

"Hunter." She smiled at him with so much love that it stole his breath. "I've known since I met you that my heart would be safe with you. I love you with everything I am and will be. I love your humor and your compassion. I love your body and your mind. I especially love the niceness you keep pretending you don't want to have. Will you be my best friend and lover forever? Will you marry me?"

He slid the ring on her finger, swept her into his arms, and kissed her.

"You'd better say yes," Meara called out from outside the room.

Alice started to laugh. "We'd be afraid to say no, now."

"I'll love you forever, even with your ferrets and raccoons and demon-dragons, Alice Darlington. You made my life whole when you stepped into it with that silly raccoon."

She gave him a thoughtful look. "Alice Darlington Evans has a nice ring to it. And I was thinking we could add snake and rat rescue, now that we have all that money."

"Maybe in a different building," he said, trying not to grimace. "Now kiss me until I forget how scared I was that you wouldn't wake up."

She grinned at him. "Could those maybe be naked kisses?"

"I think that could be arranged," he said, instantly going hard.

Just as he bent his head to hers, she jerked back and stared at him, wide-eyed. "I'm a *vampire*."

"I know."

"I can *fly*."

He started to get a bad feeling. "Well, maybe, with some practice, but—"

"Ryan," she shouted, leaping up. "Let's go jump off the roof!"

Hunter leaned back in his chair and smiled.

It was going to be a *wonderful* life.

EPILOGUE

Later that night, Meara called a war council but only invited Bane and Edge. She waited until after Ryan had gone to sleep and Hunter and Alice had driven off to her house, where they were probably doing anything *but* sleeping. She waited, standing next to her piano in the parlor, until the men walked into the room.

"Edge, tell Bane what you learned."

Edge's face was grim. "First, I learned I'm not anywhere near as smart as I think I am. I'm sorry for that. For my false intel putting Alice—all of us—in danger."

"Enough of that," Meara said. "Tell him the rest."

"Neville pulled off the impossible," Edge said. "He managed to avoid all charges, and Interpol is even considering appointing him to be some kind of special consultant."

"He used blood magic on them," Bane said, frowning. "If he's out, he'll be after us again soon."

"Enough is enough," Meara told him. "We're going to take the fight to him. Hit him where it hurts."

Bane narrowed his eyes. "What does that mean?"

She glanced at Edge, who nodded.

"Edge and I are going to London. The Chamber is going down."

ACKNOWLEDGMENTS

Thank you to my amazing team at Entangled: Liz Pelletier, Lydia Sharp, Jessica Turner, Bree Archer (Whee! That cover art!), Meredith Johnson, Heather Riccio, Riki Cleveland, Debbie Suzuki, Curtis Svehlak, and Katie Clapsadl—and HOLY CRAP, thanks to Hannah Lindsey, who copy edited this book while Hurricane Ida battered at her door! You are all wonderful beyond reason, super talented, and work SO hard, all while being kinder than any neurotic author deserves. Thank you for all of your hard work on my behalf. (And for putting up with me when I make up words.)

To my agent, Kevan Lyon: Thanks for your kindness and understanding. Depression is hell, but having you on my team helps a lot.

To my readers: Thank you for being part of my worlds and for loving and talking about my books for all these years. I appreciate you more than I can ever say.

To Judd, Connor, and Lauren: I love you more than the metaverse. Yeah, I went there. Can we go back to Alaska now?

To the dogs: No, not every package that arrives has bones in it. But thank you for furry cuddles when life was dark.

And, to Liz: I owe you a kidney.

AUTHOR'S NOTE: This book has no real people in it, I promise. Whoever the governor of Georgia is at time of publication, I seriously doubt they have ever had vampires visit their yacht. But of course, in Savannah, one never knows…

A modern-day Game of Thrones *meets JR Ward's Black Dagger Brotherhood series.*

by Abigail Owen

Kasia Amon is a master at hiding. Who—and what—she is makes her a mark for the entire supernatural world. *Especially* dragon shifters. To them, she's treasure to be taken and claimed. A golden ticket to their highest throne. But she can't stop bursting into flames, *and* there's a sexy dragon shifter in town hunting for her...

As a rogue dragon, Brand Astarot has spent his life in the dark, shunned by his own kind, concealing his true identity. Only his dangerous reputation ensures his survival. Delivering a phoenix to the feared Blood King will bring him one step closer to the revenge he's waited centuries to take. No *way* is he letting the feisty beauty get away.

But when Kasia sparks a white-hot need in him that's impossible to ignore, Brand begins to form a new plan: claim her for himself…and take back his birthright.

AMARA
an imprint of Entangled Publishing LLC